1

Uncle's Dream; and The Permanent Husband

by Fyodor Dostoyevsky

Copyright © 7/30/2015
Jefferson Publication

ISBN-13: 978-1515295822

Printed in the United States of America

Contents

CHAPTER I.

Maria Alexandrovna Moskaleva was the principal lady of Mordasoff—there was no doubt whatever on that point! She always bore herself as though *she* did not care a fig for anyone, but as though no one else could do without *her*. True, there were uncommonly few who loved her—in fact I may say that very many detested her; still, everyone was afraid of her, and that was what she liked!

Now, why did Maria Alexandrovna, who dearly loves scandal, and cannot sleep at night unless she has heard something new and piquant the day before,—why or how did she know how to bear herself so that it would never strike anyone, looking at her, to suppose that the dignified lady was the most inveterate scandal-monger in the world—or at all events in Mordasoff? On the contrary, anyone would have said at once, that scandals and such-like pettiness must vanish in her presence; and that scandal-mongers, caught red-handed by Maria Alexandrovna, would blush and tremble, like schoolboys at the entrance of the master; and that the talk would immediately be diverted into channels of the loftiest and most sublime subjects so soon as she entered the room. Maria Alexandrovna knew many deadly and scandalous secrets of certain other Mordasoff inhabitants, which, if she liked to reveal them at any convenient opportunity, would produce results little less terrible than the earthquake of Lisbon. Still, she was very quiet about the secrets she knew, and never let them out except in cases of absolute need, and then only to her nearest and dearest friends. She liked to hint that she knew certain things, and frighten people out of their wits; preferring to keep them in a state of perpetual terror, rather than crush them altogether.

This was real talent—the talent of tactics.

We all considered Maria Alexandrovna as our type and model of irreproachable *comme-il-faut*! She had no rival in this respect in Mordasoff! She could kill and annihilate and pulverize any rival with a single word. We have seen her do it; and all the while she would look as though she had not even observed that she had let the fatal word fall.

Everyone knows that this trait is a speciality of the highest circles.

Her circle of friends was large. Many visitors to Mordasoff left the town again in an ecstasy over her reception of them, and carried on a correspondence with her afterwards! Somebody even addressed some poetry to her, which she showed about the place with great pride. The novelist who came to the town used to read his novel to her of an evening, and ended by dedicating it to her; which produced a very agreeable effect. A certain German professor, who came from Carlsbad to inquire into the question of a little worm with horns which abounds in our part of the world, and who wrote and published four large quarto volumes about this same little insect, was so delighted and ravished with her amiability and kindness that to this very day he carries on a most improving correspondence upon moral subjects from far Carlsbad!

Some people have compared Maria Alexandrovna, in certain respects, with Napoleon. Of course it may have been her enemies who did so, in order to bring Maria Alexandrovna to scorn; but all I can say is, How is it that Napoleon, when he rose to his highest, that *too* high estate of his, became giddy and fell? Historians of the old school have ascribed this to the fact that he was not only not of royal blood, but was not even a gentleman! and therefore when he rose too high, he thought of his proper place, the ground, became giddy and fell! But why did not Maria Alexandrovna's head whirl? And how was it that she could always keep her place as the first lady of Mordasoff?

People have often said this sort of thing of Maria Alexandrovna; for instance: "Oh—yes, but how would she act under such and such difficult circumstances?" Yet, when the circumstances arose, Maria Alexandrovna invariably rose also to the emergency! For instance, when her husband—Afanassy Matveyevitch—was obliged to throw up his appointment, out of pure incapacity and feebleness of intellect, just before the government inspector came down to look into matters, all Mordasoff danced with delight to think that she would be down on her knees to this inspector, begging and beseeching and weeping and praying—in fact, that she would drop her wings and fall; but, bless you, nothing of the sort happened! Maria Alexandrovna quite understood that her husband was beyond praying for: he must retire. So she only rearranged her affairs a little, in such a manner that she lost not a scrap of her influence in the place, and her house still remained the acknowledged head of all Mordasoff Society!

The procurer's wife, Anna Nicolaevna Antipova, the sworn foe of Maria Alexandrovna, though a friend so far as could be judged outside, had already blown the trumpet of victory over her rival! But when Society found that Maria Alexandrovna was extremely difficult to put down, they were obliged to conclude that the latter had struck her roots far deeper than they had thought for.

As I have mentioned Afanassy Matveyevitch, Maria Alexandrovna's husband, I may as well add a few words about him in this place.

Firstly, then, he was a most presentable man, so far as exterior goes, and a very high-principled person besides; but in critical moments he used to lose his head and stand looking like a sheep which has come across a new gate. He looked very majestic and dignified in his dress-coat and white tie at dinner parties, and so on; but his dignity only lasted until he opened his mouth to speak; for then—well, you'd better have shut your ears, ladies and gentlemen, when he began to talk—that's all! Everyone agreed that he was quite unworthy to be Maria Alexandrovna's husband. He only sat in his place by virtue of his wife's genius. In my humble opinion he ought long ago to have been derogated to the office of frightening sparrows in the kitchen garden. There, and only there, would he have been in his proper sphere, and doing some good to his fellow countrymen.

Therefore, I think Maria Alexandrovna did a very wise thing when she sent him away to her village, about a couple of miles from town, where she possessed a property of some hundred and twenty souls—which, to tell the truth, was all she had to keep up the respectability and grandeur of her noble house upon!

Everybody knew that Afanassy was only kept because he had earned a salary and perquisites; so that when he ceased to earn the said salary and perquisites, it surprised no-one to learn that he was sent away—"returned empty" to the village, as useless and fit for nothing! In fact, everyone praised his wife for her soundness of judgment and decision of character!

Afanassy lived in clover at the village. I called on him there once and spent a very pleasant hour. He tied on his white ties, cleaned his boots himself (not because he had no-one to do it for him, but for the sake of art, for he loved to have them *shine*), went to the bath as often as he could, had tea four times a day, and was as contented as possible.

Do you remember, a year and a half ago, the dreadful stories that were afoot about Zenaida, Maria Alexandrovna's and Afanassy's daughter? Zenaida was undoubtedly a fine, handsome, well-educated girl; but she was now twenty-three years old, and not married yet. Among the reasons put forth for Zenaida being still a maid, one of the strongest was those dark rumours about a strange attachment, a year and a half ago, with the schoolmaster of the place—rumours not hushed up even to this day. Yes, to this very day they tell of a love-letter, written by Zina, as she was called, and handed all about Mordasoff. But kindly tell me, who ever saw this letter? If it went from hand to hand what became of it? Everyone seems to have heard of it, but no one ever saw it! At all events, *I* have never met anyone who actually saw the letter with his own eyes. If you drop a hint to Maria Alexandrovna about it, she simply does not understand you.

Well, supposing that there *was* something, and that Zina did write such a letter; what dexterity and skill of Maria Alexandrovna, to have so ably nipped the bud of the scandal! I feel sure that Zina *did* write the letter; but Maria Alexandrovna has managed so well that there is not a trace, not a shred of evidence of the existence of it. Goodness knows how she must have worked and planned to save the reputation of this only daughter of hers; but she managed it somehow.

As for Zina not having married, there's nothing surprising in that. Why, what sort of a husband could be found for her in Mordasoff? Zina ought to marry a reigning prince, if anyone! Did you ever see such a beauty among beauties as Zina? I think not. Of course, she was very proud—too proud.

There was Mosgliakoff—some people said she was likely to end by marrying *him*; but I never thought so. Why, what was there in Mosgliakoff? True, he was young and good looking, and possessed an estate of a hundred and fifty souls, and was a Petersburg swell; but, in the first place, I don't think there was much inside his head. He was such a funny, new-idea sort of man. Besides, what is an estate of a hundred and fifty souls, according to present notions? Oh, no; that's a marriage that never could come off.

There, kind reader, all you have just read was written by me some five months ago, for my own amusement. I admit, I am rather partial to Maria Alexandrovna; and I wished to write some sort of laudatory account of that charming woman, and to mould it into the form of one of those playful "letters to a friend," purporting to have been written in the old golden days (which will never return—thank Heaven!) to one of the periodicals of the time, "The Northern Bee," or some such paper. But since I have no "friend," and since I am, besides, naturally of a timid disposition, and especially so as to my literary efforts, the essay remained on my writing-table, as a memorial of my early literary attempts and in memory of the peaceful occupation of a moment or two of leisure.

Well, five months have gone by, and lo! great things have happened at Mordasoff!

Prince K—— drove into the town at an early hour one fine morning, and put up at Maria Alexandrovna's house! The prince only stayed three days, but his visit proved pregnant with the most fatal consequences. I will say more—the prince brought about what was, in a certain sense, a revolution in the town, an account of which revolution will, of course, comprise some of the most important events that have ever happened in Mordasoff; and I have determined at last, after many heart-sinkings and flutterings, and much doubt, to arrange the story into the orthodox literary form of a novel, and present it to the indulgent Public! My tale will include a narrative of the Rise and Greatness and Triumphant Fall of Maria Alexandrovna, and of all her House in Mordasoff, a theme both worthy of, and attractive to any writer!

Of course I must first explain why there should have been anything extraordinary in the fact that Prince K—— came to Mordasoff, and put up at Maria Alexandrovna's mansion. And in order to do this, I must first be allowed to say a few words about this same Prince K——. This I shall now do. A short biography of the nobleman is absolutely necessary to the further working out of my story. So, reader, you must excuse me.

CHAPTER II.

I will begin, then, by stating that Prince K—— was not so very, very old, although, to look at him, you would think he *must* fall to pieces every moment, so decayed, or rather, worn-out was he. At Mordasoff all sorts of strange things were told of him. Some declared that the old prince's wits had forsaken him. All agreed that it was passing strange that the owner of a magnificent property of four thousand souls, a man of rank, and one who could have, if he liked, a great influence, and play a great part in his country's affairs; that such a man should live all alone upon his estate, and make an absolute hermit of himself, as did Prince K——. Many who had known him a few years before insisted upon it that he was very far from loving solitude then, and was as unlike a hermit as anyone could possibly be.

However, here is all I have been able to learn authentically as to his antecedents, etc.:—

Some time or other, in his younger days—which must have been a mighty long while ago,—the prince made a most brilliant entry into life. He knocked about and enjoyed himself, and sang romantic songs, and wrote epigrams, and led a fast life generally, very often abroad, and was full of gifts and intellectual capacity.

Of course he very soon ran through his means, and when old age approached, he suddenly found himself almost penniless. Somebody recommended him to betake himself to his country seat, which was about to be sold by public auction. So off he went with that intention; but called in at Mordasoff, and stopped there six months. He liked this provincial life, and while in our town he spent every farthing he had left in the world, continuing his reckless life as of old, galivanting about, and forming intimacies with half the ladies of Mordasoff.

He was a kind-hearted, good sort of a man, but, of course, not without certain princely failings, which, however, were accounted here to be nothing but evidences of the highest breeding, and for this reason caused a good effect instead of aversion. The ladies, especially, were in a state of perpetual ecstasy over their dear guest. They cherished the fondest and tenderest recollections of him. There were also strange traditions and rumours about the prince. It was said that he spent more than half the day at his toilet table; and that he was, in fact, made up of all sorts of little bits. No one could say when or how he had managed to fall to pieces so completely.

He wore a wig, whiskers, moustache, and even an "espagnole," all false to a hair, and of a lovely raven black; besides which he painted and rouged every day. It was even said that he managed to do away with his wrinkles by means of *hidden springs*—hidden somehow in his wig. It was said, further, that he wore stays, in consequence of the want of a rib which he had lost in Italy, through being caused to fly, involuntarily, out of a window during a certain love affair. He limped with his left foot, and it was whispered that the said foot was a cork one—a very scientific member, made for him in place of the real one which came to grief during another love affair, in Paris this time. But what will not people say? At all events, I know for a fact that his right eye was a glass one; beautifully made, I confess, but still—glass. His teeth were false too.

For whole days at a time he used to wash himself in all sorts of patent waters and scents and pomades.

However, no one could deny that even then he was beginning to indulge in senile drivel and chatter. It appeared his career was about over; he had seen his best days, everyone knew that he had not a copeck left in the world!

Then, suddenly and unexpectedly, an old relative of his—who had always lived in Paris, but from whom he never had had the slightest hope of inheritance—died, after having buried her legal heir exactly a month before! The prince, to his utter astonishment, turned out to be the next heir, and a beautiful property of four thousand serfs, just forty miles from Mordasoff, became his—absolutely and unquestionably!

He immediately started off to Petersburg, to see to his affairs. Before he departed, however, the ladies of our town gave him a magnificent subscription banquet. They tell how bewitching and delightful the prince was at this last dinner; how he punned and joked and told the most *unusual* stories; and how he promised to come to Donchanovo (his new property) very soon, and gave his word that on his arrival he would give endless balls and garden parties and picnics and fireworks and entertainments of all kinds, for his friends here.

For a whole year after his departure, the ladies of the place talked of nothing but these promised festivities; and awaited the arrival of the "dear old man" with the utmost impatience. At last the prince arrived; but to the disappointment and astonishment of everyone, he did not even call in at Mordasoff on the way; and on his arrival at Donchanovo he shut himself up there, as I have expressed it before, like a very hermit.

All sorts of fantastic rumours were bruited about, and from this time the prince's life and history became most secret, mysterious, and incomprehensible.

In the first place, it was declared that the prince had not been very successful in St. Petersburg; that many of his relations—future heirs and heirs presumptive, and so on, had wished to put the Prince under some kind of restraint, on the plea of "feebleness of intellect;" probably fearing that he would run through this property as he had done with the last! And more, some of them went so far as to suggest that he should be popped into a lunatic asylum; and he was only saved by the interference of one of the nearest of kin, who pointed out that the poor old prince was more than half dead already, and that the rest of him must inevitably soon die too; and that then the property would come down to them safely enough without the need of the lunatic asylum. I repeat, what will not people say? Especially at our place, Mordasoff! All this, it was said, had frightened the prince dreadfully; so that his nature seemed to change entirely, and he came down to live a hermit life at Donchanovo.

Some of our Mordasoff folk went over to welcome him on his arrival; but they were either not received at all or received in the strangest fashion. The prince did not recognise his old friends: many people explained that he did not *wish* to recognise them. Among other visitors to Donchanovo was the Governor.

On the return of the latter from his visit, he declared that the prince was undoubtedly a little "off his head." The Governor always made a face if anyone reminded him of this visit of his to Donchanovo. The ladies were dreadfully offended.

At last an important fact was revealed: namely, that there was with the prince, and apparently in authority over him, some unknown person of the name of Stepanida Matveyevna, who had come down with him from St. Petersburg; an elderly fat woman in a calico dress, who went about with the house-keys in her hand; and that the prince obeyed this woman like a little child, and did not dare take a step without her leave; that she washed him and dressed him and soothed and petted him just like a nurse with a baby; and lastly, that she kept all visitors away from him, even relations—who, little by little, had begun to pervade the place rather too frequently, for the purpose of seeing that all was right.

It was said that this person managed not only the prince, but his estate too: she turned off bailiffs and clerks, she encashed the rents, she looked after things in general—and did it well, too; so that the peasants blessed their fate under her rule.

As for the prince, it was rumoured that he spent his days now almost entirely at his toilet-table, trying on wigs and dress-coats, and that the rest of his time was spent playing cards and games with Stepanida Matveyevna, and riding on a quiet old English mare. On such occasions his nurse always accompanied him in a covered droshky, because the prince liked to ride out of bravado, but was most unsafe in his saddle.

He had been seen on foot too, in a long great coat and a straw hat with a wide brim; a pink silk lady's tie round his neck, and a basket on his arm for mushrooms and flowers and berries, and so on, which he collected. The nurse accompanied him, and a few yards behind walked a manservant, while a carriage was in attendance on the high road at the side. When any peasant happened to meet him, and with low bow, and hat in hand, said, "Good morning, your highness—our beloved Sun, and Father of us all," or some such Russian greeting, he would stick his eye-glass in his eye, nod his head and say, with great urbanity, and in French, "Bon jour, mon ami, bon jour!"

Lots of other rumours there were—in fact, our folks could not forget that the prince lived so near them.

What, then, must have been the general amazement when one fine day it was trumpeted abroad that the prince—their curious old hermit-prince, had arrived at Mordasoff, and put up at Maria Alexandrovna's house!

Agitation and bewilderment were the order of the day; everybody waited for explanations, and asked one another what could be the meaning of this mystery? Some proposed to go and see for themselves; all agreed that it was *most* extraordinary. The ladies wrote notes to each other, came and whispered to one another, and sent their maids and husbands to find out more.

What was particularly strange was, why had the prince put up at Maria Alexandrovna's, and not somewhere else? This fact annoyed everyone; but, most of all, Mrs. Antipova, who happened to be a distant relative of the prince.

However, in order to clear up all these mysteries and find an answer to all these questions, we must ourselves go and see Maria Alexandrovna. Will you follow me in, kind reader? It is only ten in the morning, certainly, as you point out; but I daresay she will receive such intimate friends, all the same. Oh, yes; she'll see us all right.

CHAPTER III.

It is ten o'clock in the morning, and we are at Maria Alexandrovna's, and in that room which the mistress calls her "salon" on great occasions; she has a boudoir besides.

In this salon the walls are prettily papered, and the floor is nicely painted; the furniture is mostly red; there is a fireplace, and on the mantelpiece a bronze clock with some figure—a Cupid—upon it, in dreadfully bad taste. There are large looking-glasses between the windows. Against the back wall there stands a magnificent grand piano—Zina's—for Zina is a musician. On a table in the middle of the room hisses a silver tea-urn, with a very pretty tea-set alongside of it.

There is a lady pouring out tea, a distant relative of the family, and living with Maria Alexandrovna in that capacity, one Nastasia Petrovna Ziablova. She is a widow of over thirty, a brunette with a fresh-looking face and lively black eyes, not at all bad looking.

She is of a very animated disposition, laughs a great deal, is fond of scandal, of course; and can manage her own little affairs very nicely. She has two children somewhere, being educated. She would much like to marry again. Her last husband was a military man.

Maria Alexandrovna herself is sitting at the fire in a very benign frame of mind; she is dressed in a pale-green dress, which becomes her very well; she is unspeakably delighted at the arrival of the Prince, who, at this moment, is sitting upstairs, at his toilet table. She is so happy, that she does not even attempt to conceal her joy. A young man is standing before her and relating something in an animated way; one can see in his eyes that he wishes to curry favour with his listener.

This young fellow is about twenty-five years old, and his manners are decidedly good, though he has a silly way of going into raptures, and has, besides, a good deal too much of the "funny man" about him. He is well dressed and his hair is light; he is not a bad-looking fellow. But we have already heard of this gentleman: he is Mr. Mosgliakoff. Maria Alexandrovna considers him rather a stupid sort of a man, but receives him very well. He is an aspirant for the hand of her daughter Zina, whom, according to his own account, he loves to distraction. In his conversation, he refers to Zina every other minute, and does his best to bring a smile to her lips by his witty remarks; but the girl is evidently very cool and indifferent with him. At this moment she is standing away at the side near the piano, turning over the leaves of some book.

This girl is one of those women who create a sensation amounting almost to amazement when they appear in society. She is lovely to an almost impossible extent, a brunette with splendid black eyes, a grand figure and divine bust. Her shoulders and arms are like an antique statue; her gait that of an empress. She is a little pale to-day; but her lips, with the gleam of her pearly teeth between them, are things to dream of, if you once get a sight of them. Her expression is severe and serious.

Mr. Mosgliakoff is evidently afraid of her intent gaze; at all events, he seems to cower before her when she looks at him. She is very simply dressed, in a white muslin frock—the white suits her admirably. But then, *everything* suits her! On her finger is a hair ring: it does not look as though the hair was her mother's, from the colour. Mosgliakoff has never dared to ask her whose hair it is. This morning she seems to be in a peculiarly depressed humour; she appears to be very much preoccupied and silent: but her mother is quite ready to talk enough for both; albeit she glances continually at Zina, as though anxious for her, but timidly, too, as if afraid of her.

"I am *so* pleased, Pavel Alexandrovitch," she chirps to Mosgliakoff; "*so* happy, that I feel inclined to cry the news out of the window to every passer-by. Not to speak of the delightful surprise—to both Zina and myself—of seeing you a whole fortnight sooner than we expected you—that, of course, 'goes without saying'; but I am so, *so* pleased that you should have brought this dear prince with you. You don't know how I love that fascinating old man. No, no! You would never believe it. You young people don't understand this sort of rapture; you never would believe me, assure you as much as ever I pleased.

"Don't you remember, Zina, how much he was to me at that time—six years ago? Why, I was his guide, his sister, his mother! There was something delightfully ingenuous and ennobling in our intimacy—one might say *pastoral*; I don't know what to call it—it was delightful. That is why the poor dear prince thinks of *my* house, and only mine, with gratitude, now. Do you know, Pavel Alexandrovitch, perhaps you have *saved* him by thus bringing him to me? I have thought of him with quaking of heart all these six years—you'd hardly believe it,—and *dreamed* of him, too. They say that wretch of a woman has bewitched and ruined him; but you've got him out of the net at last. We must make the best of our opportunity now, and save him outright. Do tell me again, how did you manage it? Describe your meeting and all in detail; I only heard the chief point of the story just now, and I do so like details. So, he's still at his toilet table now, is he?—"

"Yes. It was all just as I told you, Maria Alexandrovna!" begins Mosgliakoff readily—delighted to repeat his story ten times over, if required—"I had driven all night, and not slept a wink. You can imagine what a hurry I was in to arrive here," he adds, turning to Zina; "in a word, I swore at the driver, yelled for fresh horses, kicked up a row at every post station: my adventures would fill a volume. Well, exactly at six o'clock in the morning I arrived at the last station, Igishova. 'Horses, horses!' I shouted, 'let's have fresh horses quick; I'm not going to get out.' I frightened the post-station man's wife out of her wits; she had a small baby in her arms, and I have an idea that its mother's fright will affect said baby's supply of the needful. Well, the sunrise was splendid—fine frosty morning—lovely! but I hadn't time to look at anything. I got my horses—I had to deprive some other traveller of his pair; he was a professor, and we nearly fought a duel about it.

"They told me some prince had driven off a quarter of an hour ago. He had slept here, and was driving his own horses; but I didn't attend to anything. Well, just seven miles from town, at a turn of the road, I saw that some surprising event had happened. A huge travelling carriage was lying on its side; the coachman and two flunkeys stood outside it, apparently dazed, while from inside the carriage came heart-rending lamentations and cries. I thought I'd pass by and let them all be—; it was no affair of mine: but humanity insisted, and would not take a denial. (I think it is Heine says that humanity shoves its nose in everywhere!) So I stopped; and my driver and myself, with the other fellows, lifted the carriage on to its legs again, or perhaps I should say wheels, as it had no legs.

"I thought to myself, 'This is that very prince they mentioned!' So, I looked in. Good Heavens! it was our prince! Here was a meeting, if you like! I yelled at him, 'Prince—uncle!' Of course he hardly knew me at the first glance, but he very soon recognised me. At least, I don't believe he knows who I am really, even *now*; I think he takes me for someone else, not a relation. I saw him last seven years ago, as a boy; I remember *him*, because he struck me so; but how was he to remember *me*? At all events, I told him my name, and he embraced me ecstatically; and all the while he himself was crying and trembling with fright. He really was *crying*, I'll take my oath he was! I saw it with my own eyes.

"Well, we talked a bit, and at last I persuaded him to get into my trap with me, and call in at Mordasoff, if only for one day, to rest and compose his feelings. He told me that Stepanida Matveyevna had had a letter from Moscow, saying that her father, or daughter, or both, with all her family, were dying; and that she had wavered for a long time, and at last determined to go away for ten days. The prince sat out one day, and then another, and then a third, measuring wigs, and powdering and pomading himself; then he grew sick of it, and determined to go and see an old friend, a priest called Misael, who lived at the Svetozersk Hermitage. Some of the household, being afraid of the great Stepanida's wrath, opposed the prince's proposed journey; but the latter insisted, and started last night after dinner. He slept at Igishova, and went off this morning again, at sunrise. Just at the turn going down to the Reverend Mr. Misael's, the carriage went over, and the prince was very nearly shot down the ravine."

"Then I step in and save the prince, and persuade him to come and pay a visit to our mutual friend, Maria Alexandrovna (of whom the prince told me that she is the most delightful and charming woman he has ever known). And so here we are, and the prince is now upstairs attending to his wigs and so on, with the help of his valet, whom he took along with him, and whom he always would and will take with him wherever he goes; because he would sooner die than appear before ladies without certain little secret touches which require the valet's hand. There you are, that's the whole story."

"Why, what a humourist he is, isn't he, Zina?" said the lady of the house. "How beautifully you told the story! Now, listen, Paul: one question; explain to me clearly how you are related to the prince; you call him uncle!"

"I really don't know, Maria Alexandrovna; seventh, cousin I think, or something of that sort. My aunt knows all about it; it was she who made me go down to see him at Donchanova, when I got kicked out by Stepanida! I simply call him 'uncle,' and he answers me; that's about all our relationship."

"Well, I repeat, it was Providence that made you bring him straight to my house as you did. I tremble to think of what might have happened to the poor dear prince if somebody else, and not I, had got hold of him! Why, they'd have torn him to pieces among them, and picked his bones! They'd have pounced on him as on a new-found mine; they might easily have robbed him; they are capable of it. You have no idea, Paul, of the depth of meanness and greediness to which the people of this place have fallen!"

"But, my dear good Maria Alexandrovna—as if he would ever *think* of bringing him anywhere but to yourself," said the widow, pouring out a cup of tea; "you don't suppose he would have taken the prince to Mrs. Antipova's, surely, do you?"

"Dear me, how very long he is coming out," said Maria Alexandrovna, impatiently rising from her chair; "it really is quite strange!"

"Strange! what, of uncle? Oh dear, no! he'll probably be another five hours or so putting himself together; besides, since he has no memory whatever, he has very likely quite forgotten that he has come to your house! Why, he's a most extraordinary man, Maria Alexandrovna."

"Oh don't, don't! Don't talk like that!"

"Why not, Maria Alexandrovna? He is a lump of composition, not a man at all! Remember, you haven't seen him for six years, and I saw him half an hour ago. He is half a corpse; he's only the memory of a man; they've forgotten to bury him! Why, his eye is made of glass, and his leg of cork, and he goes on wires; he even talks on wires!"

Maria Alexandrovna's face took a serious expression. "What nonsense you talk," she said; "and aren't you ashamed of yourself, you, a young man and a relation too—to talk like that of a most honourable old nobleman! not to mention his incomparable personal goodness and kindness" (her voice here trembled with emotion). "He is a relic, a chip, so to speak, of our old aristocracy. I know, my dear young friend, that all this flightiness on your part, proceeds from those 'new ideas' of which you are so fond of talking; but, goodness me, I've seen a good deal more of life than you have: I'm a mother; and though I see the greatness and nobleness, if you like, of these 'new ideas,' yet I can understand the practical side of things too! Now, this gentleman is an old man, and that is quite enough to render him ridiculous in your eyes. You, who talk of emancipating your serfs, and 'doing something for posterity,' indeed! I tell you what it is, it's your Shakespeare! You stuff yourself full of Shakespeare, who has long ago outlived his time, my dear Paul; and who, if he lived now, with all his wisdom, would never make head or tail of our way of life!"

"If there be any chivalry left in our modern society, it is only in the highest circles of the aristocracy. A prince is a prince either in a hovel or in a palace! *You* are more or less a representative of the highest circles; your extraction is aristocratic. I, too, am not altogether a stranger to the upper ten, and it's a bad fledgling that fouls its own nest! However, my dear Paul, you'll forget your Shakespeare yet, and you'll understand all this much better than I can explain it. I foresee it! Besides, I'm sure you are only joking; you did not mean what you said. Stay here, dear Paul, will you? I'm just going upstairs to make inquiries after the prince, he may want something." And Maria Alexandrovna left the room hurriedly.

"Maria Alexandrovna seems highly delighted that Mrs. Antipova, who thinks so much of herself, did not get hold of the prince!" remarked the widow; "Mrs. Antipova must be gnashing her teeth with annoyance just now! She's a relation, too, as I've been pointing out to Maria Alexandrovna."

Observing that no one answered her, and casting her eyes on Zina and Mosgliakoff, the widow suddenly recollected herself, and discreetly left the room, as though to fetch something. However, she rewarded herself for her discretion, by putting her ear to the keyhole, as soon as she had closed the door after her.

Pavel Alexandrovitch immediately turned to Zina. He was in a state of great agitation; his voice shook.

"Zenaida Afanassievna, are you angry with me?" he began, in a timid, beseechful tone.

"With you? Why?" asked Zina, blushing a little, and raising her magnificent eyes to his face.

"For coming earlier. I couldn't help it; I couldn't wait another fortnight; I dreamed of you every night; so I flew off to learn my fate. But you are frowning, you are angry;—oh; am I really not to hear anything definite, even now?"

Zina distinctly and decidedly frowned.

"I supposed you would speak of this," she said, with her eyes drooped again, but with a firm and severe voice, in which some annoyance was perceptible; "and as the expectation of it was very tedious, the sooner you had your say, the better! You insist upon an answer again, do you? Very well, I say *wait*, just as I said it before. I now repeat, as I did then, that I have not as yet decided, and cannot therefore promise to be your wife. You cannot force a girl to such a decision, Pavel Alexandrovitch! However, to relieve your mind, I will add, that I do not as yet refuse you absolutely; and pray observe that I give you thus much hope of a favourable reply, merely out of forced deference to your impatience and agitation; and that if I think fit afterwards to reject you altogether, you are not to blame me for having given you false hopes. So now you know."

"Oh, but—but—what's the use of that? What hope am I to get out of that, Zina?" cried Mosgliakoff in piteous tones.

"Recollect what I have said, and draw whatever you please from the words; that's your business. I shall add nothing. I do not refuse you; I merely say—wait! And I repeat, I reserve the free right of rejecting you afterwards if I choose so to do. Just one more word: if you come here before the fixed time relying on outside protection, or even on my mother's influence to help you gain your end, let me tell you, you make a great mistake; if you worry me now, I shall refuse you outright. I hope we understand each other now, and that I shall hear no more of this, until the period I named to you for my decision." All this was said quietly and drily, and without a pause, as if learnt by rote. Paul felt foolish; but just at this moment Maria Alexandrovna entered the room, and the widow after her.

"I think he's just coming, Zina! Nastasia Petrovna, make some new tea quick, please!" The good lady was considerably agitated.

"Mrs. Antipova has sent her maid over to inquire about the prince already. How angry she must be feeling just now," remarked the widow, as she commenced to pass over the tea-urn.

"And what's that to me!" replied Maria Alexandrovna, over her shoulder. "Just as though *I* care what she thinks! *I* shall not send a maid to her kitchen to inquire, I assure you! And I am surprised, downright *surprised*, that, not only you, but all the town, too, should suppose that that wretched woman is my enemy! I appeal to you, Paul—you know us both. Why should I be her enemy, now? Is it a question of precedence? Pooh! I don't care about precedence! She may be first, if she likes, and I shall be readiest of all to go and congratulate her on the fact. Besides, it's all nonsense! Why, I take her part; I *must* take her part. People malign her; *why* do you all fall upon her so? Because she's young, and likes to be smart; is that it? Dear me, I think finery is a good bit better than some other failings—like Natalia Dimitrievna's, for instance, who has a taste for things that cannot be mentioned in polite society. Or is it that Mrs. Antipova goes out too much, and never stays at home? My goodness! why, the woman has never had any education; naturally she doesn't care to sit down to read, or anything of that sort. True, she coquets and makes eyes at everybody who looks at her. But why do people tell her that she's pretty? especially as she only has a pale face, and nothing else to boast of.

"She is amusing at a dance, I admit; but why do people tell her that she dances the polka so well? She wears hideous hats and things; but it's not her fault that nature gave her no gift of good taste. She talks scandal; but that's the custom of the place—who doesn't here? That fellow, Sushikoff, with his whiskers, goes to see her pretty often while her husband plays cards, but that *may* be merely a trumped-up tale; at all events I always say so, and take her part in every way! But, good heavens! here's the prince at last! 'Tis he, 'tis he! I recognise him! I should know him out of a thousand! At last I see you! At last, my Prince!" cried Maria Alexandrovna,—and she rushed to greet the prince as he entered the room.

CHAPTER IV.

At first sight you would not take this prince for an old man at all, and it is only when you come near and take a good look at him, that you see he is merely a dead man working on wires. All the resources of science are brought to bear upon this mummy, in order to give it the appearance of life and youth. A marvellous wig, glorious whiskers, moustache and napoleon—all of the most raven black—cover half his face. He is painted and powdered with very great skill, so much so that one can hardly detect any wrinkles. What has become of them, goodness only knows.

He is dressed in the pink of fashion, just as though he had walked straight out of a tailor's fashion-page. His coat, his gloves, tie, his waistcoat, his linen, are all in perfect taste, and in the very last mode. The prince limps slightly, but so slightly that one would suppose he did it on purpose because *that* was in fashion too. In his eye he wears a glass—in the eye which is itself glass already.

He was soaked with scent. His speech and manner of pronouncing certain syllables was full of affectation; and this was, perhaps, all that he retained of the mannerisms and tricks of his younger days. For if the prince had not quite lost his wits as yet, he had certainly parted with nearly every vestige of his memory, which—alas!—is a thing which no amount of perfumeries and wigs and rouge and tight-lacing will renovate. He continually forgets words in the midst of conversation, and loses his way, which makes it a matter of some difficulty to carry on a conversation with him. However, Maria Alexandrovna has confidence in her inborn dexterity, and at sight of the prince she flies into a condition of unspeakable rapture.

"Oh! but you've not changed, you've not changed a *bit*!" she cries, seizing her guest by both hands, and popping him into a comfortable arm-chair. "Sit down, dear Prince, do sit down! Six years, prince, six whole long years since we saw each other, and not a letter, not a little tiny scrap of a note all the while. *Oh*, how naughty you have been, prince! And *how* angry I have been with you, my dear friend! But, tea! tea! Good Heavens, Nastasia Petrovna, tea for the prince, quick!"

"Th—thanks, thanks; I'm very s—orry!" stammered the old man (I forgot to mention that he stammered a little, but he did even this as though it were the fashion to do it). "Very s—sorry; fancy, I—I wanted to co—come last year, but they t—told me there was cho—cho—cholera here."

"There was foot and mouth disease here, uncle," put in Mosgliakoff, by way of distinguishing himself. Maria Alexandrovna gave him a severe look.

"Ye—yes, foot and mouth disease, or something of that s—sort," said the prince; "so I st—stayed at home. Well, and how's your h—husband, my dear Anna Nic—Nicolaevna? Still at his proc—procuror's work?"

"No, prince!" said Maria Alexandrovna, a little disconcerted. "My husband is not a procurer."

"I'll bet anything that uncle has mixed you up with Anna Nicolaevna Antipova," said Mosgliakoff, but stopped suddenly on observing the look on Maria Alexandrovna's face.

"Ye—yes, of course, Anna Nicolaevna. A—An. What the deuce! I'm always f—forgetting; Antipova, Antipova, of course," continued the prince.

"No, prince, you have made a great mistake," remarked Maria Alexandrovna, with a bitter smile. "I am not Anna Nicolaevna at all, and I confess I should never have believed that you would not recognise me. You have astonished me, prince. I am your old friend, Maria Alexandrovna Moskaloff. Don't you remember Maria Alexandrovna?"

"M—Maria Alexandrovna! think of that; and I thought she was w—what's her name. Y—yes, Anna Vasilievna! *C'est délicieux.* W—why I thought you were going to take me to this A—Anna Matveyevna. Dear me! *C'est ch—charmant!* It often happens so w—with me. I get taken to the wrong house; but I'm v—very pleased, v—very pleased! So you're not Nastasia Va—silievna? How interesting."

"I'm Maria Alexandrovna, prince; *Maria Alexandrovna*! Oh! how naughty you are, Prince, to forget your best, best friend!"

"Ye—es! ye—yes! best friend; best friend, for—forgive me!" stammered the old man, staring at Zina.

"That's my daughter Zina. You are not acquainted yet, prince. She wasn't here when you were last in the town, in the year —— you know."

"Oh, th—this is your d—daughter!" muttered the old man, staring hungrily at Zina through his glasses. "Dear me, dear me. *Ch—charmante, ch—armante!* But what a lo—ovely girl," he added, evidently impressed.

"Tea! prince," remarked Maria Alexandrovna, directing his attention to the page standing before him with the tray. The prince took a cup, and examined the boy, who had a nice fresh face of his own.

"Ah! this is your l—little boy? Wh—what a charming little b—boy! and does he be—behave nicely?"

"But, prince," interrupted Maria Alexandrovna, impatiently, "what is this dreadful occurrence I hear of? I confess I was nearly beside myself with terror when I heard of it. Were you not hurt at all? *Do* take care. One cannot make light of this sort of thing."

"Upset, upset; the c—coachman upset me!" cried the prince, with unwonted vivacity. "I thought it was the end of the world, and I was fri—frightened out of my wits. I didn't expect it; I didn't, indeed! and my co—oachman is to blame for it all. I trust you, my friend, to lo—ok into the matter well. I feel sure he was making an attempt on my life!"

"All right, all right, uncle," said Paul; "I'll see about it. But look here—forgive him, just this once, uncle; just this once, won't you?"

"N—not I! Not for anything! I'm sure he wants my life, he and Lavrenty too. It's—it's the 'new ideas;' it's Com—Communism, in the fullest sense of the word. I daren't meet them anywhere."

"You are right, you are quite right, prince," cried Maria Alexandrovna. "You don't know how I suffer myself from these wretched people. I've just been obliged to change two of my servants; and you've no idea how *stupid* they are, prince."

"Ye—yes! quite so!" said the prince, delighted—as all old men are whose senile chatter is listened to with servility. "But I like a fl—flunky to look stupid; it gives them presence. There's my Terenty, now. You remember Terenty, my friend? Well, the f—first time I ever looked at him I said, 'You shall be my ha—hall porter.' He's stupid, phen—phen—omenally stupid, he looks like a she—sheep; but his dig—dignity and majesty are wonderful. When I look at him he seems to be composing some l—learned dis—sertation. He's just like the German philosopher, Kant, or like some fa—fat old turkey, and that's just what one wants in a serving-man."

Maria Alexandrovna laughed, and clapped her hands in the highest state of ecstasy; Paul supported her with all his might; Nastasia Petrovna laughed too; and even Zina smiled.

"But, prince, how clever, how witty, how *humorous* you are!" cried Maria Alexandrovna. "What a wonderful gilt of remarking the smallest refinements of character. And for a man like you to eschew all society, and shut yourself up for five years! With such talents! Why, prince, you could *write*, you could be an author. You could emulate Von Vezin, Gribojedoff, Gogol!"

"Ye—yes! ye—yes!" said the delighted prince. "I can reproduce things I see, very well. And, do you know, I used to be a very wi—witty fellow indeed, some time ago. I even wrote a play once. There were some very smart couplets, I remember; but it was never acted."

"Oh! how nice it would be to read it over, especially just *now*, eh, Zina? for we are thinking of getting up a play, you must know, prince, for the benefit of the 'martyrs of the Fatherland,' the wounded soldiers. There, now, how handy your play would come in!"

"Certainly, certainly. I—I would even write you another. I think I've quite forgotten the old one. I remember there were two or three such epigrams that (here the prince kissed his own hand to convey an idea of the exquisite wit of his lines) I recollect when I was abroad I made a real furore. I remember Lord Byron well; we were great friends; you should have seen him dance the mazurka one day during the Vienna Congress."

"Lord Byron, uncle?—Surely not!"

"Ye—yes, Lord Byron. Perhaps it was not Lord Byron, though, perhaps it was someone else; no, it wasn't Lord Byron, it was some Pole; I remember now. A won—der-ful fellow that Pole was! He said he was a C—Count, and he turned out to be a c—cook—shop man! But he danced the mazurka won—der—fully, and broke his leg at last. I recollect I wrote some lines at the time:—

"Our little Pole

Danced like blazes."

—How did it go on, now? Wait a minute! No, I can't remember."

"I'll tell you, uncle. It must have been like this," said Paul, becoming more and more inspired:—

"But he tripped in a hole,

Which stopped his crazes."

10

"Ye—yes, that was it, I think, or something very like it. I don't know, though—perhaps it wasn't. Anyhow, the lines were very sm—art. I forget a good deal of what I have seen and done. I'm so b—busy now!"

"But do let me hear how you have employed your time in your solitude, dear prince," said Maria Alexandrovna. "I must confess that I have thought of you so often, and often, that I am burning with impatience to hear more about you and your doings."

"Employed my time? Oh, very busy; very busy, ge—generally. One rests, you see, part of the day; and then I imagine a good many things."

"I should think you have a very strong imagination, haven't you, uncle?" remarked Paul.

"Exceptionally so, my dear fellow. I sometimes imagine things which amaze even myself! When I was at Kadueff,—by-the-by, you were vice-governor of Kadueff, weren't you?"

"I, uncle! Why, what are you thinking of?"

"No? Just fancy, my dear fellow! and I've been thinking all this time how f—funny that the vice-governor of Kadueff should be here with quite a different face: he had a fine intelligent, dig—dignified face, you know. A wo—wonderful fellow! Always writing verses, too; he was rather like the Ki—King of Diamonds from the side view, but—"

"No, prince," interrupted Maria Alexandrovna. "I assure you, you'll ruin yourself with the life you are leading! To make a hermit of oneself for five years, and see no one, and hear no one: you're a lost man, dear prince! Ask any one of those who love you, they'll all tell you the same; you're a lost man!"

"No," cried the prince, "really?"

"Yes, I assure you of it! I am speaking to you as a sister—as a friend! I am telling you this because you are very dear to me, and because the memory of the past is sacred to me. No, no! You must change your way of living; otherwise you will fall ill, and break up, and die!"

"Gracious heavens! Surely I shan't d—die so soon?" cried the old man. "You—you are right about being ill; I am ill now and then. I'll tell you all the sy—symptoms! I'll de—detail them to you. Firstly I—"

"Uncle, don't you think you had better tell us all about it another day?" Paul interrupted hurriedly. "I think we had better be starting just now, don't you?"

"Yes—yes, perhaps, perhaps. But remind me to tell you another time; it's a most interesting case, I assure you!"

"But listen, my dear prince!" Maria Alexandrovna resumed, "why don't you try being doctored abroad?"

"Ab—road? Yes, yes—I shall certainly go abroad. I remember when I was abroad, about '20; it was delightfully g—gay and jolly. I very nearly married a vi—viscountess, a French woman. I was fearfully in love, but som—somebody else married her, not I. It was a very s—strange thing. I had only gone away for a coup—couple of hours, and this Ger—German baron fellow came and carried her off! He went into a ma—madhouse afterwards!"

"Yes, dear prince, you must look after your health. There are such good doctors abroad; and—besides, the mere change of life, what will not that alone do for you! You *must* desert your dear Donchanovo, if only for a time!"

"C—certainly, certainly! I've long meant to do it. I'm going to try hy—hydropathy!"

"Hydropathy?"

"Yes. I've tried it once before: I was abroad, you know, and they persuaded me to try drinking the wa—waters. There wasn't anything the matter with me, but I agreed, just out of deli—delicacy for their feelings; and I did seem to feel easier, somehow. So I drank, and drank, and dra—ank up a whole waterfall; and I assure you if I hadn't fallen ill just then I should have been quite well, th—thanks to the water! But, I confess, you've frightened me so about these ma—maladies and things, I feel quite put out. I'll come back d—directly!"

"Why, prince, where are you off to?" asked Maria Alexandrovna in surprise.

"Directly, directly. I'm just going to note down an i—idea!"

"What sort of idea?" cried Paul, bursting with laughter.

Maria Alexandrovna lost all patience.

"I cannot understand what you find to laugh at!" she cried, as the old man disappeared; "to laugh at an honourable old man, and turn every word of his into ridicule—presuming on his angelic good nature. I assure you I *blushed* for you, Paul Alexandrovitch! Why, what do you see in him to laugh at? I never saw anything funny about him!"

"Well, I laugh because he does not recognise people, and talks such nonsense!"

"That's simply the result of his sad life, of his dreadful five years' captivity, under the guardianship of that she-devil! You should *pity*, not laugh at him! He did not even know *me*; you saw it yourself. I tell you it's a crying shame; he must be saved, at all costs! I recommend him to go abroad so that he may get out of the clutches of that—beast of a woman!"

"Do you know what—we must find him a wife!" cried Paul.

"Oh, Mr. Mosgliakoff, you are too bad; you really are too bad!"

"No, no, Maria Alexandrovna; I assure you, this time I'm speaking in all seriousness. Why *not* marry him off? Isn't it rather a brilliant idea? What harm can marriage do him? On the contrary, he is in that position that such a step alone can save him! In the first place, he will get rid of that fox of a woman; and, secondly, he may find some girl, or better still some widow—kind, good, wise and gentle, and poor, who will look after him as his own daughter would, and who will be sensible of the honour he does her in making her his wife! And what could be better for the old fellow than to have such a person about him, rather than the—woman he has now? Of course she must be nice-looking, for uncle appreciates good looks; didn't you observe how he stared at Miss Zina?"

"But how will you find him such a bride?" asked Nastasia Petrovna, who had listened intently to Paul's suggestion.

11

"What a question! Why, you yourself, if you pleased! and why not, pray? In the first place, you are good-looking, you are a widow, you are generous, you are poor (at least I don't think you are very rich). Then you are a very reasonable woman: you'll learn to love him, and take good care of him; you'll send that other woman to the deuce, and take your husband abroad, where you will feed him on pudding and lollipops till the moment of his quitting this wicked world, which will be in about a year, or in a couple of months perhaps. After that, you emerge a princess, a rich widow, and, as a prize for your goodness to the old gentleman, you'll marry a fine young marquis, or a governor-general, or somebody of the sort! There—that's a pretty enough prospect, isn't it?"

"Tfu! Goodness me! I should fall in love with him at once, out of pure gratitude, if he only proposed to me!" said the widow, with her black eyes all ablaze; "but, of course, it's all nonsense!"

"Nonsense, is it? Shall I make it sound sense, then, for you? Ask me prettily, and if I don't make you his betrothed by this evening, you may cut my little finger off! Why, there's nothing in the world easier than to talk uncle into anything you please! He'll only say, 'Ye—yes, ye—yes,' just as you heard him now! We'll marry him so that he doesn't know anything about it, if you like? We'll deceive him and marry him, if you please! Any way you like, it can be done! Why, it's for his own good; it's out of pity for himself! Don't you think, seriously, Nastasia Petrovna, that you had better put on some smart clothes in any case?"

Paul's enthusiasm amounted by now to something like madness, while the widow's mouth watered at his idea, in spite of her better judgment.

"I know, I know I look horridly untidy!" she said. "I go about anyhow, nowadays! There's nothing to dress for. Do I really look like a regular cook?"

All this time Maria Alexandrovna sat still, with a strange expression on her face. I shall not be far wrong if I say that she listened to Paul's wild suggestion with a look of terror, almost: she was confused and startled; at last she recollected herself, and spoke.

"All this is very nice, of course; but at the same time it is utter nonsense, and perfectly out of the question!" she observed cuttingly.

"Why, why, my good Maria Alexandrovna? Why is it such nonsense, or why out of the question?"

"For many reasons; and, principally because you are, as the prince is also, a guest in my house; and I cannot permit anyone to forget their respect towards my establishment! I shall consider your words as a joke, Paul Alexandrovitch, and nothing more! Here comes the prince—thank goodness!"

"Here I am!" cried the old man as he entered. "It's a wo—wonderful thing how many good ideas of all s—sorts I'm having to-day! and another day I may spend the whole of it without a single one! As—tonishing? not one all day!"

"Probably the result of your accident, to-day, uncle! Your nerves got shaken up, you see, and ——"

"Ye—yes, I think so, I think so too; and I look on the accident as pro—fitable, on the whole; and therefore I'm going to excuse the coachman. I don't think it was an at—tempt on my life, after all, do you? Besides, he was punished a little while a—go, when his beard was sh—shaved off!"

"Beard shaved off? Why, uncle, his beard is as big as a German state!"

"Ye—yes, a German state, you are very happy in your ex—pressions, my boy! but it's a fa—false one. Fancy what happened: I sent for a price-current for false hair and beards, and found advertisements for splendid ser—vants' and coachmen's beards, very cheap—extraordinarily so! I sent for one, and it certainly was a be—auty. But when we wanted to clap it on the coachman, we found he had one of his own t—twice as big; so I thought, shall I cut off his, or let him wear it, and send this one b—back? and I decided to shave his off, and let him wear the f—false one!"

"On the theory that art is higher than nature, I suppose uncle?"

"Yes, yes! Just so—and I assure you, when we cut off his beard he suffered as much as though we were depriving him of all he held most dear! But we must be go—going, my boy!"

"But I hope, dear prince, that you will only call upon the governor!" cried Maria Alexandrovna, in great agitation. "You are *mine* now, Prince; you belong to *my* family for the whole of this day! Of course I will say nothing about the society of this place. Perhaps you are thinking of paying Anna Nicolaevna a visit? I will not say a word to dissuade you; but at the same time I am quite convinced that—time will show! Remember one thing, dear Prince, that I am your sister, your nurse, your guardian for to-day at least, and oh!—I tremble for you. You don't know these people, Prince, as I do! You don't know them fully: but time will teach you all you do not know."

"Trust me, Maria Alexandrovna!" said Paul, "it shall all be exactly as I have promised you!"

"Oh—but you're such a weathercock! I can never trust *you*! I shall wait for you at dinner time, Prince; we dine early. How sorry I am that my husband happens to be in the country on such an occasion! How happy he would have been to see you! He esteems you so highly, Prince; he is so sincerely attached to you!"

"Your husband? dear me! So you have a h—husband, too!" observed the old man.

"Oh, prince, prince! how forgetful you are! Why, you have *quite*, quite forgotten the past! My husband, Afanassy Matveyevitch, surely you must remember him? He is in the country: but you have seen him thousands of times before! Don't you remember—Afanassy Matveyevitch!"

"Afanassy Matveyevitch. Dear me!—and in the co—country! how very charming! So you have a husband! dear me, I remember a vaudeville very like that, something about—

"The husband's here,

And his wife at Tvere."

Charming, charming—such a good rhyme too; and it's a most ri—diculous story! Charming, charming; the wife's away, you know, at Jaroslaf or Tv—— or somewhere, and the husband is——is——Dear me! I'm afraid I've forgotten what we were talking about! Yes, yes—

we must be going, my boy! *Au revoir, madame; adieu, ma charmante demoiselle*" he added, turning to Zina, and putting the ends of her fingers to his lips.

"Come back to dinner,—to dinner, prince! don't forget to come back here quick!" cried Maria Alexandrovna after them as they went out; "be back to dinner!"

CHAPTER V.

"Nastasia Petrovna, I think you had better go and see what is doing in the kitchen!" observed Maria Alexandrovna, as she returned from seeing the prince off. "I'm sure that rascal Nikitka will spoil the dinner! Probably he's drunk already!" The widow obeyed.

As the latter left the room, she glanced suspiciously at Maria Alexandrovna, and observed that the latter was in a high state of agitation. Therefore, instead of going to look after Nikitka, she went through the "Salon," along the passage to her own room, and through that to a dark box-room, where the old clothes of the establishment and such things were stored. There she approached the locked door on tiptoe; and stifling her breath, she bent to the keyhole, through which she peeped, and settled herself to listen intently. This door, which was always kept shut, was one of the three doors communicating with the room where Maria Alexandrovna and Zina were now left alone. Maria Alexandrovna always considered Nastasia an untrustworthy sort of woman, although extremely silly into the bargain. Of course she had suspected the widow—more than once—of eavesdropping; but it so happened that at the moment Madame Moskaleva was too agitated and excited to think of the usual precautions.

She was sitting in her arm-chair and gazing at Zina. Zina felt that her mother was looking at her, and was conscious of an unpleasant sensation at her heart.

"Zina!"

Zina slowly turned her head towards the speaker, and lifted her splendid dark eyes to hers.

"Zina, I wish to speak to you on a most important matter!"

Zina adopted an attentive air, and sat still with folded hands, waiting for light. In her face there was an expression of annoyance as well as irony, which she did her best to hide.

"I wish to ask you first, Zina, what you thought of *that* Mosgliakoff, to-day?"

"You have known my opinion of him for a long time!" replied Zina, surlily.

"Yes, yes, of course! but I think he is getting just a little *too* troublesome, with his continual bothering you—"

"Oh, but he says he is in love with me, in which case his importunity is pardonable!"

"Strange! You used not to be so ready to find his offences pardonable; you used to fly out at him if ever I mentioned his name!"

"Strange, too, that you always defended him, and were so very anxious that I should marry him!—and now you are the first to attack him!"

"Yes; I don't deny, Zina, that I did wish, then, to see you married to Mosgliakoff! It was painful to me to witness your continual grief, your sufferings, which I can well realize—whatever you may think to the contrary!—and which deprived me of my rest at night! I determined at last that there was but one great change of life that would ever save you from the sorrows of the past, and that change was matrimony! We are not rich; we cannot afford to go abroad. All the asses in the place prick their long ears, and wonder that you should be unmarried at twenty-three years old; and they must needs invent all sorts of stories to account for the fact! As if I would marry you to one of our wretched little town councillors, or to Ivan Ivanovitch, the family lawyer! There are no husbands for *you* in this place, Zina! Of course Paul Mosgliakoff is a silly sort of a fellow, but he is better than these people here: he is fairly born, at least, and he has 150 serfs and landed property, all of which is better than living by bribes and corruption, and goodness knows what jobbery besides, as these do! and that is why I allowed my eyes to rest on him. But I give you my solemn word, I never had any real sympathy for him! and if Providence has sent you someone better now, oh, my dear girl, how fortunate that you have not given your word to Mosgliakoff! You didn't tell him anything for certain to-day, did you, Zina?"

"What is the use of beating about the bush, when the whole thing lies in a couple of words?" said Zina, with some show of annoyance.

"Beating about the bush, Zina? Is that the way to speak to your mother? But what am I? You have long ceased to trust to your poor mother! You have long looked upon me as your enemy, and not as your mother at all!"

"Oh, come mother! you and I are beyond quarrelling about an expression! Surely we understand one another by now? It is about time we did, anyhow!"

"But you offend me, my child! you will not believe that I am ready to devote *all, all* I can give, in order to establish your destiny on a safe and happy footing!"

Zina looked angrily and sarcastically at her mother.

"Would not you like to marry me to this old prince, now, in order to establish my destiny on a safe and happy footing?"

"I have not said a word about it; but, as you mention the fact, I will say that if you *were* to marry the prince it would be a very happy thing for you, and—"

"Oh! Well, I consider the idea utter nonsense!" cried the girl passionately. "Nonsense, humbug! and what's more, I think you have a good deal too much poetical inspiration, mamma; you are a woman poet in the fullest sense of the term, and they call you by that name here! You are always full of projects; and the impracticability and absurdity of your ideas does not in the least discourage you. I felt, when the prince was sitting here, that you had that notion in your head. When Mosgliakoff was talking nonsense there about marrying the old man to somebody I read all your thoughts in your face. I am ready to bet any money that you are thinking of it now, and that you have come to me now about this very question! However, as your perpetual projects on my behalf are beginning to weary me to death, I must beg you not to say one word about it, not *one word*, mamma; do you hear me? *not one word*; and I beg you will remember what I say!" She was panting with rage.

"You are a child, Zina; a poor sorrow-worn, sick child!" said Maria Alexandrovna in tearful accents. "You speak to your poor mother disrespectfully; you wound me deeply, my dear; there is not another mother in the world who would have borne what I have to bear from you every day! But you are suffering, you are sick, you are sorrowful, and I am your mother, and, first of all, I am a Christian woman! I must bear it all, and forgive it. But one word, Zina: if I had really thought of the union you suggest, why would you consider it so impracticable and absurd? In my opinion, Mosgliakoff has never said a wiser thing than he did to-day, when he declared that marriage was what alone could save the prince,—not, of course, marriage with that slovenly slut, Nastasia; there he certainly *did* make a fool of himself!"

"Now look here, mamma; do you ask me this out of pure curiosity, or with design? Tell me the truth."

"All I ask is, why does it appear to you to be so absurd?"

"Good heavens, mother, you'll drive me wild! What a fate!" cried Zina, stamping her foot with impatience. "I'll tell you why, if you can't see for yourself. Not to mention all the other evident absurdities of the plan, to take advantage of the weakened wits of a poor old man, and deceive him and marry him—an old cripple, in order to get hold of his money,—and then every day and every hour to wish for his death, is, in my opinion, not only nonsense, but so mean, *so* mean, mamma, that I—I can't congratulate you on your brilliant idea; that's all I can say!"

There was silence for one minute.

"Zina, do you remember all that happened two years ago?" asked Maria Alexandrovna of a sudden.

Zina trembled.

"Mamma!" she said, severely, "you promised me solemnly never to mention that again."

"And I ask you now, as solemnly, my dear child, to allow me to break that promise, just once! I have never broken it before. Zina! the time has come for a full and clear understanding between us! These two years of silence have been terrible. We cannot go on like this. I am ready to pray you, on my knees, to let me speak. Listen, Zina, your own mother who bore you beseeches you, on her knees! And I promise you faithfully, Zina, and solemnly, on the word of an unhappy but adoring mother, that never, under any circumstances, not even to save my life, will I ever mention the subject again. This shall be the last time, but it is absolutely necessary!"

Maria Alexandrovna counted upon the effect of her words, and with reason:

"Speak, then!" said Zina, growing whiter every moment.

"Thank you, Zina!——Two years ago there came to the house, to teach your little brother Mitya, since dead, a tutor——"

"Why do you begin so solemnly, mamma? Why all this eloquence, all these quite unnecessary details, which are painful to me, and only too well known to both of us?" cried Zina with a sort of irritated disgust.

"Because, my dear child, I, your mother, felt in some degree bound to justify myself before you; and also because I wish to present this whole question to you from an entirely new point of view, and not from that mistaken position which you are accustomed to take up with regard to it; and because, lastly, I think you will thus better understand the conclusion at which I shall arrive upon the whole question. Do not think, dear child, that I wish to trifle with your heart! No, Zina, you will find in me a real mother; and perhaps, with tears streaming from your eyes, you will ask and beseech at my feet—at the feet of the '*mean woman*,' as you have just called me,—yes, and pray for that reconciliation which you have rejected so long! That's why I wish to recall all, Zina, *all* that has happened, from the very beginning; and without this I shall not speak at all!"

"Speak, then!" repeated Zina, cursing the necessity for her mother's eloquence from the very bottom of her heart.

"I continue then, Zina!——This tutor, a master of the parish school, almost a boy, makes upon you what is, to me, a totally inexplicable impression. I built too much upon my confidence in your good sense, or your noble pride, and principally upon the fact of his insignificance—(I must speak out!)—to allow myself to harbour the slightest suspicion of you! And then you suddenly come to me, one fine day, and state that you intend to marry the man! Zina, it was putting a knife to my heart! I gave a shriek and lost consciousness.

"But of course you remember all this. Of course I thought it my duty to use all my power over you, which power you called tyranny. Think for yourself—a boy, the son of a deacon, receiving a salary of twelve roubles a month—a writer of weak verses which are printed, out of pity, in the 'library of short readings.' A man, a boy, who could talk of nothing but that accursed Shakespeare,—this boy to be the husband of Zenaida Moskaloff! Forgive me, Zina, but the very thought of it all makes me *wild*!

"I rejected him, of course. But no power would stop *you*; your father only blinked his eyes, as usual, and could not even understand what I was telling him about. You continue your relations with this boy, even giving him rendezvous, and, worst of all, you allow yourself to correspond with him!

"Rumours now begin to flit about town: I am assailed with hints; they blow their trumpets of joy and triumph; and suddenly all my fears and anticipations are verified! You and he quarrel over something or other; he shows himself to be a boy (I can't call him a man!), who is utterly unworthy of you, and threatens to show your letters all over the town! On hearing this threat, you, beside yourself with irritation, boxed his ears. Yes, Zina, I am aware of even that fact! I know all, all! But to continue—the wretched boy shows one of your letters the very same day to that ne'er-do-well Zanshin, and within an hour Natalie Dimitrievna holds it in her hands—my deadly enemy! The same evening the miserable fellow attempts to put an end to himself, in remorse. In a word, there is a fearful scandal stirred up. That slut, Nastasia, comes panting to me with the dreadful news; she tells me that Natalie Dimitrievna has had your letter for a whole hour. In a couple of hours the whole town will learn of your foolishness! I bore it all. I did not fall down in a swoon; but oh, the blows, the blows you dealt to my heart, Zina! That shameless scum of the earth, Nastasia, says she will get the letter back for two hundred roubles! I myself run over, in thin shoes, too, through the snow to the Jew Baumstein, and pledge my diamond clasps—a keepsake of my dear mother's! In a couple of hours the letter is in my hands! Nastasia had stolen it; she had broken open a desk, and your honour was safe!

14

"But what a dreadful day you had sentenced me to live! I noticed some grey hairs among my raven locks for the first time, next morning! Zina, you have judged this boy's action yourself now! You can admit now, and perhaps smile a bitter smile over the admission, that it was beyond the limits of good sense to wish to entrust your fate to this youth.

"But since that fatal time you are wretched, my child, you are miserable! You cannot forget him, or rather not him—for he was never worthy of you,—but you cannot forget the phantom of your past joy! This wretched young fellow is now on the point of death—consumption, they say; and you, angel of goodness that you are! you do not wish to marry while he is alive, because you fear to harass him in his last days; because to this day he is miserable with jealousy, though I am convinced that he never loved you in the best and highest sense of the word! I know well that, hearing of Mosgliakoff's proposal to you, he has been in a flutter of jealousy, and has spied upon you and your actions ever since; and you—you have been merciful to him, my child. And oh! God knows how I have watered my pillow with tears for you!"

"Oh, mother, do drop all this sort of thing!" cried Zina, with inexpressible agony in her tone. "Surely we needn't hear all about your pillow!" she added, sharply. "Can't we get on without all this declamation and pirouetting?"

"You do not believe me, Zina! Oh! do not look so unfriendly at me, my child! My eyes have not been dry these two years. I have hidden my tears from you; but I am changed, Zina mine, much changed and in many ways! I have long known of your feelings, Zina, but I admit I have only lately realized the depth of your mental anguish. Can you blame me, my child, if I looked upon this attachment of yours as romanticism—called into being by that accursed Shakespeare, who shoves his nose in everywhere where he isn't wanted?

"What mother would blame me for my fears of that kind, for my measures, for the severity of my judgment? But now, understanding as I do, and realizing your two years' sufferings, I can estimate the depth of your real feelings. Believe me, I understand you far better than you understand yourself! I am convinced that you love not him—not this unnatural boy,—but your lost happiness, your broken hopes, your cracked idol!

"I have loved too—perhaps more deeply than yourself; I, too, have suffered, I, too, have lost my exalted ideals and seen them levelled with the earth; and therefore who can blame me now—and, above all, can *you* blame me now,—if I consider a marriage with the prince to be the one saving, the one *essential* move left to you in your present position"?

Zina listened to this long declamation with surprise. She knew well that her mother never adopted this tone without good reason. However this last and unexpected conclusion fairly amazed her.

"You don't mean to say you seriously entertain the idea of marrying me to this prince?" she cried bewildered, and gazing at her mother almost with alarm; "that this is no mere idea, no project, no flighty inspiration, but your deliberate intention? I *have* guessed right, then? And pray, *how* is this marriage going to save me? and *why* is it essential to me in my present position? And—and what has all this to do with what you have been talking about?——I cannot understand you, mother,—not a bit!"

"And *I* can't understand, angel mine, how you *cannot* see the connection of it all!" cried Maria Alexandrovna, in her turn. "In the first place, you would pass into new society, into a new world. You would leave for ever this loathsome little town, so full of sad memories for you; where you meet neither friends nor kindness; where they have bullied and maligned you; where all these—these *magpies* hate you because you are good looking! You could go abroad this very spring, to Italy, Switzerland, Spain!—to Spain, Zina, where the Alhambra is, and where the Guadalquiver flows—no wretched little stream like this of ours!"

"But, one moment, mother; you talk as though I were married already, or at least as if the prince had made me an offer!"

"Oh, no—oh dear, no! don't bother yourself about that, my angel! I know what I'm talking about! Let me proceed. I've said my 'firstly;' now, then, for my 'secondly!' I understand, dear child, with what loathing you would give your hand to that Mosgliakoff!——"

"I know, without your telling me so, that I shall never be *his* wife!" cried Zina, angrily, and with flashing eyes.

"If only you knew, my angel, how I understand and enter into your loathing for him! It is dreadful to vow before the altar that you will love a man whom you *cannot* love—how dreadful to belong to one whom you cannot esteem! And he insists on your *love*—he only marries you for love. I can see it by the way he looks at you! Why deceive ourselves? I have suffered from the same thing for twenty-five years; your father ruined me—he, so to speak, sucked up my youth! You have seen my tears many a time!——"

"Father's away in the country, don't touch *him*, please!" said Zina.

"I know you always take his part! Oh, Zina, my very heart trembled within me when I thought to arrange your marriage with Mosgliakoff for financial reasons! I trembled for the consequences. But with the prince it is different, you need not deceive him; you cannot be expected to give him your *love*, not your *love*—oh, no! and he is not in a state to ask it of you!"

"Good heavens, what nonsense! I do assure you you are in error from the very first step—from the first and most important step! Understand, that I do not care to make a martyr of myself for some unknown reason! Know, also, that I shall not marry anyone at all; I shall remain a maid. You have bitten my head off for the last two years because I would not marry. Well, you must accept the fact, and make the best of it; that's all I can say, and so it shall be!"

"But Zina, darling—my Zina, don't be so cross before you have heard me out! What a hot-headed little person you are, to be sure! Let me show you the matter from my point of view, and you'll agree with me—you really will! The prince will live a year—two at most; and surely it is better to be a young widow than a decayed old maid! Not to mention the fact that you will be a princess—free, rich, independent! I dare say you look with contempt upon all these calculations—founded upon his death; but I am a mother, and what mother will blame me for my foresight?

"And if you, my angel of kindness, are unwilling to marry, even now, out of tenderness for that wretched boy's feelings, oh, think, think how, by marrying this prince, you will rejoice his heart and soothe and comfort his soul! For if he has a single particle of commonsense, he must understand that jealousy of this old man were *too* absurd—*too* ridiculous! He will understand that you marry him—for money, for convenience; that stern necessity compels you to it!

15

"And lastly, he will understand that—that,—well I simply wish to say, that, upon the prince's death, you will be at liberty to marry whomsoever you please."

"That's a truly simple arrangement! All I have to do is to marry this prince, rob him of his money, and then count upon his death in order to marry my lover! You are a clever arithmetician, mamma; you do your sums and get your totals nicely. You wish to seduce me by offering me this! Oh, I understand you, mamma—I understand you well! You cannot resist the expression of your noble sentiments and exalted ideas, even in the manufacture of a nasty business. Why can't you say simply and straightforwardly, 'Zina, this is a dirty affair, but it will pay us, so please agree with me?' at all events, that would be candid and frank on your part."

"But, my dear child, why, *why* look at it from this point of view? Why look at it under the light of suspicion as *deceit*, and low cunning, and covetousness? You consider my calculations as meanness, as deceit; but, by all that is good and true, where is the meanness? Show me the deceit. Look at yourself in the glass: you are so beautiful, that a kingdom would be a fair price for you! And suddenly you, you, the possessor of this divine beauty, sacrifice yourself, in order to soothe the last years of an old man's life! You would be like a beautiful star, shedding your light over the evening of his days. You would be like the fresh green ivy, twining in and about his old age; not the stinging nettle that this wretched woman at his place is, fastening herself upon him, and thirstily sucking his blood! Surely his money, his rank are not worthy of being put in the scales beside *you*? Where is the meanness of it; where is the deceit of all this? You don't know what you are saying, Zina."

"I suppose they *are* worthy of being weighed against me, if I am to marry a cripple for them! No, mother, however you look at it, it is deceit, and you can't get out of *that*!"

"On the contrary, my dear child, I can look at it from a high, almost from an exalted—nay, Christian—point of view. You, yourself, told me once, in a fit of temporary insanity of some sort, that you wished to be a sister of charity. You had suffered; you said your heart could love no more. If, then, you cannot love, turn your thoughts to the higher aspect of the case. This poor old man has also suffered—he is unhappy. I have known him, and felt the deepest sympathy towards him—akin to love,—for many a year. Be his friend, his daughter, be his plaything, even, if you like; but warm his old heart, and you are doing a good work—a virtuous, kind, noble work of love.

"He may be funny to look at; don't think of that. He's but half a man—pity him! You are a Christian girl—do whatever is right by him; and this will be medicine for your own heart-wounds; employment, action, all this will heal you too, and where is the deceit here? But you do not believe me. Perhaps you think that I am deceiving myself when I thus talk of duty and of action. You think that I, a woman of the world, have no right to good feeling and the promptings of duty and virtue. Very well, do not trust me, if you like: insult me, do what you please to your poor mother; but you will have to admit that her words carry the stamp of good sense,—they are saving words! Imagine that someone else is talking to you, not I. Shut your eyes, and fancy that some invisible being is speaking. What is worrying you is the idea that all this is for money—a sort of sale or purchase. Very well, then *refuse* the money, if it is so loathsome to your eyes. Leave just as much as is absolutely necessary for yourself, and give the rest to the poor. Help *him*, if you like, the poor fellow who lies there a-dying!"

"He would never accept my help!" muttered Zina, as though to herself.

"He would not, but his mother would!" said Maria Alexandrovna. "She would take it, and keep her secret. You sold your ear-rings, a present from your aunt, half a year or so ago, and helped her; *I* know all about it! I know, too, that the woman washes linen in order to support her unfortunate son!"

"He will soon be where he requires no more help!"

"I know, I understand your hints." Maria Alexandrovna sighed a real sigh. "They say he is in a consumption, and must die.

"But *who* says so?

"I asked the doctor the other day, because, having a tender heart, Zina, I felt interested in the poor fellow. The doctor said that he was convinced the malady was *not* consumption; that it was dangerous, no doubt, but still *not* consumption, only some severe affection of the lungs. Ask him yourself! He certainly told me that under different conditions—change of climate and of his style of living,—the sick man might well recover. He said—and I have read it too, somewhere, that off Spain there is a wonderful island, called Malaga—I think it was Malaga; anyhow, the name was like some wine, where, not only ordinary sufferers from chest maladies, but even consumptive patients, recover entirely, solely by virtue of the climate, and that sick people go there on purpose to be cured.

"Oh, but Spain—the Alhambra alone—and the lemons, and the riding on mules. All this is enough in itself to impress a poetical nature. You think he would not accept your help, your money—for such a journey? Very well—deceit is permissible where it may save a man's life.

"Give him hope, too! Promise him your love; promise to marry him when you are a widow! Anything in the world can be said with care and tact! Your own mother would not counsel you to an ignoble deed, Zina. You will do as I say, to save this boy's life; and with this object, everything is permissible! You will revive his hope; he will himself begin to think of his health, and listen to what the doctor says to him. He will do his best to resuscitate his dead happiness; and if he gets well again, even if you never marry him, you will have saved him—raised him from the dead!

"I can look at him with some sympathy. I admit I can, now! Perhaps sorrow has changed him for the better; and I say frankly, if he should be worthy of you when you become a widow, marry him, by all means! You will be rich then, and independent. You can not only cure him, but, having done so, you can give him position in the world—a career! Your marriage to him will then be possible and pardonable, not, as now, an absolute impossibility!

"For what would become of both of you were you to be capable of such madness *now*? Universal contempt, beggary; smacking little boys, which is part of his duty; the reading of Shakespeare; perpetual, hopeless life in Mordasoff; and lastly his certain death, which will undoubtedly take place before long unless he is taken away from here!

"While, if you resuscitate him—if you raise him from the dead, as it were, you raise him to a good, useful, and virtuous life! He may then enter public life—make himself rank, and a name! At the least, even if he must die, he will die happy, at peace with himself, in your arms—for he will be by then assured of your love and forgiveness of the past, and lying beneath the scent of myrtles and lemons, beneath the tropical sky of the South. Oh, Zina, all this is within your grasp, and all—all is *gain*. Yes, and all to be had by merely marrying this prince."

Maria Alexandrovna broke off, and for several minutes there was silence; not a word was said on either side: Zina was in a state of indescribable agitation. I say indescribable because I will not attempt to describe Zina's feelings: I cannot guess at them; but I *think* that Maria Alexandrovna had found the road to her heart.

Not knowing how her words had sped with her daughter, Maria Alexandrovna now began to work her busy brain to imagine and prepare herself for every possible humour that Zina might prove to be in; but at last she concluded that she had happened upon the right track after all. Her rude hand had touched the sorest place in Zina's heart, but her crude and absurd sentimental twaddle had not blinded her daughter. "However, that doesn't matter"—thought the mother. "All I care to do is to make her *think*; I wish my ideas to stick!" So she reflected, and she gained her end; the effect was made—the arrow reached the mark. Zina had listened hungrily as her mother spoke; her cheeks were burning, her breast heaved.

"Listen, mother," she said at last, with decision; though the sudden pallor of her face showed clearly what the decision had cost her. "Listen mother——" But at this moment a sudden noise in the entrance hall, and a shrill female voice, asking for Maria Alexandrovna, interrupted Zina, while her mother jumped up from her chair.

"Oh! the devil fly away with this magpie of a woman!" cried the latter furiously. "Why, I nearly drove her out by force only a fortnight ago!" she added, almost in despair. "I can't, I can't receive her now. Zina, this question is too important to be put off: she must have news for me or she never would have dared to come. I won't receive the old —— Oh! *how* glad I am to see you, dear Sophia Petrovna. What lucky chance brought *you* to see me? What a *charming* surprise!" said Maria Alexandrovna, advancing to receive her guest.

Zina escaped out of the room.

CHAPTER VI.

Mrs. Colonel Tarpuchin, or Sophia Petrovna, was only morally like a magpie; she was more akin to the sparrow tribe, viewed physically. She was a little bit of a woman of fifty summers or so, with lively eyes, and yellow patches all over her face. On her little wizened body and spare limbs she wore a black silk dress, which was perpetually on the rustle: for this little woman could never sit still for an instant.

This was the most inveterate and bitterest scandal-monger in the town. She took her stand on the fact that she was a Colonel's wife, though she often fought with her husband, the Colonel, and scratched his face handsomely on such occasions.

Add to this, that it was her custom to drink four glasses of "vodki" at lunch, or earlier, and four more in the evening; and that she hated Mrs. Antipova to madness.

"I've just come in for a minute, *mon ange*," she panted; "it's no use sitting down—no time! I wanted to let you know what's going on, simply that the whole town has gone mad over this prince. Our 'beauties,' you know what I mean! are all after him, fishing for him, pulling him about, giving him champagne—you would not believe it! *would* you now? How on earth you could ever have let him out of the house, I can't understand! Are you aware that he's at Natalia Dimitrievna's at this moment?"

"At *Natalia Dimitrievna's*?" cried Maria Alexandrovna jumping up. "Why, he was only going to see the Governor, and then call in for one moment at the Antipova's!"

"Oh, yes, just for one moment—of course! Well, catch him if you can, there! That's all I can say. He found the Governor 'out,' and went on to Mrs. Antipova's, where he has promised to dine. There Natalia caught him—she is never away from Mrs. Antipova nowadays,—and persuaded him to come away with her to lunch. So there's your prince! catch him if you can!"

"But how—Mosgliakoff's with him—he promised—"

"Mosgliakoff, indeed,—why, he's gone too! and they'll be playing at cards and clearing him out before he knows where he is! And the things Natalia is saying, too—out loud if you please! She's telling the prince to his face that you, *you* have got hold of him with certain views—*vous comprenez*?"

"She calmly tells him this to his face! Of course he doesn't understand a word of it, and simply sits there like a soaked cat, and says 'Ye—yes!' And would you believe it, she has trotted out her Sonia—a girl of fifteen, in a dress down to her knees—my word on it? Then she has sent for that little orphan—Masha; she's in a short dress too,—why, I swear it doesn't reach her knees. I looked at it carefully through my pince-nez! She's stuck red caps with some sort of feathers in them on their heads, and set them to dance some silly dance to the piano accompaniment for the prince's benefit! You know his little weakness as to our sex,—well, you can imagine him staring at them through his glass and saying, '*Charmant!*—What figures!' Tfu! They've turned the place into a music hall! Call that a dance! I was at school at Madame Jarne's, I know, and there were plenty of princesses and countesses there with me, too; and I know I danced before senators and councillors, and earned their applause, too: but as for this dance—it's a low can-can, and nothing more! I simply *burned* with shame,—I couldn't stand it, and came out."

"How! have you been at Natalia Dimitrievna's? Why, you——!"

"What!—she offended me last week? is that what you you mean? Oh, but, my dear, I *had* to go and have a peep at the prince—else, when should I have seen him? As if I would have gone *near* her but for this wretched old prince. Imagine—chocolate handed round and *me left out*. I'll let her have it for that, some day! Well, good-bye, *mon ange*: I must hurry off to Akulina, and let her know all about it. You may say good-bye to the prince; he won't come near you again now! He has no memory left, you know, and Mrs. Antipova will simply carry him off bodily to her house. He'll think it's all right——They're all afraid of you, you know; they think that you want to get hold of him— you understand! Zina, you know!"

"*Quelle horreur!*"

"Oh, yes, I know! I tell you—the whole town is talking about it! Mrs. Antipova is going to make him stay to dinner—and then she'll just keep him! She's doing it to spite *you*, my angel. I had a look in at her back premises. *Such* arrangements, my dear. Knives clattering, people running about for champagne. I tell you what you must do—go and grab him as he comes out from Natalia Dimitrievna's to Antipova's to dinner. He promised *you* first, he's *your* guest. Tfu! don't you be laughed at by this brace of chattering magpies—good for nothing baggage, both of them. 'Procuror's lady,' indeed! Why, I'm a Colonel's wife. Tfu!—*Mais adieu, mon ange.* I have my own sledge at the door, or I'd go with you."

Having got rid of this walking newspaper, Maria Alexandrovna waited a moment, to free herself of a little of her super-abundant agitation. Mrs. Colonel's advice was good and practical. There was no use losing time,—none to lose, in fact. But the greatest difficulty of all was as yet unsettled.

Maria Alexandrovna flew to Zina's room.

Zina was walking up and down, pale, with hands folded and head bent on her bosom: there were tears in her eyes, but Resolve was there too, and sparkled in the glance which she threw on her mother as the latter entered the room. She hastily dried her tears, and a sarcastic smile played on her lips once more.

"Mamma," she began, anticipating her mother's speech "you have already wasted much of your eloquence over me—too much! But you have not blinded me; I am not a child. To do the work of a sister of mercy, without the slightest call thereto,—to justify one's meanness—meanness proceeding in reality from the purest egotism, by attributing to it noble ends,—all this is a sort of Jesuitism which cannot deceive me. Listen! I repeat, all *this could not deceive me*, and I wish you to understand that!"

"But, dearest child!" began her mother, in some alarm.

"Be quiet, mamma; have patience, and hear me out. In spite of the full consciousness that all this is pure Jesuitism, and in spite of my full knowledge of the absolutely ignoble character of such an act, I accept your proposition in full,—you hear me—*in full*; and inform you hereby, that I am ready to marry the prince. More! I am ready to help you to the best of my power in your endeavours to lure the prince into making me an offer. Why do I do this? You need not know that; enough that I have consented. I have consented to the whole thing—to bringing him his boots, to serving him; I will dance for him, that my meanness may be in some sort atoned. I shall do all I possibly can so that he shall never regret that he married me! But in return for my consent I insist upon knowing *how* you intend to bring the matter about? Since you have spoken so warmly on the subject—I know you!—I am convinced you must have some definite plan of operation in your head. Be frank for once in your life; your candour is the essential condition upon which alone I give my consent. I shall not decide until you have told me what I require!"

Maria Alexandrovna was so surprised by the unexpected conclusion at which Zina arrived, that she stood before the latter some little while, dumb with amazement, and staring at her with all her eyes. Prepared to have to combat the stubborn romanticism of her daughter—whose obstinate nobility of character she always feared,—she had suddenly heard this same daughter consent to all that her mother had required of her.

Consequently, the matter had taken a very different complexion. Her eyes sparkled with delight:

"Zina, Zina!" she cried; "you are my life, my——"

She could say no more, but fell to embracing and kissing her daughter.

"Oh, mother, I don't *want* all this kissing!" cried Zina, with impatience and disgust. "I don't need all this rapture on your part; all I want is a plain answer to my question!"

"But, Zina, I love you; I adore you, darling, and you repel me like this! I am working for your happiness, child!"

Tears sparkled in her eyes. Maria Alexandrovna really loved her daughter, in her own way, and just now she actually felt deeply, for once in her life—thanks to her agitation, and the success of her eloquence.

Zina, in spite of her present distorted view of things in general, knew that her mother loved her; but this love only annoyed her; she would much rather—it would have been easier for her—if it had been hate!

"Well, well; don't be angry, mamma—I'm so excited just now!" she said, to soothe her mother's feelings.

"I'm not angry, I'm not angry, darling! I know you are much agitated!" cried Maria Alexandrovna. "You say, my child, that you wish me to be candid: very well, I will; I will be *quite* frank, I assure you. But you might have trusted me! Firstly, then, I must tell you that I have no actually organized plan yet—no *detailed* plan, that is. You must understand, with that clever little head of yours, you must see, Zina, that I *cannot* have such a plan, all cut out. I even anticipate some difficulties. Why, that magpie of a woman has just been telling me all sorts of things. We ought to be quick, by the bye; you see, I am quite open with you! But I swear to you that the end shall be attained!" she added, ecstatically. "My convictions are not the result of a poetical nature, as you told me just now; they are founded on facts. I rely on the weakness of the prince's intellect—which is a canvas upon which one can stitch any pattern one pleases!

"The only fear is, we may be interfered with! But a fool of a woman like that is not going to get the better of *me*!" she added, stamping her foot, and with flashing eyes. "That's my part of the business, though; and to manage it thoroughly I must begin as soon as possible—in fact, the whole thing, or the most important part of it, must be arranged this very day!"

"Very well, mamma; but now listen to one more piece of candour. Do you know why I am so interested in your plan of operations, and do not trust it? because I am not sure of myself! I have told you already that I consent to this——meanness; but I must warn you that if I find the details of your plan of operations *too* dirty, too mean and repulsive, I shall not be able to stand it, and shall assuredly throw you over. I know that this is a new pettiness, to consent to a wicked thing and then fear the dirt in which it floats! But what's to be done? So it will be, and I warn you!"

"But Zina, dear child, where is the wickedness in this?" asked Maria Alexandrovna timidly. "It is simply a matter of a marriage for profit; everybody does it! Look at it in this light, and you will see there is nothing particular in it; it is good 'form' enough!"

"Oh, mamma, don't try to play the fox over me! Don't you see that I have consented to everything—to *everything*? What else do you require of me? Don't be alarmed if I call things by their proper names! For all you know it may be my only comfort!" And a bitter smile played over her lips.

"Very well, very well, dear! we may disagree as to ideas and yet be very fond of one another. But if you are afraid of the working of my plan, and dread that you will see any baseness or meanness about it, leave it all to me, dear, and I guarantee you that not a particle of dirt shall soil you! Your hands shall be clean! As if I would be the one to compromise you! Trust me entirely, and all shall go grandly and with dignity; all shall be done worthily; there shall be no scandal—even if there be a whisper afterwards, we shall all be out of the way, far off! We shall not stay here, of course! Let them *howl* if they like, *we* won't care. Besides, they are not worth bothering about, and I wonder at your being so frightened of these people, Zina. Don't be angry with me! how can you be so frightened, with your proud nature?"

"I'm not frightened; you don't understand me a bit!" said Zina, in a tone of annoyance.

"Very well, darling; don't be angry. I only talk like this because these people about here are always stirring up mud, if they can; while you—this is the first time in your life you have done a mean action.—*Mean* action! What an old fool I am! On the contrary, this is a most generous, *noble* act! I'll prove this to you once more, Zina. Firstly, then, it all depends upon the point of view you take up——"

"Oh! bother your proofs, mother. I've surely had enough of them by now," cried Zina angrily, and stamped her foot on the floor.

"Well, darling, I won't; it was stupid of me—I won't!"

There was another moment's silence. Maria Alexandrovna looked into her daughter's eyes as a little dog looks into the eyes of its mistress.

"I don't understand how you are going to set about it," said Zina at last, in a tone of disgust. "I feel sure you will only plunge yourself into a pool of shame! I'm not thinking of these people about here. I despise their opinions; but it would be very ignominious for *you*."

"Oh! if that's all, my dear child, don't bother your head about it: please, *please* don't! Let us be agreed about it, and then you need not fear for me. Dear me! if you but knew, though, what things I have done, and kept my skin whole! I tell you this is *nothing* in comparison with *real* difficulties which I have arranged successfully. Only let me try. But, first of all we must get the prince *alone*, and that as soon as possible. That's the first move: all the rest will depend upon the way we manage this. However, I can foresee the result. They'll all rise against us; but I'll manage *them* all right! I'm a little nervous about Mosgliakoff. He——"

"Mosgliakoff!" said Zina, contemptuously.

"Yes, but don't you be afraid, Zina! I'll give you my word I'll work him so that he shall help us himself. You don't know me yet, my Zina. My child, when I heard about this old prince having arrived this morning, the idea, as it were, shone out all at once in my brain! Who would have thought of his really coming to us like this! It is a chance such as you might wait for a thousand years in vain. Zina, my angel! there's no shame in what you are doing. What *is* wrong is to marry a man whom you loathe. Your marriage with the prince will be no *real* marriage; it is simply a domestic contract. It is he, the old fool, who gains by it. It is *he* who is made unspeakably, immeasurably happy. Oh! Zina, how lovely you look to-day. If I were a man I would give you half a kingdom if you but raised your finger for it! *Asses* they all are! Who wouldn't kiss a hand like this?" and Maria Alexandrovna kissed her daughter's hand warmly. "Why, this is my own flesh and blood, Zina. What's to be done afterwards? You won't part with me, will you? You won't drive your old mother away when you are happy yourself? No, darling, for though we have quarrelled often enough, you have not such another friend as I am, Zina! You——"

"Mamma, if you've made up your mind to it all, perhaps it is time you set about making some move in the matter. We are losing time," said Zina, impatiently.

"Yes, it is, it is indeed time; and here am I gabbling on while they are all doing their best to seduce the prince away from us. I must be off at once. I shall find them, and bring the prince back by force, if need be. Good-bye, Zina, darling child. Don't be afraid, and don't look sad, dear; please don't! It will be all well, nay, *gloriously* well! Good-bye, good-bye!"

Maria Alexandrovna made the sign of the Cross over Zina, and dashed out of the room. She stopped one moment at her looking-glass to see that all was right, and then, in another minute, was seated in her carriage and careering through the Mordasoff streets. Maria Alexandrovna lived in good style, and her carriage was always in waiting at that hour in case of need.

"No, no, my dears! it's not for *you* to outwit me," she thought, as she drove along. "Zina agrees; so half the work is done. Oh, Zina, Zina! so your imagination is susceptible to pretty little visions, is it? and I *did* treat her to a pretty little picture. She was really touched at last; and how lovely the child looked to-day! If I had her beauty I should turn half Europe topsy-turvy. But wait a bit, it's all right. Shakespeare will fly away to another world when you're a princess, my dear, and know a few people. What does she know? Mordasoff and the tutor! And what a princess she will make. I *love* to see her pride and pluck. She looks at you like any queen. And not to know her own good! However, she soon will. Wait a bit; let this old fool die, and then the boy, and I'll marry her to a reigning prince yet! The only thing I'm afraid of is—haven't I trusted her too much? Didn't I allow my feelings to run away with me too far? I am anxious about her. I am anxious, anxious!"

Thus Maria Alexandrovna reflected as she drove along. She was a busy woman, was Maria Alexandrovna.

Zina, left alone, continued her solitary walk up and down the room with folded hands and thoughtful brow. She had a good deal to think of! Over and over again she repeated, "It's time—it's time—oh, it's time!" What did this ejaculation mean? Once or twice tears glistened on her long silken eyelashes, and she did not attempt to wipe them away.

Her mother worried herself in vain, as far as Zina was concerned; for her daughter had quite made up her mind:—she was ready, come what might!

"Wait a bit!" said the widow to herself, as she picked her way out of her hiding-place, after having observed and listened to the interview between Zina and her mother. "And I was thinking of a wedding dress for myself; I positively thought the prince would really come my way! So much for *my* wedding dress—what a fool I was! Oho! Maria Alexandrovna—I'm a baggage, am I—and a beggar;—and I took a bribe of two hundred roubles from you, did I? And I didn't spend it on expenses connected with your precious daughter's letter, did I? and break open a desk for your sake with my own hands! Yes, madam; I'll teach you what sort of a baggage Nastasia Petrovna is; both of you shall know her a little better yet! Wait a bit!"

CHAPTER VII.

Maria Alexandrovna's genius had conceived a great and daring project.

To marry her daughter to a rich man, a prince, and a cripple; to marry her secretly, to take advantage of the senile feebleness of her guest, to marry her daughter to this old man *burglariously*, as her enemies would call it,—was not only a daring, it was a downright audacious, project.

Of course, in case of success, it would be a profitable undertaking enough; but in the event of *non*-success, what an ignominious position for the authors of such a failure.

Maria Alexandrovna knew all this, but she did not despair. She had been through deeper mire than this, as she had rightly informed Zina.

Undoubtedly all this looked rather too like a robbery on the high road to be altogether pleasant; but Maria Alexandrovna did not dwell much on this thought. She had one very simple but very pointed notion on the subject: namely, this—"*once married they can't be unmarried again.*"

It was a simple, but very pleasant reflection, and the very thought of it gave Maria Alexandrovna a tingling sensation in all her limbs. She was in a great state of agitation, and sat in her carriage as if on pins and needles. She was anxious to begin the fray: her grand plan of operations was drawn up; but there were thousands of small details to be settled, and these must depend upon circumstances. She was not agitated by fear of failure—oh dear, no! all she minded was delay! she feared the delay and obstructions that might be put in her way by the Mordasoff ladies, whose pretty ways she knew so well! She was well aware that probably at this moment the whole town knew all about her present intentions, though she had not revealed them to a living soul. She had found out by painful experience that nothing, not the most secret event, could happen in her house in the morning but it was known at the farthest end of the town by the evening.

Of course, no anticipation, no presentiment, deterred or deceived Maria Alexandrovna: she might feel such sensations at times, but she despised them. Now, this is what had happened in the town this morning, and of which our heroine was as yet only partly informed. About mid-day, that is, just three hours after the prince's arrival at Mordasoff, extraordinary rumours began to circulate about the town.

Whence came they? Who spread them? None could say; but they spread like wild-fire. Everyone suddenly began to assure his neighbour that Maria Alexandrovna had engaged her daughter to the prince; that Mosgliakoff had notice to quit, and that all was settled and signed, and the penniless, twenty-three-year-old Zina was to be the princess.

Whence came this rumour? Could it be that Maria Alexandrovna was so thoroughly known that her friends could anticipate her thoughts and actions under any given circumstances?

The fact is, every inhabitant of a provincial town lives under a glass case; there is no possibility of his keeping anything whatever secret from his honourable co-dwellers in the place. They know *everything*; they know it, too, better than he does himself. Every provincial person should be a psychologist by nature; and that is why I have been surprised, often and often, to observe when I am among provincials that there is not a great number of psychologists—as one would expect,—but an infinite number of dreadful asses. However, this a digression.

The rumour thus spread, then, was a thunder-like and startling shock to the Mordasoff system. Such a marriage—a marriage with this prince—appeared to all to be a thing so very desirable, so brilliant, that the strange side of the affair had not seemed to strike anyone as yet!

One more circumstance must be noticed. Zina was even more detested in the place than her mother; why, I don't know. Perhaps her beauty was the prime cause. Perhaps, too, it was that Maria Alexandrovna was, as it were, one of themselves, a fruit of their own soil: if she was to go away she might even be missed; she kept the place alive more or less—it might be dull without her! But with Zina it was quite a different matter: she lived more in the clouds than in the town of Mordasoff. She was no company for these good people; she could not pair with them. Perhaps she bore herself towards them, unconsciously though, too haughtily.

And now this same Zina, this haughty girl, about whom there were certain scandalous stories afloat, this same Zina was to become a millionaire, a princess, and a woman of rank and eminence!

In a couple of years she might marry again, some duke, perhaps, or a general, maybe a Governor; their own Governor was a widower, and very fond of the ladies! Then she would be the first lady of their province! Why, the very thought of such a thing would be intolerable: in fact, this rumour of Zina's marriage with the prince aroused more irritation in Mordasoff than any other piece of gossip within the memory of man!

People told each other that it was a sin and a shame, that the prince was crazy, that the old man was being deceived, caught, robbed—anything you like; that the prince must be saved from the bloodthirsty talons he had floundered into; that the thing was simply robbery, immorality. And why were any others worse than Zina? Why should not somebody else marry the prince?

Maria Alexandrovna only guessed at all this at present—but that was quite enough. She knew that the whole town would rise up and use all and every means to defeat her ends. Why, they had tried to "confiscate" the prince already; she would have to retrieve him by force, and if she should succeed in luring or forcing him back now, she could not keep him tied to her apron-strings for ever. Again, what was to prevent this whole troop of Mordasoff gossips from coming *en masse* to her salon, under such a plausible plea, too, that she would not be able to turn them out. She knew well that if kicked out of the door these good people would get in at the window—a thing which had actually happened before now at Mordasoff.

In a word, there was not an hour, not a moment to be lost; and meanwhile things were not even begun. A brilliant idea now struck Maria Alexandrovna. We shall hear what this idea was in its proper place, meanwhile I will only state that my heroine dashed through the streets of Mordasoff, looking like a threatening storm-cloud as she swept along full of the stern and implacable resolve that the prince should come back if she had to drag him, and fight for him; and that all Mordasoff might fall in ruins but she should have her way!

Her first move was successful—it could not have been more so.

She chanced to meet the prince in the street, and carried him off to dinner with her.

If my reader wishes to know *how* this feat was accomplished with such a circle of enemies about and around her, and how she managed to make such a fool of Mrs. Antipova, then I must be allowed to point out that such a question is an insult to Maria Alexandrovna. As if *she* were not capable of outwitting any Antipova that ever breathed!

She simply "arrested" the prince at her rival's very door, as he alighted there with Mosgliakoff, in spite of the latter's terror of a scandal, and in spite of everything else; and she popped the old man into the carriage beside her. Of course the prince made very little resistance, and as usual, forgot all about the episode in a couple of minutes, and was as happy as possible.

At dinner he was hilarious to a degree; he made jokes and fun, and told stories which had no ends, or which he tacked on to ends belonging to other stories, without remarking the fact.

He had had three glasses of champagne at lunch at Natalie Dimitrievna's. He now took more wine, and his old head whirled with it. Maria Alexandrovna plied him well. The dinner was very good: the mistress of the house kept the company alive with most bewitching airs and manners,—at least so it should have been, but all excepting herself and the prince were terribly dull on this occasion. Zina sat silent and grave. Mosgliakoff was clearly off his feed: he was very thoughtful; and as this was unusual Maria Alexandrovna was considerably anxious about him. The widow looked cross and cunning; she continually made mysterious signs to Mosgliakoff on the sly; but the latter took no notice of them.

If the mistress herself had not been so amiable and bewitching, the dinner party might have been mistaken for a lunch at a funeral!

Meanwhile Maria Alexandrovna's condition of mind was in reality excited and agitated to a terrible degree. Zina alone terrified her by her tragic look and tearful eyes. And there was another difficulty—for that accursed Mosgliakoff would probably sit about and get in the way of business! One could not well set about it with him in the room!

So, Maria Alexandrovna rose from the table in some agitation.

But what was her amazement, her joyful surprise, when Mosgliakoff came up to her after dinner, of his own accord, and suddenly and most unexpectedly informed her that he must—to his infinite regret—leave the house on important business for a short while.

"Why, where are you going to?" she asked, with great show of regret.

"Well, you see," began Mosgliakoff, rather disconcerted and uncomfortable, "I have to—*may* I come to you for advice?"

"What is it—what is it?"

"Why, you see, my godfather Borodueff—you know the man; I met him in the street to-day, and he is dreadfully angry with me, says I am grown so *proud*, that though I have been in Mordasoff three times I have never shown my nose inside his doors. He asked me to come in for a cup of tea at five—it's four now. He has no children, you know,—and he is worth a million of roubles—*more*, they say; and if I marry Zina—you see,—and he's seventy years old now!"

"Why, my good boy, of course, of course!—what are you thinking of? You must not neglect that sort of thing—go at once, of course! I *thought* you looked preoccupied at dinner. You ought to have gone this morning and shewn him that you cared for him, and so on. Oh, you boys, you boys!" cried Maria Alexandrovna with difficulty concealing her joy.

"Thanks, thanks, Maria Alexandrovna! you've made a man of me again! I declare I quite feared telling you—for I know you didn't think much of the connection.—He is a common sort of old fellow, I know! So good-bye—my respects to Zina, and apologies—I must be off, of course I shall be back soon!"

"Good-bye—take my blessing with you; say something polite to the old man for me; I have long changed my opinion of him; I have grown to like the real old Russian style of the man. *Au revoir, mon ami, au revoir!*"

"Well, it *is* a mercy that the devil has carried him off, out of the way!" she reflected, flushing with joy as Paul took his departure out of the room. But Paul had only just reached the hall and was putting on his fur coat when to him appeared—goodness knows whence—the widow, Nastasia Petrovna. She had been waiting for him.

"Where are you going to?" she asked, holding him by the arm.

"To my godfather Borodueff's—a rich old fellow; I want him to leave me money. Excuse me—I'm in rather a hurry!"

Mosgliakoff was in a capital humour!

"Oh! then say good-bye to your betrothed!" remarked the widow, cuttingly.

"And why 'good-bye'?"

"Why; you think she's yours already, do you? and they are going to marry her to the prince! I heard them say so myself!"

"To the prince? Oh, come now, Nastasia Petrovna!"

"Oh, it's not a case of 'come now' at all! Would you like to see and hear it for yourself? Put down your coat, and come along here,—this way!"

"Excuse me, Nastasia Petrovna, but I don't understand what you are driving at!"

"Oh! you'll understand fast enough if you just bend down here and listen! The comedy is probably just beginning!"

"What comedy?"

"Hush! don't talk so loud! The comedy of humbugging *you*. This morning, when you went away with the prince, Maria Alexandrovna spent a whole hour talking Zina over into marrying the old man! She told her that nothing was easier than to lure the prince into marrying her; and all sorts of other things that were enough to make one sick! Zina agreed. You should have heard the pretty way in which *you* were spoken of! They think you simply a fool! Zina said plump out that she would never marry you! Listen now, listen!"

"Why—why—it would be most godless cunning," Paul stammered, looking sheepishly into Nastasia's eyes.

"Well, just you listen—you'll hear that, and more besides!"

"But how am I to listen?"

"Here, bend down here. Do you see that keyhole!"

"Oh! but, Nastasia Petrovna, I can't eavesdrop, you know!"

"Oh, nonsense, nonsense! Put your pride in your pocket! You've come, and you must listen now!"

"Well, at all events——"

"Oh! if you can't bear to be an eavesdropper, let it alone, and be made a fool of! One goes out of one's way solely out of pity for you, and you must needs make difficulties! What is it to me? I'm not doing this for myself! *I* shall leave the house before night, in any case!"

Paul, steeling his heart, bent to the keyhole.

His pulses were raging and throbbing. He did not realise what was going on, or what he was doing, or where he was.

CHAPTER VIII.

"So you were very gay, prince, at Natalia Dimitrievna's?" asked Maria Alexandrovna, surveying the battlefield before her; she was anxious to begin the conversation as innocently as possible; but her heart beat loud with hope and agitation.

After dinner the Prince had been carried off to the salon, where he was first received in the morning. Maria Alexandrovna prided herself on this room, and always used it on state occasions.

The old man, after his six glasses of champagne, was not very steady on his legs; but he talked away all the more, for the same reason.

Surveying the field of battle before the fray, Maria Alexandrovna had observed with satisfaction that the voluptuous old man had already begun to regard Zina with great tenderness, and her maternal heart beat high with joy.

"Oh! ch—charming—very gay indeed!" replied the prince, "and, do you know, Nat—alia Dimitrievna is a wo—wonderful woman, a ch—charming woman!"

Howsoever busy with her own high thoughts and exalted ideas, Maria Alexandrovna's heart waxed wrathful to hear such a loud blast of praise on her rival's account.

"Oh! Prince," she began, with flashing eyes, "if Natalia Dimitrievna is a charming woman in your eyes, then I really don't know *what* to think! After such a statement, dear Prince, you must not claim to know society here—no, no!"

"Really! You sur—pr—prise me!"

"I assure you—I assure you, *mon cher* Prince! Listen Zina, I must just tell the prince that absurd story about what Natalia Dimitrievna did when she was here last week. Dearest prince, I am not a scandal-monger, but I must, I really *must* tell you this, if only to make you laugh, and to show you a living picture, as it were, of what people are like in this place! Well, last week this Natalia Dimitrievna came to call upon me. Coffee was brought in, and I had to leave the room for a moment—I forget why—at all events, I went out. Now, I happened to have remarked how much sugar there was in the silver sugar basin; it was quite full. Well, I came back in a few minutes—looked at the sugar basin, and!——three lumps—three little wretched lumps at the very bottom of the basin, prince!—and she was all alone in the room, mind! Now that woman has a large house of her own, and lots of money! Of course this is merely a funny story—but you can judge from this what sort of people one has to deal with here!"

"N—no! you don't mean it!" said the prince, in real astonishment. "What a gr—eedy woman! Do you mean to say she ate it all up?"

"There, prince, and that's your 'charming woman!' What do you think of *that* nice little bit of lady-like conduct? I think I should have died of shame if I had ever allowed myself to do such a dirty thing as that!"

"Ye—yes, ye—yes! but, do you know, she is a real '*belle femme*' all the same!"

"What! Natalia Dimitrievna? My dear prince; why, she is a mere tub of a woman! Oh! prince, prince! what have you said? I expected far better taste of *you*, prince!"

"Ye—yes, tub—tub, of course! but she's a n—nice figure, a nice figure! And the girl who danced—oh! a nice figure too, a very nice figure of a wo—woman!"

"What, Sonia? Why she's a mere child, prince? She's only thirteen years old."

"Ye—yes, ye—yes, of course; but her figure de—velops very fast—charming, charming! And the other da—ancing girl, she's de—veloping too—nicely: she's dirty rather—she might have washed her hands, but very at—tractive, charming!" and the prince raised his glass again and hungrily inspected Zina. "*Mais quelle charmante personne!*—what a lovely girl!" he muttered, melting with satisfaction.

"Zina, play us something, or—better still, sing us a song! How she sings, prince! she's an artiste—a real artiste; oh if you only knew, dear prince," continued Maria Alexandrovna, in a half whisper, as Zina rose to go to the piano with her stately but quiet gait and queenly composure, which evidently told upon the old man; "if you only knew what a daughter that is to me! how she can love; how tender, how affectionate she is to me! what taste she has, what a heart!"

"Ye—yes! ye—yes! taste. And do you know, I have only known one woman in all my life who could compare with her in love—liness. It was the late C—ountess Nainsky: she died thirty years ago, a w—onderful woman, and her beauty was quite sur—passing. She married her co—ook at last."

"Her cook, prince?"

"Ye—yes, her cook, a Frenchman, abroad. She bought him a count's title a—broad; he was a good-looking fellow enough, with little moustaches——"

"And how did they get on?"

"Oh, very well indeed; however, they p—arted very soon; they quarrelled about some sa—sauce. He robbed her—and bo—olted."

"Mamma, what shall I play?" asked Zina.

"Better sing us something, Zina. *How* she sings, prince! Do you like music?"

"Oh, ye—yes! charming, charming. I love music pass—sionately. I knew Beethoven, abroad."

"Knew Beethoven!" cried Maria Alexandrovna, ecstatically. "Imagine, Zina, the prince knew Beethoven! Oh, prince, did you really, *really* know the great Beethoven?"

"Ye—yes, we were great friends, Beet—hoven and I; he was always taking snuff—such a funny fellow!"

"What, Beethoven?"

"Yes, Beethoven; or it may have been some other German fellow—I don't know; there are a great many Germans there. I forget."

"Well, what shall I sing, mamma?" asked Zina again.

"Oh Zina darling, do sing us that lovely ballad all about knights, you know, and the girl who lived in a castle and loved a troubadour. Don't you know! Oh, prince, how I do *love* all those knightly stories and songs, and the castles! Oh! the castles, and life in the middle ages, and the troubadours, and heralds and all. Shall I accompany you, Zina? Sit down near here, prince. Oh! those castles, those castles!"

"Ye—yes, ye—yes, castles; I love ca—astles too!" observed the prince, staring at Zina all the while with the whole of his one eye, as if he would like to eat her up at once. "But, good heavens," he cried, "that song! I know that s—song. I heard that song years—years ago! Oh! how that song reminds me of so—omething. Oh, oh."

I will not attempt to describe the ecstatic state of the prince while Zina sang.

She warbled an old French ballad which had once been all the fashion. Zina sang it beautifully; her lovely face, her glorious eyes, her fine sweet contralto voice, all this went to the prince's heart at once; and her dark thick hair, her heaving bosom, her proud, beautiful, stately figure as she sat at the piano, and played and sang, quite finished him. He never took his eyes off her, he panted with excitement. His old heart, partially revivified with champagne, with the music, and with awakening recollections (and who is there who has no beloved memories of the past?), his old heart beat faster and faster. It was long since it had last beat in this way. He was ready to fall on his knees at her feet, when Zina stopped singing, and he was almost in tears with various emotions.

"Oh, my charming, charming child," he cried, putting his lips to her fingers, "you have ra—vished me quite—quite! I remember all now. Oh charming, charming child!——"

The poor prince could not finish his sentence.

Maria Alexandrovna felt that the moment had arrived for her to make a move.

"Why, *why* do you bury yourself alive as you do, prince?" she began, solemnly. "So much taste, so much vital energy, so many rich gifts of the mind and soul—and to hide yourself in solitude all your days; to flee from mankind, from your friends. Oh, it is unpardonable! Prince, bethink yourself. Look up at life again with open eyes. Call up your dear memories of the past; think of your golden youth—your golden, careless, happy days of youth! Wake them, wake them from the dead, Prince! and wake yourself, too; and recommence life among men and women and society! Go abroad—to Italy, to Spain, oh, to Spain, Prince! You must have a guide, a heart that will love and respect, and sympathize with you! You have friends; summon them about you! Give the word, and they will rally round you in crowds! I myself will be the first to throw up everything, and answer to your cry! I remembered our old friendship, my Prince; and I will sacrifice husband, home, all, and follow you. Yes, and were I but young and lovely, like my daughter here, I would be your fellow, your friend, your *wife*, if you said but the word!"

"And I am convinced that you were a most charming creature in your day, too!" said the prince, blowing his nose violently. His eyes were full of tears.

"We live again in our children," said Maria Alexandrovna, with great feeling. "I, too, have my guardian angel, and that is this child, my daughter, Prince, the partner of my heart and of all my thoughts! She has refused seven offers because she is unwilling to leave me! So that she will go too, when you accompany me abroad."

"In that case, I shall certainly go abroad," cried the prince with animation. "As—suredly I shall go! And if only I could ve—venture to hope—oh! you be—witching child, charming, be—witching child!" And the prince recommenced to kiss Zina's fingers. The poor old man was evidently meditating going down on his knees before her.

"But, Prince," began Maria Alexandrovna again, feeling that the opportunity had arrived for another display of eloquence. "But, Prince, you say, 'If only I could flatter myself into indulging any hope!' Why, what a strange man you are, Prince. Surely you do not suppose that you are unworthy the flattering attention of *any* woman! It is not only youth that constitutes true beauty. Remember that you are, so to speak, a chip of the tree of aristocracy. You are a representative of all the most knightly, most refined taste and culture and manners. Did not Maria fall in love with the old man Mazeppa? I remember reading that Lauzun, that fascinating marquis of the court of Louis (I forget which), when he was an old, bent and bowed man, won the heart of one of the youngest and most beautiful women about the court.

"And who told you you are an old man? Who taught you that nonsense? Do men like you ever grow old? You, with your wealth of taste and wit, and animation and vital energy and brilliant manners! Just you make your appearance at some watering-place abroad with a young wife on your arm—some lovely young girl like my Zina, for instance—of course I merely mention her as an example, nothing more,—and you will see at once what a colossal effect you will produce: you, a scion of our aristocracy; she a beauty among beauties! You will lead her triumphantly on your arm; she, perhaps, will sing in some brilliant assemblage; you will delight the company with your wit. Why, all the people of the place will crowd to see you! All Europe will ring with your renown, for every newspaper and feuilleton at the Waters will be full of you. And yet you say, 'If I could but *venture* to *hope*,' indeed!"

"The feuilletons! yes—ye—yes, and the newspapers," said the prince, growing more and more feeble with love, but not understanding half of Maria Alexandrovna's tall talk. "But, my child, if you're not tired, do repeat that song which you have just sung so cha—armingly once more."

"Oh! but, Prince, she has other lovely songs, still prettier ones; don't you remember *L'Hirondelle*? You must have heard it, haven't you?"

"Ye—yes, I remember it; at least I've for—gotten it. No, no! the one you have just sung. I don't want the Hir—ondelle! I want that other song," whined the prince, just like any child.

Zina sang again.

This time the prince could not contain himself; he fell on his knees at her feet, he cried, he sobbed:

"Oh, my beautiful *chatelaine*!" he cried in his shaky old voice—shaky with old age and emotion combined. "Oh, my charming, charming *chatelaine*! oh, my dear child! You have re—minded me of so much that is long, long passed! I always thought then that things must be fairer in the future than in the present. I used to sing duets with the vis—countess in this very ballad! And now, oh! I don't know what to do, I don't know *what* to do!"

The prince panted and choked as he spoke; his tongue seemed to find it difficult to move; some of his words were almost unintelligible. It was clear that he was in the last stage of emotional excitement. Maria Alexandrovna immediately poured oil on the fire.

"Why, Prince, I do believe you are falling in love with my Zina," she cried, feeling that the moment was a solemn one.

The prince's reply surpassed her fondest expectations.

"I am madly in love with her!" cried the old man, all animated, of a sudden. He was still on his knees, and he trembled with excitement as he spoke. "I am ready to give my life for her! And if only I could hope, if only I might have a little hope—I,—but, lift me up; I feel so weak. I—if only she would give me the hope that I might offer her my heart, I—she should sing ballads to me every day; and I could look at her, and look and gaze and gaze at her.——Oh, my God! my God!"

"Prince, Prince! you are offering her your hand. You want to take her from me, my Zina! my darling, my *ange*, my own dear child, Zina! No, Zina, no, I can't let you go! They must tear you from me, Zina. They must tear you first from your mother's arms!"

Maria Alexandrovna sprang to her daughter, and caught her up in a close embrace, conscious, withal, of serious physical resistance on Zina's part. The fond mother was a little overdoing it.

Zina felt this with all her soul, and she looked on at the whole comedy with inexpressible loathing.

However, she held her tongue, and that was all the fond mother required of her.

"She has refused nine men because she will not leave me!" said Maria. "But this time, I fear—my heart tells me that we are doomed to part! I noticed just now how she looked at you, Prince. You have impressed her with your aristocratic manner, with your refinement. Oh! Prince, you are going to separate us—I feel it, I feel it!"

"I ad—ore her!" murmured the poor old man, still trembling like an autumnal leaf.

"And you'll consent to leave your mother!" cried Maria Alexandrovna, throwing herself upon her daughter once more. Zina made haste to bring this, to her, painful scene to an end. She stretched her pretty hand silently to the prince, and even forced herself to smile. The prince reverently took the little hand into his own, and covered it with kisses.

"I am only this mo—ment beginning to live," he muttered, in a voice that seemed choking with rapture and ecstasy.

"Zina," began Maria Alexandrovna, solemnly, "look well at this man! This is the most honest and upright and noble man of all the men I know. He is a knight of the middle ages! But she knows it, Prince, she knows it too well; to my grief I say it. Oh! why did you come here? I am surrendering my treasure to you—my angel! Oh! take care of her, Prince. Her mother entreats you to watch over her. And what mother could blame my grief!"

"Enough, mamma! that's enough," said Zina, quietly.

"Protect her from all hurt and insult, Prince! Can I rely upon your sword to flash in the face of the vile scandal-monger who dares to offend my Zina?"

"Enough, mother, I tell you! am I——?"

"Ye—yes, ye—yes, it shall flash all right," said the prince. "But I want to be married now, at once. I—I'm only just learning what it is to live. I want to send off to Donchanovo at once. I want to send for some di—iamonds I have there. I want to lay them at her feet.——I——"

"What noble ardour! what ecstasy of love! what noble, generous feelings you have, Prince!" cried Maria Alexandrovna. "And you could bury yourself—*bury* yourself, far from the world and society! I shall remind you of this a thousand times! I go mad when I think of that *hellish* woman."

"What could I do? I was fri—ghtened!" stammered the prince in a whining voice: "they wanted to put me in a lu—unatic asylum! I was dreadfully alarmed!"

"In a lunatic asylum? Ah, the scoundrels! oh, the inhuman wretches! Ah, the low cunning of them! Yes, Prince; I had heard of it. But the lunacy was in these people, not in *you*. Why, *why* was it—what for?"

"I don't know myself, what it was for," replied the poor old man, feebly sinking into his chair; "I was at a ball, don't you know, and told some an—ecdote or other and they didn't like it; and so they got up a scandal and a ro—ow."

"Surely that was not all, Prince?"

"No;—the—I was playing cards with Prince Paul De—mentieff, and I was cleared out: you see, I had two kings and three quee—ns, three kings and two qu—eens; or I should say—one king—and some queens—I know I had——."

"And it was for this? Oh, the hellish inhumanity of some people! You are weeping, Prince; but be of good cheer—it is all over now! Now I shall be at hand, dearest Prince,—I shall not leave Zina; and we shall see which of them will dare to say a word to you, *then*! And do you know, my Prince, your marriage will expose them! it will shame them! They will see that you are a man—that a lovely girl like our Zina would never have married a madman! You shall raise your head proudly now, and look them straight in the face!"

"Ye—yes; I shall look them straight in the f—ace!" murmured the prince, slowly shutting his eyes.

Maria Alexandrovna saw that her work was done: the prince was tired out with love and emotion. She was only wasting her eloquence!

"Prince, you are disturbed and tired, I see you are!" she said; "you must rest, you must take a good rest after so much agitation," she added, bending over him maternally.

"Ye—yes, ye—yes; I should like to lie down a little," said the old man.

"Of course, of course! you must lie down! those agitating scenes——stop, I will escort you myself, and arrange your couch with my own hands! Why are you looking so hard at that portrait, Prince? That is my mother's picture; she was an angel—not a woman! Oh, why is she not among us at this joyful moment!"

"Ye—yes; charming—charming! Do you know, I had a mother too,—a princess, and imagine! a re—markably, a re—markably fat woman she was; but that is not what I was going to say,——I—I feel a little weak, and——Au revoir, my charming child—to-morrow—to-day—I will—I—I—Au revoir, au revoir!" Here the poor old fellow tried to kiss his hand, but slipped, and nearly fell over the threshold of the door.

"Take care, dear Prince—take care! lean on my arm!" cried Maria Alexandrovna.

"Charming, ch—arming!" he muttered, as he left the room. "I am only now le—learning to live!"

Zina was left alone.

A terrible oppression weighed down her heart. She felt a sensation of loathing which nearly suffocated her. She despised herself—her cheeks burned. With folded hands, and teeth biting hard into her lips, she stood in one spot, motionless. The tears of shame streamed from her eyes,——and at this moment the door opened, and Paul Mosgliakoff entered the room!

CHAPTER IX.

He had heard all—*all*.

He did not actually enter the room, but stood at the door, pale with excitement and fury. Zina looked at him in amazement.

"So that's the sort of person you are!" he cried panting. "At last I have found you out, have I?"

"Found me out?" repeated Zina, looking at him as though he were a madman. Suddenly her eyes flashed with rage. "How dare you address me like that?" she cried, advancing towards him.

"I have heard all!" said Mosgliakoff solemnly, but involuntarily taking a step backwards.

"You heard? I see—you have been eavesdropping!" cried Zina, looking at him with disdain.

"Yes, I have been eavesdropping! Yes—I consented to do a mean action, and my reward is that I have found out that you, too, are——I don't know how to express to you what I think you!" he replied, looking more and more timid under Zina's eyes.

"And supposing that you *have* heard all: what right have you to blame me? What right have you to speak to me so insolently, in any case?"

"*I!*—*I?* what right have *I?* and *you* can ask me this? You are going to marry this prince, and I have no right to say a word! Why, you gave me your promise—is that nothing?"

"When?"

"How, when?"

"Did not I tell you that morning, when you came to me with your sentimental nonsense—did I not tell you that I could give you no decided answer?"

"But you did not reject me; you did not send me away. I see—you kept me hanging in reserve, in case of need! You lured me into your net! I see, I see it all!"

An expression of pain flitted over Zina's careworn face, as though someone had suddenly stabbed her to the heart; but she mastered her feelings.

"If I didn't turn you out of the house," she began deliberately and very clearly, though her voice had a scarcely perceptible tremor in it, "I refrained from such a course purely out of pity. You begged me yourself to postpone, to give you time, not to say you 'No,' to study you better, and 'then,' you said, 'then, when you know what a fine fellow I am, perhaps you will not refuse me!' These were your own words, or very like them, at the very beginning of your courtship!—you cannot deny them! And now you dare to tell me that I 'lured you into my net,' just as though you did not notice my expression of loathing when you made your appearance this morning! You came a fortnight sooner than I expected you, and I did not hide my disgust; on the contrary, I made it evident—you must have noticed it—I know you did; because you asked me whether I was angry because you had come sooner than you promised! Let me tell you that people who do not, and do not *care* to, hide their loathing for a man can hardly be accused of luring that man into their net! You dare to tell me that I was keeping you in reserve! Very well; my answer to that is, that I judged of you like this: 'Though he may not be endowed with much intellect, still he may turn out to be a good enough fellow; and if so, it might be possible to marry him.' However, being persuaded, now, that you are a fool, and a *mischievous* fool into the bargain,—having found out this fact, to my great joy,—it only remains for me now to wish you every happiness and a pleasant journey. Good-bye!"

With these words Zina turned her back on him, and deliberately made for the door.

Mosgliakoff, seeing that all was lost, boiled over with fury.

"Oh! so I'm a fool!" he yelled; "I'm a fool, am I? Very well, good-bye! But before I go, the whole town shall know of this! They shall all hear how you and your mother made the old man drunk, and then swindled him! I shall let the whole world know it! You shall see what Mosgliakoff can do!"

Zina trembled and stopped, as though to answer; but on reflection, she contented herself by shrugging her shoulders; glanced contemptuously at Mosgliakoff, and left the room, banging the door after her.

At this moment Maria Alexandrovna made her appearance. She heard Mosgliakoff's exclamation, and, divining at once what had happened, trembled with terror. Mosgliakoff still in the house, and near the prince! Mosgliakoff about to spread the news all over the town! At this moment, when secrecy, if only for a short time, was essential! But Maria Alexandrovna was quick at calculations: she thought, with an eagle flight of the mind, over all the circumstances of the case, and her plan for the pacification of Mosgliakoff was ready in an instant!

"What is it, *mon ami*?" she said, entering the room, and holding out her hand to him with friendly warmth.

"How—'*mon ami*?' " cried the enraged Mosgliakoff. "*Mon ami*, indeed! the moment after you have abused and reviled me like a pickpocket! No, no! Not quite so green, my good lady! I'm not to be so easily imposed upon again!"

"I am sorry, extremely sorry, to see you in such a *strange* condition of mind, Paul Alexandrovitch! What expressions you use! You do not take the trouble to choose your words before ladies—oh, fie!"

"Before ladies? Ho ho! You—you are—you are anything you like—but not a lady!" yelled Mosgliakoff.

I don't quite know what he meant, but it was something very terrible, you may be sure!

Maria Alexandrovna looked benignly in his face:

"Sit down!" she said, sorrowfully, showing him a chair, the same that the old prince had reclined in a quarter of an hour before.

"But listen, *will* you listen, Maria Alexandrovna? You look at me just as though you were not the least to blame; in fact, as though *I* were the guilty party! Really, Maria Alexandrovna, this is a little *too* much of a good thing! No human being can stand that sort of thing, Maria Alexandrovna! You must be aware of that fact!"

"My dear friend," replied Maria Alexandrovna—"you will allow me to continue to call you by that name, for you have no better friend than I am!—my friend, you are suffering—you are amazed and bewildered; your heart is sore, and therefore the tone of your remarks to me is perhaps not surprising. But I have made up my mind to open my heart to you, especially as I am, perhaps, in some degree to blame before you. Sit down; let us talk it over!"

Maria Alexandrovna's voice was tender to a sickly extent. Her face showed the pain she was suffering. The amazed Mosgliakoff sat down beside her in the arm-chair.

"You hid somewhere, and listened, I suppose?" she began, looking reproachfully into his face.

"Yes I did, of course I did; and a good thing too! What a fool I should have looked if I hadn't! At all events now I know what you have been plotting against me!" replied the injured man, rudely; encouraging and supporting himself by his own fury.

"And you—and you—with your principles, and with your bringing up, could condescend to such an action—Oh, oh!"

Mosgliakoff jumped up.

"Maria Alexandrovna, this is a little too much!" he cried. "Consider what *you* condescend to do, with *your* principles, and *then* judge of other people."

"One more question," she continued, without replying to his outburst: "who recommended you to be an eavesdropper; who told you anything; who is the spy here? That's what I wish to know!"

"Oh, excuse me; that I shall *not* tell you!"

"Very well; I know already. I said, Paul, that I was in some degree to blame before you. But if you look into the matter you will find that if I am to blame it is solely in consequence of my anxiety to do you a good turn!"

"*What?* a good turn—*me*? No, no, madam! I assure you I am not to be caught again! I'm not quite such a fool!"

He moved so violently in his arm-chair that it shook again.

"Now, do be cool, if you can, my good friend. Listen to me attentively, and you will find that what I say is only the bare truth. In the first place I was anxious to inform you of all that has just taken place, in which case you would have learned everything, down to the smallest detail, without being obliged to descend to eavesdropping! If I did not tell you all before, it was simply because the whole matter was in an embryo condition in my mind. It was then quite possible that what *has* happened would never happen. You see, I am quite open with you.

"In the second place, do not blame my daughter. She loves you to distraction; and it was only by the exercise of my utmost influence that I persuaded her to drop you, and accept the prince's offer."

"I have just had the pleasure of receiving convincing proof of her 'love to distraction!' " remarked Mosgliakoff, ironically and bitterly.

"Very well. But how did you speak to *her*? As a lover should speak? Again, ought *any* man of respectable position and tone to speak like that? You insulted and wounded her!"

"Never mind about my 'tone' now! All I can say is that this morning, when I went away with the prince, in spite of both of you having been as sweet as honey to me before, you reviled me behind my back like a pickpocket! *I* know all about it, you see!"

"Yes, from the same dirty source, I suppose?" said Maria Alexandrovna, smiling disdainfully. "Yes, Paul, I *did* revile you: I pitched into you considerably, and I admit it frankly. But it was simply that I was *bound* to blacken you before her. Why? Because, as I have said, I required her to consent to leave you, and this consent was so difficult to tear from her! Short-sighted man that you are! If she had not loved you, why should I have required so to blacken your character? Why should I have been obliged to take this extreme step? Oh! you don't know all! I was forced to use my fullest maternal authority in order to erase you from her heart; and with all my influence and skill I only succeeded in erasing your dear image superficially and partially! If you saw and heard all just now, it cannot have escaped you that Zina did not once, by either word or gesture, encourage or confirm my words to the prince? Throughout the whole scene she said not one word. She sang, but like an automaton! Her whole soul was in anguish, and at last, out of pity for her, I took the prince away. I am sure, she cried, when I left her alone! When you entered the room you must have observed tears in her eyes?"

Mosgliakoff certainly did recall the fact that when he rushed into the room Zina was crying.

"But you—*you*—why were *you* so against me, Maria Alexandrovna?" he cried. "Why did you revile me and malign me, as you admit you did?"

"Ah, now that's quite a different question. Now, if you had only asked me reasonably at the beginning, you should have had your answer long ago! Yes, you are right. It was I, and I alone, who did it all. Do not think of Zina in the matter. Now, *why* did I do it? I reply, in the first place, for Zina's sake. The prince is rich, influential, has great connections, and in marrying him Zina will make a brilliant match. Very well; then if the prince dies—as perhaps he will die soon, for we are all mortal,—Zina is still young, a widow, a princess, and probably very rich. Then she can marry whom she pleases; she may make another brilliant match if she likes. But of course she will marry the man she loves, and loved before, the man whose heart she wounded by accepting the prince. Remorse alone would be enough to make her marry the man whom she had loved and so deeply injured!"

"Hem!" said Paul, gazing at his boots thoughtfully.

"In the second place," continued Maria, "and I will put this shortly, because, though you read a great deal of your beloved Shakespeare, and extract his finest thoughts and ideals, yet you are very young, and cannot, perhaps, apply what you read. You may not understand my feelings in this matter: listen, however. *I* am giving my Zina to this prince partly for the prince's own sake, because I wish to save him by this marriage. We are old friends; he is the dearest and best of men, he is a knightly, chivalrous gentleman, and he lives helpless and miserable in the claws of that devil of a woman at Donchanovo! Heaven knows that I persuaded Zina into this marriage by putting it to her that she would be performing a great and noble action. I represented her as being the stay and the comfort and the darling and the idol of a poor old man, who probably would not live another year at the most! I showed her that thus his last days should be made happy with love and light and friendship, instead of wretched with fear and the society of a detestable woman. Oh! do not blame Zina. She is guiltless. I am not—I admit it; for if there have been calculations it is I who have made them! But I calculated for her, Paul; for her, not myself! I have outlived my time; I have thought but for my child, and what mother could blame me for this?" Tears sparkled in the fond mother's eyes. Mosgliakoff listened in amazement to all this eloquence, winking his eyes in bewilderment.

"Yes, yes, of course! You talk well, Maria Alexandrovna, but you forget—you gave me your word, you encouraged me, you gave me my hopes; and where am I now? I have to stand aside and look a fool!"

"But, my dear Paul, you don't surely suppose that I have not thought of you too! Don't you see the huge, immeasurable gain to yourself in all this? A gain so vast that I was bound in your interest to act as I did!"

"Gain for me! How so?" asked Paul, in the most abject state of confusion and bewilderment.

"Gracious Heavens! do you mean to say you are really so simple and so short-sighted as to be unable to see *that*?" cried Maria Alexandrovna, raising her eyes to the ceiling in a pious manner. "Oh! youth, youth! That's what comes of steeping one's soul in Shakespeare! You ask me, my dear friend Paul, where is the gain to you in all this. Allow me to make a little digression. Zina loves you—that is an undoubted fact. But I have observed that at the same time, and in spite of her evident love, she is not quite sure of your good feeling and devotion to her; and for this reason she is sometimes cold and self-restrained in your presence. Have you never observed this yourself, Paul?"

"Certainly; I did this very day; but go on, what do you deduce from that fact?"

"There, you see! you have observed it yourself: then of course I am right. She is not quite sure of the *lasting* quality of your feeling for her! I am a mother, and I may be permitted to read the heart of my child. Now, then, supposing that instead of rushing into the room and reproaching, vilifying, even *swearing* at and insulting this sweet, pure, beautiful, proud being, instead of hurling contempt and vituperation at her head—supposing that instead of all this you had received the bad news with composure, with tears of grief, maybe; perhaps even with despair—but at the same time with noble composure of soul——"

"H'm!"

"No, no—don't interrupt me! I wish to show you the picture as it is. Very well, supposing, then, that you had come to her and said, 'Zina, I love you better than my life, but family considerations must separate us; I understand these considerations—they are devised for your greater happiness, and I dare not oppose them. Zina, I forgive you; be happy, if you can!'—think what effect such noble words would have wrought upon her heart!"

"Yes—yes, that's all very true, I quite understand that much! but if I *had* said all this, I should have had to go all the same, without satisfaction!"

"No, no, no! don't interrupt me! I wish to show you the *whole* picture in all its detail, in order to impress you fully and satisfactorily. Very well, then, imagine now that you meet her in society some time afterwards: you meet perhaps at a ball—in the brilliant light of a ball-room, under the soothing strains of music, and in the midst of worldly women and of all that is gay and beautiful. You alone are sad—thoughtful—pale,—you lean against some pillar (where you are visible, however!) and watch her. She is dancing. You hear the strains of Strauss, and the wit and merriment around you, but you are sad and wretched.

"What, think you, will Zina make of it? With what sort of eyes will she gaze on you as you stand there? 'And I could doubt this man!' she will think, 'this man who sacrificed all, all, for my sake—even to the mortal wounding of his heart!' Of course the old love will awake in her bosom and will swell with irresistible power!"

Maria Alexandrovna stopped to take breath. Paul moved violently from side to side of his chair.

"Zina now goes abroad for the benefit of the prince's health—to Italy—to Spain," she continued, "where the myrtle and the lemon tree grow, where the sky is so blue, the beautiful Guadalquiver flows! to the land of love, where none can live without loving; where roses and kisses—so to speak—breathe in the very air around. You follow her—you sacrifice your business, friends, everything, and follow her. And so your love grows and increases with irresistible might. Of course that love is irreproachable—innocent—you will languish for one another—you will meet frequently; of course others will malign and vilify you both, and call your love by baser names—but your love is innocent, as I have purposely said; I am her mother—it is not for me to teach you evil, but good. At all events the prince is not in the condition to keep a very sharp look-out upon you; but if he did, as if there would be the slightest ground for base suspicion? Well, the prince dies at last, and then, who will marry Zina, if not yourself? You are so distant a relative of the prince's that there could be no obstacle to the match; you marry her—she is young still, and rich. You are a grandee in an instant! you, too, are rich now! I will take care that the prince's will is made as it should be; and lastly, Zina, now convinced of your loyalty and faithfulness, will look on you hereafter as her hero, as her paragon of virtue and self-sacrifice! Oh! you must be blind,—*blind*, not to observe and calculate your own profit when it lies but a couple of strides from you, grinning at you, as it were, and saying, 'Here, I am yours, take me! Oh, Paul, Paul!' "

"Maria Alexandrovna!" cried Mosgliakoff, in great agitation and excitement, "I see it all! I have been rude, and a fool, and a scoundrel too!" He jumped up from his chair and tore his hair.

"Yes, and unbusinesslike, that's the chief thing—unbusinesslike, and blindly so!" added Maria Alexandrovna.

"I'm an ass! Maria Alexandrovna," he cried in despair. "All is lost now, and I loved her to madness!"

"Maybe all is not lost yet!" said this successful orator softly, and as though thinking out some idea.

"Oh! if only it could be so! help me—teach me. Oh! save me, save me!"

Mosgliakoff burst into tears.

"My dear boy," said Maria Alexandrovna, sympathetically, and holding out her hand, "you acted impulsively, from the depth and heat of your passion—in fact, out of your great love for her; you were in despair, you had forgotten yourself; she must understand all that!"

"Oh! I love her madly! I am ready to sacrifice everything for her!" cried Mosgliakoff.

"Listen! I will justify you before her."

"Oh, Maria Alexandrovna!"

"Yes, I will. I take it upon myself! You come with me, and you shall tell her exactly what I said!"

"Oh, how kind, how good you are! Can't we go at once, Maria Alexandrovna?"

"Goodness gracious, no! What a very green hand you are, Paul! She's far too proud! she would take it as a new rudeness and impertinence! To-morrow I shall arrange it all comfortably for you: but now, couldn't you get out of the way somewhere for a while, to that godfather of yours, for instance? You could come back in the evening, if you pleased; but my advice would be to stay away!"

"Yes, yes! I'll go—of course! Good heavens, you've made a man of me again!—Well, but look here—one more question:—What if the prince does *not* die so soon?"

"Oh, my dear boy, how delightfully naïve you are! On the contrary, we must pray for his good health! We must wish with all our hearts for long life to this dear, good, and chivalrous old man! I shall be the first to pray day and night for the happiness of my beloved daughter! But alas! I fear the prince's case is hopeless; you see, they must visit the capital now, to bring Zina out into society.—I dreadfully fear that all this may prove fatal to him; however, we'll pray, Paul, we can't do more, and the rest is in the hands of a kind Providence. You see what I mean? Very well—good-bye, my dear boy, bless you! Be a man, and wait patiently—be a man, that's the chief thing! I never doubted your generosity of character; but be brave—good-bye!" She pressed his hand warmly, and Mosgliakoff walked out of the room on tip-toes.

"There goes *one* fool, got rid of satisfactorily!" observed Maria Alexandrovna to herself,—"but there are more behind——!"

At this moment the door opened, and Zina entered the room. She was paler than usual, and her eyes were all ablaze.

"Mamma!" she said, "be quick about this business, or I shall not be able to hold out. It is all so dirty and mean that I feel I must run out of the house if it goes on. Don't drive me to desperation! I warn you—don't weary me out—don't weary me out!"

"Zina—what is it, my darling? You—you've been listening?" cried Maria Alexandrovna, gazing intently and anxiously at her daughter.

"Yes, I have; but you need not try to make me ashamed of myself as you succeeded in doing with that fool. Now listen: I solemnly swear that if you worry and annoy me by making me play various mean and odious parts in this comedy of yours,—I swear to you that I will throw up the whole business and put an end to it in a moment. It is quite enough that I have consented to be a party in the main and essence of the base transactions; but—but—I did not know myself, I am poisoned and suffocated with the stench of it!"—So saying, she left the room and banged the door after her.

Maria Alexandrovna looked fixedly after her for a moment, and reflected.

"I must make haste," she cried, rousing herself; "*she* is the greatest danger and difficulty of all! If these detestable people do not let us alone, instead of acting the town-criers all over the place (as I fear they are doing already!)—all will be lost! She won't stand the worry of it—she'll drop the business altogether!—At all hazards, I must get the prince to the country house, and that quickly, too! I shall be off there at once, first, and bring my fool of a husband up: he shall be made useful for once in his life! Meanwhile the prince shall have his sleep out, and when he wakes up I shall be back and ready to cart him away bodily!"

She rang the bell.

"Are the horses ready?" she inquired of the man.

"Yes, madam, long ago!" said the latter.

She had ordered the carriage the moment after she had taken the prince upstairs.

28

Maria Alexandrovna dressed hurriedly, and then looked in at Zina's room for a moment, before starting, in order to tell her the outlines of her plan of operations, and at the same time to give Zina a few necessary instructions. But her daughter could not listen to her. She was lying on her bed with face hidden in the pillows, crying, and was tearing her beautiful hair with her long white hands: occasionally she trembled violently for a moment, as though a blast of cold had passed through all her veins. Her mother began to speak to her, but Zina did not even raise her head!

Having stood over her daughter in a state of bewilderment for some little while, Maria Alexandrovna left the room; and to make up for lost time bade the coachman drive like fury, as she stepped into the carriage.

"I don't quite like Zina having listened!" she thought as she rattled away. "I gave Mosgliakoff very much the same argument as to herself: she is proud, and may easily have taken offence! H'm! Well, the great thing is to be in time with all the arrangements,—before people know what I am up to! Good heavens, fancy, if my fool of a husband were to be out!!"

And at the very thought of such a thing, Maria Alexandrovna's rage so overcame her that it was clear her poor husband would fare badly for his sins if he proved to be not at home! She twisted and turned in her place with impatience,—the horses almost galloped with the carriage at their heels.

CHAPTER X.

On they flew.

I have said already that this very day, on her first drive after the prince, Maria Alexandrovna had been inspired with a great idea! and I promised to reveal this idea in its proper place. But I am sure the reader has guessed it already!—It was, to "confiscate" the prince in her turn, and carry him off to the village where, at this moment, her husband Afanassy Matveyevitch vegetated alone.

I must admit that our heroine was growing more and more anxious as the day went on; but this is often the case with heroes of all kinds, just before they attain their great ends! Some such instinct whispered to her that it was not safe to remain in Mordasoff another hour, if it could be avoided;—but once in the country house, the whole town might go mad and stand on its head, for all she cared!

Of course she must not lose time, even there! All sorts of things might happen—even the police might interfere. (Reader, I shall never believe, for my part, that my heroine really had the slightest fear of the vulgar police force; but as it has been rumoured in Mordasoff that at this moment such a thought *did* pass through her brain, why, I must record the fact.)

In a word she saw clearly that Zina's marriage with the prince must be brought about at once, without delay! It was easily done: the priest at the village should perform the ceremony; why not the day after to-morrow? or indeed, in case of need, to-morrow? Marriages had often been brought about in less time than this—in two hours, she had heard! It would be easy enough to persuade the prince that haste and simplicity would be in far better taste than all the usual pomps and vanities of common everyday weddings. In fact, she relied upon her skill in putting the matter to the old man as a fitting dramatic issue to a romantic story of love, and thus to touch the most sensitive string of his chivalrous heart.

In case of absolute need there was always the possibility of making him drunk, or rather of *keeping* him perpetually drunk. And then, come what might, Zina would be a princess! And if this marriage were fated to produce scandal among the prince's relations and friends in St. Petersburg and Moscow, Maria Alexandrovna comforted herself with the reflection that marriages in high life nearly always *were* productive of scandal; and that such a result might fairly be looked upon as "good form," and as peculiar to aristocratic circles.

Besides, she felt sure that Zina need only show herself in society, with her mamma to support her, and every one of all those countesses and princes should very soon either acknowledge her of their own accord, or yield to the head-washing that Maria Alexandrovna felt herself so competent to give to any or all of them, individually or collectively.

It was in consequence of these reflections that Maria Alexandrovna was now hastening with all speed towards her village, in order to bring back Afanassy Matveyevitch, whose presence she considered absolutely necessary at this crisis. It was desirable that her husband should appear and invite the prince down to the country: she relied upon the appearance of the father of the family, in dress-coat and white tie, hastening up to town on the first rumours of the prince's arrival there, to produce a very favourable impression upon the old man's self-respect: it would flatter him; and after such a courteous action, followed by a polite and warmly-couched invitation to the country, the prince would hardly refuse to go.

At last the carriage stopped at the door of a long low wooden house, surrounded by old lime trees. This was the country house, Maria Alexandrovna's village residence.

Lights were burning inside.

"Where's my old fool?" cried Maria Alexandrovna bursting like a hurricane into the sitting-room.

"Whats this towel lying here for?—Oh!—he's been wiping his head, has he. What, the baths again! and tea—of course tea!—always tea! Well, what are you winking your eyes at me for, you old fool?—Here, why is his hair not cropped? Grisha, Grisha!—here; why didn't you cut your master's hair, as I told you?"

Maria Alexandrovna, on entering the room, had intended to greet her husband more kindly than this; but seeing that he had just been to the baths and that he was drinking tea with great satisfaction, as usual, she could not restrain her irritable feelings.

She felt the contrast between her own activity and intellectual energy, and the stolid indifference and sheep-like contentedness of her husband, and it went to her heart!

Meanwhile the "old fool," or to put it more politely, he who had been addressed by that title, sat at the tea-urn, and stared with open mouth, in abject alarm, opening and shutting his lips as he gazed at the wife of his bosom, who had almost petrified him by her sudden appearance.

At the door stood the sleepy, fat Grisha, looking on at the scene, and blinking both eyes at periodical intervals.

"I couldn't cut his hair as you wished, because he wouldn't let me!" he growled at last. " 'You'd better let me do it!'—I said, 'or the mistress'll be down one of these days, and then we shall both catch it!' "

"No," he says, "I want it like this now, and you shall cut it on Sunday. I like it long!"

"What!—So you wish to curl it without my leave, do you! What an idea—as if you could wear curls with your sheep-face underneath! Good gracious, what a mess you've made of the place; and what's the smell—what have you been doing, idiot, eh!" cried Maria Alexandrovna, waxing more and more angry, and turning furiously upon the wretched and perfectly innocent Afanassy!

"Mam—mammy!" muttered the poor frightened master of the house, gazing with frightened eyes at the mistress, and blinking with all his might—"mammy!"

"How many times have I dinned into your stupid head that I am *not* your 'mammy.' How can I be your mammy, you idiotic pigmy? How dare you call a noble lady by such a name; a lady whose proper place is in the highest circles, not beside an ass like yourself!"

"Yes—yes,—but—but, you *are* my legal wife, you know, after all;—so I—it was husbandly affection you know——" murmured poor Afanassy, raising both hands to his head as he spoke, to defend his hair from the tugs he evidently expected.

"Oh, idiot that you are! did anyone ever hear such a ridiculous answer as that—legal wife, indeed! Who ever heard the expression '*legal* wife,' in good society—nasty low expression! And how dare you remind me that I am your wife, when I use all my power and do all I possibly can at every moment to forget the fact, eh? What are you covering your head with your hands for? Look at his hair—now: wet, as wet as reeds! it will take three hours to dry that head! How on earth am I to take him like this? How can he show his face among respectable people? What am I to do?"

And Maria Alexandrovna bit her finger-nails with rage as she walked furiously up and down the room.

It was no very great matter, of course; and one that was easily set right; but Maria Alexandrovna required a vent for her feelings and felt the need of emptying out her accumulated wrath upon the head of the wretched Afanassy Matveyevitch; for tyranny is a habit recallable at need.

Besides, everyone knows how great a contrast there is between the sweetness and refinement shown by many ladies of a certain class on the stage, as it were, of society life, and the revelations of character behind the scenes at home; and I was anxious to bring out this contrast for my reader's benefit.

Afanassy watched the movements of his terrible spouse in fear and trembling; perspiration formed upon his brow as he gazed.

"Grisha!" she cried at last, "dress your master this instant! Dress-coat, black trousers, white waistcoat and tie, quick! Where's his hairbrush—quick, quick!"

"Mam—my! Why, I've just been to the bath. I shall catch cold if I go up to town just now!"

"You won't catch cold!"

"But—mammy, my hair's quite wet!"

"We'll dry it in a minute. Here, Grisha, take this brush and brush away till he's dry,—harder—harder—much harder! There, that's better!"

Grisha worked like a man. For the greater convenience of his herculean task he seized his master's shoulder with one hand as he rubbed violently with the other. Poor Afanassy grunted and groaned and almost wept.

"Now, then, lift him up a bit. Where's the pomatum? Bend your head, duffer!—bend lower, you abject dummy!" And Maria Alexandrovna herself undertook to pomade her husband's hair, ploughing her hands through it without the slightest pity. Afanassy heartily wished that his shock growth had been cut. He winced, and groaned and moaned, but did not cry out under the painful operation.

"You suck my life-blood out of me—bend lower, you idiot!" remarked the fond wife—"bend lower still, I tell you!"

"How have I sucked your life blood?" asked the victim, bending his head as low as circumstances permitted.

"Fool!—allegorically, of course—can't you understand? Now, then, comb it yourself. Here, Grisha, dress him, quick!"

Our heroine threw herself into an arm-chair, and critically watched the ceremony of adorning her husband. Meanwhile the latter had a little opportunity to get his breath once more and compose his feelings generally; so that when matters arrived at the point where the tie is tied, he had even developed so much audacity as to express opinions of his own as to how the bow should be manufactured.

At last, having put his dress-coat on, the lord of the manor was his brave self again, and gazed at his highly ornate person in the glass with great satisfaction and complacency.

"Where are you going to take me to?" he now asked, smiling at his reflected self.

Maria Alexandrovna could not believe her ears.

"What—*what*? How *dare* you ask me where I am taking you to, sir!"

"But—mammy—I must know, you know——"

"Hold your tongue! You let me hear you call me mammy again, especially where we are going to now! you sha'n't have any tea for a month!"

The frightened consort held his peace.

"Look at that, now! You haven't got a single 'order' to put on—sloven!" she continued, looking at his black coat with contempt.

"The Government awards orders, mammy; and I am not a sloven, but a town councillor!" said Afanassy, with a sudden excess of noble wrath.

"What, what—*what*! So you've learned to argue now, have you—you mongrel, you? However, I haven't time to waste over you now, or I'd——but I sha'n't forget it. Here, Grisha, give him his fur coat and his hat—quick; and look here, Grisha, when I'm gone, get these three rooms ready, and the green room, and the corner bedroom. Quick—find your broom; take the coverings off the looking-glasses and clocks, and see that all is ready and tidy within an hour. Put on a dress coat, and see that the other men have gloves: don't lose time. Quick, now!"

She entered the carriage, followed by Afanassy. The latter sat bewildered and lost.

Meanwhile Maria Alexandrovna reflected as to how best she could drum into her husband's thick skull certain essential instructions with regard to the present situation of affairs. But Afanassy anticipated her.

"I had a very original dream to-day, Maria Alexandrovna," he observed quite unexpectedly, in the middle of a long silence.

"Tfu! idiot. I thought you were going to say something of terrific interest, from the look of you. Dream, indeed! How dare you mention your miserable dreams to me! Original, too! Listen here: if you dare so much as remind me of the word 'dream,' or say anything else, either, where we are going to-day, I—I don't know *what* I won't do to you! Now, look here: Prince K. has arrived at my house. Do you remember Prince K.?"

"Oh, yes, mammy, I remember; and why has he done us this honour?"

"Be quiet; that's not your business. Now, you are to invite him, with all the amiability you can, to come down to our house in the country, at once! That is what I am taking you up for. And if you dare so much as breathe another word of any kind, either to-day or to-morrow, or next day, without leave from me, you shall herd geese for a whole year. You're not to say a single word, mind! and that's all you have to think of. Do you understand, now?"

"Well, but if I'm asked anything?"

"Hold your tongue all the same!"

"Oh, but I can't do that—I can't do——"

"Very well, then; you can say 'H'm,' or something of that sort, to give them the idea that you are very wise indeed, and like to think well before answering."

"H'm."

"Understand me, now. I am taking you up because you are to make it appear that you have just heard of the prince's visit, and have hastened up to town in a transport of joy to express your unbounded respect and gratitude to him, and to invite him at once to your country house! Do you understand me?"

"H'm."

"I don't want you to say 'H'm' *now*, you fool! You must answer *me* when I speak!"

"All right—all right, mammy. All shall be as you wish; but why am I to ask the prince down?"

"What—what! arguing again. What business is it of yours *why* you are to invite him? How dare you ask questions!"

"Why it's all the same thing, mammy. How am I to invite him if I must not say a word?"

"Oh, I shall do all the talking. All you have to do is to bow. Do you hear? *Bow*; and hold your hat in your hand and look polite. Do you understand, or not?"

"I understand, mam—Maria-Alexandrovna."

"The prince is very witty, indeed; so mind, if he says anything either to yourself or anyone else, you are to laugh cordially and merrily. Do you hear me?"

"H'm."

"Don't say 'H'm' to *me*, I tell you. You are to answer me plainly and simply. Do you hear me, or not?"

"Yes, yes; I hear you, of course. That's all right. I only say 'H'm,' for practice; I want to get into the way of saying it. But look here, mammy, it's all very well; you say I'm not to speak, and if he speaks to me I'm to look at him and laugh—but what if he asks me a question?"

"Oh—you dense log of a man! I tell you again, you are to be quiet. *I'll* answer for you. You have simply got to look polite, and smile!"

"But he'll think I am dumb!" said Afanassy.

"Well, and what if he does. Let him! You'll conceal the fact that you are a fool, anyhow!"

"H'm, and if *other* people ask me questions?"

"No one will; there'll be no one to ask you. But if there *should* be anyone else in the room, and they ask you questions, all you have to do is to smile sarcastically. Do you know what a sarcastic smile is?"

"What, a witty sort of smile, is it, mammy?"

"I'll let you know about it! *Witty*, indeed! Why, who would think of expecting anything witty from a fool like you. No, sir, a jesting smile—*jesting* and *contemptuous*!"

"H'm."

"Good heavens. I'm afraid for this idiot," thought Maria Alexandrovna to herself. "I really think it would have been almost better to leave him behind, after all." So thinking, nervous and anxious, Maria Alexandrovna drove on. She looked out of the window, and she fidgeted, and she bustled the coachman up. The horses were almost flying through the air; but to her they appeared to be crawling. Afanassy sat silent and thoughtful in the corner of the carriage, practising his lessons. At last the carriage arrived at the town house.

Hardly, however, had Maria Alexandrovna mounted the outer steps when she became aware of a fine pair of horses trotting up—drawing a smart sledge with a hood to it. In fact, the very "turn-out" in which Anna Nicolaevna Antipova was generally to be seen.

Two ladies sat in the sledge. One of these was, of course, Mrs. Antipova herself; the other was Natalia Dimitrievna, of late the great friend and ally of the former lady.

Maria Alexandrovna's heart sank.

But she had no time to say a word, before another smart vehicle drove up, in which there reclined yet another guest. Exclamations of joy and delight were now heard.

"Maria Alexandrovna! and Afanassy Matveyevitch! Just arrived, too! Where from? How extremely delightful! And here we are, you see, just driven up at the right moment. We are going to spend the evening with you. What a delightful surprise."

The guests alighted and fluttered up the steps like so many swallows.

Maria Alexandrovna could neither believe her eyes nor her ears.

"Curse you all!" she said to herself. "This looks like a plot—it must be seen to; but it takes more than a flight of magpies like *you* to get to windward of *me*. Wait a little!!"

CHAPTER XI.

Mosgliakoff went out from Maria Alexandrovna's house to all appearances quite pacified. She had fired his ardour completely. His imagination was kindled.

He did not go to his godfather's, for he felt the need of solitude. A terrific rush of heroic and romantic thoughts surged over him, and gave him no rest.

He pictured to himself the solemn explanation he should have with Zina, then the generous throbs of his all-forgiving heart; his pallor and despair at the future ball in St. Petersburg; then Spain, the Guadalquiver, and love, and the old dying prince joining their hands with his last blessing. Then came thoughts of his beautiful wife, devoted to himself, and never ceasing to wonder at and admire her husband's heroism and exalted refinement of taste and conduct. Then, among other things, the attention which he should attract among the ladies of the highest circles, into which he would of course enter, thanks to his marriage with Zina—widow of the Prince K.: then the inevitable appointments, first as a vice-governor, with the delightful accompaniment of salary: in a word, all, *all* that Maria Alexandrovna's eloquence had pictured to his imagination, now marched in triumphant procession through his brain, soothing and attracting and flattering his self-love.

And yet—(I really cannot explain this phenomenon, however!)—and yet, no sooner did the first flush of this delightful sunrise of future delights pass off and fade away, than the annoying thought struck him: this is all very well, but it is in the future: and now, to-day, I shall look a dreadful fool. As he reflected thus, he looked up and found that he had wandered a long way, to some of the dirty back slums of the town. A wet snow was falling; now and again he met another belated pedestrian like himself. The outer circumstances began to anger Mosgliakoff, which was a bad sign; for when things are going well with us we are always inclined to see everything in a rose-coloured light.

Paul could not help remembering that up to now he had been in the habit of cutting a dash at Mordasoff. He had enjoyed being treated at all the houses he went to in the town, as Zina's accepted lover, and to be congratulated, as he often was, upon the honour of that distinction. He was proud of being her future husband; and here he was now with notice to quit. He would be laughed at. He couldn't tell everybody about the future scene in the ball-room at St. Petersburg, and the Guadalquiver, and all that! And then a thought came out into prominence, which had been uncomfortably fidgeting about in his brain for some time: "Was it all true? *Would* it really come about as Maria Alexandrovna had predicted?"

Here it struck him that Maria Alexandrovna was an amazingly cunning woman; that, however worthy she might be of universal esteem, still she was a known scandal-monger, and lied from morning to night! that, again, she probably had some good reason for wishing him out of the place to-night. He next bethought him of Zina, and of her parting look at him, which was very far from being expressive of passionate love; he remembered also, that, less than an hour ago, she had called him a fool.

As he thought of the last fact Paul stopped in his tracks, as though shot; blushed, and almost cried for very shame! At this very moment he was unfortunate enough to lose his footing on the slippery pavement, and to go head-first into a snow-heap. As he stood shaking himself dry, a whole troop of dogs, which had long trotted barking at his heels, flew at him. One of them, a wretched little half-starved beast, went so far as to fix her teeth into his fur coat and hang therefrom. Swearing and striking out, Paul cleared his way out of the yelping pack at last, in a fury, and with rent clothes; and making his way as fast as he could to the corner of the street, discovered that he hadn't the slightest idea where he was. He walked up lanes, and down streets, and round corners, and lost himself more and more hopelessly; also his temper. "The devil take all these confounded exalted ideas!" he growled, half aloud; "and the archfiend take every one of you, you and your Guadalquivers and humbug!"

Mosgliakoff was not in a pretty humour at this moment.

At last, tired and horribly angry, after two hours of walking, he reached the door of Maria Alexandrovna's house.

Observing a host of carriages standing outside, he paused to consider.

"Surely she has not a party to-night!" he thought, "and if she has, *why* has she a party?"

He inquired of the servants, and found out that Maria Alexandrovna had been out of town, and had fetched up Afanassy Matveyevitch, gorgeous in his dress-suit and white tie. He learned, further, that the prince was awake, but had not as yet made his appearance in the "salon."

On receiving this information, Paul Mosgliakoff said not a word, but quietly made his way upstairs to his uncle's room.

He was in that frame of mind in which a man determines to commit some desperate act, out of revenge, aware at the time, and wide awake to the fact that he is about to do the deed, but forgetting entirely that he may very likely regret it all his life afterwards!

Entering the prince's room, he found that worthy seated before the glass, with a perfectly bare head, but with whiskers and napoleon stuck on. His wig was in the hands of his old and grey valet, his favourite Ivan Pochomitch, and the latter was gravely and thoughtfully combing it out.

As for the prince, he was indeed a pitiable object! He was not half awake yet, for one thing; he sat as though he were still dazed with sleep; he kept opening and shutting his mouth, and stared at Mosgliakoff as though he did not know him!

"Well, how are you, uncle?" asked Mosgliakoff.

"What, it's you, is it!" said the prince. "Ye—yes; I've been as—leep a little while! Oh, heavens!" he cried suddenly, with great animation, "why, I've got no wi—ig on!"

"Oh, never mind that, uncle; I'll help you on with it, if you like!"

"Dear me; now you've found out my se—ecret! I told him to shut the door. Now, my friend, you must give me your word in—stantly, that you'll never breathe a hint of this to anyone—I mean about my hair being ar—tificial!"

"Oh, uncle! As if I could be guilty of such meanness?" cried Paul, who was anxious to please the prince, for reasons of his own.

"Ye—yes, ye—yes. Well, as I see you are a good fe—ellow, I—I'll just as—tonish you a little: I'll tell you all my secrets! How do you like my mous—tache, my dear boy?"

"Wonderful, uncle, wonderful! It astonishes me that you should have been able to keep it so long!"

"Sp—are your wonder, my friend, it's ar—tificial!"

"No!! That's difficult to believe! Well, and your whiskers, uncle! admit—you black them, now *don't* you?"

"Black them? Not—only I don't black them, but they, too, are ar—tificial!" said the Prince, regarding Mosgliakoff with a look of triumph.

"*What!* Artificial? No, no, uncle! I can't believe *that*! You're laughing at me!"

"*Parole d'honneur, mon ami!*" cried the delighted old man; "and fancy, all—everybody is taken in by them just as you were! Even Stepanida Matveyevna cannot believe they are not real, sometimes, although she often sticks them on herself! But, I am sure, my dear friend, you will keep my se—cret. Give me your word!"

"I do give you my word, uncle! But surely you do not suppose I would be so mean as to divulge it?"

"Oh, my boy! I had such a fall to-day, without you. The coachman upset me out of the carriage again!"

"How? When?"

"Why, we were driving to the mo—nastery, when?——"

"I know, uncle: that was early this morning!"

"No, no! A couple of hours ago, not more! I was driving along with him, and he suddenly took and up—set me!"

"Why, my dear uncle, you were asleep," began Paul, in amazement!

"Ye—yes, ye—yes. I did have a sleep; and then I drove away, at least I—at least I—dear me, how strange it all seems!"

"I assure you, uncle, you have been dreaming! You saw all this in a dream! You have been sleeping quietly here since just after dinner!"

"No!" And the prince reflected. "Ye—yes. Perhaps I did see it all in a dream! However, I can remember all I saw quite well. First, I saw a large bull with horns; and then I saw a pro—curor, and I think he had huge horns too. Then there was Napoleon Buonaparte. Did you ever hear, my boy, that people say I am so like Napoleon Buonaparte? But my profile is very like some old pope. What do you think about it, my bo—oy?"

"I think you are much more like Napoleon Buonaparte, uncle!"

"Why, ye—yes, of course—full face; so I am, my boy, so I am! I dreamt of him on his is—land, and do you know he was such a merry, talk—ative fellow, he quite am—used me!"

"Who, uncle—Napoleon?" asked Mosgliakoff, looking thoughtfully at the old man. A strange idea was beginning to occupy his brain— an idea which he could not quite put into shape as yet.

"Ye—yes, ye—yes, Nap—oleon. We talked about philosophical subjects. And do you know, my boy, I became quite sorry that the English had been so hard upon him. Of course, though, if one didn't chain him up, he would be flying at people's throats again! Still I'm sorry for him. Now I should have managed him quite differently. I should have put him on an uninhabited island."

"Why uninhabited, uncle?" asked Mosgliakoff, absently.

"Well, well, an inhabited one, then; but the in—habitants must be good sort of people. And I should arrange all sorts of amusements for him, at the State's charge: theatres, balle's, and so on. And, of course, he should walk about, under proper su—pervision. Then he should have tarts (he liked tarts, you know), as many tarts as ever he pleased. I should treat him like a fa—ather; and he would end by being sorry for his sins, see if he wouldn't!"

Mosgliakoff listened absently to all this senile gabble, and bit his nails with impatience. He was anxious to turn the conversation on to the subject of marriage. He did not know quite clearly why he wished to do so, but his heart was boiling over with anger.

Suddenly the old man made an exclamation of surprise.

"Why, my dear boy, I declare I've forgotten to tell you about it. Fancy, I made an offer of marriage to-day!"

"An offer of marriage, uncle?" cried Paul, brightening up.

"Why, ye—yes! an offer. Pachomief, are you going? All right! Away with you! Ye—yes, *c'est une charmante personne*. But I confess, I took the step rather rash—ly. I only begin to see that now. Dear me! dear, dear me!"

"Excuse me, uncle; but *when* did you make this offer?"

"Well, I admit I don't know exactly *when* I made it! Perhaps I dre—dreamed it; I don't know. Dear me, how very strange it all seems!"

Mosgliakoff trembled with joy: his new idea blazed forth in full developed glory.

"And *whom* did you propose to?" he asked impatiently.

"The daughter of the house, my boy; that beau—tiful girl. I—I forget what they call her. Bu—but, my dear boy, you see I—I can't possibly marry. What am I to do?"

"Oh! of course, you are done for if you marry, that's clear. But let me ask you one more question, uncle. Are you perfectly certain that you actually made her an offer of marriage?"

"Ye—yes, I'm sure of it; I—I——."

"And what if you dreamed the whole thing, just as you did that you were upset out of the carriage a second time?"

"Dear me! dear me! I—I really think I may have dreamed it; it's very awkward. I don't know how to show myself there, now. H—how could I find out, dear boy, for certain? Couldn't I get to know by some outside way whether I really did make her an offer of ma—arriage or not? Why, just you think of my dreadful po—sition!"

"Do you know, uncle, I don't think we need trouble ourselves to find out at all."

"Why, wh—what then?"

"I am convinced that you were dreaming."

"I—I think so myself, too, my dear fellow; es—pecially as I often have that sort of dream."

"You see, uncle, you had a drop of wine for lunch, and then another drop or two for dinner, don't you know; and so you may easily have——"

"Ye—yes, quite so, quite so; it may easily have been that."

"Besides, my dear uncle, however excited you may have been, you would never have taken such a senseless step in your waking moments. So far as I know you, uncle, you are a man of the highest and most deliberate judgment, and I am positive that——"

"Ye—yes, ye—yes."

"Why, only imagine—if your relations were to get to hear of such a thing. My goodness, uncle! they were cruel enough to you before. What do you suppose they would do *now*, eh?"

"Goodness gracious!" cried the frightened old prince. "Good—ness gracious! Wh—why, what would they do, do you think?"

"Do? Why, of course, they would all screech out that you had acted under the influence of insanity: in fact, that you were mad; that you had been swindled, and that you must be put under proper restraint. In fact, they'd pop you into some lunatic asylum."

Mosgliakoff was well aware of the best method of frightening the poor old man out of his wits.

"Gracious heavens!" cried the latter, trembling like a leaflet with horror. "Gra—cious heavens! would they really do that?"

"Undoubtedly; and, knowing this, uncle, think for yourself. Could you possibly have done such a thing with your eyes open? As if you don't understand what's good for you just as well as your neighbours. I solemnly affirm that you saw all this in a dream!"

"Of course, of course; un—doubtedly in a dream, un—doubtedly so! What a clever fellow you are, my dear boy; you saw it at once. I am deeply grate—ful to you for putting me right. I was really quite under the im—pression I had actually done it."

"And how glad I am that I met you, uncle, before you went in there! Just fancy, what a mess you might have made of it! You might have gone in thinking you were engaged to the girl, and behaved in the capacity of accepted lover. Think how fearfully dangerous——."

"Ye—yes, of course; most dangerous!"

"Why, remember, this girl is twenty-three years old. Nobody will marry her, and suddenly *you*, a rich and eminent man of rank and title, appear on the scene as her accepted swain. They would lay hold of the idea at once, and act up to it, and swear that you really were her future husband, and would marry you off, too. I daresay they would even count upon your speedy death, and make their calculations accordingly."

"No!"

"Then again, uncle; a man of your dignity——"

"Ye—yes, quite so, dig—nity!"

"And wisdom,—and amiability——"

"Quite so; wis—dom—wisdom!"

"And then—a prince into the bargain! Good gracious, uncle, as if a man like yourself would make such a match as *that*, if you really did mean marrying! What would your relations say?"

"Why, my dear boy, they'd simply ea—eat me up,—I—I know their cunning and malice of old! My dear fellow—you won't believe it—but I assure you I was afraid they were going to put me into a lun—atic asylum! a common ma—ad-house! Goodness me, think of that! Whatever should I have done with myself all day in a ma—ad-house?"

"Of course, of course! Well, I won't leave your side, then, uncle, when you go downstairs. There are guests there too!"

"Guests? dear me! I—I——"

"Don't be afraid, uncle; I shall be by you!"

"I—I'm *so* much obliged to you, my dear boy; you have simply sa—ved me, you have indeed! But, do you know what,—I think I'd better go away altogether!"

"To-morrow, uncle! to-morrow morning at seven! and this evening you must be sure to say, in the presence of everybody, that you are starting away at seven next morning: you must say good-bye to-night!"

"Un—doubtedly, undoubtedly—I shall go;—but what if they talk to me as though I were engaged to the young wo—oman?"

"Don't you fear, uncle! I shall be there! And mind, whatever they say or hint to you, you must declare that you dreamed the whole thing—as indeed you did, of course?"

"Ye—yes, quite so, un—doubtedly so! But, do you know my dear boy, it was a most be—witching dream, for all that! She is a wond—erfully lovely girl, my boy,—such a figure—bewitching—be—witching!"

"Well, *au revoir*, uncle! I'm going down, now, and you——"

"How! How! you are not going to leave me alone?" cried the old man, greatly alarmed.

"No, no—oh no, uncle; but we must enter the room separately. First, I will go in, and then you come down; that will be better!"

"Very well, very well. Besides, I just want to note down one little i—dea——"

"Capital, uncle! jot it down, and then come at once; don't wait any longer; and to-morrow morning——"

"And to-morrow morning away we go to the Her—mitage, straight to the Her—mitage! Charming—charm—ing! but, do you know, my boy,—she's a fas—cinating girl—she is indeed! be—witching! Such a bust! and, really, if I were to marry, I—I—really——"

"No, no, uncle! Heaven forbid!"

"Yes—yes—quite so—Heaven for—bid!—well, *au revoir*, my friend—I'll come directly; by the bye—I meant to ask you, have you read Kazanoff's Memoirs?"

"Yes, uncle. Why?"

"Yes, yes, quite so—I forget what I wanted to say——"

"You'll remember afterwards, uncle! *au revoir!*"

"*Au revoir*, my boy, *au revoir*—but, I say, it was a bewitching dream, a most be—witching dream!"

CHAPTER XII.

"Here we all are, all of us, come to spend the evening; Proskovia Ilinishna is coming too, and Luisa Karlovna and all!" cried Mrs. Antipova as she entered the salon, and looked hungrily round. She was a neat, pretty little woman! she was well-dressed, and knew it.

She looked greedily around, as I say, because she had an idea that the prince and Zina were hidden together somewhere about the room.

"Yes, and Katerina Petrovna, and Felisata Michaelovna are coming as well," added Natalia Dimitrievna, a huge woman—whose figure had pleased the prince so much, and who looked more like a grenadier than anything else. This monster had been hand and glove with little Mrs. Antipova for the last three weeks; they were now quite inseparable. Natalia looked as though she could pick her little friend up and swallow her, bones and all, without thinking.

"I need not say with what *rapture* I welcome you both to my house, and for a whole evening, too!" piped Maria Alexandrovna, a little recovered from her first shock of amazement; "but do tell me, what miracle is it that has brought you all to-day, when I had quite despaired of ever seeing anyone of you in my house again?"

"Oh, oh! my *dear* Maria Alexandrovna!" said Natalia, very affectedly, but sweetly. The attributes of sweetness and affectation were a curious contrast to her personal appearance.

"You see, dearest Maria Alexandrovna," chirped Mrs. Antipova, "we really must get on with the private theatricals question! It was only this very day that Peter Michaelovitch was saying how *bad* it was of us to have made no progress towards rehearsing, and so on; and that it was quite time we brought all our silly squabbles to an end! Well, four of us got together to-day, and then it struck us 'Let's all go to Maria Alexandrovna's, and settle the matter once for all!' So Natalia Dimitrievna let all the rest know that we were to meet here! We'll soon settle it—I don't think we should allow it to be said that we do nothing but 'squabble' over the preliminaries and get no farther, do *you*, dear Maria Alexandrovna?" She added, playfully, and kissing our heroine affectionately, "Goodness me, Zenaida, I declare you grow prettier every day!" And she betook herself to embracing Zina with equal affection.

"She has nothing else to do, but sit and grow more and more beautiful!" said Natalia with great sweetness, rubbing her huge hands together.

"Oh, the devil take them all! they know I care nothing about private theatricals—cursed magpies!" reflected Maria Alexandrovna, beside herself with rage.

"Especially, dear, as that delightful prince is with you just now. You know there is a private theatre in his house at Donchanof, and we have discovered that somewhere or other there, there are a lot of old theatrical properties and decorations and scenery. The prince was at my house to-day, but I was so surprised to see him that it all went clean out of my head and I forgot to ask him. Now we'll broach the subject before him. You must support me and we'll persuade him to send us all the old rubbish that can be found. We want to get the prince to come and see the play, too! He is sure to subscribe, isn't he—as it is for the poor? Perhaps he would even take a part; he is such a dear, kind, willing old man. If only he did, it would make the fortune of our play!"

"Of course he will take a part! why, he can be made to play *any* part!" remarked Natalia significantly.

Mrs. Antipova had not exaggerated. Guests poured in every moment! Maria Alexandrovna hardly had time to receive one lot and make the usual exclamations of surprise and delight exacted by the laws of etiquette before another arrival would be announced.

I will not undertake to describe all these good people. I will only remark that every one of them, on arrival, looked about her cunningly; and that every face wore an expression of expectation and impatience.

Some of them came with the distinct intention of witnessing some scene of a delightfully scandalous nature, and were prepared to be very angry indeed if it should turn out that they were obliged to leave the house without the gratification of their hopes.

All behaved in the most amiable and affectionate manner towards their hostess; but Maria Alexandrovna firmly braced her nerves for battle.

Many apparently natural and innocent questions were asked about the prince; but in each one might be detected some hint or insinuation.

Tea came in, and people moved about and changed places: one group surrounded the piano; Zina was requested to play and sing, but answered drily that she was not quite well—and the paleness of her face bore out this assertion. Inquiries were made for Mosgliakoff; and these inquiries were addressed to Zina.

Maria Alexandrovna proved that she had the eyes and ears of ten ordinary mortals. She saw and heard all that was going on in every corner of the room; she heard and answered every question asked, and answered readily and cleverly. She was dreadfully anxious about Zina, however, and wondered why she did not leave the room, as she usually did on such occasions.

Poor Afanassy came in for his share of notice, too. It was the custom of these amiable people of Mordasoff to do their best to set Maria Alexandrovna and her husband "by the ears;" but to-day there were hopes of extracting valuable news and secrets out of the candid simplicity of the latter.

Maria Alexandrovna watched the state of siege into which the wretched Afanassy was thrown, with great anxiety; he was answering "H'm!" to all questions put to him, as instructed; but with so wretched an expression and so extremely artificial a mien that Maria Alexandrovna could barely restrain her wrath.

"Maria Alexandrovna! your husband won't have a word to say to me!" remarked a sharp-faced little lady with a devil-may-care manner, as though she cared nothing for anybody, and was not to be abashed under any circumstances. "Do ask him to be a *little* more courteous towards ladies!"

"I really don't know myself what can have happened to him to-day!" said Maria Alexandrovna, interrupting her conversation with Mrs. Antipova and Natalia, and laughing merrily; "he is so *dreadfully* uncommunicative! He has scarcely said a word even to *me*, all day! Why don't you answer Felisata Michaelovna, Afanassy? What did you ask him?"

"But, but—why, mammy, you told me yourself"—began the bewildered and lost Afanassy. At this moment he was standing at the fireside with one hand placed inside his waistcoat, in an artistic position which he had chosen deliberately, on mature reflection,—and he was sipping his tea. The questions of the ladies had so confused him that he was blushing like a girl.

When he began the justification of himself recorded above, he suddenly met so dreadful a look in the eyes of his infuriated spouse that he nearly lost all consciousness, for terror!

Uncertain what to do, but anxious to recover himself and win back her favour once more, he said nothing, but took a gulp of tea to restore his scattered senses.

Unfortunately the tea was too hot; which fact, together with the hugeness of the gulp he took—quite upset him. He burned his throat, choked, sent the cup flying, and burst into such a fit of coughing that he was obliged to leave the room for a time, awakening universal astonishment by his conduct.

In a word, Maria Alexandrovna saw clearly enough that her guests knew all about it, and had assembled with malicious intent! The situation was dangerous! They were quite capable of confusing and overwhelming the feeble-minded old prince before her very eyes! They might even carry him off bodily—after stirring up a quarrel between the old man and herself! *Anything* might happen.

But fate had prepared her one more surprise. The door opened and in came Mosgliakoff—who, as she thought, was far enough away at his godfather's, and would not come near her to-night! She shuddered as though something had hurt her.

Mosgliakoff stood a moment at the door, looking around at the company. He was a little bewildered, and could not conceal his agitation, which showed itself very clearly in his expression.

"Why, it's Paul Alexandrovitch! and you told us he had gone to his godfather's, Maria Alexandrovna. We were told you had hidden yourself away from us, Paul Alexandrovitch!" cried Natalia.

"Hidden myself?" said Paul, with a crooked sort of a smile. "What a strange expression! Excuse me, Natalia Dimitrievna, but I never hide from anyone; I have no cause to do so, that I know of! Nor do I ever hide anyone else!" he added, looking significantly at Maria Alexandrovna.

Maria Alexandrovna trembled in her shoes.

"Surely this fool of a man is not up to anything disagreeable!" she thought. "No, no! that would be worse than anything!" She looked curiously and anxiously into his eyes.

"Is it true, Paul Alexandrovitch, that you have just been politely dismissed?—the Government service, I mean, of course!" remarked the daring Felisata Michaelovna, looking impertinently into his eyes.

"Dismissed! How dismissed? I'm simply changing my department, that's all! I am to be placed at Petersburg!" Mosgliakoff answered, drily.

"Oh! well, I congratulate you!" continued the bold young woman. "We were alarmed to hear that you were trying for a—a place down here at Mordasoff. The berths here are wretched, Paul Alexandrovitch—no good at all, I assure you!"

"I don't know—there's a place as teacher at the school, vacant, I believe," remarked Natalia.

This was such a crude and palpable insinuation that even Mrs. Antipova was ashamed of her friend, and kicked her, under the table.

"You don't suppose Paul Alexandrovitch would accept the place vacated by a wretched little schoolmaster!" said Felisata Michaelovna.

But Paul did not answer. He turned at this moment, and encountered Afanassy Matveyevitch, just returning into the room. The latter offered him his hand. Mosgliakoff, like a fool, looked beyond poor Afanassy, and did not take his outstretched hand: annoyed to the limits of endurance, he stepped up to Zina, and muttered, gazing angrily into her eyes:

"This is all thanks to you! Wait a bit; you shall see this very day whether I am a fool or not!"

"Why put off the revelation? It is clear enough already!" said Zina, aloud, staring contemptuously at her former lover.

Mosgliakoff hurriedly left her. He did not half like the loud tone she spoke in.

"Have you been to your godfather's?" asked Maria Alexandrovna at last, determined to sound matters in this direction.

"No, I've just been with uncle."

"With your uncle! What! have you just come from the prince now?"

"Oh—oh! and we were told the prince was asleep!" added Natalia Dimitrievna, looking daggers at Maria Alexandrovna.

"Do not be disturbed about the prince, Natalia Dimitrievna," replied Paul, "he is awake now, and quite restored to his senses. He was persuaded to drink a good deal too much wine, first at your house, and then here; so that he quite lost his head, which never was too strong. However, I have had a talk with him, and he now seems to have entirely recovered his judgment, thank God! He is coming down directly to take his leave, Maria Alexandrovna, and to thank you for all your kind hospitality; and to-morrow morning early we are off to the Hermitage. Thence I shall myself see him safe home to Donchanovo, in order that he may be far from the temptation to further excesses like that of to-day. There I shall give him over into the hands of Stepanida Matveyevna, who must be back at home by this time, and who will assuredly never allow him another opportunity of going on his travels, I'll answer for that!"

So saying, Mosgliakoff stared angrily at Maria Alexandrovna. The latter sat still, apparently dumb with amazement. I regret to say—it gives me great pain to record it—that, perhaps for the first time in her life, my heroine was decidedly alarmed.

"So the prince is off to-morrow morning! Dear me; why is that?" inquired Natalia Dimitrievna, very sweetly, of Maria Alexandrovna.

"Yes. How is that?" asked Mrs. Antipova, in astonishment.

"Yes; dear me! how comes that, I wonder!" said two or three voices. "How can that be? When we were told—dear me! How very strange!"

But the mistress of the house could not find words to reply in.

However, at this moment the general attention was distracted by a most unwonted and eccentric episode. In the next room was heard a strange noise—sharp exclamations and hurrying feet, which was followed by the sudden appearance of Sophia Petrovna, the fidgety guest who had called upon Maria Alexandrovna in the morning.

Sophia Petrovna was a very eccentric woman indeed—so much so that even the good people of Mordasoff could not support her, and had lately voted her out of society. I must observe that every evening, punctually at seven, this lady was in the habit of having, what she called, "a snack," and that after this snack, which she declared was for the benefit of her liver, her condition was well *emancipated*, to use no stronger term. She was in this very condition, as described, now, as she appeared flinging herself into Maria Alexandrovna's salon.

"Oho! so this is how you treat me, Maria Alexandrovna!" she shouted at the top of her voice. "Oh! don't be afraid, I shall not inflict myself upon you for more than a minute! I won't sit down. I just came in to see if what they said was true! Ah! so you go in for balls and receptions and parties, and Sophia Petrovna is to sit at home alone, and knit stockings, is she? You ask the whole town in, and leave me out, do you? Yes, and I was *mon ange*, and 'dear,' and all the rest of it when I came in to warn you of Natalia Dimitrievna having got hold of the prince! And now this very Natalia Dimitrievna, whom you swore at like a pickpocket, and who was just about as polite when she spoke of you, is here among your guests? Oh, don't mind *me*, Natalia Dimitrievna, *I* don't want your *chocolat à la santé* at a penny the ounce, six cups to the ounce! thanks, I can do better at home; t'fu, a good deal better."

"Evidently!" observed Natalia Dimitrievna.

"But—goodness gracious, Sophia Petrovna!" cried the hostess, flushing with annoyance; "what is it all about? Do show a little common sense!"

"Oh, don't bother about me, Maria Alexandrovna, thank you! I know all about it—oh, dear me, yes!—*I* know all about it!" cried Sophia Petrovna, in her shrill squeaky voice, from among the crowd of guests who now surrounded her, and who seemed to derive immense satisfaction from this unexpected scene. "Oh, yes, I know all about it, I assure you! Your friend Nastasia came over and told me all! You got hold of the old prince, made him drunk and persuaded him to make an offer of marriage to your daughter Zina—whom nobody else will marry; and I daresay you suppose you are going to be a very great lady, indeed—a sort of duchess in lace and jewellery. Tfu! Don't flatter yourself; you may not be aware that I, too, am a colonel's lady! and if you don't care to ask me to your betrothal parties, you needn't: I scorn and despise you and your parties too! I've seen honester women than you, you know! I have dined at Countess Zalichvatsky's; a chief commissioner proposed for my hand! A lot *I* care for your invitations. Tfu!"

"Look here, Sophia Petrovna," said Maria Alexandrovna, beside herself with rage; "I assure you that people do not indulge in this sort of sally at respectable houses; especially in *the condition you are now in*! And let me tell you that if you do not immediately relieve me of your presence and eloquence, I shall be obliged to take the matter into my own hands!"

"Oh, I know—you'll get your people to turn me out! Don't trouble yourself—I know the way out! Good-bye,—marry your daughter to whom you please, for all I care. And as for *you*, Natalia Dimitrievna, I will thank you not to laugh at me! I may not have been asked here, but at all events *I* did not dance a can-can for the prince's benefit. What may *you* be laughing at, Mrs. Antipova? I suppose you haven't heard that your *great friend* Lushiloff has broken his leg?—he has just been taken home. Tfu! Good-bye, Maria Alexandrovna—good luck to you! Tfu!"

Sophia Petrovna now disappeared. All the guests laughed; Maria Alexandrovna was in a state of indescribable fury.

"I think the good lady must have been drinking!" said Natalia Dimitrievna, sweetly.

"But what audacity!"

"*Quelle abominable femme!*"

"What a raving lunatic!"

"But really, what excessively improper things she says!"

"Yes, but what *could* she have meant by a 'betrothal party?' What sort of a betrothal party is this?" asked Felisata Michaelovna innocently.

"It is too bad—too bad!" Maria Alexandrovna burst out at last. "It is just such abominable women as this that sow nonsensical rumours about! it is not the fact that there *are* such women about, Felisata Michaelovna, that is so surprising; the astonishing part of the matter is that ladies can be found who support and encourage them, and believe their abominable tales, and——"

"The prince, the prince!" cried all the guests at once.

"Oh, oh, here he is—the dear, dear prince!"

"Well, thank goodness, we shall hear all the particulars now!" murmured Felisata Michaelovna to her neighbour.

CHAPTER XIII.

The prince entered and smiled benignly around.

All the agitation which his conversation with Mosgliakoff, a quarter of an hour since, had aroused in his chicken-heart vanished at the sight of the ladies.

Those gentle creatures received him with chirps and exclamations of joy. Ladies always petted our old friend the prince, and were—as a rule—wonderfully familiar with him. He had a way of amusing them with his own individuality which was astonishing! Only this morning Felisata Michaelovna had announced that she would sit on his knee with the greatest pleasure, if he liked; "because he was such a dear old pet of an old man!"

Maria Alexandrovna fastened her eyes on him, to read—if she could—if it were but the slightest indication of his state of mind, and to get a possible idea for a way out of this horribly critical position. But there was nothing to be made of *his* face; it was just as before—just as ever it was!

"Ah—h! here's the prince at last!" cried several voices. "Oh, Prince, how we have waited and waited for you!"

"With impatience, Prince, with impatience!" another chorus took up the strain.

"Dear me, how very flat—tering!" said the old man, settling himself near the tea-table.

The ladies immediately surrounded him. There only remained Natalia Dimitrievna and Mrs. Antipova with the hostess. Afanassy stood and smiled with great courtesy.

Mosgliakoff also smiled as he gazed defiantly at Zina, who, without taking the slightest notice of him, took a chair near her father, and sat down at the fireside.

"Prince, do tell us—is it true that you are about to leave us so soon?" asked Felisata Michaelovna.

"Yes, yes, *mesdames*; I am going abroad almost im—mediately!"

"Abroad, Prince, abroad? Why, what can have caused you to take such a step as that?" cried several ladies at once.

"Yes—yes, abroad," said the prince; "and do you know it is principally for the sake of the new i—deas——"

"How, new ideas? what new ideas—what does he mean?" the astonished ladies asked of one another.

"Ye—yes. Quite so—new ideas!" repeated the prince with an air of deep conviction, "everybody goes abroad now for new ideas, and I'm going too, to see if I can pick any up."

Up to this moment Maria Alexandrovna had listened to the conversation observantly; but it now struck her that the prince had entirely forgotten her existence—which would not do!

"Allow me, Prince, to introduce my husband, Afanassy Matveyevitch. He hastened up from our country seat so soon as ever he heard of your arrival in our house."

Afanassy, under the impression that he was being praised, smiled amiably and beamed all over.

"Very happy, very happy—Afanassy Mat—veyevitch!" said the prince. "Wait a moment: your name reminds me of something, Afanassy Mat—veyevitch; ye—yes, you are the man down at the village! Charming, charm—ing! Very glad, I'm sure. Do you remember, my boy," (to Paul) "the nice little rhyme we fitted out to him? What was it?"

"Oh, I know, prince," said Felisata Michaelovna—

" 'When the husband's away

The wife will play!"

"Wasn't that it? We had it last year at the theatre."

"Yes, yes, quite so, ye—yes, 'the wife will play!' That's it: charming, charming. So you are that ve—ry man? Dear me, I'm *very* glad, I'm sure," said the prince, stretching out his hand, but not rising from his chair. "Dear me, and how is your health, my dear sir?"

"H'm!"

"Oh, he's quite well, thank you, prince, *quite* well," answered Maria Alexandrovna quickly.

"Ye—yes, I see he is—he looks it! And are you still at the vill—age? Dear me, very pleased, I'm sure; why, how red he looks, and he's always laugh—ing."

Afanassy smiled and bowed, and even "scraped," as the prince spoke, but at the last observation he suddenly, and without warning or apparent reason, burst into loud fits of laughter.

The ladies were delighted. Zina flushed up, and with flashing eyes darted a look at her mother, who, in her turn, was boiling over with rage.

It was time to change the conversation.

"Did you have a nice nap, prince?" she inquired in honied accents; but at the same time giving Afanassy to understand, with very un-honied looks that he might go—well, anywhere!

"Oh, I slept won—derfully, wonderfully? And do you know, I had such a most fascinating, be—witching dream!"

"A dream? how delightful! I do so love to hear people tell their dreams," cried Felisata.

"Oh, a fas—cinating dream," stammered the old man again, "quite be—witching, but all the more a dead secret for that very reas—on."

"Oh, Prince, you don't mean to say you can't tell us?" said Mrs. Antipova. "I suppose it's an *extraordinary* dream, isn't it?"

"A dead secret!" repeated the prince, purposely whetting the curiosity of the ladies, and enjoying the fun.

"Then it *must* be interesting, oh, *dreadfully* interesting," cried other ladies.

"I don't mind taking a bet that the prince dreamed that he was kneeling at some lovely woman's feet and making a declaration of love," said Felisata Michaelovna. "Confess, now, prince, that it was so? confess, dear prince, confess."

"Yes, Prince, confess!" the chorus took up the cry. The old man listened solemnly until the last voice was hushed. The ladies' guesswork flattered his vanity wonderfully; he was as pleased as he could be. "Though I did say that my dream was a dead se—cret," he replied at last, "still I am obliged to confess, dear lady, that to my great as—tonishment you have almost exactly guessed it."

"I've guessed it, I've guessed it," cried Felisata, in a rapture of joy. "Well, prince, say what you like, but it's your *plain* duty to tell us the name of your beauty; come now, *isn't* it?"

"Of course, of course, prince."

"Is she in this town?"

"Dear prince, *do* tell us."

"*Darling* prince, do, *do* tell us; you positively *must*," was heard on all sides.

"*Mesdames, mes—dames*; if you must know, I will go so far as to say that it is the most charming, and be—witching, and vir—tuous lady I know," said the prince, unctuously.

"The most bewitching? and belonging to this place? Who *can* it be?" cried the ladies, interchanging looks and signs.

"Why, of course, the young lady who is considered the reigning beauty here," remarked Natalia Dimitrievna, rubbing her hands and looking hard at Zina with those cat's-eyes of hers. All joined her in staring at Zina.

"But, prince, if you dream those sort of things, why should not you marry somebody *bona fide*?" asked Felisata, looking around her with a significant expression.

"We would marry you off beautifully, prince!" said somebody else.

"Oh, dear prince, *do* marry!" chirped another.

"Marry, marry, *do* marry!" was now the cry on all sides.

"Ye—yes. Why should I not ma—arry!" said the old man, confused and bewildered with all the cries and exclamations around him.

"Uncle!" cried Mosgliakoff.

"Ye—yes, my boy, quite so; I un—derstand what you mean. I may as well tell you, ladies, that I am not in a position to marry again; and having passed one most delightful evening with our fascinating hostess, I must start away to-morrow to the Hermitage, and then I shall go straight off abroad, and study the question of the enlightenment of Europe."

Zina shuddered, and looked over at her mother with an expression of unspeakable anguish.

But Maria Alexandrovna had now made up her mind how to act; all this while she had played a mere waiting game, observing closely and carefully all that was said or done, although she could see only too clearly that her plans were undermined, and that her foes had come about her in numbers which were too great to be altogether pleasant.

At last, however, she comprehended the situation, she thought, completely. She had gauged how the matter stood in all its branches, and she determined to slay the hundred-headed hydra at one fell blow!

With great majesty, then, she rose from her seat, and approached the tea-table, stalking across the room with firm and dignified tread, as she looked around upon her pigmy foes. The fire of inspiration blazed in her eyes. She resolved to smite once, and annihilate this vile nest of poisonous scandal-adders: to destroy the miserable Mosgliakoff, as though he were a blackbeetle, and with one triumphant blow to reassert all her influence over this miserable old idiot-prince!

Some audacity was requisite for such a performance, of course; but Maria Alexandrovna had not even to put her hand in her pocket for a supply of that particular commodity.

"*Mesdames*," she began, solemnly, and with much dignity (Maria Alexandrovna was always a great admirer of solemnity); "*mesdames*, I have been a listener to your conversation—to your witty remarks and merry jokes—long enough, and I consider that my turn has come, at last, to put in a word in contribution.

"You are aware we have all met here accidentally (to my great joy, I must add—to my very great joy); but, though I should be the first to refuse to divulge a family secret before the strictest rules of ordinary propriety rendered such a revelation necessary, yet, as my dear guest here appears to me to have given us to understand, by covert hints and insinuations, that he is not averse to the matter becoming common property (he will forgive me if I have mistaken his intentions!)—I cannot help feeling that the prince is not only not averse, but actually desires me to make known our great family secret. Am I right, Prince?"

"Ye—yes, quite so, quite so! Very glad, ve—ry glad, I'm sure!" said the prince, who had not the remotest idea what the good lady was talking about!

Maria Alexandrovna, for greater effect, now paused to take breath, and looked solemnly and proudly around upon the assembled guests, all of whom were now listening with greedy but slightly disturbed curiosity to what their hostess was about to reveal to them.

Mosgliakoff shuddered; Zina flushed up, and arose from her seat; Afanassy, seeing that something important was about to happen, blew his nose violently, in order to be ready for any emergency.

"Yes, ladies; I am ready—nay, gratified—to entrust my family secret to your keeping!——This evening, the prince, overcome by the beauty and virtues of my daughter, has done her the honour of proposing to me for her hand. Prince," she concluded, in trembling tearful accents, "dear Prince; you must not, you cannot blame me for my candour! It is only my overwhelming joy that could have torn this dear secret prematurely from my heart: and what mother is there who will blame me in such a case as this?"

Words fail me to describe the effect produced by this most unexpected sally on the part of Maria Alexandrovna. All present appeared to be struck dumb with amazement. These perfidious guests, who had thought to frighten Maria Alexandrovna by showing her that they knew her secret; who thought to annihilate her by the premature revelation of that secret; who thought to overwhelm her, for the present, with their hints and insinuations; these guests were themselves struck down and pulverized by this fearless candour on her part! Such audacious frankness argued the consciousness of strength.

"So that the prince actually, and of his own free-will is really going to marry Zina? So they did not drink and bully and swindle him into it? So he is not to be married burglariously and forcibly? So Maria Alexandrovna is not afraid of anybody? Then we can't knock this marriage on the head—since the prince is not being married compulsorily!"

Such were the questions and exclamations the visitors now put to themselves and each other.

But very soon the whispers which the hostess's words had awakened all over the room, suddenly changed to chirps and exclamations of joy.

Natalia Dimitrievna was the first to come forward and embrace Maria Alexandrovna; then came Mrs. Antipova; next Felisata Michaelovna. All present were shortly on their feet and moving about, changing places. Many of the ladies were pale with rage. Some began to congratulate Zina, who was confused enough without; some attached themselves to the wretched Afanassy Matveyevitch. Maria Alexandrovna stretched her arms theatrically, and embraced her daughter—almost by force.

The prince alone gazed upon the company with a sort of confused wonder; but he smiled on as before. He seemed to be pleased with the scene. At sight of the mother and daughter embracing, he took out his handkerchief, and wiped his eye, in the corner of which there really was a tear.

Of course the company fell upon him with their congratulations before very long.

"I congratulate you, Prince! I congratulate you!" came from all sides at once.

"So you *are* going to be married, Prince?"

"So you *really are* going to marry?"

"Dear Prince! You really are to be married, then?"

"Ye—yes, ye—yes; quite so, quite so!" replied the old fellow, delighted beyond measure with all the rapture and atmosphere of congratulation around him; "and I confess what I like best of all, is the ve—ery kind in—terest you all take in me! I shall never forget it, never for—get it! Charming! charming! You have brought the tears to my eyes!"

"Kiss me, prince!" cried Felisata Michaelovna, in stentorian tones.

"And I con—fess further," continued the Prince, as well as the constant physical interruptions from all sides allowed him; "I confess I am beyond measure as—tonished that Maria Alexandrovna, our revered hostess, should have had the extraordinary penet—ration to guess my dream! She might have dreamed it herself, instead of me. Ex—traordinary perspicacity! Won—derful, wonderful!"

"Oh, prince; your dream again!"

"Oh, come, prince! admit—confess!" cried one and all.

"Yes, prince, it is no use concealing it now; it is time we divulged this secret of ours!" said Maria Alexandrovna, severely and decidedly. "I quite entered into your refined, allegorical manner; the delightful delicacy with which you gave me to understand, by means of subtle insinuations, that you wished the fact of your engagement to be made known. Yes, ladies, it is all true! This very evening the prince knelt at my daughter's feet, and actually, and by no means in a dream, made a solemn proposal of marriage to her!"

"Yes—yes, quite so! just exactly like that; and under the very cir—cumstances she describes: just like re—ality," said the old man. "My dear young lady," he continued, bowing with his greatest courtesy to Zina, who had by no means recovered from her amazement as yet; "my dear young lady, I swear to you, I should never have dared thus to bring your name into pro—minence, if others had not done so before me! It was a most be—witching dream! a be—witching dream! and I am doubly happy that I have been per—mitted to describe it. Charming—charming!"

"Dear me! how very curious it is: he insists on sticking to his idea about a dream!" whispered Mrs. Antipova to the now slightly paling Maria Alexandrovna. Alas! that great woman had felt her heart beating more quickly than she liked without this last little reminder!

"What does it mean?" whispered the ladies among themselves.

40

"Excuse me, prince," began Maria Alexandrovna, with a miserable attempt at a smile, "but I confess you astonish me a great deal! What is this strange idea of yours about a dream? I confess I had thought you were joking up to this moment; but—if it be a joke on your part, it is exceedingly out of place! I should like—I am *anxious* to ascribe your conduct to absence of mind, but——"

"Yes; it may really be a case of absence of mind!" put in Natalia Dimitrievna in a whisper.

"Yes—yes—of course, quite so; it may easily be absence of mind!" confirmed the prince, who clearly did not in the least comprehend what they were trying to get out of him; "and with regard to this subject, let me tell you a little an—ecdote. I was asked to a funeral at Petersburg, and I went and made a little mis—take about it and thought it was a birthday par—ty! So I brought a lovely bouquet of cam—ellias! When I came in and saw the master of the house lying in state on a table, I didn't know where to lo—ok, or what to do with my ca—mellias, I assure you!"

"Yes; but, Prince, this is not the moment for stories!" observed Maria Alexandrovna, with great annoyance. "Of course, my daughter has no need to beat up a husband; but at the same time, I must repeat that you yourself here, just by the piano, made her an offer of marriage. *I* did not ask you to do it! I may say I was amazed to hear it! However, since the episode of your proposal, I may say that I have thought of nothing else; and I have only waited for your appearance to talk the matter over with you. But now—well, I am a mother, and this is my daughter. You speak of a dream. I supposed, naturally, that you were anxious to make your engagement known by the medium of an allegory. Well, I am perfectly well aware that someone may have thought fit to confuse your mind on this matter; in fact, I may say that I have my suspicions as to the individual responsible for such a——however, kindly explain yourself, Prince; explain yourself quickly and satisfactorily. You cannot be permitted to jest in this fashion in a respectable house."

"Ye—yes—quite so, quite so; one should not jest in respectable houses," remarked the prince, still bewildered, but beginning gradually to grow a little disconcerted.

"But that is no answer to my question, Prince. I ask you to reply categorically. I insist upon your confirming—confirming here and at once—the fact that this very evening you made a proposal of marriage to my daughter!"

"Quite so—quite so; I am ready to confirm that! But I have told the com—pany all about it, and Felisata Michaelovna ac—tually guessed my dream!"

"*Not dream!* it was *not* a dream!" shouted Maria Alexandrovna furiously. "It was not a dream, Prince, but you were wide awake. Do you hear? Awake—you were *awake*!"

"Awake?" cried the prince, rising from his chair in astonishment. "Well, there you are, my friend; it has come about just as you said," he added, turning to Mosgliakoff. "But I assure you, most es—teemed Maria Alexandrovna, that you are under a del—usion. I am quite convinced that I saw the whole scene in a dream!"

"Goodness gracious!" cried Maria Alexandrovna.

"Do not disturb yourself, dear Maria Alexandrovna," said Natalia Dimitrievna, "probably the prince has forgotten; he will recollect himself by and by."

"I am astonished at you, Natalia Dimitrievna!" said the now furious hostess. "As if people forget this sort of thing! Excuse me, Prince, but are you laughing at us, or what are you doing? Are you trying to act one of Dumas' heroes, or Lauzun or Ferlacourt, or somebody? But, if you will excuse me saying so, you are a good deal too old for that sort of thing, and I assure you, your amiable little play-acting will not do here! My daughter is not a French viscountess! I tell you, this very evening and in this very spot here, my daughter sang a ballad to you, and you, amazed at the beauty of her singing, went down on your knees and made her a proposal of marriage. I am not talking in my sleep, am I? Surely I am wide awake? Speak, Prince, am I asleep, or not?"

"Ye—yes, of course, of course—quite so. I don't know," said the bewildered old man. "I mean, I don't think I am drea—ming now; but, a little while ago I *was* asleep, you see; and while asleep I had this dream, that I——"

"Goodness me, Prince, I tell you you were *not* dreaming. *Not dreaming*, do you hear? *Not* dreaming! What on earth do you mean? Are you raving, Prince, or what?"

"Ye—yes; deuce only knows. I don't know! It seems to me I'm getting be—wildered," said the prince, looking around him in a state of considerable mental perturbation.

"But, my dear Prince, how can you possibly have *dreamed* this, when I can tell you all the minutest details of your proposal and of the circumstances attending it? You have not told any of us of these details. How could I possibly have known what you dreamed?"

"But, perhaps the prince *did* tell someone of his dream, in detail," remarked Natalia Dimitrievna.

"Ye—yes, quite so—quite so! Perhaps I did tell someone all about my dream, in detail," said the now completely lost and bewildered prince.

"Here's a nice comedy!" whispered Felisata Michaelovna to her neighbour.

"My goodness me! this is too much for *anybody's* patience!" cried Maria Alexandrovna, beside herself with helpless rage. "Do you hear me, Prince? She sang you a ballad—*sang you a ballad*! Surely you didn't dream that too?"

"Certainly—cer—tainly, quite so. It really did seem to me that she sang me a ballad," murmured the prince; and a ray of recollection seemed to flash across his face. "My friend," he continued, addressing Mosgliakoff, "I believe I forgot to tell you, there was a ballad sung—a ballad all about castles and knights; and some trou—badour or other came in. Of course, of course, I remember it all quite well. I recoll—ect I did turn over the ballad. It puzzles me much, for now it seems as though I had really heard the ballad, and not dreamt it all."

"I confess, uncle," said Mosgliakoff, as calmly as he could, though his voice shook with agitation, "I confess I do not see any difficulty in bringing your actual experience and your dream into strict conformity; it is consistent enough. You probably *did* hear the ballad. Miss Zenaida sings beautifully; probably you all adjourned into this room and Zenaida Afanassievna sang you the song. Of course, I was not there myself, but in all probability this ballad reminded you of old times; very likely it reminded you of that very vicomtesse with whom you used once to sing, and of whom you were speaking to-day; well, and then, when you went up for your nap and lay down, thinking of

41

the delightful impressions made upon you by the ballad and all, you dreamed that you were in love and made an offer of marriage to the lady who had inspired you with that feeling."

Maria Alexandrovna was struck dumb by this display of barefaced audacity.

"Why, ye—yes, my boy, yes, of course; that's exactly how it really wa—as!" cried the prince, in an ecstasy of delight. "Of course it was the de—lightful impressions that caused me to dream it. I certainly re—member the song; and then I went away and dreamed about my pro—posal, and that I really wished to marry! The viscountess was there too. How beautifully you have unravelled the diffi—culty, my dear boy. Well, now I am quite convinced that it was all a dream. Maria Alex—androvna! I assure you, you are under a delu—usion: it was a dream. I should not think of trifling with your feelings otherwise."

"Oh, indeed! Now I perceive very clearly whom we have to thank for making this dirty mess of our affairs!" cried Maria Alexandrovna, beside herself with rage, and turning to Mosgliakoff: "You are the man, sir—the *dishonest* person. It is you who stirred up this mud! It is you that puzzled an unhappy old idiot into this eccentric behaviour, because you yourself were rejected! But we shall be quits, my friend, for this offence! You shall pay, you shall pay! Wait a bit, my dishonest friend; wait a bit!"

"Maria Alexandrovna!" cried Mosgliakoff, blushing in his turn until he looked as red as a boiled lobster, "your words are so, so——to such an extent—I really don't know how to express my opinion of you. No lady would ever permit herself to—to—. At all events I am but protecting my relative. You must allow that to *allure* an old man like this is, is——."

"Quite so, quite so; *allure*," began the prince, trying to hide himself behind Mosgliakoff.

"Afanassy Matveyevitch!" cried Maria Alexandrovna, in unnatural tones; "do you hear, sir, how these people are shaming and insulting me? Have you *quite* exempted yourself from all the responsibilities of a man? Or are you actually a—a wooden block, instead of the father of a family? What do you stand blinking there for? eh! Any other husband would have wiped out such an insult to his family with the blood of the offender long ago."

"Wife!" began Afanassy, solemnly, delighted, and proud to find that a need for him had sprung up for once in his life. "Wife, are you quite certain, now, that *you* did not dream all this? You might so easily have fallen asleep and dreamed it, and then muddled it all up with what really happened, you know, and so——"

But Afanassy Matveyevitch was never destined to complete his ingenious, but unlucky guess.

Up to this moment the guests had all restrained themselves, and had managed, cleverly enough, to keep up an appearance of solid and judicial interest in the proceedings. But at the first sound, almost, of Afanassy's voice, a burst of uncontrollable laughter rose like a tempest from all parts of the room.

Maria Alexandrovna, forgetting all the laws of propriety in her fury, tried to rush at her unlucky consort; but she was held back by force, or, doubtless, she would have scratched out that gentleman's eyes.

Natalia Dimitrievna took advantage of the occasion to add a little, if only a little, drop more of poison to the bitter cup.

"But, dear Maria Alexandrovna," she said, in the sweetest honied tones, "perhaps it may be that it really *was* so, as your husband suggests, and that you are actually under a strange delusion?"

"How! What was a delusion?" cried Maria Alexandrovna, not quite catching the remark.

"Why, my dear Maria, I was saying, *mightn't* it have been so, dear, after all? These sort of things *do* happen sometimes, you know!"

"*What* sort of things do happen, eh? What are you trying to do with me? What am I to make of you?"

"Why, perhaps, dear, you really *did* dream it all!"

"What? *dream* it! *I* dreamed it? And you dare suggest such a thing to me—straight to my face?"

"Oh, why not? Perhaps it really was the case," observed Felisata Michaelovna.

"Ye—yes, quite so, very likely it act—ually *was* the case," muttered the old prince.

"He, too—gracious Heaven!" cried poor Maria Alexandrovna, wringing her hands.

"Dear me, how you do worry yourself, Maria Alexandrovna. You should remember that dreams are sent us by a good Providence. If Providence so wills it, there is no more to be said. Providence gives the word, and we can neither weep nor be angry at its dictum."

"Quite so, quite so. We can't be a—angry about it," observed the prince.

"Look here; do you take me for a lunatic, or not?" said Maria Alexandrovna. She spoke with difficulty, so dreadfully was she panting with fury. It was more than flesh and blood could stand. She hurriedly grasped a chair, and fell fainting into it. There was a scene of great excitement.

"She has fainted in obedience to the laws of propriety!" observed Natalia Dimitrievna to Mrs. Antipova. But at this moment—at this moment when the general bewilderment and confusion had reached its height, and when the scene was strained to the last possible point of excitement, another actor suddenly stepped to the front; one who had been silent hitherto, but who immediately threw quite a different complexion on the scene.

CHAPTER XIV.

Zenaida, or Zina Afanassievna, was an individual of an extremely romantic turn of mind.

I don't know whether it really was that she had read too much of "that fool Shakespeare," with her "little tutor fellow," as Maria Alexandrovna insisted; but, at all events she was very romantic. However, never, in all her experience of Mordasoff life, had Zina before made such an ultra-romantic, or perhaps I might call it *heroic*, display as on the occasion of the sally which I am now about to describe.

Pale, and with resolution in her eyes, yet almost trembling with agitation, and wonderfully beautiful in her anger and scorn, she stepped to the front.

Gazing around at all, defiantly, she approached her mother in the midst of the sudden silence which had fallen on all present. Her mother roused herself from her swoon at the first indication of a projected movement on Zina's part, and she now opened her eyes.

"Mamma!" cried Zina, "why should we deceive anyone? Why befoul ourselves with more lies? Everything is so foul already that surely it is not worth while to bemean ourselves any further by attempting to gloss over the filth!"

"Zina, Zina! what are you thinking of? *Do* recollect yourself!" cried Maria Alexandrovna, frightened out of her wits, and jumping briskly up from her chair.

"I told you, mamma—I told you before, that I should not be able to last out the length of this shameful and ignominious business!" continued Zina. "Surely we need no further bemean and befoul ourselves! I will take it all on myself, mamma. I am the basest of all, for lending myself, of my own free will, to this abominable intrigue! You are my mother; you love me, I know, and you wished to arrange matters for my happiness, as you thought best, and according to your lights. *Your* conduct, therefore, is pardonable; but mine! oh, no! never, never!"

"Zina, Zina! surely you are not going to tell the whole story? Oh! woe, woe! I felt that the knife would pierce my heart!"

"Yes, mamma, I shall tell all; I am disgraced, you—we all of us are disgraced——"

"Zina, you are exaggerating! you are beside yourself; and you don't know what you are saying. And why say anything about it? The ignominy and disgrace is not on our side, dear child; I will show in a moment that it is not on our side!"

"No, mamma, no!" cried Zina, with a quiver of rage in her voice, "I do not wish to remain silent any longer before these—persons, whose opinion I despise, and who have come here for the purpose of laughing at us. I do not wish to stand insult from any one of them; none of them have any right to throw dirt at me; every single one of them would be ready at any moment to do things thirty times as bad as anything either I or you have done or would do! Dare they, *can* they constitute themselves our judges?"

"Listen to that!"

"There's a pretty little speech for you!"

"Why, that's *us* she's abusing"!

"A nice sort of creature she is herself!"

These and other such-like exclamations greeted the conclusion of Zina's speech.

"Oh, she simply doesn't know what she's talking about!" observed Natalia Dimitrievna.

We will make a digression, and remark that Natalia Dimitrievna was quite right there!

For if Zina did not consider these women competent to judge herself, why should she trouble herself to make those exposures and admissions which she proposed to reveal in their presence? Zina was in much too great a hurry. (She always was,—so the best heads in Mordasoff had agreed!) All might have been set right; all might have been satisfactorily arranged! Maria Alexandrovna was a great deal to blame this night, too! She had been too much "in a hurry," like her daughter,—and too arrogant! She should have simply raised the laugh at the old prince's expense, and turned him out of the house! But Zina, in despite of all common sense (as indicated above), and of the sage opinions of all Mordasoff, addressed herself to the prince:

"Prince," she said to the old man, who actually rose from his arm-chair to show his respect for the speaker, so much was he struck by her at this moment!—"Prince forgive us; we have deceived you; we entrapped you——"

"*Will* you be quiet, you wretched girl?" cried Maria Alexandrovna, wild with rage.

"My dear young lady—my dear child, my darling child!" murmured the admiring prince.

But the proud haughty character of Zina had led her on to cross the barrier of all propriety;—she even forgot her own mother who lay fainting at her feet—a victim to the self-exposure her daughter indulged in.

"Yes, prince, we both cheated you. Mamma was in fault in that she determined that I must marry you; and I in that I consented thereto. We filled you with wine; I sang to you and postured and posed for your admiration. We tricked you, a weak defenceless old man, we *tricked* you (as Mr. Mosgliakoff would express it!) for the sake of your wealth, and your rank. All this was shockingly mean, and I freely admit the fact. But I swear to you, Prince, that I consented to all this baseness from motives which were *not* base. I wished,—but what a wretch I am! it is doubly mean to justify one's conduct in such a case as this! But I will tell you, Prince, that if I had accepted anything from you, I should have made it up to you for it, by being your plaything, your servant, your—your ballet dancer, your slave—anything you wished. I had sworn to this, and I should have kept my oath."

A severe spasm at the throat stopped her for a moment; while all the guests sat and listened like so many blocks of wood, their eyes and mouths wide open.

This unexpected, and to them perfectly unintelligible sally on Zina's part had utterly confounded them. The old prince alone was touched to tears, though he did not understand half that Zina said.

"But I will marry you, my beau—t—iful child, I *will* marry you, if you like"—he murmured, "and est—eem it a great honour, too! But I as—sure you it was all a dream,—what does it mat—ter what I dream? Why should you take it so to heart? I don't seem to under—stand it all; please explain, my dear friend, what it all means!" he added, to Paul.

"As for you, Pavel Alexandrovitch," Zina recommenced, also turning to Mosgliakoff, "you whom I had made up my mind, at one time, to look upon as my future husband; you who have now so cruelly revenged yourself upon me; must you needs have allied yourself to these people here, whose object at all times is to humiliate and shame me? And you said that you loved me! However, it is not for me to preach moralities to you, for I am worse than all! I wronged you, distinctly, in holding out false hopes and half promises. I never loved you, and if I had agreed to be your wife, it would have been solely with the view of getting away from here, out of this accursed town, and free of all

43

this meanness and baseness. However, I swear to you that had I married you, I should have been a good and faithful wife! You have taken a cruel vengeance upon me, and if that flatters your pride, then——"

"Zina!" cried Mosgliakoff.

"If you still hate me——"

"Zina!!"

"If you ever did love me——"

"Zenaida Afanassievna!"

"Zina, Zina—my child!" cried Maria Alexandrovna.

"I am a blackguard, Zina—a blackguard, and nothing else!" cried Mosgliakoff; while all the assembled ladies gave way to violent agitation. Cries of amazement and of wrath broke upon the silence; but Mosgliakoff himself stood speechless and miserable, without a thought and without a word to plead for him!

"I am an ass, Zina," he cried at last, in an outburst of wild despair,—"an ass! oh far, far worse than an ass. But I will prove to you, Zina, that even an ass can behave like a generous human being! Uncle, I cheated you! I, I—it was I who cheated you: you were *not* asleep,—you were wide awake when you made this lady an offer of marriage! And I—scoundrel that I was—out of revenge because I was rejected by her myself, persuaded you that you had dreamed it all!"

"Dear me, what wonderful and interesting revelations we are being treated to now!" whispered Natalia to Mrs. Antipova.

"My dear friend," replied the prince, "com—pose yourself, do! I assure you—you quite start—led me with that sudden ex—clamation of yours! Besides, you are labouring under a delusion;—I will marr—y the lady, of course, if ne—cessary. But you told me, yourself, it was all a dre—eam!"

"Oh, how am I to tell you? Do show me, somebody, how to explain to him! Uncle, uncle! this is an important matter—a most important family affair! Think of that, uncle—just try to realise that——"

"Wait a bit, my boy—wait a bit: let me think! First there was my coachman, Theophile——"

"Oh, never mind Theophile now, for goodness sake!"

"Of course we need not waste time over The—ophile. Well—then came Na—poleon; and then we seemed to be sitting at tea, and some la—dy came and ate up all our su—gar!"

"But, uncle!" cried Mosgliakoff, at his wits' end, "it was Maria Alexandrovna herself told us that anecdote about Natalia Dimitrievna! I was here myself and heard it!—I was a blackguard, and listened at the keyhole!"

"How, Maria Alexandrovna!" cried Natalia, "you've told the prince too, have you, that I stole sugar out of your basin? So I come to you to steal your sugar, do I, eh! do I?"

"Get away from me!" cried Maria Alexandrovna, with the abandonment of utter despair.

"Oh, dear no! I shall do nothing of the sort, Maria Alexandrovna! I steal your sugar, do I? I tell you you shall not talk of me like that, madam—you dare not! I have long suspected you of spreading this sort of rubbish abroad about me! Sophia Petrovna came and told me all about it. So I stole your sugar, did I, eh?"

"But, my dear la—dies!" said the prince, "it was only part of a dream! What do my dreams matter?——"

"Great tub of a woman!" muttered Maria Alexandrovna through her teeth.

"What! what! I'm a tub, too, am I?" shrieked Natalia Dimitrievna. "And what are you yourself, pray? Oh, I have long known that you call me a tub, madam. Never mind!—at all events my husband is a man, madam, and not a fool, like yours!"

"Ye—yes—quite so! I remember there *was* something about a tub, too!" murmured the old man, with a vague recollection of his late conversation with Maria Alexandrovna.

"What—*you*, too? *you* join in abusing a respectable woman of noble extraction, do you? How dare you call me names, prince—you wretched old one-legged misery! I'm a tub am I, you one-legged old abomination?"

"Wha—at, madam, I one-legged?"

"Yes—one-legged and toothless, sir; that's what you are!"

"Yes, and one-eyed too!" shouted Maria Alexandrovna.

"And what's more, you wear stays instead of having your own ribs!" added Natalia Dimitrievna.

"His face is all on wire springs!"

"He hasn't a hair of his own to swear by!"

"Even the old fool's moustache is stuck on!" put in Maria Alexandrovna.

"Well, Ma—arie Alexandrovna, give me the credit of having a nose of my ve—ry own, at all events!" said the prince, overwhelmed with confusion under these unexpected disclosures. "My friend, it must have been you betrayed me! *you* must have told them that my hair is stuck on?"

"Uncle, what an idea, I——!"

"My dear boy, I can't stay here any lon—ger, take me away somewhere—*quelle société*! Where have you brought me to, eh?—Gracious Hea—eaven, what dreadful soc—iety!"

"Idiot! scoundrel!" shrieked Maria Alexandrovna.

"Goodness!" said the unfortunate old prince. "I can't quite remember just now what I came here for at all—I suppose I shall reme—mber directly. Take me away, quick, my boy, or I shall be torn to pieces here! Besides, I have an i—dea that I want to make a note of——"

"Come along, uncle—it isn't very late; I'll take you over to an hotel at once, and I'll move over my own things too."

"Ye—yes, of course, a ho—tel! Good-bye, my charming child; you alone, you—are the only vir—tuous one of them all; you are a no—oble child. Good-bye, my charming girl! Come along, my friend;—oh, good gra—cious, what people!"

I will not attempt to describe the end of this disagreeable scene, after the prince's departure.

The guests separated in a hurricane of scolding and abuse and mutual vituperation, and Maria Alexandrovna was at last left alone amid the ruins and relics of her departed glory.

Alas, alas! Power, glory, weight—all had disappeared in this one unfortunate evening. Maria Alexandrovna quite realised that there was no chance of her ever again mounting to the height from which she had now fallen. Her long preeminence and despotism over society in general had collapsed.

What remained to her? Philosophy? She was wild with the madness of despair all night! Zina was dishonoured—scandals would circulate, never-ceasing scandals; and—oh! it was dreadful!

As a faithful historian, I must record that poor Afanassy was the scapegoat this night; he "caught it" so terribly that he eventually disappeared; he had hidden himself in the garret, and was there starved to death almost, with cold, all night.

The morning came at last; but it brought nothing good with it! Misfortunes never come singly.

CHAPTER XV.

If fate makes up its mind to visit anyone with misfortune, there is no end to its malice! This fact has often been remarked by thinkers; and, as if the ignominy of last night were not enough, the same malicious destiny had prepared for this family more, yea, and worse—evils to come!

By ten o'clock in the morning a strange and almost incredible rumour was in full swing all over the town: it was received by society, of course, with full measure of spiteful joy, just as we all love to receive delightfully scandalous stories of anyone about us.

"To lose one's sense of shame to such an extent!" people said one to another.

"To humiliate oneself so, and to neglect the first rules of propriety! To loose the bands of decency altogether like this, really!" etc., etc.

But here is what had happened.

Early in the morning, something after six o'clock, a poor piteous-looking old woman came hurriedly to the door of Maria Alexandrovna's house, and begged the maid to wake Miss Zina up as quickly, as possible,—only Miss Zina, and very quietly, so that her mother should not hear of it, if possible.

Zina, pale and miserable, ran out to the old woman immediately.

The latter fell at Zina's feet and kissed them and begged her with tears to come with her at once to see poor Vaísia, her son, who had been so bad, so bad all night that she did not think he could live another day.

The old woman told Zina that Vaísia had sent to beg her to come and bid him farewell in this his death hour: he conjured her to come by all the blessed angels, and by all their past—otherwise he must die in despair.

Zina at once decided to go, in spite of the fact that, by so doing, she would be justifying all the scandal and slanders disseminated about her in former days, as to the intercepted letter, her visits to him, and so on. Without a word to her mother, then, she donned her cloak and started off with the old woman, passing through the whole length of the town, into one of the poorest slums of Mordasof—and stopped at a little low wretched house, with small miserable windows, and snow piled round the basement for warmth.

In this house, in a tiny room, more than half of which was occupied by an enormous stove, on a wretched bed, and covered with a miserably thin quilt, lay a young man, pale and haggard: his eyes were ablaze with the fire of fever, his hands were dry and thin, and he was breathing with difficulty and very hoarsely. He looked as though he might have been handsome once, but disease had put its finger on his features and made them dreadful to look upon and sad withal, as are so many dying consumptive patients' faces.

His old mother who had fed herself for a year past with the conviction that her son would recover, now saw at last that Vaísia was not to live. She stood over him, bowed down with her grief—tearless, and looked and looked, and could not look enough; and felt, but could not realize, that this dear son of hers must in a few days be buried in the miserable Mordasof churchyard, far down beneath the snow and frozen earth!

But Vaísia was not looking at her at this moment! His poor suffering face was at rest now, and happy; for he saw before him the dear image which he had thought of, dreamed of, and loved through all the long sad nights of his illness, for the last year and a half! He realised that she forgave him, and had come, like an angel of God, to tell him of her forgiveness, here, on his deathbed.

She pressed his hands, wept over him, stood and smiled over him, looked at him once more with those wonderful eyes of hers, and all the past, the undying ever-present past rose up before the mind's eye of the dying man. The spark of life flashed up again in his soul, as though to show, now that it was about to die out for ever on this earth, how hard, how hard it was to see so sweet a light fade away.

"Zina, Zina!" he said, "my Zina, do not weep; don't grieve, Zina, don't remind me that I must die! Let me gaze at you, so—so,—and feel that our two souls have come together once more—that you have forgiven me! Let me kiss your dear hands again, as I used, and so let me die without noticing the approach of death.

"How thin you have grown, Zina! and how sweetly you are looking at me now, my Zina! Do you remember how you used to laugh, in bygone days? Oh, Zina, my angel, I shall not ask you to forgive me,—I will not remember anything about—that, you know what! for if you do forgive me, I can never forgive myself!

45

"All the long, long nights, Zina, I have lain here and thought, and thought; and I have long since decided that I had better die, Zina; for I am not fit to live!"

Zina wept, and silently pressed his hands, as though she would stop him talking so.

"Why do you cry so?" continued the sick man. "Is it because I am dying? but all the past is long since dead and buried, Zina, my angel! You are wiser than I am, you know I am a bad, wicked man; surely you cannot love me still? Do you know what it has cost me to realise that I am a bad man? I, who have always prided myself before the world—and what on? Purity of heart, generosity of aim! Yes, Zina, so I did, while we read Shakespeare; and in theory I was pure and generous. Yet, how did I prove these qualities in practice?"

"Oh, don't! don't!" sobbed Zina, "you are not fair to yourself: don't talk like this, please don't!"

"Don't stop me, Zina! You forgave me, my angel; I know you forgave me long ago, but you must have judged me, and you know what sort of man I really am; and that is what tortures me so! I am unworthy of your love, Zina! And you were good and true, not only in theory, but in practice too! You told your mother you would marry me, and no one else, and you would have kept your word! Do you know, Zina, I never realized before what you would sacrifice in marrying me! I could not even see that you might die of hunger if you did so! All I thought of was that you would be the bride of a great poet (in the future), and I could not understand your reasons for wishing to delay our union! So I reproached you and bullied you, and despised you and suspected you, and at last I committed the crime of showing your letter! I was not even a scoundrel at that moment! I was simply a worm-man. Ah! how you must have despised me! No, it is well that I am dying; it is well that you did not marry me! I should not have understood your sacrifice, and I should have worried you, and perhaps, in time, have learned to hate you, and ... but now it is good, it is best so! my bitter tears can at least cleanse my heart before I die. Ah! Zina! Zina! love me, love me as you did before for a little, little while! just for the last hour of my life. I know I am not worthy of it, but—oh, my angel, my Zina!"

Throughout this speech Zina, sobbing herself, had several times tried to stop the speaker; but he would not listen. He felt that he must unburden his soul by speaking out, and continued to talk—though with difficulty, panting, and with choking and husky utterance.

"Oh, if only you had never seen me and never loved me," said Zina, "you would have lived on now! Ah, *why* did we ever meet?"

"No, no, darling, don't blame yourself because I am dying! think of all my self-love, my romanticism! I am to blame for all, myself! Did they ever tell you my story in full? Do you remember, three years ago, there was a criminal here sentenced to death? This man heard that a criminal was never executed whilst ill! so he got hold of some wine, mixed tobacco in it, and drank it. The effect was to make him so dreadfully sick, with blood-spitting, that his lungs became affected; he was taken to a hospital, and a few weeks after he died of virulent consumption! Well, on that day, you know, after the letter, it struck me that I would do the same; and why do you think I chose consumption? Because I was afraid of any more sudden death? Perhaps. But, oh, Zina! believe me, a romantic nonsense played a great part in it; at all events, I had an idea that it would be striking and grand for me to be lying here, dying of consumption, and you standing and wringing your hands for woe that *love* should have brought me to this! You should come, I thought, and beg my pardon on your knees, and I should forgive you and die in your arms!"

"Oh, don't! don't!" said Zina, "don't talk of it now, dear! you are not really like that. Think of our happy days together, think of something else—not that, not that!"

"Oh, but it's so bitter to me, darling; and that's why I must speak of it. I havn't seen you for a year and a half, you know, and all that time I have been alone; and I don't think there was one single minute of all that time when I have not thought of you, my angel, Zina! And, oh! how I longed to do something to earn a better opinion from you! Up to these very last days I have never believed that I should really die; it has not killed me all at once, you know. I have long walked about with my lungs affected. For instance, I have longed to become a great poet suddenly, to publish a poem such as has never appeared before on this earth; I intended to pour my whole soul and being into it, so that wherever I was, or wherever *you* were, I should always be with you and remind you of myself in my poems! And my greatest longing of all was that you should think it all over and say to yourself at last some day, 'No, he is not such a wretch as I thought, after all!' It was stupid of me, Zina, stupid—stupid—wasn't it, darling?"

"No, no, Vaísia—no!" cried Zina. She fell on his breast and kissed his poor hot, dry hands.

"And, oh! how jealous I have been of you all this time, Zina! I think I should have died if I had heard of your wedding. I kept a watch over you, you know; I had a spy—there!" (he nodded towards his mother). "She used to go over and bring me news. You never loved Mosgliakoff—now *did* you, Zina? Oh, my darling, my darling, will you remember me when I am dead? Oh, I know you will; but years go by, Zina, and hearts grow cold, and yours will cool too, and you'll forget me, Zina!"

"No, no, never! I shall never marry. You are my first love, and my only—only—undying love!"

"But all things die, Zina, even our memories, and our good and noble feelings die also, and in their place comes reason. No, no, Zina, be happy, and live long. Love another if you can, you cannot love a poor dead man for ever! But think of me now and then, if only seldom; don't think of my faults: forgive them! For oh, Zina, there was good in that sweet love of ours as well as evil. Oh, golden, golden days never to be recalled! Listen, darling, I have always loved the sunset hour—remember me at that time, will you? Oh no, no! why must I die? oh *how* I should love to live on now. Think of that time—oh, just think of it! it was all spring then, the sun shone so bright, the flowers were so sweet, ah me! and look, now—look!"

And the poor thin finger pointed to the frozen window-pane. Then he seized Zina's hand and pressed it tight over his eyes, and sighed bitterly—bitterly! His sobs nearly burst his poor suffering breast.... And so he continued suffering and talking all the long day. Zina comforted and soothed him as she best could, but she too was full of deadly grief and pain. She told him—she promised him—never to forget; that she would never love again as she loved him; and he believed her and wept, and smiled again, and kissed her hands. And so the day passed.

Meanwhile, Maria Alexandrovna had sent some ten times for Zina, begging her not to ruin her reputation irretrievably. At last, at dusk, she determined to go herself; she was out of her wits with terror and grief.

Having called Zina out into the next room, she proceeded to beg and pray her, on her knees, "to spare this last dagger at her heart!"

Zina had come out from the sick-room ill: her head was on fire,—she heard, but could not comprehend, what her mother said; and Marie Alexandrovna was obliged to leave the house again in despair, for Zina had determined to sit up all night with Vaísia.

She never left his bedside, but the poor fellow grew worse and worse. Another day came, but there was no hope that the sick man would see its close. His old mother walked about as though she had lost all control of her actions; grief had turned her head for the time; she gave her son medicines, but he would none of them! His death agony dragged on and on! He could not speak now, and only hoarse inarticulate sounds proceeded from his throat. To the very last instant he stared and stared at Zina, and never took his eyes off her; and when their light failed them he still groped with uncertain fingers for her hand, to press and fondle it in his own!

Meanwhile the short winter day was waning! And when at even the last sunbeam gilded the frozen window-pane of the little room, the soul of the sufferer fled in pursuit of it out of the emaciated body that had kept it prisoner.

The old mother, seeing that there was nothing left her now but the lifeless body of her beloved Vaísia, wrung her hands, and with a loud cry flung herself on his dead breast.

"This is your doing, you viper, you cursed snake," she yelled to Zina, in her despair; "it was you ruined and killed him, you wicked, wretched girl." But Zina heard nothing. She stood over the dead body like one bereft of her senses.

At last she bent over him, made the sign of the Cross, kissed him, and mechanically left the room. Her eyes were ablaze, her head whirled. Two nights without sleep, combined with her turbulent feelings, were almost too much for her reason; she had a sort of confused consciousness that all her past had just been torn out of her heart, and that a new life was beginning for her, dark and threatening.

But she had not gone ten paces when Mosgliakoff suddenly seemed to start up from the earth at her feet.

He must have been waiting for her here.

"Zenaida Afanassievna," he began, peering all around him in what looked like timid haste; it was still pretty light. "Zenaida Afanassievna, of course I am an ass, or, if you please, perhaps not quite an ass, for I really think I am acting rather generously this time. Excuse my blundering, but I am rather confused, from a variety of causes."

Zina glanced at him almost unconsciously, and silently went on her way. There was not much room for two on the narrow pavement, and as Zina did not make way for Paul, the latter was obliged to walk on the road at the side, which he did, never taking his eyes off her face.

"Zenaida Afanassievna," he continued, "I have thought it all over, and if you are agreeable I am willing to renew my proposal of marriage. I am even ready to forget all that has happened; all the ignominy of the last two days, and to forgive it—but on one condition: that while we are still here our engagement is to remain a strict secret. You will depart from this place as soon as ever you can, and I shall quietly follow you. We will be married secretly, somewhere, so that nobody shall know anything about it; and then we'll be off to St. Petersburg by express post—don't take more than a small bag—eh? What say you, Zenaida Afanassievna; tell me quick, please, I can't stay here. We might be seen together, you know."

Zina did not answer a word; she only looked at Mosgliakoff; but it was such a look that he understood all instantly, bowed, and disappeared down the next lane.

"Dear me," he said to himself, "what's the meaning of this? The day before yesterday she became so jolly humble, and blamed herself all round. I've come on the wrong day, evidently!"

Meanwhile event followed event in Mordasof.

A very tragical circumstance occurred.

The old prince, who moved over to the hotel with Mosgliakoff, fell very ill that same night, dangerously ill. All Mordasof knew of it in the morning; the doctor never left his side. That evening a consultation of all the local medical talent was held over the old man (the invitations to which were issued in Latin); but in spite of the Latin and all they could do for him, the poor prince was quite off his head; he raved and asked his doctor to sing him some ballad or other; raved about wigs, and occasionally cried out as though frightened.

The Mordasof doctors decided that the hospitality of the town had given the prince inflammation of the stomach, which had somehow "gone to the head."

There might be some subordinate moral causes to account for the attack; but at all events he ought to have died long ago; and so he would certainly die now.

In this last conclusion they were not far wrong; for the poor old prince breathed his last three days after, at the hotel.

This event impressed the Mordasof folk considerably. No one had expected such a tragical turn of affairs. They went in troops to the hotel to view the poor old body, and there they wagged their heads wisely and ended by passing severe judgment upon "the murderers of the unfortunate Prince,"—meaning thereby, of course, Maria Alexandrovna and her daughter. They predicted that this matter would go further. Mosgliakoff was in a dreadful state of perturbation: he did not know what to do with the body. Should he take it back to Donchanof! or what? Perhaps he would be held responsible for the old man's death, as he had brought him here? He did not like the look of things. The Mordasof people were less than useless for advice, they were all far too frightened to hazard a word.

But suddenly the scene changed.

One fine evening a visitor arrived—no less a person than the eminent Prince Shepetiloff, a young man of thirty-five, with colonel's epaulettes, a relative of the dead man. His arrival created a great stir among all classes at Mordasof.

It appeared that this gentleman had lately left St. Petersburg, and had called in at Donchanof. Finding no one there, he had followed the prince to Mordasof, where the news and circumstances of the old man's death fell upon him like a thunder-clap!

Even the governor felt a little guilty while detailing the story of the prince's death: all Mordasof felt and looked guilty.

This visitor took the matter entirely into his own hands, and Mosgliakoff made himself scarce before the presence of the prince's real nephew, and disappeared, no one knew whither.

47

The body was taken to the monastery, and all the Mordasof ladies flocked thither to the funeral. It was rumoured that Maria Alexandrovna was to be present, and that she was to go on her knees before the coffin, and loudly pray for pardon; and that all this was in conformity with the laws of the country.

Of course this was all nonsense, and Maria Alexandrovna never went near the place!

I forgot to state that the latter had carried off Zina to the country house, not deeming it possible to continue to live in the town. There she sat, and trembled over all the second-hand news she could get hold of as to events occurring at Mordasof.

The funeral procession passed within half a mile of her country house; so that Maria Alexandrovna could get a good view of the long train of carriages looking black against the white snow roads; but she could not bear the sight, and left the window.

Before the week was out, she and her daughter moved to Moscow, taking Afanassy Matveyevitch with them; and, within a month, the country house and town house were both for sale.

And so Mordasof lost its most eminent inhabitant for ever!

Afanassy Matveyevitch was said to be for sale with the country house.

A year—two years went by, and Mordasof had quite forgotten Maria Alexandrovna, or nearly so! Alas! so wags the world! It was said that she had bought another estate, and had moved over to some other provincial capital; where, of course, she had everybody under her thumb; that Zina was not yet married; and that Afanassy Matveyevitch—but why repeat all this nonsense? None of it was true; it was but rumour!——

It is three years since I wrote the last words of the above chronicles of Mordasof, and whoever would have believed that I should have to unfold my MS., and add another piece of news to my narrative?

Well, to business!—

Let's begin with Paul Mosgliakoff.—After leaving Mordasof, he went straight to St. Petersburg, where he very soon obtained the clerkship he had applied for. He then promptly forgot all about Mordasof, and the events enacted there. He enjoyed life, went into society, fell in love, made another offer of marriage, and had to swallow another snub; became disgusted with Petersburg life, and joined an expedition to one of the remote quarters of our vast empire.

This expedition passed through its perils of land and water, and arrived in due course at the capital of the remote province which was its destination.

There the members were well received by the governor, and a ball was arranged for their entertainment.

Mosgliakoff was delighted. He donned his best Petersburg uniform, and proceeded to the large ball-room with the full intention of producing a great and startling effect. His first duty was to make his bow to the governor-general's lady, of whom it was rumoured that she was young, and very lovely.

He advanced then, with some little "swagger," but was suddenly rooted to the spot with amazement. Before him stood Zina, beautifully dressed, proud and haughty, and sparkling with diamonds! She did not recognize him; her eyes rested a moment on his face, and then passed on to glance at some other person.

Paul immediately departed to a safe and quiet corner, and there button-holed a young civilian whom he questioned, and from whom he learned certain most interesting facts. He learned that the governor-general had married a very rich and very lovely lady in Moscow, two years since; that his wife was certainly very beautiful, but, at the same time, excessively proud and haughty, and danced with none but generals. That the governor's lady had a mother, a lady of rank and fashion, who had followed them from Moscow; that this lady was very clever and wise, but that even she was quite under the thumb of her daughter; as for the general (the governor), he doted on his wife.

Mosgliakoff inquired after our old friend Afanassy; but in their "remote province" nothing was known of that gentleman.

Feeling a little more at home presently, Paul began to walk about the room, and shortly espied Maria Alexandrovna herself. She was wonderfully dressed, and was surrounded by a bevy of ladies who evidently dwelt in the glory of her patronage: she appeared to be exceedingly amiable to them—wonderfully so!

Paul plucked up courage and introduced himself. Maria Alexandrovna seemed to give a shudder at first sight of him, but in an instant she was herself again. She was kind enough to recognise Paul, and to ask him all sorts of questions as to his Petersburg experiences, and so on. She never said a word about Mordasof, however. She behaved as though no such place existed.

After a minute or so, and having dropped a question as to some Petersburg prince whom Paul had never so much as heard of, she turned to speak to another young gentleman standing by, and in a second or two was entirely oblivious of Mosgliakoff. With a sarcastic smile our friend passed on into the large hall. Feeling offended—though he knew not why—he decided not to dance. So he leant his back against one of the pillars, and for a couple of hours did nothing but follow Zina about with his eyes. But alas! all the grace of his figure and attitude, and all the fascinations of his general appearance were lost upon her, she never looked at him.

At last, with legs stiff from standing, tired, hungry, and feeling miserable generally, he went home. Here he tossed about half the night thinking of the past, and next morning, having the chance of joining a branch party of his expedition, he accepted the opportunity with delight, and left the town at once.

The bells tinkled, the horses trotted gaily along, kicking up snowballs as they went. Paul Mosgliakoff fell to thinking, then he fell to snoring, and so he continued until the third station from the start; there he awoke fresh and jolly, and with the new scenery came newer, and healthier, and pleasanter thoughts.

THE END OF "UNCLE'S DREAM."

THE PERMANENT HUSBAND.

CHAPTER I.

Summer had come, and Velchaninoff, contrary to his expectations, was still in St. Petersburg. His trip to the south of Russia had fallen through, and there seemed no end to the business which had detained him.

This business—which was a lawsuit as to certain property—had taken a very disagreeable aspect. Three months ago the thing had appeared to be by no means complicated—in fact, there had seemed to be scarcely any question as to the rights and wrongs of the matter, but all seemed to change suddenly.

"Everything else seems to have changed for the worse, too!" said Velchaninoff to himself, over and over again.

He was employing a clever lawyer—an eminent man, and an expensive one, too; but in his impatience and suspicion he began to interfere in the matter himself. He read and wrote papers—all of which the lawyer put into his waste-paper basket—*holus bolus*; called in continually at the courts and offices, made inquiries, and confused and worried everybody concerned in the matter; so at least the lawyer declared, and begged him for mercy's sake to go away to the country somewhere.

But he could not make up his mind to do so. He stayed in town and enjoyed the dust, and the hot nights, and the closeness of the air of St. Petersburg, things which are enough to destroy anyone's nerves. His lodgings were somewhere near the Great Theatre; he had lately taken them, and did not like them. Nothing went well with him; his hypochondria increased with each day, and he had long been a victim to that disorder.

Velchaninoff was a man who had seen a great deal of the world; he was not quite young, thirty-eight years old—perhaps thirty-nine, or so; and all this "old age," as he called it, had "fallen upon him quite unawares." However, as he himself well understood, he had aged more in the *quality* than in the number of the years of his life; and if his infirmities were really creeping upon him, they must have come from within and not from outside causes. He looked young enough still. He was a tall, stout man, with light-brown thick hair, without a suspicion of white about it, and a light beard that reached half way down his chest. At first sight you might have supposed him to be of a lax, careless disposition or character, but on studying him more closely you would have found that, on the contrary, the man was decidedly a stickler for the proprieties of this world, and withal brought up in the ways and graces of the very best society. His manners were very good—free but graceful—in spite of this lately-acquired habit of grumbling and reviling things in general. He was still full of the most perfect, aristocratic self-confidence: probably he did not himself suspect to how great an extent this was so, though he was a most decidedly intelligent, I may say clever, even talented man. His open, healthy-looking face was distinguished by an almost feminine refinement, which quality gained him much attention from the fair sex. He had large blue eyes—eyes which ten years ago had known well how to persuade and attract; such clear, merry, careless eyes they had been, that they invariably brought over to his side any person he wished to gain. Now, when he was nearly forty years old, their ancient, kind, frank expression had died out of them, and a certain cynicism—a cunning—an irony very often, and yet another variety of expression, of late—an expression of melancholy or pain, undefined but keen, had taken the place of the earlier attractive qualities of his eyes. This expression of melancholy especially showed itself when he was alone; and it was a strange fact that the gay, careless, happy fellow of a couple of years ago, the man who could tell a funny story so inimitably, should now love nothing so well as to be all alone. He intended to throw up most of his friends—a quite unnecessary step, in spite of his present financial difficulties. Probably his vanity was to blame for this intention: he could not bear to see his old friends in his present position; with his vain suspicious character it would be most unpalatable to him.

But his vanity began to change its nature in solitude. It did not grow less, on the contrary; but it seemed to develop into a special type of vanity which was unlike its old self. This new vanity suffered from entirely different causes, "*higher* causes, if I may so express it," he said, "and if there really be higher and lower motives in this world."

He defined these "higher things" as matters which he could not laugh at, or turn to ridicule when happening in his own individual experience. Of course it would be quite another thing with the same subjects in society; by *himself* he could not ridicule then; but put him among other people, and he would be the first to tear himself from all of those secret resolutions of his conscience made in solitude, and laugh them to scorn.

Very often, on rising from his bed in the morning, he would feel ashamed of the thoughts and feelings which had animated him during the long sleepless night—and his nights of late had been sleepless. He seemed suspicious of everything and everybody, great and small, and grew mistrustful of himself.

One fact stood out clearly, and that was that during those sleepless nights his thoughts and opinions took huge leaps and bounds, sometimes changing entirely from the thoughts and opinions of the daytime. This fact struck him very forcibly; and he took occasion to consult an eminent medical friend. He spoke in fun, but the doctor informed him that the fact of feelings and opinions changing during meditations at night, and during sleeplessness, was one long recognised by science; and that that was especially the case with persons of strong thinking power, and of acute feelings. He stated further that very often the beliefs of a whole life are uprooted under the melancholy influence of night and inability to sleep, and that often the most fateful resolutions are made under the same influence; that sometimes this impressionability to the mystic influence of the dark hours amounted to a malady, in which case measures must be taken, the radical manner of living should be changed, diet considered, a journey undertaken if possible, etc., etc.

Velchaninoff listened no further, but he was sure that in his own case there was decided malady.

Very soon his morning meditations began to partake of the nature of those of the night, but they were more bitter. Certain events of his life now began to recur to his memory more and more vividly; they would strike him suddenly, and without apparent reason: things which had been forgotten for ten or fifteen years—some so long ago that he thought it miraculous that he should have been able to recall them at all. But that was not all—for, after all, what man who has seen any life has not hundreds of such recollections of the past? The principal point was that all this past came back to him now with an absolutely new light thrown upon it, and he seemed to look at it from an entirely new and unexpected point of view. Why did some of his acts appear to him now to be nothing better than crimes? It was not merely in the judgment of his intellect that these things appeared so to him now—had it been only his poor sick mind, he would not have trusted it; but his whole being seemed to condemn him; he would curse and even weep over these recollections of the past! If anyone had told him a couple of years since that he would *weep* over anything, he would have laughed the idea to scorn.

At first he recalled the unpleasant experiences of his life: certain failures in society, humiliations; he remembered how some designing person had so successfully blackened his character that he was requested to cease his visits to a certain house; how once, and not so very long ago, he had been publicly insulted, and had not challenged the offender; how once an epigram had been fastened to his name by some witty person, in the midst of a party of pretty women and he had not found a reply; he remembered several unpaid debts, and how he had most stupidly run through two very respectable fortunes.

Then he began to recall facts belonging to a "higher" order. He remembered that he had once insulted a poor old grey-headed clerk, and that the latter had covered his face with his hands and cried, which Velchaninoff had thought a great joke at the time, but now looked upon in quite another light. Then he thought how he had once, merely for fun, set a scandal going about the beautiful little wife of a certain schoolmaster, and how the husband had got to hear the rumour. He (Velchaninoff) had left the town shortly after and did not know how the matter had ended; but now he fell to wondering and picturing to himself the possible consequences of his action; and goodness knows where this theme would not have taken him to if he had not suddenly recalled another picture: that of a poor girl, whom he had been ashamed of and never thought of loving, but whom he had betrayed and forsaken, her and her child, when he left St. Petersburg. He had afterwards searched for this girl and her baby for a whole year, but never found them.

Of this sort of recollections there were, alas! but too many; and each one seemed to bring along with it a train of others. His vanity began to suffer, little by little, under these memories. I have said that his vanity had developed into a new type of vanity. There were moments (few albeit) in which he was not even ashamed of having no carriage of his own, now; or of being seen by one of his former friends in shabby clothes; or when, if seen and looked at by such a person contemptuously, he was high-minded enough to suppress even a frown. Of course such moments of self-oblivion were rare; but, as I said before, his vanity began little by little to change away from its former quarters and to centre upon one question which was perpetually ranging itself before his intellect. "There is some power or other," he would muse, sarcastically, "somewhere, which is extremely interested in my morals, and sends me these damnable recollections and tears of remorse! Let them come, by all means; but they have not the slightest effect on me! for I haven't a scrap of independence about me, in spite of my wretched forty years, I know that for certain. Why, if it were to happen so that I should gain anything by spreading another scandal about that schoolmaster's wife, (for instance, that she had accepted presents from me, or something of that sort), I should certainly spread it without a thought."

But though no other opportunity ever did occur of maligning the schoolmistress, yet the very thought alone that *if* such an opportunity were to occur he would inevitably seize it was almost fatal to him at times. He was not tortured with memory at every moment of his life; he had intervals of time to breathe and rest in. But the longer he stayed, the more unpleasant did he find his life in St. Petersburg. July came in. At certain moments he felt inclined to throw up his lawsuit and all, and go down to the Crimea; but after an hour or so he would despise his own idea, and laugh at himself for entertaining it.

"These thoughts won't be driven away by a mere journey down south," he said to himself, "when they have once begun to annoy me; besides, if I am easy in my conscience now, I surely need not try to run away from any such worrying recollections of past days!" "Why should I go after all?" he resumed, in a strain of melancholy philosophizing; "this place is a very heaven for a hypochondriac like myself, what with the dust and the heat, and the discomfort of this house, what with the nonsensical swagger and pretence of all these wretched little 'civil servants' in the departments I frequent! Everyone is delightfully candid—and candour is undoubtedly worthy of all respect! I *won't* go away—I'll stay and die here rather than go!"

CHAPTER II.

It was the third of July. The heat and closeness of the air had become quite unbearable. The day had been a busy one for Velchaninoff—he had been walking and driving about without rest, and had still in prospect a visit in the evening to a certain state councillor who lived somewhere on the Chornaya Riéchka (black stream), and whom he was anxious to drop in upon unexpectedly.

At six o'clock our hero issued from his house once more, and trudged off to dine at a restaurant on the Nefsky, near the police-bridge—a second-rate sort of place, but French. Here he took his usual corner, and ordered his usual dinner, and waited.

He always had a rouble[1] dinner, and paid for his wine extra, which moderation he looked upon as a discreet sacrifice to the temporary financial embarrassment under which he was suffering.

He regularly went through the ceremony of wondering how he could bring himself to eat "such nastiness," and yet as regularly he demolished every morsel, and with excellent show of appetite too, just as though he had eaten nothing for three days.

"This appetite can't be healthy!" he murmured to himself sometimes, observing his own voracity. However, on this particular occasion, he sat down to his dinner in a miserably bad humour: he threw his hat angrily away somewhere, tipped his chair back,—and reflected.

He was in the sort of humour that if his next neighbour—dining at the little table near him—were to rattle his plate, or if the boy serving him were to make any little blunder, or, in fact, if any little petty annoyance were to put him out of a sudden, he was quite capable of shouting at the offender, and, in fact, of kicking up a serious row on the smallest pretext.

Soup was served to him. He took up his spoon, and was about to commence operations, when he suddenly threw it down again, and started from his seat. An unexpected thought had struck him, and in an instant he had realized why he had been plunged in gloom and mental perturbation during the last few days. Goodness knows why he thus suddenly became inspired, as it were, with the truth; but so it was. He jumped from his chair, and in an instant it all stood out before him as plain as his five fingers! "It's all that hat!" he muttered to himself; "it's all simply and solely that damnable round hat, with the crape band round it; that's the reason and cause of all my worries these last days!"

He began to think; and the more he thought, the more dejected he became, and the more astonishing appeared the "remarkable circumstance of the hat."

"But, hang it all, there *is* no circumstance!" he growled to himself. "What circumstance do I mean? There's been nothing in the nature of an event or occurrence!"

The fact of the matter was this: Nearly a fortnight since, he had met for the first time, somewhere about the corner of the Podiacheskaya, a gentleman with crape round his hat. There was nothing particular about the man—he was just like all others; but as he passed Velchaninoff he had stared at him so fixedly that it was impossible to avoid noticing him, and more than noticing—observing him attentively.

The man's face seemed to be familiar to Velchaninoff. He had evidently seen him somewhere and at some time or other.

"But one sees thousands of people during one's life," thought Velchaninoff; "one can't remember every face!" So he had gone on his way, and before he was twenty yards further, to all appearances he had forgotten all about the meeting, in spite of the strength of the first impression made upon him.

And yet he had *not* forgotten; for the impression remained all day, and a very original impression it was, too,—a kind of objectless feeling of anger against he knew not what. He remembered his exact feelings at this moment, a fortnight after the occurrence: how he had been puzzled by the angry nature of his sentiments at the time, and puzzled to such an extent that he had never for a moment connected his ill-humour with the meeting of the morning, though he had felt as cross as possible all day. But the gentleman with the crape band had not lost much time about reminding Velchaninoff of his existence, for the very next day he met the latter again, on the Nefsky Prospect and again he had stared in a peculiarly fixed way at him.

Velchaninoff flared up and spat on the ground in irritation—Russian like, but a moment after he was wondering at his own wrath. "There are faces, undoubtedly," he reflected, "which fill one with disgust at first sight; but I certainly *have* met that fellow somewhere or other."

"Yes, I *have* met him before!" he muttered again, half an hour later.

And again, as on the last occasion, he was in a vile humour all that evening, and even went so far as to have a bad dream in the night; and yet it never entered his head to imagine that the cause of his bad temper on both occasions had been the accidental meeting with the gentleman in mourning, although on the second evening he had remembered and thought of the chance encounter two or three times.

He had even flared up angrily to think that "such a dirty-looking cad" should presume to linger in his memory so long; he would have felt it humiliating to himself to imagine for a moment that such a wretched creature could possibly be in any way connected with the agitated condition of his feelings.

Two days later the pair had met once more at the landing place of one of the small Neva ferry steamers.

On the third occasion Velchaninoff was ready to swear that the man recognised him, and had pressed through the crowd towards him; had even dared to stretch out his hand and call him by name. As to this last fact he was not quite certain, however. "At all events, who the deuce *is* he?" thought Velchaninoff, "and why can't the idiot come up and speak to me if he really does recognise me; and if he so much wishes to do so?" With these thoughts Velchaninoff had taken a droshky and started off for the Smolney Monastery, where his lawyer lived.

Half an hour later he was engaged in his usual quarrel with that gentleman.

But that same evening he was in a worse humour than ever, and his night was spent in fantastic dreams and imaginings, which were anything but pleasant. "I suppose it's bile!" he concluded, as he paid his matutinal visit to the looking-glass.

This was the third meeting.

Then, for five days there was not a sign of the man; and yet, much to his distaste, Velchaninoff could not, for the life of him, avoid thinking of the man with the crape band.

He caught himself musing over the fellow. "What have I to do with him?" he thought. "What can his business in St. Petersburg be?—he looks busy: and whom is he in mourning for? He clearly recognises me, but I don't know in the least who he is! And why do such people as he is put crape on their hats? it doesn't seem 'the thing' for them, somehow! I believe I shall recognise this fellow if I ever get a good close look at him!"

And there came over him that sensation we all know so well—the same feeling that one has when one can't for the life of one think of the required word; every other word comes up; associations with the right word come up; occasions when one has used the word come up; one wanders round and round the immediate vicinity of the word wanted, but the actual word itself will not appear, though you may break your head to get at it!

"Let's see, now: it was—yes—some while since. It was—where on earth was it? There was a—oh! devil take whatever there was or wasn't there! What does it matter to me?" he broke off angrily of a sudden. "I'm not going to lower myself by thinking of a little cad like that!"

He felt very angry; but when, in the evening, he remembered that he had been so upset, and recollected the cause of his anger, he felt the disagreeable sensation of having been caught by someone doing something wrong.

This fact puzzled and annoyed him.

51

"There must be some reason for my getting so angry at the mere recollection of that man's face," he thought, but he didn't finish thinking it out.

But the next evening he was still more indignant; and this time, he really thought, with good cause. "Such audacity is unparalleled!" he said to himself.

The fact of the matter is, there had been a fourth meeting with the man of the crape hat band. The latter had apparently arisen from the earth and confronted him. But let me explain what had happened.

It so chanced that Velchaninoff had just met, accidentally, that very state-councillor mentioned a few pages back, whom he had been so anxious to see, and on whom he had intended to pounce unexpectedly at his country house. This gentleman evidently avoided Velchaninoff, but at the same time was most necessary to the latter in his lawsuit. Consequently, when Velchaninoff met him, the one was delighted, while the other was very much the reverse. Velchaninoff had immediately button-holed him, and walked down the street with him, talking; doing his very utmost to keep the sly old fox to the subject on which it was so necessary that he should be pumped. And it was just at this most important moment, when Velchaninoff's intellect was all on the *qui vive* to catch up the slightest hints of what he wished to get at, while the foxy old councillor (aware of the fact) was doing his best to reveal nothing, that the former, taking his eyes from his companion's face for one instant, beheld the gentleman of the crape hatband walking along the other side of the road, and looking at him—nay, *watching* him, evidently—and apparently smiling!

"Devil take him!" said Velchaninoff, bursting out into fury at once, while the "old fox" instantly disappeared, "and I should have succeeded in another minute. Curse that dirty little hound! he's simply spying me. I'll—I'll hire somebody to—I'll take my oath he laughed at me! D—n him, I'll thrash him. I wish I had a stick with me. I'll—I'll buy one! I won't leave this matter so. Who the deuce is he? I *will* know! Who is he?"

At last, three days after this fourth encounter, we find Velchaninoff sitting down to dinner at his restaurant, as recorded a page or two back, in a state of mind bordering upon the furious. He could not conceal the state of his feelings from himself, in spite of all his pride. He was obliged to confess at last, that all his anxiety, his irritation, his state of agitation generally, must undoubtedly be connected with, and absolutely attributed to, the appearance of the wretched-looking creature with the crape hatband, in spite of his insignificance.

"I may be a hypochondriac," he reflected, "and I may be inclined to make an elephant out of a gnat; but how does it help me? What use is it to me if I persuade myself to believe that *perhaps* all this is fancy? Why, if every dirty little wretch like that is to have the power of upsetting a man like myself, why—it's—it's simply unbearable!"

Undoubtedly, at this last (fifth) encounter of to-day, the elephant had proved himself a very small gnat indeed. The "crape man" had appeared suddenly, as usual, and had passed by Velchaninoff, but without looking up at him this time; indeed, he had gone by with downcast eyes, and had even seemed anxious to pass unobserved. Velchaninoff had turned rapidly round and shouted as loud as ever he could at him.

"Hey!" he cried. "You! Crape hatband! You want to escape notice this time, do you? Who are you?"

Both the question and the whole idea of calling after the man were absurdly foolish, and Velchaninoff knew it the moment he had said the words. The man had turned round, stopped for an instant, lost his head, smiled—half made up his mind to say something,—had waited half a minute in painful indecision, then twisted suddenly round again, and "bolted" without a word. Velchaninoff gazed after him in amazement. "What if it be *I* that haunt *him*, and not he me, after all?" he thought. However, Velchaninoff ate up his dinner, and then drove off to pounce upon the town councillor at the latter's house, if he could.

The councillor was not in; and he was informed that he would scarcely be at home before three or four in the morning, because he had gone to a "name's-day party."

Velchaninoff felt that this was too bad! In his rage he determined to follow and hunt the fellow up at the party: he actually took a droshky, and started off with that wild idea; but luckily he thought better of it on the way, got out of the vehicle and walked away towards the "Great Theatre," near which he lived. He felt that he must have motion; also he *must* absolutely sleep well this coming night: in order to sleep he must be tired; so he walked all the way home—a fairly long walk, and arrived there about half-past ten, as tired as he could wish.

His lodging, which he had taken last March, and had abused ever since, apologising to himself for living "in such a hole," and at the same time excusing himself for the fact by the reflection that it was only for a while, and that he had dropped quite accidentally into St. Petersburg—thanks to that cursed lawsuit!—his lodging, I say, was by no means so bad as he made it out to be!

The entrance certainly was a little dark, and dirty-looking, being just under the arch of the gateway. But he had two fine large light rooms on the second floor, separated by the entrance hall: one of these rooms overlooked the yard and the other the street. Leading out of the former of these was a smaller room, meant to be used as a bedroom; but Velchaninoff had filled it with a disordered array of books and papers, and preferred to sleep in one of the large rooms, the one overlooking the street, to wit.

His bed was made for him, every day, upon the large divan. The rooms were full of good furniture, and some valuable ornaments and pictures were scattered about, but the whole place was in dreadful disorder; the fact being that at this time Velchaninoff was without a regular servant. His one domestic had gone away to stay with her friends in the country; he thought of taking a man, but decided that it was not worth while for a short time; besides he hated flunkeys, and ended by making arrangements with his dvornik's sister Martha, who was to come up every morning and "do out" his rooms, he leaving the key with her as he went out each day. Martha did absolutely nothing towards tidying the place and robbed him besides, but he didn't care, he liked to be alone in the house. But solitude is all very well within certain limits, and Velchaninoff found that his nerves could not stand all this sort of thing at certain bilious moments; and it so fell out that he began to loathe his room more and more every time he entered it.

However, on this particular evening he hardly gave himself time to undress; he threw himself on his bed, and determined that nothing should make him think of *anything*, and that he would fall asleep at once.

And, strangely enough, his head had hardly touched the pillow before he actually was asleep; and this was the first time for a month past that such a thing had occurred.

52

He awoke at about two, considerably agitated; he had dreamed certain very strange dreams, reminding him of the incoherent wanderings of fever.

The subject seemed to be some crime which he had committed and concealed, but of which he was accused by a continuous flow of people who swarmed into his rooms for the purpose. The crowd which had already collected within was enormous, and yet they continued to pour in in such numbers that the door was never shut for an instant.

But his whole interest seemed to centre in one strange looking individual,—a man who seemed to have once been very closely and intimately connected with him, but who had died long ago and now reappeared for some reason or other.

The most tormenting part of the matter was that Velchaninoff could not recollect who this man was,—he could not remember his name,—though he recollected the fact that he had once dearly loved him. All the rest of the people swarming into the room seemed to be waiting for the final word of this man,—either the condemnation or the justification of Velchaninoff was to be pronounced by him,—and everyone was impatiently waiting to hear him speak.

But he sat motionless at the table, and would not open his lips to say a word of any sort.

The uproar continued, the general annoyance increased, and, suddenly, Velchaninoff himself strode up to the man in a fury, and smote him because he would not speak. Velchaninoff felt the strangest satisfaction in having thus smitten him; his heart seemed to freeze in horror for what he had done, and in acute suffering for the crime involved in his action,—but in that very sensation of freezing at the heart lay the sense of satisfaction which he felt.

Exasperated more and more, he struck the man a second and a third time; and then—in a sort of intoxication of fury and terror, which amounted to actual insanity, and yet bore within it a germ of delightful satisfaction, he ceased to count his blows, and rained them in without ceasing.

He felt he must destroy, annihilate, demolish all this.

Suddenly something strange happened; everyone present had given a dreadful cry and turned expectantly towards the door, while at the same moment there came three terrific peals of the hall-bell, so violent that it appeared someone was anxious to pull the bell-handle out.

Velchaninoff awoke, started up in a second, and made for the door; he was persuaded that the ring at the bell had been no dream or illusion, but that someone had actually rung, and was at that moment standing at the front door.

"It would be *too* unnatural if such a clear and unmistakable ring should turn out to be nothing but an item of a dream!" he thought. But, to his surprise, it proved that such was nevertheless the actual state of the case! He opened the door and went out on to the landing; he looked downstairs and about him, but there was not a soul to be seen. The bell hung motionless. Surprised, but pleased, he returned into his room. He lit a candle, and suddenly remembered that he had left the door closed, but not locked and chained. He had often returned home before this evening and forgotten to lock the door behind him, without attaching any special significance to the fact; his maid had often respectfully protested against such neglect while with him. He now returned to the entrance hall to make the door fast; before doing so he opened it, however, and had one more look about the stairs. He then shut the door and fastened the chain and hook, but did not take the trouble to turn the key in the lock.

Some clock struck half-past two at this moment, so that he had had three hours' sleep—more or less.

His dream had agitated him to such an extent that he felt unwilling to lie down again at once; he decided to walk up and down the room two or three times first, just long enough to smoke a cigar. Having half-dressed himself, he went to the window, drew the heavy curtains aside and pulled up one of the blinds, it was almost full daylight. These light summer nights of St. Petersburg always had a bad effect upon his nerves, and of late they had added to the causes of his sleeplessness, so that a few weeks since he had invested in these thick curtains, which completely shut out the light when drawn close.

Having thus let in the sunshine, quite oblivious of the lighted candle on the table, he commenced to walk up and down the room. Still feeling the burden of his dream upon him, its impression was even now at work upon his mind, he still felt a painfully guilty sensation about him, caused by the fact that he had allowed himself to raise his hand against "that man" and strike him. "But, my dear sir!" he argued with himself, "it was not a man at all! the whole thing was a dream! what's the use of worrying yourself for nothing?"

Velchaninoff now became obstinately convinced that he was a sick man, and that to his sickly state of body was to be attributed all his perturbation of mind. He was an invalid.

It had always been a weak point with Velchaninoff that he hated to think of himself as growing old or infirm; and yet in his moments of anger he loved to exaggerate one or the other in order to worry himself.

"It's old age," he now muttered to himself, as he paced up and down the room. "I'm becoming an old fogey—that's the fact of the matter! I'm losing my memory—see ghosts, and have dreams, and hear bells ring—curse it all! I know these dreams of old, they always herald fever with me. I dare swear that the whole business of this man with the crape hatband has been a dream too! I was perfectly right yesterday, he isn't haunting me the least bit in the world; it is I that am haunting *him*! I've invented a pretty little ghost-story about him and then climb under the table in terror at my own creation! Why do I call him a little cad, too? he may be a most respectable individual for all I know! His face is a disagreeable one, certainly, though there is nothing hideous about it! He dresses just like anyone else. I don't know— there's something about his look—There I go again! What the devil have I got to do with his look? what a fool I am—just as though I could not live without the dirty little wretch—curse him!"

Among other thoughts connected with this haunting crape-man was one which puzzled Velchaninoff immensely; he felt convinced that at some time or other he had known the man, and known him very intimately; and that now the latter, when meeting him, always laughed at him because he was aware of some great secret of his former life, or because he was amused to see Velchaninoff's present humiliating condition of poverty.

Mechanically our hero approached the window in order to get a breath of fresh air—when he was suddenly seized with a violent fit of shuddering;—a feeling came over him that something unusual and unheard-of was happening before his very eyes.

He had not had time to open the window when something he saw caused him to slip behind the corner of the curtain, and hide himself.

The man in the crape hatband was standing on the opposite side of the street.

He was standing with his face turned directly towards Velchaninoff's window, but evidently unaware of the latter's presence there, and was carefully examining the house, and apparently considering some question connected with it.

He seemed to come to a decision after a moment's thought, and raised his finger to his forehead; then he looked quietly about him, and ran swiftly across the road on tiptoe. He reached the gate, and entered it; this gate was often left open on summer nights until two or three in the morning.

"He's coming to me," muttered Velchaninoff, and with equal caution he left the window, and ran to the front door; arrived in the hall, he stood in breathless expectation before the door, and placed his trembling hand carefully upon the hook which he had fastened a few minutes since, and stood listening for the tread of the expected footfall on the stairs. His heart was beating so loud that he was afraid he might miss the sound of the cautious steps approaching.

He could understand nothing of what was happening, but it seemed clear that his dream was about to be realised.

Velchaninoff was naturally brave. He loved risk for its own sake, and very often ran into useless dangers, with no one by to see, to please himself. But this was different, somehow; he was not himself, and yet he was as brave as ever, but with something added. He made out every movement of the stranger from behind his own door.

"Ah!—there he comes!—he's on the steps now!—here he comes!—he's up now!—now he's looking down stairs and all about, and crouching down! Aha! there's his hand on the door-handle—he's trying it!—he thought he would find it unlocked!—then he must know that I *do* leave it unlocked sometimes!—He's trying it again!—I suppose he thinks the hook may slip!—he doesn't care to go away without doing anything!"

So ran Velchaninoff's thoughts, and so indeed followed the man's actions. There was no doubt about it, someone was certainly standing outside and trying the door-handle, carefully and cautiously pulling at the door itself, and, in fact, endeavouring to effect an entrance; equally sure was it that the person so doing must have his own object in trying to sneak into another man's house at dead of night. But Velchaninoff's plan of action was laid, and he awaited the proper moment; he was anxious to seize a good opportunity—slip the hook and chain—open the door wide, suddenly, and stand face to face with this bugbear, and then ask him what the deuce he wanted there.

No sooner devised than executed.

Awaiting the proper moment, Velchaninoff suddenly slipped the hook, pushed the door wide, and almost tumbled over the man with the crape hatband!

CHAPTER III.

The crape-man stood rooted to the spot dumb with astonishment.

Both men stood opposite one another on the landing, and both stared in each other's eyes, silent and motionless.

So passed a few moments, and suddenly, like a flash of lightning, Velchaninoff became aware of the identity of his guest.

At the same moment the latter seemed to guess that Velchaninoff had recognised him. Velchaninoff could see it in his eyes. In one instant the visitor's whole face was all ablaze with its very sweetest of smiles.

"Surely I have the pleasure of speaking to Aleksey Ivanovitch?" he asked, in the most dulcet of voices, comically inappropriate to the circumstances of the case.

"Surely you are Pavel Pavlovitch Trusotsky?" asked Velchaninoff, in return, after a pause, and with an expression of much perplexity.

"I had the pleasure of your acquaintance ten years ago at T——, and, if I may remind you of the fact, we were almost intimate friends."

"Quite so—oh yes! but it is now three o'clock in the morning, and you have been trying my lock for the last ten minutes."

"Three o'clock!" cried the visitor, looking at his watch with an air of melancholy surprise.

"Why, so it is! dear me—three o'clock! forgive me, Aleksey Ivanovitch! I ought to have found it out before thinking of paying you a visit. I will do myself the honour of calling to explain another day, and now I—."

"Oh no;—no, no! If you are to explain at all let's have it at once; this moment!" interrupted Velchaninoff warmly. "Kindly step in here, into the room! You must have meant to come in, you know; you didn't come here at night, like this, simply for the pleasure of trying my lock?"

He felt excited, and at the same time was conscious of a sort of timidity; he could not collect his thoughts. He was ashamed of himself for it. There was no danger, no mystery about the business, nothing but the silly figure of Pavel Pavlovitch.

And yet he could not feel satisfied that there was nothing particular in it; he felt afraid of something to come, he knew not what or when.

However, he made the man enter, seated him in a chair, and himself sat down on the side of his bed, a yard or so off, and rested his elbows on his knees while he quietly waited for the other to begin. He felt irritated; he stared at his visitor and let his thoughts run. Strangely enough, the other never opened his mouth; he seemed to be entirely oblivious of the fact that it was his duty to speak. Nay, he was even looking enquiringly at Velchaninoff as though quite expecting that the latter would speak to *him*!

Perhaps he felt a little uncomfortable at first, somewhat as a mouse must feel when he finds himself unexpectedly in the trap.

Velchaninoff very soon lost his patience.

"Well?" he cried, "you are not a fantasy or a dream or anything of that kind, are you? You aren't a corpse, are you? Come, my friend, this is not a game or play. I want your explanation, please!"

The visitor fidgeted about a little, smiled, and began to speak cautiously.

"So far as I can see," he said, "the time of night of my visit is what surprises you, and that I should have come as I did; in fact, when I remember the past, and our intimacy, and all that, I am astonished myself; but the fact is, I did not mean to come in at all, and if I did so it was purely an accident."

"An accident! Why, I saw you creeping across the road on tip-toes!"

"You saw me? Indeed! Come, then you know as much or more about the matter than I do; but I see I am annoying you. This is how it was: I've been in town three weeks or so on business. I am Pavel Pavlovitch Trusotsky, you recognized me yourself, my business in town is to effect an exchange of departments. I am trying for a situation in another place—one with a large increase of salary; but all this is beside the point; the fact of the matter is, I believe I have been delaying my business on purpose. I believe if everything were settled at this moment I should still be dawdling in this St. Petersburg of yours in my present condition of mind. I go wandering about as though I had lost all interest in things, and were rather glad of the fact, in my present condition of mind."

"What condition of mind?" asked Velchaninoff, frowning.

The visitor raised his eyes to Velchaninoff's, lifted his hat from the ground beside him, and with great dignity pointed out the black crape band.

"There, sir, in *that* condition of mind!" he observed.

Velchaninoff stared stupidly at the crape, and thence at the man's face. Suddenly his face flushed up in a hot blush for a moment, and he was violently agitated.

"Not Natalia Vasilievna, surely?"

"Yes, Natalia Vasilievna! Last March! Consumption, sir, and almost suddenly—all over in two or three months—and here am I left as you see me!"

So saying, Pavel Pavlovitch, with much show of feeling, bent his bald head down and kept it bent for some ten seconds, while he held out his two hands, in one of which was the hat with the band, in explanatory emotion.

This gesture, and the man's whole air, seemed to brighten Velchaninoff up; he smiled sarcastically for one instant, not more at present, for the news of this lady's death (he had known her so long ago, and had forgotten her many a year since) had made a quite unexpected impression upon his mind.

"Is it possible!" he muttered, using the first words that came to his lips, "and pray why did you not come here and tell me at once?"

"Thanks for your kind interest, I see and value it, in spite of——"

"In spite of what?"

"In spite of so many years of separation you at once sympathised with my sorrow—and in fact with myself, and so fully too—that I feel naturally grateful. That's all I had to tell you, sir! Don't suppose I doubt my friends, you know; why, even here, in this place, I could put my finger on several very sincere friends indeed (for instance, Stepan Michailovitch Bagantoff); but remember, my dear Aleksey Ivanovitch—nine years have passed since we were acquaintances—or friends, if you'll allow me to say so—and meanwhile you have never been to see us, never written."

The guest sang all this out as though he were reading it from music, but kept his eyes fixed on the ground the while, although, of course, he saw what was going on above his eyelashes exceedingly well all the same.

Velchaninoff had found his head by this time.

With a strange sort of fascinated attention, which strengthened itself every moment, he continued to gaze at and listen to Pavel Pavlovitch, and of a sudden, when the latter stopped speaking, a flood of curious ideas swept unexpectedly through his brain.

"But look here," he cried, "how is it that I never recognized you all this while?—we've met five times, at least, in the streets!"

"Quite so—I am perfectly aware of the circumstance. You chanced to meet me two or three times, and——"

"No, no! *you* met *me*, you know—not I you!" Velchaninoff suddenly burst into a roar of laughter, and rose from his seat. Pavel Pavlovitch paused a moment, looked keenly at Velchaninoff, and then continued:

"As to your not recognizing me, in the first place you might easily have forgotten me by now; and besides, I have had small-pox since last we met, and I daresay my face is a good deal marked."

"Smallpox? why, how did you manage that?—he has had it, though, by Jove!" cried Velchaninoff. "What a funny fellow you are—however, go on, don't stop."

Velchaninoff's spirits were rising higher and higher; he was beginning to feel wonderfully light-hearted. That feeling of agitation which had lately so disturbed him had given place to quite a different sentiment. He now began to stride up and down the room, very quickly.

"I was going to say," resumed Pavel Pavlovitch, "that though I have met you several times, and though I quite intended to come and look you up, when I was arranging my visit to Petersburg, still, I was in that condition of mind, you know, and my wits have so suffered since last March, that——"

"Wits since last March,—yes, go on: wait a minute—do you smoke?"

"Oh—you know, Natalia Vasilievna, never—"

"Quite so; but since March—eh?"

"Well—I might, a cigarette or so."

"Here you are, then! Light up and go on,—go on! you interest me wonderfully."

Velchaninoff lit a cigar and sat down on his bed again. Pavel Pavlovitch paused a moment.

"But what a state of agitation you seem to be in yourself!" said he, "are you quite well?"

"Oh, curse my health!" cried Velchaninoff,—"you go on!"

The visitor observed his host's agitation with satisfaction; he went on with his share of the talking with more confidence.

"What am I to go on about?" he asked. "Imagine me, Alexey Ivanovitch—a broken man,—not simply broken, but gone at the root, as it were; a man forced to change his whole manner of living, after twenty years of married life, wandering about the dusty roads without an object,—mind lost—almost oblivious of his own self,—and yet, as it were, taking some sort of intoxicated delight in his loneliness! Isn't it natural that if I should, at such a moment of self-forgetfulness come across a friend—even a *dear* friend, I might prefer to avoid him for that moment? and isn't it equally natural that at another moment I should long to see and speak with some one who has been an eye-witness of, or a partaker, so to speak, in my never-to-be-recalled past? and to rush—not only in the day, but at night, if it so happens,—to rush to the embrace of such a man?—yes, even if one has to wake him up at three in the morning to do it! I was wrong in my time, not in my estimate of my friend, though, for at this moment I feel the full rapture of success; my rash action has been successful: I have found sympathy! As for the time of night, I confess I thought it was not twelve yet! You see, one sups of grief, and it intoxicates one,—at least, not grief, exactly, it's more the condition of mind—the new state of things that affects me."

"Dear me, how oddly you express yourself!" said Velchaninoff, rising from his seat once more, and becoming quite serious again.

"Oddly, do I? Perhaps."

"Look here: are you joking?"

"Joking!" cried Pavel Pavlovitch, in shocked surprise; "*joking*—at the very moment when I am telling you of——"

"Oh—be quiet about that! for goodness sake."

Velchaninoff started off on his journey up and down the room again.

So matters stood for five minutes or so: the visitor seemed inclined to rise from his chair, but Velchaninoff bade him sit still, and Pavel Pavlovitch obediently flopped into his seat again.

"How changed you are!" said the host at last, stopping in front of the other chair, as though suddenly struck with the idea; "fearfully changed!"

"Wonderful! you're quite another man!"

"That's hardly surprising! *nine* years, sir!"

"No, no, no! years have nothing to do with it! it's not in appearance you are so changed: it's something else!"

"Well, sir, the nine years might account for anything."

"Perhaps it's only since March, eh?"

"Ha-ha! you are playful, sir," said Pavel Pavlovitch, laughing slyly. "But, if I may ask it, wherein am I so changed?"

"Oh—why, you used to be such a staid, sober, correct Pavel Pavlovitch; such a wise Pavel Pavlovitch; and now you're a good-for-nothing sort of Pavel Pavlovitch."

Velchaninoff was in that state of irritation when the steadiest, gravest people will sometimes say rather more than they mean.

"Good-for-nothing, am I? and *wise* no longer, I suppose, eh?" chuckled Pavel Pavlovitch, with disagreeable satisfaction.

"Wise, indeed! My dear sir, I'm afraid you are not sober," replied Velchaninoff; and added to himself, "I am pretty fairly insolent myself, but I can't compare with this little cad! And what on earth is the fellow driving at?"

"Oh, my dear, good, my best of Alexey Ivanovitches," said the visitor suddenly, most excitedly, and twisting about on his chair, "and why *should* I be sober? We are not moving in the brilliant walks of society—you and I—just now. We are but two dear old friends come together in the full sincerity of perfect love, to recall and talk over that sweet mutual tie of which the dear departed formed so treasured a link in our friendship."

So saying, the sensitive gentleman became so carried away by his feelings that he bent his head down once more, to hide his emotion, and buried his face in his hat.

Velchaninoff looked on with an uncomfortable feeling of disgust.

"I can't help thinking the man is simply silly," he thought; "and yet—no, no—his face is so red he must be drunk. But drunk or not drunk, what does the little wretch want with me? That's the puzzle."

"Do you remember—oh, *don't* you remember—our delightful little evenings—dancing sometimes, or sometimes literary—at Simeon Simeonovitch's?" continued the visitor, gradually removing his hat from before his face, and apparently growing more and more enthusiastic over the memories of the past, "and our little readings—you and she and myself—and our first meeting, when you came in to ask for information about something connected with your business in the town, and commenced shouting angrily at me; don't you remember—when suddenly in came Natalia Vasilievna, and within ten minutes you were our dear friend, and so remained for exactly a year? Just like Turgenieff's story 'The Provincialka!'"

Velchaninoff had continued his walk up and down the room during this *tirade*, with his eyes on the ground, listening impatiently and with disgust—but listening *hard*, all the same.

"It never struck me to think of 'The Provincialka' in connection with the matter," he interrupted. "And look here, why do you talk in that sneaking, whining sort of voice? You never used to do that. Your whole manner is unlike yourself."

"Quite so, quite so. I used to be more silent, I know. I used to love to listen while others talked. You remember how well the dear departed talked—the wit and grace of her conversation. As to The Provincialka, I remember she and I used often to compare your friendship for us to certain episodes in that piece, and especially to the doings of one Stupendief. It really was remarkably like that character and his doings."

"What Stupendief do you mean, confound it all?" cried Velchaninoff, stamping his foot with rage. The name seemed to have evoked certain most irritating thoughts in his mind.

"Why, Stupendief, don't you know, the 'husband' in 'Provincialka,' " whined Pavel Pavlovitch, in the very sweetest of tones; "but that belongs to another set of fond memories—after you departed, in fact, when Mr. Bagantoff had honoured us with his friendship, just as you had done before him, only that his lasted five whole years."

"Bagantoff? What Bagantoff? Do you mean that same Bagantoff who was serving down in your town? Why, he also——"

"Yes, yes! quite so. He also, he also!" cried the enthusiastic Pavel Pavlovitch, seizing upon Velchaninoff's accidental slip. "Of course! So that there you are—there's the whole company. Bagantoff played the 'count,' the dear departed was the 'Provincialka,' and I was the 'husband,' only that the part was taken away from me, for incapacity, I suppose!"

"Yes; fancy *you* a Stupendief. You're a—you're first a Pavel Pavlovitch Trusotsky!" said Velchaninoff, contemptuously, and very unceremoniously. "But look here! Bagantoff is in town; I know he is, for I have seen him. Why don't you go to see *him* as well as myself?"

"My dear sir, I've been there every day for the last three weeks. He won't receive me; he's ill, and can't receive! And, do you know, I have found out that he really is very ill! Fancy my feelings—a five-year's friend! Oh, my dear Alexey Ivanovitch! you don't know what my feelings are in my present condition of mind. I assure you, at one moment I long for the earth to open and swallow me up, and the next I feel that I *must* find one of those old friends, eyewitnesses of the past, as it were, if only to weep on his bosom, only to weep, sir—give you my word."

"Well, that's about enough for to-night; don't you think so?" said Velchaninoff, cuttingly.

"Oh, too—too much!" cried the other, rising. "It must be four o'clock; and here am I agitating your feelings in the most selfish way."

"Now, look here; I shall call upon you myself, and I hope that you will then——but, tell me honestly, are you drunk to-night?"

"Drunk! not the least in the world!"

"Did you drink nothing before you came here, or earlier?"

"Do you know, my dear Alexey Ivanovitch, you are quite in a high fever!"

"Good-night. I shall call to-morrow."

"And I have noticed it all the evening, really quite delirious!" continued Pavel Pavlovitch, licking his lips, as it were, with satisfaction as he pursued this theme. "I am really quite ashamed that I should have allowed myself to be so awkward as to agitate you. Well, well; I'm going! Now you must lie down at once and go to sleep."

"You haven't told me where you live," shouted Velchaninoff after him as he left the room.

"Oh, didn't I? Pokrofsky Hotel."

Pavel Pavlovitch was out on the stairs now.

"Stop!" cried Velchaninoff, once more. "You are not 'running away,' are you?"

"How do you mean, 'running away?' " asked Pavel Pavlovitch, turning round at the third step, and grinning back at him, with his eyes staring very wide open.

Instead of replying, Velchaninoff banged the door fiercely, locked and bolted it, and went fuming back into his room. Arrived there, he spat on the ground, as though to get rid of the taste of something loathsome.

He then stood motionless for at least five minutes, in the centre of the room; after which he threw himself upon his bed, and fell asleep in an instant.

The forgotten candle burned itself out in its socket.

CHAPTER IV.

Velchaninoff slept soundly until half-past nine, at which hour he started up, sat down on the side of his bed, and began to think.

His thoughts quickly fixed themselves upon the death of "that woman."

The agitating impression wrought upon his mind by yesterday's news as to her death had left a painful feeling of mental perturbation.

This morning the whole of the events of nine years back stood out before his mind's eye with extraordinary distinctness.

He had loved this woman, Natalia Vasilievna—Trusotsky's wife,—he had loved her, and had acted the part of her lover during the time which he had spent in their provincial town (while engaged in business connected with a legacy); he had lived there a whole year, though his business did not require by any means so long a visit; in fact, the tie above mentioned had detained him in the place.

He had been so completely under the influence of this passion, that Natalia Vasilievna had held him in a species of slavery. He would have obeyed the slightest whim or the wildest caprice of the woman, at that time. He had never, before or since, experienced anything approaching to the infatuation she had caused.

When the time came for departing, Velchaninoff had been in a state of such absolute despair, though the parting was to have been but a short one, that he had begged Natalia Vasilievna to leave all and fly across the frontier with him; and it was only by laughing him out of the idea (though she had at first encouraged it herself, probably for a joke), and by unmercifully chaffing him, that the lady eventually persuaded Velchaninoff to depart alone.

However, he had not been a couple of months in St. Petersburg before he found himself asking himself that question which he had never to this day been able to answer satisfactorily, namely, "*Did* he love this woman at all, or was it nothing but the infatuation of the moment?" He did not ask this question because he was conscious of any new passion taking root in his heart; on the contrary, during those first two months in town he had been in that condition of mind that he had not so much as looked at a woman, though he had met hundreds, and had returned to his old society ways at once. And yet he knew perfectly well that if he were to return to T—— he would instantly fall into the meshes of his passion for Natalia Vasilievna once more, in spite of the question which he could not answer as to the reality of his love for her.

Five years later he was as convinced of this fact as ever, although the very thought of it was detestable to him, and although he did not remember the name of Natalia Vasilievna but with loathing.

He was ashamed of that episode at T——. He could not understand how he (Velchaninoff) could ever have allowed himself to become the victim of such a stupid passion. He blushed whenever he thought of the shameful business—blushed, and even wept for shame.

He managed to forget his remorse after a few more years—he felt sure that he had "lived it down;" and yet now, after nine years, here was the whole thing resuscitated by the news of Natalia's death.

At all events, however, now, as he sat on his bed with agitating thoughts swarming through his brain, he could not but feel that the fact of her being dead was a consolation, amidst all the painful reflections which the mention of her name had called up.

"Surely I am a little sorry for her?" he asked himself.

Well, he certainly did not feel that sensation of hatred for her now; he could think of her and judge her now without passion of any kind, and therefore more justly.

He had long since been of opinion that in all probability there had been nothing more in Natalia Vasilievna than is to be found in every lady of good provincial society, and that he himself had created the whole "fantasy" of his worship and her worshipfulness; but though he had formed this opinion, he always doubted its correctness, and he still felt that doubt now. Facts existed to contradict the theory. For instance, this Bagantoff had lived for several years at T——, and had been no less a victim to passion for this woman, and had been as helpless as Velchaninoff himself under her witchery. Bagantoff, though a young idiot (as Velchaninoff expressed it), was nevertheless a scion of the very highest society in St. Petersburg. His career was in St. Petersburg, and it was significant that such a man should have wasted five important years of his life at T—— simply out of love for this woman. It was said that he had only returned to Petersburg even then because the lady had had enough of him; so that, all things considered, there must have been something which rendered Natalia Vasilievna preeminently attractive among women.

Yet the woman was not rich; she was not even pretty (if not absolutely *plain*!) Velchaninoff had known her when she was twenty-eight years old. Her face was capable of taking a pleasing expression, but her eyes were not good—they were too hard. She was a thin, bony woman to look at. Her mind was intelligent, but narrow and one-sided. She had tact and taste, especially as to dress. Her character was firm and overbearing. She was never wrong (in her own opinion) or unjust. The unfaithfulness towards her husband never caused her the slightest remorse; she hated corruption, and yet she was herself corrupt; and she believed in herself absolutely. Nothing could ever have persuaded her that she herself was actually depraved; Velchaninoff believed that she really did not know that her own corruption was corrupt. He considered her to be "one of those women who only exist to be unfaithful wives." Such women never remain unmarried,—it is the law of their nature to marry,—their husband is their first lover, and he is always to blame for anything that may happen afterwards; the unfaithful wife herself being invariably *absolutely* in the right, and of course perfectly innocent.

So thought Velchaninoff; and he was convinced that such a type of woman actually existed; but he was no less convinced that there also existed a corresponding type of men, born to be the husbands of such women. In his opinion the mission of such men was to be, so to speak, "permanent husbands,"—that is, to be husbands all their lives, and nothing else.

Velchaninoff had not the smallest doubt as to the existence of these two types, and Pavel Pavlovitch Trusotsky was, in his opinion, an excellent representative of the male type. Of course, the Pavel Pavlovitch of last night was by no means the same Pavel Pavlovitch as he had known at T——. He had found an extraordinary change in the man; and yet, on reflection, he was bound to admit that the change was but natural, for that he could only have remained what he was so long as his wife lived; and that now he was but a part of a whole, allowed to wander at will—that is, an imperfect being, a surprising, an incomprehensible sort of a *thing*, without proper balance.

As for the Pavel Pavlovitch of T——, this is what Velchaninoff remembered of him:

Pavel Pavlovitch had been a husband, of course,—a formality,—and that was all. If, for instance, he was a clerk of department besides, he was so merely in his capacity of, and as a part of his responsibility as—a husband. He worked for his wife, and for her social position. He had been thirty-five years old at that time, and was possessed of some considerable property. He had not shown any special talent, nor, on the other hand, any marked incapacity in his professional employment; his position had been decidedly a good one.

Natalia Vasilievna had been respected and looked up to by all; not that she valued their respect in the least,—she considered it merely as her due. She was a good hostess, and had schooled Pavel Pavlovitch into polite manners, so that he was able to receive and entertain the very best society passably well.

He might be a clever man, for all Velchaninoff knew, but as Natalia Vasilievna did not like her husband to talk much, there was little opportunity of judging. He may have had many good qualities, as well as bad; but the good ones were, so to speak, kept put away in their cases, and the bad ones were stifled and not allowed to appear. Velchaninoff remembered, for instance, that Pavel Pavlovitch had once or twice shown a disposition to laugh at those about him, but this unworthy proclivity had been very promptly subdued. He had been fond of telling stories, but this was not allowed either; or, if permitted at all, the anecdote was to be of the shortest and most uninteresting description.

Pavel Pavlovitch had a circle of private friends outside the house, with whom he was fain, at times, to taste the flowing bowl; but this vicious tendency was radically stamped out as soon as possible.

And yet, with all this, Natalia Vasilievna appeared, to the uninitiated, to be the most obedient of wives, and doubtless considered herself so. Pavel Pavlovitch may have been desperately in love with her,—no one could say as to this.

Velchaninoff had frequently asked himself during his life at T——, whether Pavel Pavlovitch ever suspected his wife of having formed the tie with himself, of which mention has been made. Velchaninoff had several times questioned Natalia Vasilievna on this point, seriously enough; but had invariably been told, with some show of annoyance, that her husband neither did know, nor ever could know; and that "all there might be to know was not his business!"

Another trait in her character was that she never laughed at Pavel Pavlovitch, and never found him funny in any sense; and that she would have been down on any person who dared to be rude to him, at once!

Pavel Pavlovitch's reference to the pleasant little readings enjoyed by the trio nine years ago was accurate; they used to read Dickens' novels together. Velchaninoff or Trusotsky reading aloud, while Natalia Vasilievna worked. The life at T—— had ended suddenly, and so far as Velchaninoff was concerned, in a way which drove him almost to the verge of madness. The fact is, he was simply turned out—although it was all managed in such a way that he never observed that he was being thrown over like an old worn-out shoe.

A young artillery officer had appeared in the town a month or so before Velchaninoff's departure and had made acquaintance with the Trusotsky's. The trio became a quartet. Before long Velchaninoff was informed that for many reasons a separation was absolutely necessary; Natalia Vasilievna adduced a hundred excellent reasons why this had become unavoidable—and especially one which quite settled the matter. After his stormy attempt to persuade Natalia Vasilievna to fly with him to Paris—or anywhere,—Velchaninoff had ended by going to St. Petersburg alone—for two or three months at the *very most*, as he said,—otherwise he would refuse to go at all, in spite of every reason and argument Natalia might adduce.

Exactly two months later Velchaninoff had received a letter from Natalia Vasilievna, begging him to come no more to T——, because that she already loved another. As to the principal reason which she had brought forward in favour of his immediate departure, she now informed him that she had made a mistake. Velchaninoff remembered the young artilleryman, and understood,—and so the matter had ended, once and for all. A year or two after this Bagantoff appeared at T——, and an intimacy between Natalia Vasilievna and the former had sprung up which lasted for five years. This long period of constancy, Velchaninoff attributed to advancing age on the part of Natalia. He sat on the side of his bed for nearly an hour and thought. At last he roused himself, rang for Mavra and his coffee, drank it off quickly—dressed—and punctually at eleven was on his way to the Pokrofsky Hotel: he felt rather ashamed of his behaviour to Pavel Pavlovitch last night. Velchaninoff put down all that phantasmagoria of the trying of the lock and so on to Pavel Pavlovitch's drunken condition and to other reasons,—but he did not know why he was now on his way to make fresh relations with the husband of that woman, since their acquaintanceship and intercourse had come to so natural and simple a termination; yet something seemed to draw him thither—some strong current of impulse,—and he went.

CHAPTER V.

Pavel Pavlovitch was not thinking of "running away," and goodness knows why Velchaninoff should have asked him such a question last night—he did not know himself why he had said it!

He was directed to the Petrofsky Hotel, and found the building at once. At the hotel he was told that Pavel Pavlovitch had now engaged a furnished lodging in the back part of the same house.

Mounting the dirty and narrow stairs indicated, as far as the third storey, he suddenly became aware of someone crying. It sounded like the weeping of a child of some seven or eight years of age; it was a bitter, but a more or less suppressed sort of crying, and with it came the sound of a grown man's voice, apparently trying to quiet the child—anxious that its sobbing and crying should not be heard,—and yet only succeeding in making it cry the louder.

The man's voice did not seem in any way sympathetic with the child's grief; and the latter appeared to be begging for forgiveness.

Making his way into a narrow dark passage with two doors on each side of it, Velchaninoff met a stout-looking, elderly woman, in very careless morning attire, and inquired for Pavel Pavlovitch.

She tapped the door with her fingers in response to his inquiry—the same door, apparently, whence issued the noises just mentioned. Her fat face seemed to flush with indignation as she did so.

"He appears to be amusing himself in there!" she said, and proceeded downstairs.

Velchaninoff was about to knock, but thought better of it and opened the door without ceremony.

In the very middle of a room furnished with plain, but abundant furniture, stood Pavel Pavlovitch in his shirt-sleeves, very red in the face, trying to persuade a little girl to do something or other, and using cries and gestures, and what looked to Velchaninoff very like kicks, in order to effect his purpose. The child appeared to be some seven or eight years of age, and was poorly dressed in a short black stuff frock. She seemed to be in a most hysterical condition, crying and stretching out her arms to Pavel Pavlovitch, as though begging and entreating him to allow her to do whatever it might be she desired.

On Velchaninoff's appearance the scene changed in an instant. No sooner did her eyes fall on the visitor than the child made for the door of the next room, with a cry of alarm; while Pavel Pavlovitch—thrown out for one little instant—immediately relaxed into smiles of great sweetness—exactly as he had done last night, when Velchaninoff suddenly opened his front door and caught him standing outside.

"Alexey Ivanovitch!" he cried in real surprise; "who ever would have thought it! Sit down—sit down—take the sofa—or this chair,—sit down, my dear sir! I'll just put on——" and he rushed for his coat and threw it on, leaving his waistcoat behind.

"Don't stand on ceremony with me," said Velchaninoff sitting down; "stay as you are!"

"No, sir, no! excuse me—I insist upon standing on ceremony. There, now! I'm a little more respectable! Dear me, now, who ever would have thought of seeing *you* here!—not I, for one!"

Pavel Pavlovitch sat down on the edge of a chair, which he turned so as to face Velchaninoff.

"And pray *why* shouldn't you have expected me? I told you last night that I was coming this morning!"

59

"I thought you wouldn't come, sir—I did indeed; in fact, when I thought over yesterday's visit, I despaired of ever seeing you again: I did indeed, sir!"

Velchaninoff glanced round the room meanwhile. The place was very untidy; the bed was unmade; the clothes thrown about the floor; on the table were two coffee tumblers with the dregs of coffee still in them, and a bottle of champagne half finished, and with a tumbler standing alongside it. He glanced at the next room, but all was quiet there; the little girl had hidden herself, and was as still as a mouse.

"You don't mean to say you drink that stuff at this time of day?" he asked, indicating the champagne bottle.

"It's only a remnant," explained Pavel Pavlovitch, a little confused.

"My word! You *are* a changed man!"

"Bad habits, sir; and all of a sudden. All dating from that time, sir. Give you my word, I couldn't resist it. But I'm all right now—I'm not drunk—I shan't talk twaddle as I did last night; don't be afraid sir, it's all right! From that very day, sir; give you my word it is! And if anyone had told me half a year ago that I should become like this,—if they had shown me my face in a glass then as I should be *now*, I should have given them the lie, sir; I should indeed!"

"Hem! Then you *were* drunk last night?"

"Yes—I was!" admitted Pavel Pavlovitch, a little guiltily—"not exactly *drunk*, a little *beyond* drunk!—I tell you this by way of explanation, because I'm always worse *after* being drunk! If I'm only a little drunk, still the violence and unreasonableness of intoxication come out afterwards, and stay out too; and then I feel my grief the more keenly. I daresay my grief is responsible for my drinking. I am capable of making an awful fool of myself and offending people when I'm drunk. I daresay I seemed strange enough to you last night?"

"Don't you remember what you said and did?"

"Assuredly I do—I remember everything!"

"Listen to me, Pavel Pavlovitch: I have thought it over and have come to very much the same conclusion as you did yourself," began Velchaninoff gently; "besides—I believe I was a little too irritable towards you last night—too impatient,—I admit it gladly; the fact is—I am not very well sometimes, and your sudden arrival, you know, in the middle of the night——"

"In the middle of the night: you are quite right—it was!" said Pavel Pavlovitch, wagging his head assentingly; "how in the world could I have brought myself to do such a thing? I shouldn't have come in, though, if you hadn't opened the door. I should have gone as I came. I called on you about a week ago, and did not find you at home, and I daresay I should never have called again; for I am rather proud—Alexey Ivanovitch—in spite of my present state. Whenever I have met you in the streets I have always said to myself, 'What if he doesn't know me and rejects me—nine years is no joke!' and I did not dare try you for fear of being snubbed. Yesterday, thanks to that sort of thing, you know," (he pointed to the bottle), "I didn't know what time it was, and—it's lucky you are the kind of man you are, Alexey Ivanovitch, or I should despair of preserving your acquaintance, after yesterday! You remember old times, Alexey Ivanovitch!"

Velchaninoff listened keenly to all this. The man seemed to be talking seriously enough, and even with some dignity; and yet he had not believed a single word that Pavel Pavlovitch had uttered from the very first moment that he entered the room.

"Tell me, Pavel Pavlovitch," said Velchaninoff at last, "—I see you are not quite alone here,—whose little girl is that I saw when I came in?"

Pavel Pavlovitch looked surprised and raised his eyebrow; but he gazed back at Velchaninoff with candour and apparent amiability:

"Whose little girl? Why that's our Liza!" he said, smiling affably.

"What Liza?" asked Velchaninoff,—and something seemed to cause him to shudder inwardly.

The sensation was dreadfully sudden. Just now, on entering the room and seeing Liza, he had felt surprised more or less,—but had not been conscious of the slightest feeling of presentiment,—indeed he had had no special thought about the matter, at the moment.

"Why—*our* Liza!—our daughter Liza!" repeated Pavel Pavlovitch, smiling.

"Your daughter? Do you mean to say that you and Natalia Vasilievna had children?" asked Velchaninoff timidly, and in a very low tone of voice indeed!

"Of course—but—what a fool I am—how in the world should *you* know! Providence sent us the gift after you had gone!"

Pavel Pavlovitch jumped off his chair in apparently pleasurable excitement.

"I heard nothing of it!" said Velchaninoff, looking very pale.

"How should you? how should you?" repeated Pavel Pavlovitch with ineffable sweetness. "We had quite lost hope of any children—as you may remember,—when suddenly Heaven sent us this little one. And, oh! my feelings—Heaven alone knows what I felt! Just a year after you went, I think—no, wait a bit—not a year by a long way!—Let's see, you left us in October, or November, didn't you?"

"I left T—— on the twelfth of September, I remember well."

"Hum! September was it? Dear me! Well, then, let's see—September, October, November, December, January, February, March, April—to the 8th of May—that was Liza's birthday—eight months all but a bit; and if you could only have seen the dear departed, how rejoiced——"

"Show her to me—call her in!" the words seemed to tear themselves from Velchaninoff, whether he liked it or no.

"Certainly—this moment!" cried Pavel Pavlovitch, forgetting that he had not finished his previous sentence, or ignoring the fact; and he hastily left the room, and entered the small chamber adjoining.

Three or four minutes passed by, while Velchaninoff heard the rapid interchange of whispers going on, and an occasional rather louder sound of Liza's voice, apparently entreating her father to leave her alone—so Velchaninoff concluded.

At last the two came out.

"There you are—she's dreadfully shy and proud," said Pavel Pavlovitch; "just like her mother."

Liza entered the room without tears, but with eyes downcast, her father leading her by the hand. She was a tall, slight, and very pretty little girl. She raised her large blue eyes to the visitor's face with curiosity; but only glanced surlily at him, and dropped them again. There was that in her expression that one always sees in children when they look on some new guest for the first time—retiring to a corner, and looking out at him thence seriously and mistrustingly; only that there was a something in her manner beyond the usual childish mistrust—so, at least thought Velchaninoff.

Her father brought her straight up to the visitor.

"There—this gentleman knew mother very well. He was our friend; you mustn't be shy,—give him your hand!"

The child bowed slightly, and timidly stretched out her hand.

"Natalia Vasilievna never would teach her to curtsey; she liked her to bow, English fashion, and give her hand," explained Pavel Pavlovitch, gazing intently at Velchaninoff.

Velchaninoff knew perfectly well that the other was keenly examining him at this moment, but he made no attempt to conceal his agitation: he sat motionless on his chair and held the child's hand in his, gazing into her face the while.

But Liza was apparently much preoccupied, and did not take her eyes off her father's face; she listened timidly to every word he said.

Velchaninoff recognised her large blue eyes at once; but what specially struck him was the refined pallor of her face, and the colour of her hair; these traits were altogether too significant, in his eyes! Her features, on the other hand, and the set of her lips, reminded him keenly of Natalia Vasilievna. Meanwhile Pavel Pavlovitch was in the middle of some apparently most interesting tale—one of great sentiment seemingly,—but Velchaninoff did not hear a word of it until the last few words struck upon his ear:

"... So that you can't imagine what our joy was when Providence sent us this gift, Alexey Ivanovitch! She was everything to me, for I felt that if it should be the will of Heaven to deprive me of my other joy, I should still have Liza left to me; that's what I felt, sir, I did indeed!"

"And Natalia Vasilievna?" asked Velchaninoff.

"Oh, Natalia Vasilievna—" began Pavel Pavlovitch, smiling with one side of his mouth; "she never used to like to say much—as you know yourself; but she told me on her deathbed—deathbed! you know, sir—to the very day of her death she used to get so angry and say that they were trying to cure her with a lot of nasty medicines when she had nothing the matter but a simple little feverish attack; and that when Koch arrived (you remember our old doctor Koch?) he would make her all right in a fortnight. Why, five hours before she died she was talking of fixing that day three weeks for a visit to her Aunt, Liza's godmother, at her country place!" Velchaninoff here started from his seat, but still held the child's hand. He could not help thinking that there was something reproachful in the girl's persistent stare in her father's face.

"Is she ill?" he asked hurriedly, and his voice had a strange tone in it.

"No! I don't think so" said Pavel Pavlovitch; "but, you see our way of living here, and all that: she's a strange child and very nervous, besides! After her mother's death she was quite ill and hysterical for a fortnight. Just before you came in she was crying like anything; and do you know what about, sir? Do you hear me, Liza?—You listen!—Simply because I was going out, and wished to leave her behind, and because she said I didn't love her so well as I used to in her mother's time. That's what she pitches into me for! Fancy a child like this getting hold of such an idea!—a child who ought to be playing at dolls, instead of developing ideas of that sort! The thing is, she has no one to play with here."

"Then—then—are you two quite alone here?"

"Quite! a servant comes in once a day, that's all!"

"And when you go out, do you leave her quite alone?"

"Of course! What else am I to do? Yesterday I locked her in that room, and that's what all the tears were about this morning. What could I do? the day before yesterday she went down into the yard all by herself, and a boy took a shot at her head with a stone! Not only that, but she must needs go and cling on to everybody she met, and ask where I had gone to! That's not so very pleasant, you see! But I oughtn't to complain when I say I am going out for an hour and then stay out till four in the morning, as I did last night! The landlady came and let her out: she had the door broken open! Nice for my feelings, eh! It's all the result of the eclipse that came over my life; nothing but that, sir!"

"Papa!" said the child, timidly and anxiously.

"Now, then! none of that again! What did I tell you yesterday?"

"I won't; I won't!" cried the child hurriedly, clasping her hands before her entreatingly.

"Come! things can't be allowed to go on in this way!" said Velchaninoff impatiently, and with authority. "In the first place, you are a man of property; how can you possibly live in a hole like this, and in such disorder?"

"This place! Oh, but we shall probably have left this place within a week; and I've spent a lot of money here, as it is, though I may be 'a man of property;' and——"

"Very well, that'll do," interrupted Velchaninoff with growing impatience, "now, I'll make you a proposition: you have just said that you intend to stay another week—perhaps two. I have a house here—or rather I know a family where I am as much at home as at my own fireside, and have been so for twenty years. The family I mean is the Pogoryeltseffs—Alexander Pavlovitch Pogoryeltseff is a state councillor (he may be of use to you in your business!) They are now living in the country—they have a beautiful country villa; Claudia Petrovna, the lady of the house, is like a sister—like a mother to me; they have eight children. Let me take Liza down to them without loss of time! they'll receive her with joy, and they'll treat her like their own little daughter—they will, indeed!"

Velchaninoff was in a great hurry, and much excited, and he did not conceal his feelings.

"I'm afraid it's impossible!" said Pavel Pavlovitch with a grimace, looking straight into his visitor's eyes, very cunningly, as it seemed to Velchaninoff.

"Why! why, impossible?"

"Oh, why! to let the child go—so suddenly, you know, of course with such a sincere well-wisher as yourself—it's not that!—but a strange house—and such swells, too!—I don't know whether they would receive her!"

"But I tell you I'm like a son of the house!" cried Velchaninoff, almost angrily. "Claudia Petrovna will be delighted to take her, at one word from me! She'd receive her as though she were my own daughter. Deuce take it, sir, you know you are only humbugging me,—what's the use of talking about it?"

He stamped his foot.

"No—no! I mean to say—don't it look a little strange? Oughtn't I to call once or twice first?—such a smart house as you say theirs is—don't you see——"

"I tell you it's the simplest house in the world; it isn't 'smart' in the least bit," cried Velchaninoff; "they have a lot of children: it will make another girl of her!—I'll introduce you there myself, to-morrow, if you like. Of course you'll have to go and thank them, and all that. You shall go down every day with me, if you please."

"Oh, but——"

"Nonsense! You know it's nonsense! Now look here: you come to me this evening—I'll put you up for the night—and we'll start off early to-morrow and be down there by twelve."

"Benefactor!—and I may spend the night at your house?" cried Pavel Pavlovitch, instantly consenting to the plan with the greatest cordiality,—"you are really *too* good! And where's their country house?"

"At the Liesnoy."

"But look here, how about her dress? Such a house, you know,—a father's heart shrinks——"

"Nonsense!—she's in mourning—what else could she wear but a black dress like this? it's exactly the thing; you couldn't imagine anything more so!—you might let her have some clean linen with her, and give her a cleaner neck-handkerchief."

"Directly, directly. We'll get her linen together in a couple of minutes—it's just home from the wash!"

"Send for a carriage—can you? Tell them to let us have it at once, so as not to waste time."

But now an unexpected obstacle arose: Liza absolutely rejected the plan; she had listened to it with terror, and if Velchaninoff had, in his excited argument with Pavel Pavlovitch, had time to glance at the child's face, he would have observed her expression of absolute despair at this moment.

"I won't go!" she said, quietly but firmly.

"There—look at that! Just like her mamma!"

"I'm *not* like mamma, I'm *not* like mamma!" cried Liza, wringing her little hands in despair. "Oh, papa—papa!" she added, "if you desert me—" she suddenly threw herself upon the alarmed Velchaninoff—"If you take me away—" she cried—"I'll——"

But Liza had no time to finish her sentence, for Pavel Pavlovitch suddenly seized her by the arm and collar and hustled her into the next room with unconcealed rage. For several minutes Velchaninoff listened to the whispering going on there,—whisperings and seemingly subdued crying on the part of Liza. He was about to follow the pair, when suddenly out came Pavel Pavlovitch, and stated—with a disagreeable grin—that Liza would come directly.

Velchaninoff tried not to look at him and kept his eyes fixed on the other side of the room.

The elderly woman whom Velchaninoff had met on the stairs also made her appearance, and packed Liza's things into a neat little carpet bag.

"Is it you that are going to take the little lady away, sir?" she asked; "if so, you are doing a good deed! She's a nice quiet child, and you are saving her from goodness knows what, here!"

"Oh! come—Maria Sisevna,"—began Pavel Pavlovitch.

"Well? What? Isn't it true! Arn't you ashamed to let a girl of her intelligence see the things that you allow to go on here? The carriage has arrived for you, sir,—*you* ordered one for the Liesnoy, didn't you?"

"Yes."

"Well, good luck to you!"

Liza came out, looking very pale and with downcast eyes; she took her bag, but never glanced in Velchaninoff's direction. She restrained herself and did not throw herself upon her father, as she had done before—not even to say good-bye. She evidently did not wish to look at him.

Her father kissed her and patted her head in correct form; her lip curled during the operation, the chin trembled a little, but she did not raise her eyes to her father's.

Pavel Pavlovitch looked pale, and his hands shook; Velchaninoff saw that plainly enough, although he did his best not to see the man at all. He (Velchaninoff) had but one thought, and that was how to get away at once!

Downstairs was old Maria Sisevna, waiting to say good-bye; and more kissing was done. Liza had just climbed into the carriage when suddenly she caught sight of her father's face; she gave a loud cry and wrung her hands,—in another minute she would have been out of the carriage and away, but luckily the vehicle went on and she was too late!

CHAPTER VI.

"Are you feeling faint?" asked Velchaninoff of his companion, frightened out of his wits: "I'll tell him to stop and get you some water, shall I?"

She looked at him angrily and reproachfully.

"Where are you taking me to?" she asked coldly and abruptly.

"To a very beautiful house, Liza. There are plenty of children,—they'll all love you there, they are so kind! Don't be angry with me, Liza; I wish you well, you know!"

In truth, Velchaninoff would have looked strange at this moment to any acquaintance, if such had happened to see him!

"How—how—how—oh! *how* wicked you are!" said Liza, fighting with suppressed tears, and flashing her fine angry eyes at him.

"But Liza—I——"

"You are bad—bad—and wicked!" cried Liza. She wrung her hands.

Velchaninoff was beside himself.

"Oh, Liza, Liza! if only you knew what despair you are causing me!" he said.

"Is it true that he is coming down to-morrow?" asked the child haughtily—"is it true or not?"

"Quite true—I shall bring him down myself,—I shall take him and bring him!"

"He will deceive you somehow!" cried the child, drooping her eyes.

"Doesn't he love you, then, Liza?"

"No."

"Has he ill-treated you,—has he?"

Liza looked gloomily at her questioner, and said nothing. She then turned away from him and sat still and depressed.

Velchaninoff commenced to talk: he tried to win her,—he spoke warmly—excitedly—feverishly.

Liza listened incredulously and with a hostile air,—but still she listened. Her attention delighted him beyond measure;—he went so far as to explain to her what it meant when a man took to drink. He said that he loved her and would himself look after her father.

At last Liza raised her eyes and gazed fixedly at him.

Then Velchaninoff began to speak of her mother and of how well he had known her; and he saw that his tales attracted her. Little by little she began to reply to his questions, but very cautiously and in an obstinately monosyllabic way.

She would answer nothing to his chief inquiries; as to her former relations with her father, for instance, she maintained an obstinate silence.

While speaking to her, Velchaninoff held the child's hand in his own, as before; and she did not try to take it away.

Liza said enough to make it apparent that she had loved her father more than her mother at first, because that her father had loved the child better than her mother did; but that when her mother had died and was lying dead, Liza wept over her and kissed her, and ever since then she had loved her mother more than all—all there was in the whole world—and that every night she thought of her and loved her.

But Liza was very proud, and suddenly recollecting herself and finding that she was saying a great deal more than she had meant to reveal, she paused, and relapsed into obstinate silence once more, and gazed at Velchaninoff with something like hatred in her eyes, considering that he had beguiled her into the revelations just made.

By the end of the journey, however, her hysterical condition was nearly over, but she was very silent and sat looking morosely about her, obstinately silent and gloomy, like a little wild animal.

The fact that she was being taken to a strange house where she had never been before did not seem so far to weigh upon her; Velchaninoff saw clearly enough that other things distressed her, and principally that she was ashamed—ashamed that her father should have let her go so easily—thrown her away, as it were—into Velchaninoff's arms.

"She's ill," thought the latter, "and perhaps very ill; she has been bullied and ill-treated. Oh! that drunken, blackguardly wretch of a fellow!" He hurried on the coachman. Velchaninoff trusted greatly to the fresh air, to the garden, to the children, to the new life, now; as to the future, he was in no sort of doubt at all, his hopes were clear and defined. One thing he was quite sure of, and that was that he had never before felt what now swelled within his soul, and that the sensation would last for ever and ever.

"I have an object at last! this is Life!" he said to himself enthusiastically.

Many thoughts welled into his brain just now, but he would have none of them; he did not care to think of details at this moment, for without details the future was all so clear and so beautiful, and so safe and indestructible!

The basis of his plan was simple enough; it was simply this, in the language of his own thoughts:

"I shall so work upon that drunken little blackguard that he will leave Liza with the Pogoryeltseffs, and go away alone—at first, 'for a time,' of course!—and so Liza shall remain behind for me! what more do I want? The plan will suit him, too!—else why does he bully her like this?"

The carriage arrived at last.

It was certainly a very beautiful place. They were met first of all by a troop of noisy children, who overflowed on to the front-door steps. Velchaninoff had not been down for some time, and the delight of the little ones to see him was excessive—they were very fond of him.

The elder ones shouted, before he had left the carriage, by way of chaff:

"How's the lawsuit getting on, eh?" and the smaller gang took up the joke, and all clamoured the same question: it was a pet joke in this establishment to chaff Velchaninoff about his lawsuit. But when Liza climbed down the carriage steps, she was instantly surrounded and stared at with true juvenile curiosity. Then Claudia Petrovna and her husband came out, and both of them good-humouredly bantered Velchaninoff about his lawsuit.

Claudia Petrovna was a lady of some thirty-seven summers, stout and well-favoured, and with a sweet fresh-looking face. Her husband was a man of fifty-five, a clever and long-headed man of the world, but above all, a good and kind-hearted friend to anyone requiring kindness.

The Pogoryeltseffs' house was in the full sense of the word a "home" to Velchaninoff, as the latter had stated. There was rather more here, however; for, twenty years since Claudia had very nearly married young Velchaninoff almost a boy at that time, and a student at the university.

This had been his first experience of love—and very hot and fiery and funny—and sweet it was! The end of it was, however, that Claudia married Mr Pogoryeltseff. Five years later she and Velchaninoff had met again, and a quiet candid friendship had sprung up between them. Since then there had always been a warmth, a speciality about their friendship, a radiance which overspread it and glorified their relations one to the other. There was nothing here that Velchaninoff could remember with shame—all was pure and sweet; and this was perhaps the reason why the friendship was specially dear to Velchaninoff; he had not experienced many such platonic intimacies.

In this house Velchaninoff was simple and happy, confessed his sins, played with the children and lectured them, and never bothered his head about outside matters; he had promised the Pogoryeltseffs that he would live a few more years alone in the world, and then move over to their household for good and all; and he looked forward to that good time coming with all seriousness.

Velchaninoff now gave all the information about Liza which he thought fit, though his simple request would have been amply sufficient here.

Claudia Petrovna kissed the little "orphan," and promised to do all she possibly could for her; and the children carried Liza off to play in the garden. Half an hour passed in conversation, and then Velchaninoff rose to depart: he was in such a hurry, that his friends could not help remarking upon the fact. He had not been near them for three weeks, they said, and now he only stayed half an hour! Velchaninoff laughed and promised to come down to-morrow. Someone observed that Velchaninoff's state of agitation was remarkable, even for *him*! Whereupon the latter jumped up, seized Claudia Petrovna's hand, and, under pretence of having forgotten to tell her something most important about Liza, he led her into another room.

"Do you remember," he began, "what I told you, and only you,—even your husband does not know of it—about my year of life down at T——?"

"Oh yes! only too well! You have often spoken of it."

"No—I did not 'speak about it,' I *confessed*, and only to yourself; but I never told you the lady's name. It was Trusotsky, the wife of this Trusotsky; it is she who has died, and this little Liza is her child—*my* child!"

"Is this certain? Are you quite sure there is no mistake?" asked Claudia Petrovna, with some agitation.

"Quite, quite certain!" said Velchaninoff enthusiastically. He then gave a short, hasty, and excited narrative of all that had occurred. Claudia had heard it all before, excepting the lady's name.

The fact is, Velchaninoff had always been so afraid that one of his friends might some fine day meet Madame Trusotsky at T——, and wonder how in the world he could have loved such a woman as that, that he had never revealed her name to a single soul; not even to Claudia Petrovna, his great friend.

"And does the 'father' know nothing of it?" asked Claudia, having heard the tale out.

"N—no; he knows—you see, that's just what is bothering me now. I haven't sifted the matter as yet," resumed Velchaninoff hotly. "He must know—he *does* know. I remarked that fact both yesterday and to-day. But I wish to discover *how much* he knows. That's why I am hurrying back now; he is coming to-night. He knows all about Bagantoff; but how about myself? You know how such wives can deceive their husbands! If an angel from Heaven were to come down and convict a woman, her husband will still trust her, and give the angel the lie.

"Oh! don't nod your head at me, don't judge me! I have long since judged and convicted myself. You see, this morning I felt so sure that he knew all, that I compromised myself before him. Fancy, I was really ashamed of having been rude to him last night. He only called in to see me out of the pure unconquerably malicious desire to show me that he knew all the offence, and knew who was the offender! I behaved like a fool; I gave myself into his hands too easily; I was too heated; he came at such a feverish moment for me. I tell you, he has been bullying Liza, simply to 'let off bile,'—you understand. He needs a safety-valve for his offended feelings, and vents them upon *anyone*, even a little child!

"It is exasperation, and quite natural. We must treat him in a Christian spirit, my friend; and do you know, I wish to change my way of treating him, entirely; I wish to be particularly kind to him. That will be a good action on my part, for I am to blame before him, I know I am; there's no disguising the fact! Besides, once at T——, it so happened that I required four thousand roubles at a moment's notice. Well, the fellow gave me the money, without a receipt, at once, and with every manifestation of delight to be able to serve me! And I took the money from his hands,—I did, indeed! I took it as though he were a friend. Think of that!"

"Very well; only be careful!" said Claudia Petrovna. "You are so enthusiastic that I am really alarmed for you! Of course Liza shall now be no less than my own daughter to me; but there is so much to know and to settle yet! Above all, be very careful and observant! You are not nearly careful enough when you are happy! You are much too exalted an individual to be cautious, when you are happy!" she added with a smile.

The whole family went out to see Velchaninoff off. The children brought Liza along with them; they had been playing in the garden. They seemed to look at her now with even more perplexity then at first! The girl became dreadfully shy when Velchaninoff kissed her before all, and promised to come down next day and bring her father with him. To the last moment she did not say a single word, and never looked at him at all; but just before he was about to start she seized his hand and drew him away to one side, looking imploringly in his face: she evidently had something to say to him. Velchaninoff immediately took her into an adjoining room.

"What is it, Liza?" he asked, kindly and encouragingly; but she drew him farther away,—into the very farthest corner of the room, anxious to get well out of sight and hearing of the rest.

"What is it, Liza? What is it?"

But she was still silent, and could not make up her mind to speak; she stared with her motionless, large blue eyes, into his face, and in every lineament of her little face was betrayed the wildest terror and anxiety.

"He'll—hang himself!" she whispered at last, as though she were talking in her sleep.

"Who will hang himself?" asked Velchaninoff, in alarm.

"He will—*he*! He tried to hang himself to a hook last night!" said the child, panting with haste and excitement; "I saw it myself! To-day he tried it again,—he wishes to hang himself; he told me so!—he told me so! He wanted to, long ago; he has always wanted to do it! I saw it myself—in the night!"

"Impossible!" muttered Velchaninoff, incredulously.

Liza suddenly threw herself into his arms, kissed his hands, and cried. She could hardly breathe for sobbing; she was begging and imploring Velchaninoff, but he could not understand what she was trying to say.

Velchaninoff never afterwards forgot the terrible look of this distressed child; he thought of it waking and thought of it sleeping—how she had come to him in her despair as to her last hope, and hysterically begged and prayed him to help her! "And to think of her being so deeply attached to him!" he reflected jealously, as he drove, impatient and feverish, towards town. "She said herself that she loved her mother better;—perhaps she hates him, and doesn't love him at all! And what's all that nonsense about 'hanging himself!' What did she mean by that? As if he would hang himself, the fool! I must sift the matter—the whole matter. I must settle this business once and for ever—and quickly!"

CHAPTER VII.

He was in a great hurry to "know all." In order to lose no time about finding out what he felt he must know at once, he told the coachman to drive him straight to Trusotsky's rooms. On the way he changed his mind; "let him come to me, himself," he thought, "and meanwhile I can attend to my cursed law business."

But to-day he really felt that he was too absent to attend to anything at all; and at five o'clock he set out with the intention of dining. And at this moment, for the first time, an amusing idea struck him. What if he really only hindered his law business by meddling as he did, and hunting his wretched lawyer about the place, when the latter plainly avoided meeting him? Velchaninoff laughed merrily over this idea. "And yet," he thought; "if this notion had struck me in the evening instead of now, how angry I should have been!" He laughed again, more merrily than before. But in spite of his merriness he grew more and more thoughtful and impatient, and could settle to nothing, nor could he think out what he most wanted to reflect upon.

"I *must* have that fellow here!" he said at length; "I must read the mystery of *him* first of all, and then I can settle what to do next. There's a duel in this business!"

Returning home at seven o'clock he did not find Pavel Pavlovitch there, which fact first surprised him, then angered him, then depressed him, and at last, frightened him.

"God knows, God knows how it will all end!" he cried; first trying to settle himself on a sofa, and then marching up and down the room, and all the while looking at his watch every other minute.

At length—at about nine o'clock—Pavel Pavlovitch appeared.

"If this man was cunning enough to mean it he could not have managed better in order to put me into a state of nervousness!" thought Velchaninoff, though his heart bounded for joy to see his guest arrive.

To Velchaninoff's cordial inquiry as to why he was so late, Pavel Pavlovitch smiled disagreeably—took a seat with easy familiarity, carelessly threw his crapebound hat on a chair,—and made himself perfectly at home. Velchaninoff observed and took stock of the careless manner adopted by his visitor; it was not like yesterday. Velchaninoff then quietly, and in a few words, gave Pavel Pavlovitch an account of what he had done with Liza, of how kindly she had been received, of how good it would be for the child down there; then he led the conversation to the topic of the Pogoryeltseffs, leaving Liza out of the talking altogether, and spoke of how kind the whole family were, of how long he had known them, and so on.

Pavel Pavlovitch listened absently, occasionally looking ironically at his host from under his eyelashes.

"What an enthusiast you are!" he muttered at last, smiling very unpleasantly.

"Hum, you seem in a bad humour to-day!" remarked Velchaninoff with annoyance.

"And why shouldn't I be as wicked as my neighbours?" cried Pavel Pavlovitch suddenly! He said this so abruptly that he gave one the idea that he had pounced out of a corner where he had been lurking, on purpose to make a dash at the first opportunity.

"Oh dear me! do as you like, pray!" laughed Velchaninoff; "I only thought something had put you out, perhaps!"

"So it has," cried Pavel Pavlovitch, as though proud of the fact.

"Well, what was it?"

65

Pavel Pavlovitch waited a moment or two before he replied.

"Why it's that Stepan Michailovitch Bagantoff of ours—up to his tricks again; he's a shining light among the highest circles of society—he is!"

"Wouldn't he receive you again—or what?"

"N—no! not quite that, this time; on the contrary I was allowed to go in for the first time on record, and I had the honour of musing over his features, too!—but he happened to be a corpse, that's all!"

"What! Bagantoff dead?" cried Velchaninoff, in the greatest astonishment; though there was no particular reason why he *should* be surprised.

"Yes—my unalterable—six-years-standing friend is dead!—died yesterday at about mid-day, and I knew nothing of it! Perhaps he died just when I called there—who knows? To-morrow is the funeral! he's in his coffin at this moment! Died of nervous fever; and they let me in to see him—they did indeed!—to contemplate his features! I told them I was a great friend—and therefore they allowed me in! A pretty trick he has played me—this dear friend of six years' standing! why—perhaps I came to St. Petersburg *specially for him*!"

"Well—it's hardly worth your while to be angry with him about it, is it—he didn't die on purpose!" said Velchaninoff laughing.

"Oh, but I'm speaking out of pure sympathy—he was a *dear* friend to me! oh a *very* dear friend!"

Pavel Pavlovitch gave a smile of detestable irony and cunning.

"Do you know what, Alexey Ivanovitch," he resumed, "I think you ought to treat me to something,—I have often treated you; I used to be your host every blessed day, sir, at T——, for a whole year! Send for a bottle of wine, do—my throat is so dry!"

"With pleasure—why didn't you say so before! what would you like?"

"Don't say 'you!' say 'we'! we'll drink together of course!" said Pavel Pavlovitch defiantly, but at the same time looking into Velchaninoff's eyes with some concern.

"Shall it be champagne?"

"Of course! it isn't time for vodki yet!"

Velchaninoff rose slowly—rang the bell and gave Mavra the necessary orders.

"We'll drink to this happy meeting of friends after nine years' parting!" said Pavel Pavlovitch, with a very inappropriate and unnecessary giggle. "Why, you are the only real, true friend left to me now! Bagantoff is no more! it quite reminds one of the great poet:

"Great Patroclus is no more,

Mean Thersites liveth yet!"

—and so on,—don't you know!"

At the name "Thersites" Pavel Pavlovitch touched his own breast.

"I wish you would speak plainly, you pig of a fellow!" said Velchaninoff to himself, "I hate hints!" His own anger was on the rise, and he had long been struggling with his self-restraint.

"Look here,—tell me this, since you consider Bagantoff to have been guilty before you (as I see you do) surely you must be glad that your betrayer is dead? What are you so angry about?"

"Glad! Why should I be glad?"

"I judge by what I should imagine your feelings to be."

"Ha-ha! well, this time you are a little bit in error as to my feelings, for once! A certain sage has said 'my good enemy is dead, but I have a still better one alive! ha-ha!"

"Well but you saw him alive for five years at a stretch,—I should have thought that was enough to contemplate his features in!" said Velchaninoff angrily and contemptuously.

"Yes, but how was I to know then, sir?" snapped Pavel Pavlovitch—jumping out of an ambush once more, as it were,—delighted to be asked a question which he had long awaited; "why, what do you take me for, Alexey Ivanovitch?" at this moment there was in the speaker's face a new expression altogether, transfiguring entirely the hitherto merely disagreeably malicious look upon it.

"Do you mean to say you knew nothing of it?" said Velchaninoff in astonishment.

"How! Didn't know? As if I could have known it and——Oh, you race of Jupiters! you reckon a man to be no better than a dog, and judge of him by your own sentiments. Look here, sir,—there, look at that." So saying, he brought his fist madly down upon the table with a resounding bang, and immediately afterwards looked frightened at his own act.

Velchaninoff's face beamed.

"Listen, Pavel Pavlovitch," he said; "it is entirely the same thing to me whether you knew or did not know all about it. If you did not know, so much the more honourable is it for you; but—I can't understand why you should have selected me for your confidant."

"I wasn't talking of you; don't be angry, it wasn't about you," muttered Pavel Pavlovitch, with his eyes fixed on the ground.

At this moment, Mavra entered with the champagne.

"Here it is!" cried Pavel Pavlovitch, immensely delighted at the appearance of the wine. "Now then, tumblers my good girl, tumblers quick! Capital! Thank you, we don't require you any more, my good Mavra. What! you've drawn the cork? Excellent creature. Well, ta-ta! off with you."

Mavra's advent with the bottle so encouraged him that he again looked at Velchaninoff with some defiance.

"Now confess," he giggled suddenly, "confess that you are very curious indeed to hear about all this, and that it is by no means 'entirely the same to you,' as you declared! Confess that you would be miserable if I were to get up and go away this very minute without telling you anything more."

"Not the least in the world, I assure you!"

Pavel Pavlovitch smiled; and his smile said, as plainly as words could, "That's a lie!"

"Well, let's to business," he said, and poured out two glasses of champagne.

"Here's a toast," he continued, raising his goblet, "to the health in Paradise of our dear departed friend Bagantoff."

He raised his glass and drank.

"I won't drink such a toast as that!" said Velchaninoff; and put his glass down on the table.

"Why not? It's a very pretty toast."

"Look here, were you drunk when you came here?"

"A little; why?"

"Oh—nothing particular. Only it appeared to me that yesterday, and especially this morning, you were sincerely sorry for the loss of Natalia Vasilievna."

"And who says I am not sorry now?" cried Pavel Pavlovitch, as if somebody had pulled a string and made him snap the words out, like a doll.

"No, I don't mean that; but you must admit you may be in error about Bagantoff; and that's a serious matter!"

Pavel Pavlovitch grinned and gave a wink.

"Hey! Wouldn't you just like to know how I found out about Bagantoff, eh?"

Velchaninoff blushed.

"I repeat, it's all the same to me," he said; and added to himself, "Hadn't I better pitch him and the bottle out of the window together." He was blushing more and more now.

Pavel Pavlovitch poured himself out another glass.

"I'll tell you directly how I found out all about Mr. Bagantoff, and your burning wish shall be satisfied. For you are a fiery sort of man, you know, Alexey Ivanovitch, oh, dreadfully so! Ha-ha-ha. Just give me a cigarette first, will you, for ever since March——"

"Here's a cigarette for you."

"Ever since March I have been a depraved man, sir, and this is how it all came about. Listen. Consumption, as you know, my dear friend" (Pavel Pavlovitch was growing more and more familiar!), "is an interesting malady. One sees a man dying of consumption without a suspicion that to-morrow is to be his last day. Well, I told you how Natalia Vasilievna, up to five hours before her death, talked about going to visit her aunt, who lived thirty miles or so away, and starting in a fortnight. You know how some ladies—and gentlemen, too, I daresay—have the bad habit of keeping a lot of old rubbish by them, in the way of love-letters and so on. It would be much safer to stick them all into the fire, wouldn't it? But no, they must keep every little scrap of paper in drawers and desks, and endorse it and classify it, and tie it up in bundles, for each year and month and class! I don't know whether they find this consoling to their feelings afterwards, or what. Well, since she was arranging a visit to her aunt just five hours before her death, Natalia Vasilievna naturally did not expect to die so soon; in fact, she was expecting old Doctor Koch down till the last; and so, when Natalia Vasilievna *did* die, she left behind her a beautiful little black desk all inlaid with mother-of-pearl, and bound with silver, in her bureau; oh, a lovely little box, an heirloom left her by her grandmother, with a lock and key all complete. Well, sir, in this box everything—I mean *everything*, you know, for every day and hour for the last twenty years—was disclosed; and since Mr. Bagantoff had a decided taste for literature (indeed, he had published a passionate novel once, I am told, in a newspaper!)—consequently there were about a hundred examples of his genius in the desk, ranging over a period of five years. Some of these talented effusions were covered with pencilled remarks by Natalia Vasilievna herself! Pleasant, that, for a fond husband's feelings, sir, eh?"

Velchaninoff quickly cast his thoughts back over the past, and remembered that he had never written a single letter or a single note to Natalia Vasilievna.

He had written a couple of letters from St. Petersburg, but, according to a previous arrangement, he had addressed them to both Mr. and Mrs. Trusotsky together. He had not answered Natalia Vasilievna's last letter—which had contained his dismissal—at all.

Having ended his speech, Pavel Pavlovitch relapsed into silence, and sat smiling repulsively for a whole minute or so.

"Why don't you answer my question, my friend?" he asked, at length, evidently disturbed by Velchaninoff's silence.

"What question?"

"As to the pleasure I must have felt as a fond husband, upon opening the desk."

"Your feelings are no business of mine!" said the other bitterly, rising and commencing to stride up and down the room.

"I wouldn't mind betting that you are thinking at this very moment: 'What a pig of a fellow he is to parade his shame like this!' Ha-ha! dear me, what a squeamish gentleman you are to be sure!"

"Not at all. I was thinking nothing of the sort; on the contrary, I consider that you are—besides being more or less intoxicated—so put out by the death of the man who has injured you that you are not yourself. There's nothing surprising in it at all! I quite understand why you wish Bagantoff were still alive, and am ready to respect your annoyance, but——"

"And pray *why* do you suppose that I wish Bagantoff were alive?"

"Oh, that's your affair!"

"I'll take my oath you are thinking of a duel!"

"Devil take it, sir!" cried Velchaninoff, obliged to hold himself tighter than ever. "I was thinking that you, like every respectable person in similar circumstances, would act openly and candidly and straightforwardly, and not humiliate yourself with comical antics and silly grimaces, and ridiculous complaints and detestable innuendoes, which only heap greater shame upon you. I say I was thinking you would act like a respectable person."

"Ha-ha-ha!—but perhaps I am *not* a respectable person!"

"Oh, well, that's your own affair again and yet, if so, what in the devil's name could you want with Bagantoff alive?"

"Oh, my dear sir, I should have liked just to have a nice peep at a dear old friend, that's all. We should have got hold of a bottle of wine, and drunk it together!"

"He wouldn't have drunk with *you*!"

"Why not? *Noblesse oblige?* Why, *you* are drinking with me. Wherein is he better than you?"

"I have not drunk with you."

"Wherefore this sudden pride, sir?"

Velchaninoff suddenly burst into a fit of nervous, irritable laughter.

"Why, deuce take it all!" he cried, "you are quite a different type to what I believed. I thought you were nothing but a 'permanent husband,' but I find you are a sort of bird of prey."

"What! 'permanent husband?' What is a 'permanent husband?' " asked Pavel Pavlovitch, pricking up his ears.

"Oh—just one type of husbands—that's all, it's too long to explain. Come, you'd better get out now; it's quite time you went. I'm sick of you!"

"And bird of prey, sir; what did that mean?"

"I said you were a bird of prey for a joke."

"Yes; but—bird of prey—tell me what you mean, Alexey Ivanovitch, for goodness sake!"

"Come, come, that's quite enough!" shouted Velchaninoff, suddenly flaring up and speaking at the top of his voice. "It's time you went; get out of this, will you?"

"No, sir, it's *not* enough!" cried Pavel Pavlovitch, jumping up, too. "Even if you *are* sick of me, sir, it's not enough; for you must first drink and clink glasses with me. I won't go before you do! No, no; oh dear no! drink first; it's *not* enough yet."

"Pavel Pavlovitch, will you go to the devil or will you not?"

"With pleasure, sir. I'll go to the devil with pleasure; but first we must drink. You say you don't wish to drink *with me*; but *I wish you* to drink with me—actually *with me*."

Pavel Pavlovitch was grimacing and giggling no longer. He seemed to be suddenly transfigured again, and was as different from the Pavel Pavlovitch of but a few moments since as he could possibly be, both in appearance and in the tone of his voice; so much so that Velchaninoff was absolutely confounded.

"Come, Alexey Ivanovitch, let's drink!—don't refuse me!" continued Pavel Pavlovitch, seizing the other tightly by the hand and gazing into his face with an extraordinary expression.

It was clear there was more in this matter than the mere question of drinking a glass of wine.

"Well," muttered Velchaninoff, "but that's nothing but dregs!"

"No, there's just a couple of glasses left—it's quite clear. Now then, clink glasses and drink. There, I'll take your glass and you take mine." They touched glasses and drank.

"Oh, Alexey Ivanovitch! now that we've drunk together—oh!" Pavel Pavlovitch suddenly raised his hand to his forehead and sat still for a few moments.

Velchaninoff trembled with excitement. He thought Pavel Pavlovitch was about to disclose *all*; but Pavel Pavlovitch said nothing whatever. He only looked at him, and quietly smiled his detestable cunning smile in the other's face.

"What do you want with me, you drunken wretch?" cried Velchaninoff, furious, and stamping his foot upon the floor; "you are making a fool of me!"

"Don't shout so—don't shout! Why make such a noise?" cried Pavel Pavlovitch. "I'm not making a fool of you! Do you know what you are to me now?" and he suddenly seized Velchaninoff's hand, and kissed it before Velchaninoff could recollect himself.

"There, that's what you are to me *now*; and now I'll go to the devil."

"Wait a bit—stop!" cried Velchaninoff, recollecting himself; "there's something I wished to say to you."

Pavel Pavlovitch turned back from the door.

"You see," began Velchaninoff, blushing and keeping his eye well away from the other, "you ought to go with me to the Pogoryeltseffs to-morrow—just to thank them, you know, and make their acquaintance."

"Of course, of course; quite so!" said Pavel Pavlovitch readily, and making a gesture of the hand to imply that he knew his duty, and there was no need to remind him of it.

"Besides Liza expects you anxiously—I promised her."

"Liza?" Pavel Pavlovitch turned quickly once more upon him. "Liza? Do you know, sir, what this Liza has been to me—has been and is?" he cried passionately and almost beside himself; "but—no!—afterwards—that shall be afterwards! Meanwhile it's not enough for me, Alexey Ivanovitch, that we have drunk together; there's another satisfaction I must have, sir!" He placed his hat on a chair, and, panting with excitement, gazed at his companion with much the same expression as before.

"Kiss me, Alexey Ivanovitch!"

"Are you drunk?" cried the other, drawing back.

"Yes, I am—but kiss me all the same, Alexey Ivanovitch—oh, do! I kissed your hand just now, you know."

Alexey Ivanovitch was silent for a few moments, as though stunned by the blow of a cudgel. Then he quickly bent down to Pavel Pavlovitch (who was about the height of his shoulder), and kissed his lips, from which proceeded a disagreeably powerful odour of wine. He performed the action as though not quite certain of what he was doing.

"Well! *now, now!*" cried Pavel Pavlovitch, with drunken enthusiasm, and with his eyes flashing fiercely; "*now*—look here—I'll tell you what! I thought at that time: 'Surely not *he*, too! If *this* man,' I thought, 'if *this* man is guilty too—then whom am I ever to trust again!' "

Pavel Pavlovitch suddenly burst into tears.

"So now you must understand *how* dear a friend you are to me henceforth." With these words he took his hat and rushed out of the room.

Velchaninoff stood for several minutes in one spot, just as he had done after Pavel Pavlovitch's first visit.

"It's merely a drunken sally—nothing more!" he muttered. "Absolutely nothing further!" he repeated, when he was undressed and settled down in his bed.

CHAPTER VIII.

Next morning, while waiting for Pavel Pavlovitch, who had promised to be in good time in order to drive down to the Pogoryeltseffs with him, Velchaninoff walked up and down the room, sipped his coffee, and every other minute reflected upon one and the same idea; namely, that he felt like a man who had awaked from sleep with the deep impression of having received a box on the ear the last thing at night.

"Hm!" he thought, anxiously, "he understands the state of the case only too well; he'll take it out of me by means of Liza!" The dear image of the poor little girl danced before his eyes. His heart beat quicker when he reflected that to-day—in a couple of hours—he would see *his own* Liza once more. "Yes—there's no question about it," he said to himself; "my whole end and aim in life is *there* now! What do I care about all these 'memories' and boxes on the ear; and what have I lived for up to now?—for sorrow and discomfort—that's all! but *now*, now—it's all different!"

But in spite of his ecstatic feelings he grew more and more thoughtful.

"He is worrying me for Liza, that's plain; and he bullies Liza—he is going to take it out of me that way—for *all*! Hm! at all events I cannot possibly allow such sallies as his of last night," and Velchaninoff blushed hotly "and here's half-past eleven and he hasn't come yet." He waited long—till half-past twelve, and his anguish of impatience grew more and more keen. Pavel Pavlovitch did not appear. At length the idea began to take shape that Pavel Pavlovitch naturally would not come again for the sole purpose of another scene like that of last night. The thought filled Velchaninoff with despair. "The brute knows I am depending upon him—and what on earth am I to do now about Liza? How can I make my appearance without him?"

At last he could bear it no longer and set off to the Pokrofsky at one o'clock to look for Pavel Pavlovitch.

At the lodging, Velchaninoff was informed that Pavel Pavlovitch had not been at home all night, and had only called in at nine o'clock, stayed a quarter of an hour, and had gone out again.

Velchaninoff stood at the door listening to the servants' report, mechanically tried the handle, recollected himself, and asked to see Maria Sisevna.

The latter obeyed his summons at once.

She was a kind-hearted old creature, of generous feelings, as Velchaninoff described her afterwards to Claudia Petrovna. Having first enquired as to his journey yesterday with Liza, Maria launched into anecdotes of Pavel Pavlovitch. She declared that she would long ago have turned her lodger out neck and crop, but for the child. Pavel Pavlovitch had been turned out of the hotel for generally disreputable behaviour. "Oh, he does dreadful things!" she continued. "Fancy his telling the poor child, in anger, that she wasn't his daughter, but——"

"Oh no, no! impossible!" cried Velchaninoff in alarm.

"I heard it myself! She's only a small child, of course, but that sort of thing doesn't do before an intelligent child like her! She cried dreadfully—she was quite upset. We had a catastrophe in the house a short while since. Some commissionnaire or somebody took a room in the evening, and hung himself before morning. He had bolted with money, they say. Well, crowds of people came in to stare at him. Pavel Pavlovitch wasn't at home, but the child had escaped and was wandering about; and she must needs go with the rest to see the sight. I saw her looking at the suicide with an extraordinary expression, and carried her off at once, of course; and fancy, I hardly managed to get home with her—trembling all over she was—when off she goes in a dead faint, and it was all I could do to bring her round at all. I don't know whether she's epileptic or what—and ever since that she has been ill. When her father heard, he came and pinched her all over—he doesn't beat her; he always pinches her like that,—then he went out and got drunk somewhere, and came back and frightened her. 'I'm going to hang myself too,' he says, 'because of you. I shall hang myself on that blind string there,' he says, and he makes a loop in the string before her very eyes. The poor little thing went quite out of her mind with terror, and cried and clasped him round with her little arms. 'I'll be good—I'll be good!' she shrieks. It was a pitiful sight—it was, indeed!"

Velchaninoff, though prepared for strange revelations concerning Pavel Pavlovitch and his ways, was quite dumbfounded by these tales; he could scarcely believe his ears.

Maria Sisevna told him many more such little anecdotes. Among others, there was one occasion, when, if she (Maria) had not been by, Liza would have thrown herself out of the window.

Pavel Pavlovitch had come staggering out of the room muttering, "I shall smash her head in with a stick! I shall murder her like a dog!" and he had gone away, repeating this over and over again to himself.

Velchaninoff hired a carriage and set off towards the Pogoryeltseffs. Before he had left the town behind him, the carriage was delayed by a block at a cross road, just by a small bridge, over which was passing, at the moment, a long funeral procession. There were carriages waiting to move on on both sides of the bridge, and a considerable crowd of foot passengers besides.

The funeral was evidently of some person of considerable importance, for the train of private and hired vehicles was a very long one; and at the window of one of these carriages in the procession Velchaninoff suddenly beheld the face of Pavel Pavlovitch.

Velchaninoff would not have believed his eyes, but that Pavel Pavlovitch nodded his head and smiled to him. He seemed to be delighted to have recognised Velchaninoff; he even began to kiss his hand out of the window.

Velchaninoff jumped out of his own vehicle, and in spite of policemen, crowd, and everything else, elbowed his way to Pavel Pavlovitch's carriage window. He found the latter sitting alone.

"What are you doing?" he cried. "Why didn't you come to my house? Why are you here?"

"I'm paying a debt; don't shout so! I'm repaying a debt," said Pavel Pavlovitch, giggling and winking. "I'm escorting the mortal remains of my dear friend Stepan Michailovitch Bagantoff!"

"What absurdity, you drunken, insane creature," cried Velchaninoff louder than ever, and beside himself with outraged feeling. "Get out and come with me. Quick! get out instantly!"

"I can't. It's a debt——"

"I'll pull you out, then!" shouted Velchaninoff.

"Then I'll scream, sir, I'll scream!" giggled Pavel Pavlovitch, as merrily as ever, just as though the whole thing was a joke. However, he retreated into the further corner of the carriage, all the same.

"Look out, sir, look out! You'll be knocked down!" cried a policeman.

Sure enough, an outside carriage was making its way on to the bridge from the side, stopping the procession, and causing a commotion. Velchaninoff was obliged to spring aside, and the press of carriages and people immediately separated him from Pavel Pavlovitch. He shrugged his shoulders and returned to his own vehicle.

"It's all the same. I couldn't take such a fellow with me, anyhow," he reflected, still all of a tremble with excitement and the rage of disgust. When he repeated Maria Sisevna's story, and his meeting at the funeral, to Claudia Petrovna afterwards, the latter became buried in deep thought.

"I am anxious for you," she said at last. "You must break off all relations with that man, and as soon as possible."

"Oh, he's nothing but a drunken fool!" cried Velchaninoff passionately; "as if I am to be afraid of *him*! And how can I break off relations with him? Remember Liza!"

Meanwhile Liza was lying ill; fever had set in last night, and an eminent doctor was momentarily expected from town! He had been sent for early this morning.

These news quite upset Velchaninoff. Claudia Petrovna took him in to see the patient.

"I observed her very carefully yesterday," she said, stopping at the door of Liza's room before entering it. "She is a proud and morose child. She is ashamed of being with us, and of having been thrown over by her father. In my opinion that is the whole secret of her illness."

"How 'thrown over'? Why do you suppose that he has thrown her over?"

"The simple fact that he allowed her to come here to a strange house, and with a man who was also a stranger, or nearly so; or, at all events, with whom his relations were such that——"

"Oh, but I took her myself, almost by force."

Liza was not surprised to see Velchaninoff alone. She only smiled bitterly, and turned her hot face to the wall. She made no reply to his passionate promises to bring her father down to-morrow without fail, or to his timid attempts at consolation.

As soon as Velchaninoff left the sick child's presence, he burst into tears.

The doctor did not arrive until evening. On seeing the patient he frightened everybody by his very first remark, observing that it was a pity he had not been sent for before.

When informed that the child had only been taken ill last night, he could not believe it at first.

"Well, it all depends upon how this night is passed," he decided at last.

Having made all necessary arrangements, he took his departure, promising to come as early as possible next morning.

Velchaninoff was anxious to stay the night, but Claudia Petrovna begged him to try once more "to bring down that brute of a man."

"Try once more!" cried Velchaninoff, passionately; "why, I'll tie him hand and foot and bring him along myself!"

The idea that he would tie Pavel Pavlovitch up and carry him down in his arms overpowered Velchaninoff, and filled him with impatience to execute his frantic desire.

"I don't feel the slightest bit guilty before him any more," he said to Claudia Petrovna, at parting, "and I withdraw all my servile, abject words of yesterday—all I said to you," he added, wrathfully.

Liza lay with closed eyes, apparently asleep; she seemed to be better. When Velchaninoff bent cautiously over her in order to kiss—if it were but the edge of her bed linen—she suddenly opened her eyes, just as though she had been waiting for him, and whispered, "Take me away!"

It was but a quiet, sad petition—without a trace of yesterday's irritation; but at the same time there was that in her voice which betrayed that she made the request in the full knowledge that it could not be assented to.

No sooner did Velchaninoff, in despair, begin to assure her as tenderly as he could that what she desired was impossible, than she silently closed her eyes and said not another word, just as though she neither saw nor heard him.

Arrived in town Velchaninoff told his man to drive him to the Pokrofsky. It was ten o'clock at night.

Pavel Pavlovitch was not at his lodgings. Velchaninoff waited for him half an hour, walking up and down the passage in a state of feverish impatience. Maria Sisevna assured him at last that Pavel Pavlovitch would not come in until the small hours.

"Well, then, I'll return here before daylight," he said, beside himself with desperation, and he went home to his own rooms.

What was his amazement, when, on arriving at the gate of his house, he learned from Mavra that "yesterday's visitor" had been waiting for him ever since before ten o'clock.

"He's had some tea," she added, "and sent me for wine again—the same wine as yesterday. He gave me the money to buy it with."

CHAPTER IX.

Pavel Pavlovitch had made himself very comfortable. He was sitting in the same chair as he had occupied yesterday, smoking a cigar, and had just poured the fourth and last tumbler of champagne out of the bottle.

The teapot and a half-emptied tumbler of tea stood on the table beside him; his red face beamed with benevolence. He had taken off his coat, and sat in his shirt sleeves.

"Forgive me, dearest of friends," he cried, catching sight of Velchaninoff, and hastening to put on his coat, "I took it off to make myself thoroughly comfortable."

Velchaninoff approached him menacingly.

"You are not quite tipsy yet, are you? Can you understand what is said to you?"

Paul Pavlovitch became a little confused.

"No, not quite. I've been thinking of the dear deceased a bit, but I'm not quite drunk yet."

"Can you understand what I say?"

"My dear sir, I came here on purpose to understand you."

"Very well, then I shall begin at once by telling you that you are an ass, sir!" cried Velchaninoff, at the top of his voice.

"Why, if you begin that way where will you end, I wonder!" said Pavel Pavlovitch, clearly alarmed more than a little.

Velchaninoff did not listen, but roared again,

"Your daughter is dying—she is very ill! Have you thrown her over altogether, or not?"

"Oh, surely she isn't dying yet?"

"I tell you she's ill; very, very ill—dangerously ill."

"What, fits? or——"

"Don't talk nonsense. I tell you she is very dangerously ill. You ought to go down, if only for that reason."

"What, to thank your friends, eh? to return thanks for their hospitality? Of course, quite so; I well understand, Alexey Ivanovitch—dearest of friends!" He suddenly seized Velchaninoff by both hands, and added with intoxicated sentiment, almost melted to tears, "Alexey Ivanovitch, don't shout at me—don't shout at me, please! If you do, I may throw myself into the Neva—I don't know!—and we have such important things to talk over. There's lots of time to go to the Pogoryeltseffs another day."

Velchaninoff did his best to restrain his wrath. "You are drunk, and therefore I don't understand what you are driving at," he said sternly. "I'm ready to come to an explanation with you at any moment you like—delighted!—the the sooner the better. But first let me tell you that I am going to take my own measures to secure you. You will sleep here to-night, and to-morrow I shall take you with me to see Liza. I shall not let you go again. I shall bind you, if necessary, and carry you down myself. How do you like this sofa to sleep on?" he added, panting, and indicating a wide, soft divan opposite his own sofa, against the other wall.

"Oh—anything will do for me!"

"Very well, you shall have this sofa. Here, take these things—here are sheets, blankets, pillow" (Velchaninoff pulled all these things out of a cupboard, and tossed them impatiently to Pavel Pavlovitch, who humbly stood and received them); "now then, make your bed,—come, bustle up!"

Pavel Pavlovitch laden with bed clothes had been standing in the middle of the room with a stupid drunken leer on his face, irresolute; but at Velchaninoff's second bidding he hurriedly began the task of making his bed, moving the table away from in front of it, and smoothing a sheet over the seat of the divan. Velchaninoff approached to help him. He was more or less gratified with his guest's alarm and submission.

"Now, drink up that wine and lie down!" was his next command. He felt that he *must* order this man about, he could not help himself. "I suppose you took upon yourself to order this wine, did you?"

"I did—I did, sir! I sent for the wine, Alexey Ivanovitch, because I knew *you* would not send out again!"

"Well, it's a good thing that you knew that; but I desire that you should know still more. I give you notice that I have taken my own measures for the future, I'm not going to put up with any more of your antics."

"Oh, I quite understand, Alexey Ivanovitch, that that sort of thing could only happen once!" said Pavel Pavlovitch, giggling feebly.

At this reply Velchaninoff, who had been marching up and down the room stopped solemnly before Pavel Pavlovitch.

"Pavel Pavlovitch," he said, "speak plainly! You are a clever fellow—I admit the fact freely,—but I assure you you are going on a false track now. Speak plainly, and act like an honest man, and I give you my word of honour that I will answer all you wish to know."

Pavel Pavlovitch grinned his disagreeable grin (which always drove Velchaninoff wild) once more.

"Wait!" cried the latter. "No humbug now, please; I see through you. I repeat that I give you my word of honour to reply candidly to anything you may like to ask, and to give you every sort of satisfaction—reasonable or even unreasonable—that you please. *Oh!* how I wish I could make you understand me!"

"Since you are so very kind," began Pavel Pavlovitch, cautiously bending towards him, "I may tell you that I am very much interested as to what you said yesterday about 'bird of prey'?"

Velchaninoff spat on the ground in utter despair and disgust, and recommenced his walk up and down the room, quicker than ever.

"No, no, Alexey Ivanovitch, don't spurn my question; you don't know how interested I am in it. I assure you I came here on purpose to ask you about it. I know I'm speaking indistinctly, but you'll forgive me that. I've read the expression before. Tell me now, was Bagantoff a 'bird of prey,' or—the other thing? How is one to distinguish one from the other?"

Velchaninoff went on walking up and down, and answered nothing for some minutes.

"The bird of prey, sir," he began suddenly, stopping in front of Pavel Pavlovitch, and speaking vehemently, "is the man who would poison Bagantoff while drinking champagne with him under the cloak of goodfellowship, as you did with me yesterday, instead of escorting his wretched body to the burial ground as you did—the deuce only knows why, and with what dirty, mean, underhand, petty motives, which only recoil upon yourself and make you viler than you already are. Yes, sir, recoil upon yourself!"

"Quite so, quite so, I oughtn't to have gone," assented Pavel Pavlovitch, "but aren't you a little——"

"The bird of prey is not a man who goes and learns his grievance off by heart, like a lesson, and whines it about the place, grimacing and posing, and hanging it round other people's necks, and who spends all his time in such pettifogging. Is it true you wanted to hang yourself? Come, is it true, or not?"

"I—I don't know—I may have when I was drunk—I don't remember. You see, Alexey Ivanovitch, it wouldn't be quite nice for me to go poisoning people. I'm too high up in the service, and I have money, too, you know—and I may wish to marry again, who knows."

"Yes; you'd be sent to Siberia, which would be awkward."

"Quite so; though they say the penal servitude is not so bad as it was. But you remind me of an anecdote, Alexey Ivanovitch. I thought of it in the carriage, and meant to tell you afterwards. Well! you may remember Liftsoff at T——. He came while you were there. His younger brother—who is rather a swell, too—was serving at L—— under the governor, and one fine day he happened to quarrel with Colonel Golubenko in the presence of ladies, and of one lady especially. Liftsoff considered himself insulted, but concealed his grievance; and, meanwhile, Golubenko proposed to a certain lady and was accepted. Would you believe it, Liftsoff made great friends with Golubenko, and even volunteered to be best man at his wedding. But when the ceremony was all over, and Liftsoff approached the bridegroom to wish him joy and kiss him, as usual, he took the opportunity of sticking a knife into Golubenko. Fancy! his own best man stuck him! Well, what does the assassin do but run about the room crying. 'Oh! what have I done? Oh! what have I done?' says he, and throws himself on everyone's neck by turns, ladies and all! Ha-ha-ha! He starved to death in Siberia, sir! One is a little sorry for Golubenko; but he recovered, after all."

"I don't understand why you told me that story," said Velchaninoff, frowning heavily.

"Why, because he stuck the other fellow with a knife," giggled Pavel Pavlovitch, "which proves that he was no type, but an ass of a fellow, who could so forget the ordinary manners of society as to hang around ladies' necks, and in the presence of the governor, too—and yet he stuck the other fellow. Ha-ha-ha! He did what he intended to do, that's all, sir!"

"Go to the devil, will you—you and your miserable humbug—you miserable humbug yourself," yelled Velchaninoff, wild with rage and fury, and panting so that he could hardly get his words out. "You think you are going to alarm *me*, do you, you frightener of children—you mean beast—you low scoundrel you?—scoundrel—scoundrel—scoundrel!" He had quite forgotten himself in his rage.

Pavel Pavlovitch shuddered all over; his drunkenness seemed to vanish in an instant; his lips trembled and shook.

"Are you calling *me* a scoundrel, Alexey Ivanovitch—*you—me*?"

But Velchaninoff was himself again now.

"I'll apologise if you like," he said, and relapsed into gloomy silence. After a moment he added, "But only on condition that you yourself agree to speak out fully, and at once."

"In your place I should apologise unconditionally, Alexey Ivanovitch."

"Very well; so be it then." Velchaninoff was silent again for a while. "I apologise," he resumed; "but admit yourself, Pavel Pavlovitch, that I need not feel myself in any way bound to you after this. I mean with regard to *anything*—not only this particular matter."

"All right! Why, what is there to settle between us?" laughed Pavel Pavlovitch, without looking up.

"In that case, so much the better—so much the better. Come, drink up your wine and get into bed, for I shall not let you go now, anyhow."

"Oh, my wine—never mind my wine!" muttered Pavel Pavlovitch; but he went to the table all the same, and took up his tumbler of champagne which had long been poured out. Either he had been drinking copiously before, or there was some other unknown cause at work, but his hand shook so as he drank the wine that a quantity of it was spilled over his waistcoat and the floor. However, he drank it all, to the last drop, as though he could not leave the tumbler without emptying it. He then placed the empty glass on the table, approached his bed, sat down on it, and began to undress.

"I think perhaps I had better *not* sleep here," he said suddenly, with one boot off, and half undressed.

"Well, I *don't* think so," said Velchaninoff, who was walking up and down, without looking at him.

Pavel Pavlovitch finished undressing and lay down. A quarter of an hour later Velchaninoff also got into bed, and put the candle out.

He soon began to doze uncomfortably. Some new trouble seemed to have suddenly come over him and worried him, and at the same time he felt a sensation of shame that he could allow himself to be worried by the new trouble. Velchaninoff was just falling definitely asleep, however, when a rustling sound awoke him. He immediately glanced at Pavel Pavlovitch's bed. The room was quite dark, the blinds being down and curtains drawn; but it seemed to him that Pavel Pavlovitch was not lying in his bed; he seemed to be sitting on the side of it.

"What's the matter?" cried Velchaninoff.

"A ghost, sir," said Pavel Pavlovitch, in a low tone, after a few moments of silence.

"What? What sort of a ghost?"

"Th—there—in that room—just at the door, I seemed to see a ghost!"

"Whose ghost?" asked Velchaninoff, pausing a minute before putting the question.

"Natalia Vasilievna's!"

Velchaninoff jumped out of bed and walked to the door, whence he could see into the room opposite, across the passage. There were no curtains in that room, so that it was much lighter than his own.

"There's nothing there at all. You are drunk; lie down again!" he said, and himself set the example, rolling his blanket around him.

Pavel Pavlovitch said nothing, but lay down as he was told.

"Did you ever see any ghosts before?" asked Velchaninoff suddenly, ten minutes later.

"I think I saw one once," said Pavel Pavlovitch in the same low voice; after which there was silence once more. Velchaninoff was not sure whether he had been asleep or not, but an hour or so had passed, when suddenly he was wide awake again. Was it a rustle that awoke him? He could not tell; but one thing was evident—in the midst of the profound darkness of the room something white stood before him; not quite close to him, but about the middle of the room. He sat up in bed, and stared for a full minute.

"Is that you, Pavel Pavlovitch?" he asked. His voice sounded very weak.

There was no reply; but there was not the slightest doubt of the fact that someone was standing there.

"Is that you, Pavel Pavlovitch?" cried Velchaninoff again, louder this time; in fact, so loud that if the former had been asleep in bed he must have started up and answered.

But there was no reply again. It seemed to Velchaninoff that the white figure had approached nearer to him.

Then something strange happened; something seemed to "let go" within Velchaninoff's system, and he commenced to shout at the top of his voice, just as he had done once before this evening, in the wildest and maddest way possible, panting so that he could hardly articulate his words: "If you—drunken ass that you are—dare to think that you could frighten *me*, I'll turn my face to the wall, and not look round once the whole night, to show you how little I am afraid of you—a fool like you—if you stand there from now till morning! I despise you!" So saying, Velchaninoff twisted round with his face to the wall, rolled his blanket round him, and lay motionless, as though turned to stone. A deathlike stillness supervened.

Did the ghost stand where it was, or had it moved? He could not tell; but his heart beat, and beat, and beat—At least five minutes went by, and then, not a couple of paces from his bed, there came the feeble voice of Pavel Pavlovitch:

"I got up, Alexey Ivanovitch, to look for a little water. I couldn't find any, and was just going to look about nearer your bed——"

"Then why didn't you answer when I called?" cried Velchaninoff angrily, after a minute's pause.

"I was frightened; you shouted so, you alarmed me!"

"You'll find a caraffe and glass over there, on the little table. Light a candle."

"Oh, I'll find it without. You'll forgive me, Alexey Ivanovitch, for frightening you so; I felt thirsty so suddenly."

But Velchaninoff said nothing. He continued to lie with his face to the wall, and so he lay all night, without turning round once. Was he anxious to keep his word and show his contempt for Pavel Pavlovitch? He did not know himself why he did it; his nervous agitation and perturbation were such that he could not sleep for a long while, he felt quite delirious. At last he fell asleep, and awoke at past nine o'clock next morning. He started up just as though someone had struck him, and sat down on the side of his bed. But Pavel Pavlovitch was not to be seen. His empty, rumpled bed was there, but its occupant had flown before daybreak.

"I thought so!" cried Velchaninoff, bringing the palm of his right hand smartly to his forehead.

CHAPTER X.

The doctor's anxiety was justified; Liza grew worse, so much so that it was clear she was far more seriously ill than Velchaninoff and Claudia Petrovna had thought the day before.

When the former arrived in the morning, Liza was still conscious, though burning with fever. He assured his friend Claudia, afterwards, that the child had smiled at him and held out her little hot hand. Whether she actually did so, or whether he so much longed for her to do so that he imagined it done, is uncertain.

By the evening, however, Liza was quite unconscious, and so she remained during the whole of her illness. Ten days after her removal to the country she died.

This was a sad period for Velchaninoff; the Pogoryeltseffs were quite anxious on his account. He was with them for the greater part of the time, and during the last few days of the little one's illness, he used to sit all alone for hours together in some corner, apparently thinking of nothing. Claudia Petrovna would attempt to distract him but he hardly answered her, and conversation was clearly painful to him. Claudia was quite surprised that "all this" should affect him so deeply.

The children were the best consolation and distraction for him; with them he could even laugh and play at intervals. Every hour, at least, he would rise from his chair and creep on tip-toes to the sick-room to look at the little invalid. Sometimes he imagined that she knew him; he had no hope for her recovery—none of the family had any hope; but he never left the precincts of the child's chamber, sitting principally in the next room.

Twice, however, he had evinced great activity of a sudden; he had jumped up and started off for town, where he had called upon all the most eminent doctors of the place, and arranged consultations between them. The last consultation was on the day before Liza's death.

Claudia Petrovna had spoken seriously to him a day or two since, as to the absolute necessity of hunting up Pavel Pavlovitch Trusotsky, because in case of anything happening to Liza, she could not be buried without certain documents from him.

Velchaninoff promised to write to him, and did write a couple of lines, which he took to the Pokrofsky. Pavel Pavlovitch was not at home, as usual, but he left the letter to the care of Maria Sisevna.

At last Liza died—on a lovely summer evening, just as the sun was setting; and only then did Velchaninoff rouse himself.

When the little one was laid out, all covered with flowers, and dressed in a fair white frock belonging to one of Claudia Petrovna's children, Velchaninoff came up to the lady of the house, and told her with flashing eyes that he would now go and fetch the murderer. Regardless of all advice to put off his search until to-morrow he started for town immediately.

He knew where to find Pavel Pavlovitch. He had not been in town exclusively to find the doctors those two days. Occasionally, while watching the dying child, he had been struck with the idea that if he could only find and bring down Pavel Pavlovitch she might hear his voice and be called back, as it were, from the darkness of delirium; at such moments he had been seized with desperation, and twice he had started up and driven wildly off to town in order to find Pavel Pavlovitch.

The latter's room was the same as before, but it was useless to look for him there, for, according to Maria Sisevna's report, he was now two or three days absent from home at a stretch, and was generally to be found with some friends in the Voznecensky.

Arrived in town about ten o'clock, Velchaninoff went straight to these latter people, and securing the services of a member of the family to assist in finding Pavel Pavlovitch, set out on his quest. He did not know what he should do with Pavel Pavlovitch when found, whether he should kill him then and there, or simply inform him of the death of the child, and of the necessity for his assistance in arranging for her funeral. After a long and fruitless search Velchaninoff found Pavel Pavlovitch quite accidentally; he was quarrelling with some person in the street—tipsy as usual, and seemed to be getting the worst of the controversy, which appeared to be about a money claim.

On catching sight of Velchaninoff, Pavel Pavlovitch stretched out his arms to him and begged for help; while his opponent—observing Velchaninoff's athletic figure—made off. Pavel Pavlovitch shook his fist after him triumphantly, and hooted at him with cries of victory; but this amusement was brought to a sudden conclusion by Velchaninoff, who, impelled by some mysterious motive—which he could not analyse, took him by the shoulders, and began to shake him violently, so violently that his teeth chattered.

Pavel Pavlovitch ceased to shout after his opponent, and gazed with a stupid tipsy expression of alarm at his new antagonist. Velchaninoff, having shaken him till he was tired, and not knowing what to do next with him, set him down violently on the pavement, backwards.

"Liza is dead!" he said.

Pavel Pavlovitch sat on the pavement and stared, he was too far gone to take in the news. At last he seemed to realize.

"Dead!" he whispered, in a strange inexplicable tone. Velchaninoff was not sure whether his face was simply twitching, or whether he was trying to grin in his usual disagreeable way; but the next moment the drunkard raised his shaking hand to cross himself. He then struggled to his feet and staggered off, appearing totally oblivious of the fact that such a person as Velchaninoff existed.

However, the latter very soon pursued and caught him, seizing him once more by the shoulder.

"Do you understand, you drunken sot, that without you the funeral arrangements cannot be made?" he shouted, panting with rage.

Pavel Pavlovitch turned his head.

"The artillery—lieutenant—don't you remember him?" he muttered, thickly.

"*What?*" cried Velchaninoff, with a shudder.

"He's her father—find him! he'll bury her!"

"You liar! You said that out of pure malice. I thought you'd invent something of the sort!"

Quite beside himself with passion Velchaninoff brought down his powerful fist with all his strength on Pavel Pavlovitch's head; another moment and he might have followed up the blow and slain the man as he stood. His victim never winced, but he turned upon Velchaninoff a face of such insane terrible passion, that his whole visage looked distorted.

"Do you understand Russian?" he asked more firmly, as though his fury had chased away the effects of drunkenness. "Very well, then, you are a——!" (here followed a specimen of the very vilest language which the Russian tongue could furnish); "and now you can go back to her!" So saying he tore himself from Velchaninoff's grasp, nearly knocking himself over with the effort, and staggered away. Velchaninoff did not follow him.

Next day, however, a most respectable-looking middle-aged man arrived at the Pogoryeltseft's house, in civil uniform, and handed to Claudia Petrovna a packet addressed to her "from Pavel Pavlovitch Trusotsky."

In this packet was a sum of three hundred roubles, together with all certificates necessary for Liza's funeral. Pavel Pavlovitch had written a short note couched in very polite and correct phraseology, and thanking Claudia Petrovna sincerely "for her great kindness to the orphan—kindness for which heaven alone could recompense her." He added rather confusedly that severe illness prevented his personal presence at the funeral of his "tenderly loved and unfortunate daughter," but that he "felt he could repose all confidence (as to the ceremony being fittingly performed) in the angelic goodness of Claudia Petrovna." The three hundred roubles, he explained, were to go towards the funeral and other expenses. If there should be any of the money left after defraying all charges, Claudia Petrovna was requested to spend the same in prayers for the repose of the soul of the deceased.

Nothing further was to be discovered by questioning the messenger; and it was soon evident that the latter knew nothing, excepting that he had only consented to act as bearer of the packet, in response to the urgent appeal of Pavel Pavlovitch.

Pogoryeltseff was a little offended by the offer of money for expenses, and would have sent it back, but Claudia Petrovna suggested that a receipt should be taken from the cemetery authorities for the cost of the funeral (since one could not well refuse to allow a man to bury his own child), together with a document undertaking that the rest of the three hundred roubles should be spent in prayer for the soul of Liza.

Velchaninoff afterwards posted an envelope containing these two papers to Trusotsky's lodging.

After the funeral Velchaninoff disappeared from the country altogether. He wandered about town for a whole fortnight, knocking up against people as he went blindly through the streets. Now and then he spent a whole day lying in his bed, oblivious of the most ordinary needs and occupations; the Pogoryeltseffs often invited him to their house, and he invariably promised to come, and as invariably forgot all about it. Claudia Petrovna went as far as to call for him herself, but she did not find him at home. The same thing happened with his lawyer, who had some good news to tell him. The difference with his opponent had been settled advantageously for Velchaninoff, the former having accepted a small bonification and renounced his claim to the property in dispute. All that was wanting was the formal acquiescence of Velchaninoff himself.

Finding him at home at last, after many endeavours, the lawyer was excessively surprised to discover that Velchaninoff was as callous and cool as to the result of his (the lawyer's) labours, as he had before been ardent and excitable.

The hottest days of July had now arrived, but Velchaninoff was oblivious of everything. His grief swelled and ached at his heart like some internal boil; his greatest sorrow was that Liza had not had time to know him, and died without ever guessing how fondly he loved her. The sweet new beacon of his life, which had glimmered for a short while within his heart, was extinguished once more, and lost in eternal gloom.

The whole object of his existence, as he now told himself at every moment, should have been that Liza might feel his love about her and around her, each day, each hour, each moment of her life.

"There can be no higher aim or object than this in life," he thought, in gloomy ecstasy. "If there be other aims in life, none can be holier or better than this of mine. All my old unworthy life should have been purified and atoned for by my love for Liza; in place of myself—my sinful, worn-out, useless life—I should have bequeathed to the world a sweet, pure, beautiful being, in whose innocence all my guilt should have been absorbed, and lost, and forgiven, and in her I should have forgiven myself."

Such thoughts would flit through Velchaninoff's head as he mused sorrowfully over the memory of the dead child. He thought over all he had seen of her; he recalled her little face all burning with fever, then lying at rest in her coffin, covered with lovely flowers. He remembered that once he had noticed that one of her fingers was quite black from some bruise or pinch—goodness knows what had made it so, but it was the sight of that little finger which had filled him with longing to go straight away and *murder* Pavel Pavlovitch.

"Do you know what Liza is to me?" Pavel had said, he recollected, one day; and now he understood the exclamation. It was no pretence of love, no posturing and nonsense—it was real love! How, then, could the wretch have been so cruel to a child whom he so dearly loved? He could not bear to think of it, the question was painful, and quite unanswerable.

One day he wandered down—he knew not exactly how—to the cemetery where Liza was buried, and hunted up her grave. This was the first time he had been there since the funeral; he had never dared to go there before, fearing that the visit would be too painful. But strangely enough, when he found the little mound and had bent down and kissed it, he felt happier and lighter at heart than before.

It was a lovely evening, the sun was setting, the tall grass waved about the tombs, and a bee hummed somewhere near him. The flowers and crosses placed on the tomb by Claudia Petrovna were still there. A ray of hope blazed up in his heart for the first time for many a long day. "How light-hearted I feel," he thought, as he felt the spell of the quiet of God's Acre, and the hush of the beautiful still evening. A flow of some indefinable faith in something poured into his heart.

"This is Liza's gift," he thought; "this is Liza herself talking to me!"

It was quite dark when he left the cemetery and turned his steps homewards.

Not far from the gate of the burial ground there stood a small inn or public-house, and through the open windows he could see the people inside sitting at tables. It instantly struck Velchaninoff that one of the guests, sitting nearest to the window, was Pavel Pavlovitch, and that the latter had seen him and was observing him curiously.

He went on further, but before very long he heard footsteps pursuing him. It was, of course, Pavel Pavlovitch. Probably the unusually serene and peaceful expression of Velchaninoff's face as he went by had attracted and encouraged him.

He soon caught Velchaninoff up, and smiled timidly at him, but not with the old drunken grin. He did not appear to be in the smallest degree drunk.

"Good evening," said Pavel Pavlovitch.

"How d'ye do?" replied Velchaninoff.

CHAPTER XI.

By replying thus to Pavel Pavlovitch's greeting Velchaninoff surprised himself. It seemed strange indeed to him that he should now meet this man without any feeling of anger, and that there should be something quite novel in his feelings towards Pavel Pavlovitch—a sort of call to new relations with him.

"What a lovely evening!" said Pavel Pavlovitch, looking observantly into the other's eyes.

"So you haven't gone away yet!" murmured Velchaninoff, not in a tone of inquiry, but as though musing upon the fact as he continued to walk on.

"I've been a good deal delayed; but I've obtained my petition, my new post, with rise of salary. I'm off the day after to-morrow for certain."

"What? You've obtained the new situation?"

"And why not?" said Pavel Pavlovitch, with a crooked smile.

"Oh, I meant nothing particular by my remark!" said Velchaninoff frowning, and glancing sidelong at his companion. To his surprise Pavel Pavlovitch, both in dress and appearance, even down to the hat with the crape band, was incomparably neater and tidier-looking than he was wont to be a fortnight since.

"Why was he sitting in the public-house then?" thought Velchaninoff. This fact puzzled him much.

"I wished to let you know of my other great joy, Alexey Ivanovitch!" resumed Pavel.

"Joy?"

"I'm going to marry."

"What?"

"Yes, sir! after sorrow, joy! It is ever thus in life. Oh! Alexey Ivanovitch, I should so much like if—but you look as though you were in a great hurry."

"Yes, I am in a hurry, and I am ill besides." He felt as though he would give anything to get rid of the man; the feeling of readiness to develop new and better relations with him had vanished in a moment.

"I should so much like——"

Pavel Pavlovitch did not finish his sentence; Velchaninoff kept silence and waited.

"In that case, perhaps another time—if we should happen to meet."

"Yes, yes, another time," said Velchaninoff quickly, continuing to move along, and never looking at his companion.

Nothing was said for another minute or two. Pavel Pavlovitch continued to trot alongside.

"In that case, *au revoir*," he blurted, at last. "*Au revoir!* I hope——"

Velchaninoff did not think it necessary to hear him complete his sentence; he left Pavel, and returned home much agitated. The meeting with "that fellow" had been too much for his present state of mind. As he lay down upon his bed the thought came over him once more: "Why was that fellow there, close to the cemetery?" He determined to go down to the Pogoryeltseffs' next morning; not that he felt inclined to go—any sympathy was intolerably painful to him,—but they had been so kind and so anxious about him, that he must really make up his mind to go. But next day, while finishing his breakfast, he felt terribly disinclined for the visit; he felt, as it were, shy of meeting them for the first time after his grief. "Shall I go or not?" he was saying to himself, as he sat at his table. When suddenly, to his extreme amazement, in walked Pavel Pavlovitch.

In spite of yesterday's *rencontre*, Velchaninoff could not have believed that this man would ever enter his rooms again; and when he now saw him appear, he gazed at him in such absolute astonishment, that he simply did not know what to say. But Pavel Pavlovitch took the management of the matter into his own hands; he said "good morning," and sat down in the very same chair which he had occupied on his last visit, three weeks since.

This circumstance reminded Velchaninoff too painfully of that visit, and he glared at his visitor with disgust and some agitation.

"You are surprised, I see!" said Pavel Pavlovitch, reading the other's expression.

He seemed to be both freer, more at his ease, and yet more timid than yesterday. His outward appearance was very curious to behold; for Pavel Pavlovitch was not only *neatly* dressed, he was "got up" in the pink of fashion. He had on a neat summer overcoat, with a pair of light trousers and a white waistcoat; his gloves, his gold eye-glasses (quite a new acquisition), and his linen were quite above all criticism; he wafted an odour of sweet scent when he moved. He looked funny, but his appearance awakened strange thoughts besides.

"Of course I have surprised you, Alexey Ivanovitch," he said, twisting himself about; "I see it. But in my opinion there should be a something exalted, something higher—untouched and unattainable by petty discords, or the ordinary conditions of life, between man and man. Don't you agree with me, sir?"

"Pavel Pavlovitch, say what you have to say as quickly as you can, and without further ceremony," said Velchaninoff, frowning angrily.

"In a couple of words, sir," said Pavel, hurriedly, "I am going to be married, and I am now off to see my bride—at once. She lives in the country; and what I desire is, the profound honour of introducing *you* to the family, sir; in fact, I have come here to petition you, sir" (Pavel Pavlovitch bent his head deferentially)—"to beg you to go down with me."

"Go down with you? Where to?" cried the other, his eyes starting out of his head.

"To their house in the country, sir. Forgive me, my dear sir, if I am too agitated, and confuse my words; but I am so dreadfully afraid of hearing you refuse me."

He looked at Velchaninoff plaintively.

"You wish me to accompany you to see your bride?" said Velchaninoff, staring keenly at Pavel Pavlovitch; he could not believe either his eyes or his ears.

"Yes—yes, sir!" murmured Pavel, who had suddenly become timid to a painful degree. "Don't be angry, Alexey Ivanovitch, it is not my audacity that prompts me to ask you this; I do it with all humility, and conscious of the unusual nature of my petition. I—I thought perhaps you would not refuse my humble request."

"In the first place, the thing is absolutely out of the question," said Velchaninoff, turning away in considerable mental perturbation.

"It is only my immeasurable longing that prompts me to ask you. I confess I have a reason for desiring it, which reason I propose to reveal to you afterwards; just now I——"

"The thing is quite impossible, however you may look at it. You must admit yourself that it is so!" cried Velchaninoff. Both men had risen from their chairs in the excitement of the conversation.

"Not at all—not at all; it is quite possible, sir. In the first place, I merely propose to introduce you as my friend; and in the second place, you know the family already, the Zachlebnikoff's—State Councillor Zachlebnikoff!"

"What? how so?" cried Velchaninoff. This was the very man whom he had so often tried to find at home, and whom he never succeeded in hunting down—the very lawyer who had acted for his adversary in the late legal proceedings.

"Why, certainly—certainly!" cried Pavel Pavlovitch, apparently taking heart at Velchaninoff's extreme display of amazement. "The very same man whom I saw you talking to in the street one day; when I watched you from the other side of the road, I was waiting my turn to speak to him then. We served in the same department twelve years since. I had no thought of all this that day I saw you with him; the whole idea is quite new and sudden—only a week old."

"But—excuse me; why, surely this is a most respectable family, isn't it?" asked Velchaninoff, naïvely.

"Well, and what if it is respectable?" said Pavel, with a twist.

"Oh, no—of course, I meant nothing; but, so far as I could judge from what I saw, there——"

"They remember—they remember your coming down," cried Pavel delightedly. "I told them all sorts of flattering things about you."

"But, look here, how are you to marry within three months of your late wife's death?"

"Oh! the wedding needn't be at once. The wedding can come off in nine or ten months, so that I shall have been in mourning exactly a year. Believe me, my dear sir, it's all most charming—first place, Fedosie Petrovitch has known me since I was a child; he knew my late wife; he knows how much income I have; he knows all about my little private capital, and all about my new increase of salary. So that you see the whole thing is a mere matter of weights and scales."

"Is she a daughter of his, then?"

"I'll tell you all about it," said Pavel, licking his lips with pleasure. "May I smoke a cigarette? Now, you see, men like Fedosie Petrovitch Zachlebnikoff are much valued in the State; but, excepting for a few perquisites allowed them, the pay is wretched; they live well enough, but they cannot possibly lay by money. Now, imagine, this man has eight daughters and only one little boy: if he were to die there would be nothing but a wretched little pension to keep the lot of them. Just imagine now—*boots* alone for such a family, eh? Well, out of these eight girls five are marriageable, the eldest is twenty-four already (a splendid girl, she is, you shall see her for yourself). The sixth is a girl of fifteen, still at school. Well, all those five elder girls have to be trotted about and shown off, and what does all that sort of thing cost the poor father, sir? They must be married. Then suddenly I appear on the scene—the first probable bridegroom in the family, and they all know that I have money. Well, there you are, sir—the thing's done."

Pavel Pavlovitch was intoxicated with enthusiasm.

"Are you engaged to the eldest?"

"N—no;—not the eldest. I am wooing the sixth girl, the one at school."

"What?" cried Velchaninoff, laughing in spite of himself. "Why, you say yourself she's only fifteen years old."

"Fifteen *now*, sir; but she'll be sixteen in nine months—sixteen and three months—so why not? It wouldn't be quite nice to make the engagement public just yet, though; so there's to be nothing formal at present, it's only a private arrangement between the parents and myself so far. Believe me, my dear sir, the whole thing is apple-pie, regular and charming."

"Then it isn't quite settled yet?"

"Oh, *quite* settled—quite settled. Believe me, it's all as right and tight as——"

"Does *she* know?"

"Well, you see, just for form's sake, it is not actually talked about—to her I mean,—but she *knows* well enough. Oh! now you *will* make me happy this once, Alexey Ivanovitch, won't you?" he concluded, with extreme timidity of voice and manner.

"But why should *I* go with you? However," added Velchaninoff impatiently, "as I am not going in any case, I don't see why I should hear any reasons you may adduce for my accompanying you."

"Alexey Ivanovitch!——"

"Oh, come! you don't suppose I am going to sit down in a carriage with you alongside, and drive down there! Come, just think for yourself!"

The feeling of disgust and displeasure which Pavel Pavlovitch had awakened in him before, had now started into life again after the momentary distraction of the man's foolery about his bride. He felt that in another minute or two he might kick the fellow out before he realized what he was doing. He felt angry with himself for some reason or other.

"Sit down, Alexey Ivanovitch, sit down! You shall not repent it!" said Pavel Pavlovitch in a wheedling voice. "No, no, no!" he added, deprecating the impatient gesture which Velchaninoff made at this moment. "Alexey Ivanovitch, I entreat you to pause before you decide definitely. I see you have quite misunderstood me. I quite realize that I am not for you, nor you for me! I am not quite so absurd as to be unaware of that fact. The service I ask of you now shall not compromise you in any way for the future. I am going away the day after to-morrow, for certain; let this one day be an exceptional one for me, sir. I came to you founding my hopes upon the generosity and nobility of your heart, Alexey Ivanovitch—upon those special tender feelings which may, perhaps, have been aroused in you by late events. Am I explaining myself clearly, sir; or do you still misunderstand me?"

The agitation of Pavel Pavlovitch was increasing with every moment.

Velchaninoff gazed curiously at him.

"You ask a service of me," he said thoughtfully, "and insist strongly upon my performance of it. This is very suspicious, in my opinion; I must know more."

"The whole service I ask is merely that you will come with me; and I promise, when we return that I will lay bare my heart to you as though we were at a confessional. Trust me this once, Alexey Ivanovitch!"

But Velchaninoff still held out, and the more obstinately because he was conscious of a certain worrying feeling which he had had ever since Pavel Pavlovitch began to talk about his bride. Whether this feeling was simple curiosity, or something quite inexplicable, he knew not. Whatever it was it urged him to agree, and go. And the more the instinct urged him, the more he resisted it.

He sat and thought for a long time, his head resting on his hand, while Pavel Pavlovitch buzzed about him and continued to repeat his arguments.

"Very well," he said at last, "very well, I'll go." He was agitated almost to trembling pitch. Pavel was radiant.

"Then, Alexey Ivanovitch, change your clothes—dress up, will you? Dress up in your own style—you know so well how to do it."

Pavel Pavlovitch danced about Velchaninoff as he dressed. His state of mind was exuberantly blissful.

"What in the world does the fellow mean by it all?" thought Velchaninoff.

"I'm going to ask you one more favour yet, Alexey Ivanovitch," cried the other. "You've consented to come; you must be my guide, sir, too."

"For instance, how?"

"Well, for instance, here's an important question—the crape. Which ought I to do—tear it off, or leave it on?"

"Just as you like."

"No, I want your opinion. What should you do yourself, if you were wearing crape, under the circumstances? My own idea was, that if I left it on, I should be giving a proof of the fidelity of my affections. A very flattering recommendation, eh, sir?"

"Oh, take it off, of course."

"Do you really think it's a matter of 'of course'?" Pavel Pavlovitch reflected. "No," he continued, "do you know, I think I'd rather leave it on."

"Well, do as you like! He doesn't trust me, at all events, which is one good thing," thought Velchaninoff.

They left the house at last. Pavel looked over his companion's smart costume with intense satisfaction. Velchaninoff was greatly surprised at Pavel's conduct, but not less so at his own. At the gate there stood a very superior open carriage.

"H'm! so you had a carriage in waiting, had you? Then you were quite convinced that I would consent to come down with you, I suppose?"

"I took the carriage for my own use, but I was nearly sure you would come," said Pavel Pavlovitch, who wore the air of a man whose cup of happiness is full to the brim.

"Don't you think you are a little too sanguine in trusting so much to my benevolence?" asked Velchaninoff, as they took their seats and started. He smiled as he spoke, but his heart was full of annoyance.

"Well, Alexey Ivanovitch, it is not for *you* to call me a fool for that," replied Pavel, firmly and impressively.

"H'm! and Liza?" thought Velchaninoff, but he chased the idea away, he felt as though it were sacrilege to think of her here; and immediately another thought came in, namely, how small, how petty a creature he must be himself to harbour such a thought—such a mean, paltry sentiment in connection with Liza's sacred name. So angry was he, that he felt as though he must stop the carriage and get out, even though it cost him a struggle with Pavel Pavlovitch to do so.

But at this moment Pavel spoke, and the old feeling of desire to go with him re-entered his soul. "Alexey Ivanovitch," Pavel said, "are you a judge of articles of value?"

"What sort of articles?"

"Diamonds."

"Yes."

"I wish to take down a present with me. What do you think? Ought I to give her one, or not?"

"Quite unnecessary, I should think."

"But I wish to do it, badly. The only thing is, what shall I give?—a whole set, brooch, ear-rings, bracelet, and all, or only one article?"

"How much do you wish to spend?"

"Oh, four or five hundred roubles."

"Bosh!"

"What, too much?"

"Buy one bracelet for about a hundred."

This advice depressed Pavel Pavlovitch; he grew wondrous melancholy. He was terribly anxious to spend a lot of money, and buy the whole set. He insisted upon the necessity of doing so.

A shop was reached and entered, and Pavel bought a bracelet after all, and that not the one he chose himself, but the one which his companion fixed upon. Pavel wished to buy both. When the shopman, who originally asked one hundred and seventy five, let the bracelet go for a hundred and fifty roubles, Pavel Pavlovitch was anything but pleased. He was most anxious to spend a lot of money on the young lady, and would have gladly paid two hundred roubles for the same goods, on the slightest encouragement.

"It doesn't matter, my being in a hurry to give her presents, does it?" he began excitedly, when they were back in the carriage, and rolling along once more. "They are not 'swells' at all; they live most simply. Innocence loves presents," he continued, smiling cunningly. "You laughed just now, Alexey Ivanovitch, when I said that the girl was only fifteen; but, you know, what specially struck me about her was, that she still goes to school, with a sweet little bag in her hand, containing copy books and pencils. Ha-ha-ha! It was the little satchel that 'fetched' me. I do love innocence, Alexey Ivanovitch. I don't care half so much for good looks as for innocence. Fancy, she and her friend were sitting in the corner there, the other day, and roared with laughter because the cat jumped from a cupboard on to the sofa, and fell down all of a heap. Why, it smells of fresh apples, that does, sir. Shall I take off the crape, eh?"

"Do as you like!"

"Well, I'll take it off!" He took his hat, tore the crape off, and threw the latter into the road.

Velchaninoff remarked that as he put his hat on his bald head once more, he wore an expression of the simplest and frankest hope and delight.

"Is he *really* that sort of man?" thought Velchaninoff with annoyance. "He surely *can't* be trundling me down here without some underhand motive—impossible! He *can't* be trusting entirely to my generosity?" This last idea seemed to fill him with indignation. "What *is* this clown of a fellow?" he continued to reflect. "Is he a fool, an idiot, or simply a 'permanent husband'? I can't make head or tail of it all!"

CHAPTER XII.

The Zachlebnikoffs were certainly, as Velchaninoff had expressed it, a most respectable family. Zachlebnikoff himself was a most eminently dignified and "solid" gentleman to look at. What Pavel Pavlovitch had said as to their resources was, however, quite true; they lived well, but if paterfamilias were to die, it would be very awkward for the rest.

Old Zachlebnikoff received Velchaninoff most cordially. He was no longer the legal opponent; he appeared now in a far more agreeable guise.

"I congratulate you," he said at once, "upon the issue. I did my best to arrange it so, and your lawyer was a capital fellow to deal with. You have your sixty thousand without trouble or worry, you see; and if we hadn't squared it we might have fought on for two or three years."

Velchaninoff was introduced to the lady of the house as well—an elderly, simple-looking, worn woman. Then the girls began to troop in, one by one and occasionally two together. But, somehow, there seemed to be even more than Velchaninoff had been led to expect; ten or a dozen were collected already—he could not count them exactly. It turned out that some were friends from the neighbouring houses.

The Zachlebnikoffs' country house was a large wooden structure of no particular style of architecture, but handsome enough, and was possessed of a fine large garden. There were, however, two or three other houses built round the latter, so that the garden was common property for all, which fact resulted in great intimacy between the Zachlebnikoff girls and the young ladies of the neighbouring houses.

Velchaninoff discovered, almost from the first moment, that his arrival—in the capacity of Pavel Pavlovitch's friend, desiring an introduction to the family—was expected, and looked forward to as a solemn and important occasion.

Being an expert in such matters he very soon observed that there was even more than this in his reception. Judging from the extra politeness of the parents, and by the exceeding smartness of the young ladies, he could not help suspecting that Pavel Pavlovitch had been improving the occasion, and that he had—not, of course, in so many words—given to understand that Velchaninoff was a single man—dull and disconsolate, and had represented him as likely enough at any moment to change his manner of living and set up an establishment, especially as he had just come in for a considerable inheritance. He thought that Katerina Fedosievna, the eldest girl—twenty-four years of age, and a splendid girl according to Pavel's description—seemed rather "got up to kill," from the look of her. She was eminent, even among her well-dressed sisters, for special elegance of costume, and for a certain originality about the make-up of her abundant hair.

The rest of the girls all looked as though they were well aware that Velchaninoff was making acquaintance with the family "for Katie," and had come down "to have a look at her." Their looks and words all strengthened the impression that they were acting with this supposition in view, as the day went on.

Katerina Fedosievna was a fine tall girl, rather plump, and with an extremely pleasing face. She seemed to be of a quiet, if not actually sleepy, disposition.

"Strange, that such a fine girl should be unmarried," thought Velchaninoff, as he watched her with much satisfaction.

All the sisters were nice-looking, and there were several pretty faces among the friends assembled. Velchaninoff was much diverted by the presence of all these young ladies.

Nadejda Fedosievna, the school-girl and bride elect of Pavel Pavlovitch, had not as yet condescended to appear. Velchaninoff awaited her coming with a degree of impatience which surprised and amused him. At last she came, and came with effect, too, accompanied by a lively girl, her friend—Maria Nikitishna—who was considerably older than herself and a very old friend of the family, having been governess in a neighbouring house for some years. She was quite one of the family, and boasted of about twenty-three years of age. She was much esteemed by all the girls, and evidently acted at present as guide, philosopher, and friend to Nadia (Nadejda). Velchaninoff saw at the first glance that all the girls were against Pavel Pavlovitch, friends and all; and when Nadia came in, it did not take him long to discover that she absolutely *hated* him. He observed, further, that Pavel Pavlovitch either did not, or *would not*, notice this fact.

Nadia was the prettiest of all the girls—a little *brunette*, with an impudent audacious expression; she might have been a Nihilist from the independence of her look. The sly little creature had a pair of flashing eyes and a most charming smile, though as often as not her smile was more full of mischief and wickedness than of amiability; her lips and teeth were wonders; she was slender but well put together, and the expression of her face was thoughtful though at the same time childish.

"Fifteen years old" was imprinted in every feature of her face and every motion of her body. It appeared afterwards that Pavel Pavlovitch had actually seen the girl for the first time with a little satchel in her hand, coming back from school. She had ceased to carry the satchel since that day.

The present brought down by Pavel Pavlovitch proved a failure, and was the cause of a very painful impression.

Pavel Pavlovitch no sooner saw his bride elect enter the room than he approached her with a broad grin on his face. He gave his present with the preface that he "offered it in recognition of the agreeable sensation experienced by him at his last visit upon the occasion of Nadejda Fedosievna singing a certain song to the pianoforte," and there he stopped in confusion and stood before her lost and miserable, shoving the jeweller's box into her hand. Nadia, however, would not take the present, and drew her hands away.

She approached her mother imperiously (the latter looked much put out), and said aloud: "I won't take it, mother." Nadia was blushing with shame and anger.

"Take it and say 'thank you' to Pavel Pavlovitch for it," said her father quietly but firmly. He was very far from pleased.

"Quite unnecessary, quite unnecessary!" he muttered to Pavel Pavlovitch.

Nadia, seeing there was nothing else to be done, took the case and curtsied—just as children do, giving a little bob down and then a bob up again, as if she had been on springs.

One of the sisters came across to look at the present whereupon Nadia handed it over to her unopened, thereby showing that she did not care so much as to look at it herself.

The bracelet was taken out and handed around from one to the other of the company; but all examined it silently, and some even ironically, only the mother of the family muttered that the bracelet was "very pretty."

Pavel Pavlovitch would have been delighted to see the earth open and swallow him up.

Velchaninoff helped the wretched man out of the mess. He suddenly began to talk loudly and eloquently about the first thing that struck him, and before five minutes had passed he had won the attention of everyone in the room. He was a wonderfully clever society talker. He had the knack of putting on an air of absolute sincerity, and of impressing his hearers with the belief that he considered them equally sincere; he was able to act the simple, careless, and happy young fellow to perfection. He was a master of the art of interlarding his talk with occasional flashes of real wit, apparently spontaneous but actually pre-arranged, and very likely *stale*, in so far that he had himself made the joke before.

But to-day he was particularly successful; he felt that he must talk on and talk well, and he knew that before many moments were past he should succeed in monopolizing all eyes and all ears—that no joke should be laughed at but his own, and no voice heard but his.

And sure enough the spell of his presence seemed to produce a wonderful effect; in a while the talking and laughter became general, with Velchaninoff as the centre and motor of all. Mrs. Zachlebnikoff's kind face lighted up with real pleasure, and Katie's pretty eyes were alight with absolute fascination, while her whole visage glowed with delight.

Only Nadia frowned at him, and watched him keenly from beneath her dark lashes. It was clear that she was prejudiced against him. This last fact only roused Velchaninoff to greater exertions. The mischievous Maria Nikitishna, however, as Nadia's ally, succeeded in playing off a successful piece of chaff against Velchaninoff; she pretended that Pavel Pavlovitch had represented Velchaninoff as the friend of his childhood, thereby making the latter out to be some seven or eight years older than he really was. Velchaninoff liked the look of Maria, notwithstanding.

Pavel Pavlovitch was the picture of perplexity. He quite understood the success which his "friend" was achieving, and at first he felt glad and proud of that success, laughing at the jokes and taking a share of the conversation; but for some reason or other he gradually relapsed into thoughtfulness, and thence into melancholy—which fact was sufficiently plain from the expression of his lugubrious and careworn physiognomy.

"Well, my dear fellow, you are the sort of guest one need not exert oneself to entertain," said old Zachlebnikoff at last, rising and making for his private study, where he had business of importance awaiting his attention; "and I was led to believe that you were the most morose of hypochondriacs. Dear me! what mistakes one does make about other people, to be sure!"

There was a grand piano in the room, and Velchaninoff suddenly turned to Nadia and remarked:

"You sing, don't you?"

"Who told you I did?" said Nadia curtly.

"Pavel Pavlovitch."

"It isn't true; I only sing for a joke—I have no voice."

"Oh, but I have no voice either, and yet I sing!"

"Well, you sing to us first, and then I'll sing," said Nadia, with sparkling eyes; "not now though—after dinner. I hate music," she added, "I'm so sick of the piano. We have singing and strumming going on all day here;—and Katie is the only one of us all worth hearing!"

Velchaninoff immediately attacked Katie, and besieged her with petitions to play. This attention from him to her eldest daughter so pleased mamma that she flushed up with satisfaction.

Katie went to the piano, blushing like a school-girl, and evidently much ashamed of herself for blushing; she played some little piece of Haydn's correctly enough but without much expression.

When she had finished Velchaninoff praised the music warmly—Haydn's music generally, and this little piece in particular. He looked at Katie too, with admiration, and his expression seemed to say. "By Jove, you're a fine girl!" So eloquent was his look that everyone in the room was able to read it, and especially Katie herself.

"What a pretty garden you have!" said Velchaninoff after a short pause, looking through the glass doors of the balcony. "Let's all go out; may we?"

"Oh, yes! do let's go out!" cried several voices together. He seemed to have hit upon the very thing most desired by all.

So they all adjourned into the garden, and walked about there until dinner-time; and Velchaninoff had the opportunity of making closer acquaintance with some of the girls of the establishment. Two or three young fellows "dropped in" from the neighbouring houses—a student, a school-boy, and another young fellow of about twenty in a pair of huge spectacles. Each of these young fellows immediately attached himself to the particular young lady of his choice.

The young man in spectacles no sooner arrived than he went aside with Nadia and Maria Nikitishna, and entered into an animated whispering conversation with them, with much frowning and impatience of manner.

This gentleman seemed to consider it his mission to treat Pavel Pavlovitch with the most ineffable contempt.

Some of the girls proposed a game. One of them suggested "Proverbs," but it was voted dull; another suggested acting, but the objection was made that they never knew how to finish off.

"It may be more successful with you," said Nadia to Velchaninoff confidentially. "You know we all thought you were Pavel Pavlovitch's friend, but it appears that he was only boasting. I am *very* glad you have come—for a certain reason!" she added, looking knowingly into Velchaninoff's face, and then retreating back again to Maria's wing, blushing.

"We'll play 'Proverbs' in the evening," said another, "and we'll all chaff Pavel Pavlovitch; *you* must help us too!"

"We *are* so glad you're come—it's so dull here as a rule," said a third, a funny-looking red-haired girl, whose face was comically hot, with running apparently. Goodness knows where she had dropped from; Velchaninoff had not observed her arrive.

Pavel Pavlovitch's agitation increased every moment. Meanwhile Velchaninoff took the opportunity of making great friends with Nadia. She had ceased to frown at him as before, and had now developed the wildest of spirits, dancing and jumping about, singing and whistling, and occasionally even catching hold of his hand in her innocent friendliness.

She was very happy indeed, apparently; but she took no more notice of Pavel Pavlovitch than if he had not been there at all.

Pavel Pavlovitch was very jealous of all this, and once or twice when Nadia and Velchaninoff talked apart, he joined them and rudely interrupted their conversation by interposing his anxious face between them.

Katia could not help being fully aware by this time that their charming guest had not come in for her sake, as had been believed by the family; indeed, it was clear that Nadia interested him so much that she excluded everyone else, to a considerable extent, from his attention. However, in spite of this, her good-natured face retained its amiability of expression all the same. She seemed to be happy enough witnessing the happiness of the rest and listening to the merry talk; she could not take a large share in the conversation herself, poor girl!

"What a fine girl your sister, Katerina Fedosievna is," remarked Velchaninoff to Nadia.

"Katia? I should think so! there is no better girl in the world. She's our family angel! I'm in love with her myself!" replied Nadia enthusiastically.

At last, dinner was announced, and a very good dinner it was, several courses being added for the benefit of the guests: a bottle of tokay made its appearance, and champagne was handed round in honour of the occasion. The good humour of the company was general, old Zachlebnikoff was in high spirits, having partaken of an extra glass of wine this evening. So infectious was the hilarity that even Pavel Pavlovitch took heart of grace and made a pun. From the end of the table where he sat beside the lady of the house, there suddenly came a loud laugh from the delighted girls who had been fortunate enough to hear the virgin attempt.

"Papa, papa, Pavel Pavlovitch has made a joke!" cried several at once: "he says that there is quite a 'galaxy of gals' here!"

"Oho! *he's* made a pun too, has he?" cried the old fellow. "Well, what is it, let's have it!" He turned to Pavel Pavlovitch with beaming face, prepared to roar over the latter's joke.

"Why, I tell you, he says there's quite a 'galaxy of gals.' "

"Well, go on, where's the joke?" repeated papa, still dense to the merits of the pun, but beaming more and more with benevolent desire to see it.

"Oh, papa, how stupid you are not to see it. Why 'gals' and 'galaxy,' don't you see?—he says there's quite a gal-axy of gals!"

"Oh! oh!" guffawed the old gentleman, "Ha-ha! Well, we'll hope he'll make a better one next time, that's all."

"Pavel Pavlovitch can't acquire all the perfections at once," said Maria Nikitishna. "Oh, my goodness! he's swallowed a bone—look!" she added, jumping up from her chair.

The alarm was general, and Maria's delight was great.

Poor Pavel Pavlovitch had only choked over a glass of wine, which he seized and drank to hide his confusion; but Maria declared that it was a fishbone—that she had seen it herself, and that people had been known to die of swallowing a bone just like that.

"Clap him on the back!" cried somebody.

It appeared that there were numerous kind friends ready to perform this friendly office, and poor Pavel protested in vain that it was nothing but a common choke. The belabouring went on until the coughing fit was over, and it became evident that mischievous Maria was at the bottom of it all.

After dinner old Mr. Zachlebnikoff retired for his post-prandial nap, bidding the young people enjoy themselves in the garden as best they might.

"You enjoy yourself, too!" he added to Pavel Pavlovitch, tapping the latter's shoulder affably as he went by.

When the party were all collected in the garden once more, Pavel suddenly approached Velchaninoff: "One moment," he whispered, pulling the latter by the coat-sleeve.

The two men went aside into a lonely by-path.

"None of that *here*, please; I won't allow it here!" said Pavel Pavlovitch in a choking whisper.

"None of what? Who?" asked Velchaninoff, staring with all his eyes.

Pavel Pavlovitch said nothing more, but gazed furiously at his companion, his lips trembling in a desperate attempt at a pretended smile. At this moment the voices of several of the girls broke in upon them, calling them to some game. Velchaninoff shrugged his shoulders and re-joined the party. Pavel followed him.

"I'm sure Pavel Pavlovitch was borrowing a handkerchief from you, wasn't he? He forgot his handkerchief last time too. Pavel Pavlovitch has forgotten his handkerchief again, and he has a cold as usual!" cried Maria.

"Oh, Pavel Pavlovitch, why didn't you say so?" cried Mrs. Zachlebnikoff, making towards the house; "you shall have one at once."

In vain poor Pavel protested that he had two of those necessary articles, and was *not* suffering from a cold. Mrs. Zachlebnikoff was glad of the excuse for retiring to the house, and heard nothing. A few moments afterwards a maid pursued Pavel with a handkerchief, to the confusion of the latter gentleman.

A game of "proverbs" was now proposed. All sat down, and the young man with spectacles was made to retire to a considerable distance and wait there with his nose close up against the wall and his back turned until the proverb should have been chosen and the words arranged. Velchaninoff was the next in turn to be the questioner.

Then the cry arose for Pavel Pavlovitch, and the latter, who had more or less recovered his good humour by this time, proceeded to the spot indicated; and, resolved to do his duty like a man, took his stand with his nose to the wall, ready to stay there motionless until called. The red-haired young lady was detailed to watch him, in case of fraud on his part.

No sooner, however, had the wretched Pavel taken up his position at the wall, than the whole party took to their heels and ran away as fast as their legs could carry them.

"Run quick!" whispered the girls to Velchaninoff, in despair, for he had not started with them.

"Why, what's happened? What's the matter?" asked the latter, keeping up as best he could.

"Don't make a noise! we want to get away and let him go on standing there—that's all."

Katia, it appeared, did not like this practical joke. When the last stragglers of the party arrived at the end of the garden, among them Velchaninoff, the latter found Katia angrily scolding the rest of the girls.

"Very well," she was saying, "I won't tell mother this time; but I shall go away myself: it's too bad! What will the poor fellow's feelings be, standing all alone there, and finding us fled!"

And off she went. The rest, however, were entirely unsympathizing, and enjoyed the joke thoroughly. Velchaninoff was entreated to appear entirely unconscious when Pavel Pavlovitch should appear again, just as though nothing whatever had happened. It was a full quarter of an hour before Pavel put in an appearance, two thirds, at least, of that time he must have stood at the wall. When he reached the party he found everyone busy over a game of *Goriélki*, laughing and shouting and making themselves thoroughly happy.

Wild with rage, Pavel Pavlovitch again made straight for Velchaninoff, and tugged him by the coat-sleeve.

"One moment, sir!"

"Oh, my goodness! he's always coming in with his 'one moments'!" said someone.

"A handkerchief wanted again probably!" shouted someone else after the pair as they retired.

"Come now, this time it was you! You were the originator of this insult!" muttered Pavel, his teeth chattering with fury.

Velchaninoff interrupted him, and strongly recommended Pavel to bestir himself to be merrier.

"You are chaffed because you get angry," he said; "if you try to be jolly instead of sulky you'll be let alone!"

To his surprise these words impressed Pavel deeply; he was quiet at once, and returned to the party with a guilty air, and immediately began to take part in the games engaged in once more. He was not further bullied at present, and within half an hour his good humour seemed quite re-established.

To Velchaninoff's astonishment, however, he never seemed to presume to speak to Nadia, although he kept as close to her, on all occasions, as he possibly could. He seemed to take his position as quite natural, and was not put out by her contemptuous air towards him.

Pavel Pavlovitch was teased once more, however, before the evening ended.

A game of "Hide-and-seek" was commenced, and Pavel had hidden in a small room in the house. Being observed entering there by someone, he was locked in, and left there raging for an hour. Meanwhile, Velchaninoff learned the "special reason" for Nadia's joy at his arrival. Maria conducted him to a lonely alley, where Nadia was awaiting him alone.

"I have quite convinced myself," began the latter, when they were left alone, "that you are not nearly so great a friend of Pavel Pavlovitch as he gave us to understand. I have also convinced myself that you alone can perform a certain great service for me. Here is his horrid bracelet" (she drew the case out of her pocket)—"I wish to ask you to be so kind as to return it to him; I cannot do so myself, because I am quite determined never to speak to him again all my life. You can tell him so from me, and better add that he is not to worry me with any more of his nasty presents. I'll let him know something else I have to say through other channels. Will you do this for me?"

"Oh, for goodness sake, spare me!" cried Velchaninoff, almost wringing his hands.

"How spare you?" cried poor Nadia. Her artificial tone put on for the occasion had collapsed at once before this check, and she was nearly crying. Velchaninoff burst out laughing.

"I don't mean—I should be delighted, you know—but the thing is, I have my own accounts to settle with him!"

"I knew you weren't his friend, and that he was lying. I shall never marry him—never! You may rely on that! I don't understand how he could dare—at all events, you really *must* give him back this horrid bracelet. What am I to do if you don't? I *must* have it given back to him this very day. He'll catch it if he interferes with father about me!"

At this moment the spectacled young gentleman issued from the shrubs at their elbow.

"You are bound to return the bracelet!" he burst out furiously, upon Velchaninoff, "if only out of respect to the rights of woman——"

He did not finish the sentence, for Nadia pulled him away from beside Velchaninoff with all her strength.

"How stupid you are," she cried; "go away. How dare you listen? I told you to stand a long way off!" She stamped her foot with rage, and for some while after the young fellow had slunk away she continued to walk along with flashing eyes, furious with indignation. "You wouldn't believe how stupid he is!" she cried at last. "You laugh, but think of my feelings!"

"That's not *he*, is it?" laughed Velchaninoff.

"Of course not. How could you imagine such a thing! It's only his friend, and how he can choose such friends I can't understand! They say he is a 'future motive-power,' but I don't see it. Alexey Ivanovitch, for the last time—I have no one else to ask—will you give the bracelet back or not?"

"Very well, I will. Give it to me!"

"Oh, you dear, good Alexey Ivanovitch, thanks!" she cried, enthusiastic with delight. "I'll sing all the evening for that! I sing beautifully, you know! I was telling you a wicked story before dinner. Oh, I *wish* you would come down here again; I'd tell you *all*, then, and lots of other things besides—for you are a dear, kind, good fellow, like—like Katia!"

And sure enough when they reached home she sat down and sang a couple of songs in a voice which, though entirely untrained, was of great natural sweetness and considerable strength.

When the party returned from the garden they had found Pavel Pavlovitch drinking tea with the old folks on the balcony. He had probably been talking on serious topics, as he was to take his departure the day after to-morrow for nine months. He never so much as glanced at Velchaninoff and the rest when they entered; but he evidently had not complained to the authorities, and all was quiet as yet. But, when Nadia began to sing, he came in. Nadia did not answer a single one of his questions, but he did not seem offended by this, and took his stand behind her chair. Once there, his whole appearance gave it to be understood that that was his own place by right, and that he allowed none to dispute it.

"It's Alexey Ivanovitch's turn to sing now!" cried the girls, when Nadia's song was finished, and all crowded round to hear Velchaninoff, who sat down to accompany himself. He chose a song of Glinke's, too much neglected nowadays; it ran:—

"When from your merry lips

Tenderness flows," &c.

Velchaninoff seemed to address the words to Nadia exclusively, but the whole party stood around him. His voice had long since gone the way of all flesh, but it was clear that he must have had a good one once, and it so happened that Velchaninoff had heard this particular song many years ago, from Glinkes' own lips, when a student at the university, and remembered the great effect that it had made upon him when he first heard it. The song was full of the most intense passion of expression, and Velchaninoff sang it well, with his eyes fixed upon Nadia.

Amid the applause that followed the completion of the performance, Pavel Pavlovitch came forward, seized Nadia's hand and drew her away from the proximity of Velchaninoff; he then returned to the latter at the piano, and, with every evidence of frantic rage, whispered to him, his lips all of a tremble,

"One moment with you!"

Velchaninoff, seeing that the man was capable of worse things in his then frame of mind, took Pavel's hand and led him out through the balcony into the garden—quite dark now.

"Do you understand, sir, that you must come away at once—*this very minute*?" said Pavel Pavlovitch.

"No, sir, I do not!"

"Do you remember," continued Pavel in his frenzied whisper, "do you remember that you begged me to tell you *all, everything*—down to the smallest details? Well, the time has come for telling you all—come!"

Velchaninoff considered a moment, glanced once more at Pavel Pavlovitch, and consented to go.

"Oh! stay and have another cup of tea!" said Mrs. Zachlebnikoff, when this decision was announced.

"Pavel Pavlovitch, why are you taking Alexey Ivanovitch away?" cried the girls, with angry looks. As for Nadia, she looked so cross with Pavel, that the latter felt absolutely uncomfortable; but he did not give in.

"Oh, but I am very much obliged to Pavel Pavlovitch," said Velchaninoff, "for reminding me of some most important business which I must attend to this very evening, and which I might have forgotten," laughed Velchaninoff, as he shook hands with his host and made his bow to the ladies, especially to Katia, as the family thought.

"You must come again soon!" said the host; "we have been so glad to see you; it was so good of you to come!"

"Yes, *so* glad!" said the lady of the house.

"Do come again soon!" cried the girls, as Pavel Pavlovitch and Velchaninoff took their seats in the carriage; "Alexey Ivanovitch, *do* come back soon!" And with these voices in their ears they drove away.

CHAPTER XIII.

In spite of Velchaninoff's apparently happy day, the feeling of annoyance and suffering at his heart had hardly actually left him for a single moment. Before he sang the song he had not known what to do with himself, or suppressed anger and melancholy—perhaps that was the reason why he had sung with so much feeling and passion.

"To think that I could so have lowered myself as to forget everything!" he thought—and then despised himself for thinking it; "it is more humiliating still to cry over what is done," he continued. "Far better to fly into a passion with someone instead."

"Fool!" he muttered—looking askance at Pavel Pavlovitch, who sat beside him as still as a mouse. Pavel Pavlovitch preserved a most obstinate silence—probably concentrating and ranging his energies. He occasionally took his hat off, impatiently, and wiped the perspiration from his forehead.

Once—and once only—Pavel spoke, to the coachman, he asked whether there was going to be a thunder-storm.

"Wheugh!" said the man, "I should think so! It's been a steamy day—just the day for it!"

By the time town was reached—half-past ten—the whole sky was overcast.

"I am coming to your house," said Pavel to Velchaninoff, when almost at the door.

"Quite so; but I warn you, I feel very unwell to-night!"

"All right—I won't stay too long."

When the two men passed under the gateway, Pavel Pavlovitch disappeared into the 'dvornik's' room for a minute, to speak to Mavra.

"What did you go in there for?" asked Velchaninoff severely as they mounted the stairs and reached his own door.

"Oh—nothing—nothing at all,—just to tell them about the coachman.——"

"Very well. Mind, I shall not allow you to drink!"

Pavel Pavlovitch did not answer.

Velchaninoff lit a candle, while Pavel threw himself into a chair;—then the former came and stood menacingly before him.

"I may have told you I should have *my* last word to say to-night, as well as you!" he said with suppressed anger in his voice and manner: "Here it is. I consider conscientiously that things are square between you and me, now; and therefore there is no more to be said, understand me, about *anything*. Since this is so, had you not better go, and let me close the door after you?"

"Let's cry 'quits' first, Alexey Ivanovitch," said Pavel Pavlovitch, gazing into Velchaninoff's eyes with great sweetness.

"Quits?" cried the latter, in amazement; "you strange man, what are we to cry quits about? Are you harping upon your promise of a 'last word'?"

"Yes."

"Oh, well, we have nothing more to cry quits for. We have been quits long since," said Velchaninoff.

"Dear me, do you really think so?" cried Pavel Pavlovitch, in a shrill, sharp voice, pressing his two hands tightly together, finger to finger, as he held them up before his breast.

Velchaninoff said nothing. He rose from his seat and began to walk up and down the room. The word "Liza" resounded through and through his soul like the voice of a bell.

"Well, what is there that you still consider unsettled between us?" he asked at last, looking angrily at Pavel, who had never ceased to follow him with his eyes—always holding his hands before his breast, finger tip to finger tip.

"Don't go down there any more," said Pavel, almost in a whisper, and rising from his seat with every indication of humble entreaty.

"*What!* is *that* all?" cried Velchaninoff, bursting into an angry laugh; "good heavens, man, you have done nothing but surprise me all day." He had begun in a tone of exasperation, but he now abruptly changed both voice and expression, and continued with an air of deep feeling. "Listen," he said, "listen to me. I don't think I have ever felt so deeply humiliated as I am feeling now, in consequence of the events of to-day. In the first place, that I should have condescended to go down with you at all, and in the second place, all that happened there. It has been such a day of pettifogging—pitiful pettifogging. I have profaned and lowered myself by taking a share in it all, and forgetting—— Well, it's done now. But look here—you fell upon me to-day, unawares—upon a sick man. Oh, you needn't excuse yourself; at all events I shall certainly *not* go there again. I have not the slightest interest in so doing," he concluded, with an air of decision.

"No, really!" cried Pavel Pavlovitch, making no secret of his delight and exultation.

Velchaninoff glanced contemptuously at him, and recommenced his march up and down the room.

"You have determined to be happy under any circumstances, I suppose?" he observed, after a pause. He could not resist making the remark disdainfully.

"Yes, I have," said Pavel, quietly.

"It's no business of mine that he's a fool and a knave, out of pure idiocy!" thought Velchaninoff. "I can't help hating him, though I feel that he is not even worth hating."

"I'm a permanent husband," said Pavel Pavlovitch, with the most exquisitely servile irony, at his own expense. "I remember you using that expression, Alexey Ivanovitch, long ago, when you were with us at T——. I remember many of your original phrases of that time, and when you spoke of 'permanent husbands,' the other day, I recollected the expression."

At this point Mavra entered the room with a bottle of champagne and two glasses.

"Forgive me, Alexey Ivanovitch," said Pavel, "you know I can't get on without it. Don't consider it an audacity on my part—think of it as a mere bit of by-play unworthy your notice."

"Well," consented Velchaninoff, with a look of disgust, "but I must remind you that I don't feel well, and that—"

"One little moment—I'll go at once, I really will—I *must* just drink *one* glass, my throat is so——"

He seized the bottle eagerly, and poured himself out a glass, drank it greedily at a gulp, and sat down. He looked at Velchaninoff almost tenderly.

"What a nasty looking beast!" muttered the latter to himself.

"It's all her friends that make her like that," said Pavel, suddenly, with animation.

"What? Oh, you refer to the lady. I——"

"And, besides, she is so very young still, you see," resumed Pavel. "I shall be her slave—she shall see a little society, and a bit of the world. She will change, sir, entirely."

"I mustn't forget to give him back the bracelet, by-the-bye," thought Velchaninoff, frowning, as he felt for the case in his coat pocket.

"You said just now that I am determined to be happy, Alexey Ivanovitch," continued Pavel, confidentially, and with almost touching earnestness. "I *must* marry, else what will become of me? You see for yourself" (he pointed to the bottle), "and that's only a hundredth part of what I demean myself to nowadays. I cannot get on without marrying again, sir; I *must* have a new faith. If I can but believe in some one again, sir, I shall rise—I shall be saved."

"Why are you telling *me* all this?" exclaimed Velchaninoff, very nearly laughing in his face; it seemed so absurdly inconsistent.

"Look here," he continued, roaring the words out, "let me know now, once for all, why did you drag me down there? what good was I to do you there?"

"I—I wished to try——," began Pavel, with some confusion.

"Try what?"

"The effect, sir. You see, Alexey Ivanovitch, I have only been visiting there a week" (he grew more and more confused), "and yesterday, when I met you, I thought to myself that I had never seen her yet in society; that is, in the society of other *men* besides myself—a stupid idea, I know it is—I was very anxious to try—you know my wretchedly jealous nature." He suddenly raised his head and blushed violently.

"He *can't* be telling me the truth!" thought Velchaninoff; he was struck dumb with surprise.

"Well, go on!" he muttered at last.

"Well, I see it was all her pretty childish nature, sir—that and her friends together. You must forgive my stupid conduct towards yourself to-day, Alexey Ivanovitch. I will never do it again—never again, sir, I assure you!"

"I shall never be there to give you the opportunity," replied Velchaninoff with a laugh.

"That's partly why I say it," said Pavel.

"Oh, come! I'm not the only man in the world you know!" said the other irritably.

"I am sorry to hear you say that, Alexey Ivanovitch. My esteem for Nadejda is such that I——"

"Oh, forgive me, forgive me! I meant nothing, I assure you! Only it surprises me that you should have expected so much of me—that you trusted me so completely."

"I trusted you entirely, sir, solely on account of—all that has passed."

"So that you still consider me the most honourable of men?" Velchaninoff paused, the naïve nature of his sudden question surprised even himself.

"I always did think you that, sir!" said Pavel, hanging his head.

"Of course, quite so—I didn't mean quite that—I wanted to say, in spite of all prejudices you may have formed, you——"

"Yes, in spite of all prejudices!"

"And when you first came to Petersburg?" asked Velchaninoff, who himself felt the monstrosity of his own inquisitive questions, but could not resist putting them.

"I considered you the most honourable of men when I first came to Petersburg, sir; no less. I always respected you, Alexey Ivanovitch!"

Pavel Pavlovitch raised his eyes and looked at his companion without the smallest trace of confusion.

Velchaninoff suddenly felt cowed and afraid. He was anxious that nothing should result—nothing disagreeable—from this conversation, since he himself was responsible for having initiated it.

"I loved you, Alexey Ivanovitch; all that year at T—— I loved you—you did not observe it," continued Pavel Pavlovitch, his voice trembling with emotion, to the great discomfiture of his companion. "You did not observe my affection, because I was too lowly a being to deserve any sort of notice; but it was unnecessary that you should observe my love. Well, sir, and all these nine years I have thought of you, for I have never known such a year of life as that year was." (Pavel's eyes seemed to have a special glare in them at this point.) "I remembered many of your sayings and expressions, sir, and I thought of you always as a man imbued with the loftiest sentiments, and gifted with knowledge and intellect, sir—of the highest order—a man of grand ideas. 'Great ideas do not proceed so frequently from greatness of intellect, as from elevation of taste and feeling.' You yourself said that, sir, once. I dare say you have forgotten the fact, but you did say it. Therefore I always thought of you, sir, as a man of taste and feeling; consequently I concluded—consequently I trusted you, in spite of everything."

Pavel Pavlovitch's chin suddenly began to tremble. Velchaninoff was frightened out of his wits. This unexpected tone must be put an end to at all hazards.

"Enough, Pavel Pavlovitch!" he said softly, blushing violently and with some show of irritation. "And why—why (Velchaninoff suddenly began to shout passionately)—why do you come hanging round the neck of a sick man, a worried man—a man who is almost out of his wits with fever and annoyance of all sorts, and drag him into this abyss of lies and mirage and vision and shame—and unnatural, disproportionate, distorted nonsense! Yes, sir, that's the most shameful part of the whole business—the disproportionate nonsense of what you say! You know it's all humbug; both of us are mean wretches—both of us; and if you like I'll prove to you at once that not only you don't love me, but that you loathe and hate me with all your heart, and that you are a liar, whether you know it or not! You took me down to see your bride, not—not a bit in the world to try how she would behave in the society of other men—absurd idea!—You simply saw me, yesterday, and your vile impulse led you to carry me off there in order that you might show me the girl, and say, as it were. There, look at that! She's to be mine! Try your hand *there* if you can! It was nothing but your challenge to me! You may not have known it, but this was so, as I say; and you felt the impulse which I have described. Such a challenge could not be made without hatred; consequently you hate me."

Velchaninoff almost *rushed* up and down the room as he shouted the above words; and with every syllable the humiliating consciousness that he was allowing himself to descend to the level of Pavel Pavlovitch afflicted him and tormented him more and more!

"I was only anxious to be at peace with you, Alexey Ivanovitch!" said Pavel sadly, his chin and lips working again.

Velchaninoff flew into a violent rage, as if he had been insulted in the most unexampled manner.

"I tell you once more, sir," he cried, "that you have attached yourself to a sick and irritated man, in order that you may surprise him into saying something unseemly in his madness! We are, I tell you, man, we are men of different worlds. Understand me! between us two there is a grave," he hissed in his fury, and stopped.

"And how do you know,—sir," cried Pavel Pavlovitch, his face suddenly becoming all twisted, and deadly white to look at, as he strode up to Velchaninoff, "how do you know what that grave means to me, sir, here!" (He beat his breast with terrible earnestness, droll though he looked.) "Yes, sir, we both stand on the brink of the grave, but on my side there is more, sir, than on yours—yes, more, more, more!" he hissed, beating his breast without pause—"more than on yours—the grave means more to me than to you!"

But at this moment a loud ring at the bell brought both men to their senses. Someone was ringing so loud that the bell-wire was in danger of snapping.

"People don't ring like that for me, observed Velchaninoff angrily."

"No more they do for me, sir! I assure you they don't!" said Pavel Pavlovitch anxiously. He had become the quiet timid Pavel again in a moment. Velchaninoff frowned and went to open the door.

"Mr. Velchaninoff, if I am not mistaken?" said a strange voice, apparently belonging to some young and very self-satisfied person, at the door.

"What is it?"

"I have been informed that Mr. Trusotsky is at this moment in your rooms. I must see him at once."

Velchaninoff felt inclined to send this self-satisfied looking young gentleman flying downstairs again; but he reflected—refrained, stood aside and let him in.

"Here is Mr. Trusotsky. Come in."

CHAPTER XIV.

A young fellow of some nineteen summers entered the room; he might have been even younger, to judge by his handsome but self-satisfied and very juvenile face.

He was not badly dressed, at all events his clothes fitted him well; in stature he was a little above the middle height; he had thick black hair, and dark, bold eyes—and these were the striking features of his face. Unfortunately his nose was a little too broad and tip-tilted, otherwise he would have been a really remarkably good-looking young fellow.—He came in with some pretension.

"I believe I have the opportunity of speaking to Mr. Trusotsky?" he observed deliberately, and bringing out the word opportunity with much apparent satisfaction, as though he wished to accentuate the fact that he could not possibly be supposed to feel either honour or pleasure in meeting Mr. Trusotsky. Velchaninoff thought he knew what all this meant; Pavel Pavlovitch seemed to have an inkling of the state of affairs, too. His expression was one of anxiety, but he did not show the white feather.

"Not having the honour of your acquaintance," he said with dignity, "I do not understand what sort of business you can have with me."

"Kindly listen to me first, and you can then let me know your ideas on the subject," observed the young gentleman, pulling out his tortoiseshell glasses, and focusing the champagne bottle with them. Having deliberately inspected that object, he put up his glasses again, and fixing his attention once more upon Pavel Pavlovitch, remarked:

"Alexander Loboff."

"What about Alexander Loboff?"

"That's my name. You've not heard of me?"

"No."

"H'm! Well, I don't know when you should have, now I think of it; but I've come on important business concerning yourself. I suppose I can sit down? I'm tired."

"Oh, pray sit down," said Velchaninoff, but not before the young man had taken a chair. In spite of the pain at his heart Velchaninoff could not help being interested in this impudent youngling.

There seemed to be something in his good-looking, fresh young face that reminded him of Nadia.

"You can sit down too," observed Loboff, indicating an empty seat to Pavel Pavlovitch, with a careless nod of his head.

"Thank you; I shall stand."

"Very well, but you'll soon get tired. You need not go away, I think, Mr. Velchaninoff."

"I have nowhere to go to, my good sir, I am at home."

"As you like; I confess I should prefer your being present while I have an explanation with this gentleman. Nadejda Fedosievna has given you a flattering enough character, sir, to me."

"Nonsense; how could she have had time to do so?"

"Immediately after you left. Now, Mr. Trusotsky, this is what I wish to observe," he continued to Pavel, the latter still standing in front of him; "we, that is Nadejda Fedosievna and myself, have long loved one another, and have plighted our troth. You have suddenly come between us as an obstruction; I have come to tell you that you had better clear out of the way at once. Are you prepared to adopt my suggestion?"

Pavel Pavlovitch took a step backward in amazement; his face paled visibly, but in a moment a spiteful smile curled his lip.

"Not in the slightest degree prepared, sir," he said, laconically.

"Dear me," said the young fellow, settling himself comfortably in his chair, and throwing one leg over the other.

"Indeed, I do not know whom I am speaking to," added Pavel Pavlovitch, "so that it can't hardly be worth your while to continue."

So saying he sat down at last.

"I *said* you'd get tired," remarked the youth. "I informed you just now," he added, "that my name is Alexander Loboff, and that Nadejda and I have plighted our troth; consequently you cannot truthfully say, as you did say just now, that you don't know who I am, nor can you honestly assert that you do not see what we can have to talk about. Not to speak of myself—there is Nadejda Fedosievna to be considered—the lady to whom you have so impudently attached yourself: that alone is matter sufficient for explanation between us."

All this the young fellow rattled off carelessly enough, as if the thing were so self-evident that it hardly needed mentioning. While talking, he raised his eye-glass once more, and inspected some object for an instant, putting the glass back in his pocket immediately afterwards.

"Excuse me, young man," began Pavel Pavlovitch: but the words "young man" were fatal.

"At any other moment," observed the youth, "I should of course forbid your calling me 'young man' at once; but you must admit that in this case my youth is my principal advantage over yourself, and that even this very day you would have given anything—nay, at the moment when you presented your bracelet—to be just a little bit younger."

"Cheeky young brat!" muttered Velchaninoff.

"In any case," began Pavel Pavlovitch, with dignity, "I do not consider your reasons as set forth—most questionable and improper reasons at the best—sufficient to justify the continuance of this conversation. I see your 'business' is mere childishness and nonsense: to-morrow I shall have the pleasure of an explanation with Mr. Zachlebnikoff, my respected friend. Meanwhile, sir, perhaps you will make it convenient to—depart."

"That's the sort of man he is," cried the youth, hotly, turning to Velchaninoff: "he is not content with being as good as kicked out of the place, and having faces made at him, but he must go down again to-morrow to carry tales about us to Mr. Zachlebnikoff. Do you not prove by this, you obstinate man, that you wish to carry off the young lady by force? that you desire to *buy* her of people who preserve—thanks to the relics of barbarism still triumphant among us—a species of power over her? Surely she showed you sufficiently clearly that she *despises* you? You have had your wretched tasteless present of to-day—that bracelet thing—returned to you; what more do you want?"

"Excuse me, no bracelet has been, or can be returned to me," said Pavel Pavlovitch, with a shudder of anxiety, however.

"How so? hasn't Mr. Velchaninoff given it to you?"

"Oh, the deuce take you, sir," thought Velchaninoff. "Nadejda Fedosievna certainly did give me this case for you, Pavel Pavlovitch," he said; "I did not wish to take it, but she was anxious that I should: here it is, I'm very sorry."

He took out the case and laid it down on the table before the enraged Pavel Pavlovitch.

"How is it you have not handed it to him before?" asked the young man severely.

"I had no time, as you may conclude," said Velchaninoff with a frown.

"H'm! Strange circumstance!"

"*What*, sir?"

"Well, you must admit it *is* strange! However, I am quite prepared to believe that there has been some mistake."

Velchaninoff would have given worlds to get up and drub the impertinent young rascal and drag him out of the house by the ear; but he could not contain himself, and burst out laughing. The boy immediately followed suit and laughed too.

But for Pavel Pavlovitch it was no laughing matter.

If Velchaninoff had seen the ferocious look which the former cast at him at the moment when he and Loboff laughed, he would have realized that Pavel Pavlovitch was in the act of passing a fatal limit of forbearance. He did not see the look; but it struck him that it was only fair to stand up for Pavel now.

"Listen, Mr. Loboff," he said, in friendly tones, "not to enter into the consideration of other matters, I may point out that Mr. Trusotsky brings with him, in his wooing of Miss Zachlebnikoff, a name and circumstances fully well-known to that esteemed family; in the second place, he brings a fairly respectable position in the world; and thirdly, he brings wealth. Therefore he may well be surprised to find himself confronted by such a rival as yourself—a gentleman of great wealth, doubtless, but at the same time so very young, that he could not possibly look upon you as a serious rival; therefore, again, he is quite right in begging you to bring the conversation to an end."

87

"What do you mean by 'so very young'? I was nineteen a month since; by the law I might have been married long ago. That's a sufficient answer to your argument."

"But what father would consent to allowing his daughter to marry you *now*—even though you may be a Rothschild to come, or a benefactor to humanity in the future. A man of nineteen years old is not capable of answering for himself and yet you are ready to take on your own responsibility another being—in other words, a being who is as much a child as you are yourself. Why, it is hardly even honourable on your part, is it? I have presumed to address you thus, because you yourself referred the matter to me as a sort of arbiter between yourself and Pavel Pavlovitch."

"Yes, by-the-bye, 'Pavel Pavlovitch,' I forgot he was called that," remarked the youth. "I wonder why I thought of him all along as 'Vassili Petrovitch.' Look here, sir (addressing Velchaninoff), you have not surprised me in the least. I knew you were all tarred with one brush. It is strange that you should have been described to me as a man of some originality. However, to business. All that you have said is, of course, utter nonsense; not only is there nothing 'dishonourable' about my intentions, as you permitted yourself to suggest, but the fact of the matter is entirely the reverse, as I hope to prove to you by-and-bye. In the first place, we have promised each other marriage, besides which I have given her my word that if she ever repents of her promise she shall have her full liberty to throw me over. I have given her surety to that effect before witnesses."

"I bet anything your friend—what's his name?—Predposiloff invented that idea," cried Velchaninoff.

"He-he-he!" giggled Pavel Pavlovitch contemptuously.

"What is that person giggling about? You are right, sir, it was Predposiloff's idea. But I don't think you and I quite understand one another, do we? and I had such a good report of you. How old are you? Are you fifty yet?"

"Stick to business, if you please."

"Forgive the liberty. I did not mean anything offensive. Well, to proceed. I am no millionaire, and I am no great benefactor to humanity (to reply to your arguments), but I shall manage to keep myself and my wife. Of course I have nothing now; I was brought up, in fact, in their house from my childhood."

"How so?"

"Oh, because I am a distant relative of this Mr. Zachlebnikoff's wife. When my people died, he took me in and sent me to school. The old fellow is really quite a kind-hearted man, if you only knew it."

"I do know it!"

"Yes, he's an old fogey rather, but a kind-hearted old fellow; but I left him four months ago and began to keep myself. I first joined a railway office at ten roubles a month, and am now in a notary's place at twenty-five. I made him a formal proposal for her a fortnight since. He first laughed like mad, and afterwards fell into a violent rage, and Nadia was locked up. She bore it heroically. He had been furious with me before for throwing up a post in his department which he procured for me. You see he is a good and kind old fellow at home, but get him in his office and—oh, my word!—he's a sort of *Jupiter Tonans*! I told him straight out that I didn't like his ways; but the great row was—thanks to the second chief at the office; he said I insulted him, but I only told him he was an ignorant beggar. So I threw them all up, and went in for the notary business. Listen to that! What a clap! We shall have a thunder-storm directly! What a good thing I arrived before the rain! I came here on foot, you know, all the way, nearly at a run, too!"

"How in the world did you find an opportunity of speaking to Miss Nadia then? especially since you are not allowed to meet."

"Oh, one can always get over the railing; then there's that red-haired girl, she helps, and Maria Nikitishna—oh, but she's a snake, that girl! What's the matter? Are you afraid of the thunder-storm?"

"No, I'm ill—seriously ill!"

Velchaninoff had risen from his seat with a fearful sudden pain in his chest, and was trying to walk up and down the room.

"Oh, really! then I'm disturbing you. I shall go at once," said the youth, jumping up.

"No, you don't disturb me!" said Velchaninoff ceremoniously.

"How not; of course I do, if you've got the stomach ache! Well now, Vassili—what's your name—Pavel Pavlovitch, let's conclude this matter. I will formulate my question for once into words which will adapt themselves to your understanding: Are you prepared to renounce your claim to the hand of Nadejda Fedosievna before her parents, and in my presence, with all due formality?"

"No, sir; not in the slightest degree prepared," said Pavel Pavlovitch witheringly; "and allow me to say once more that all this is childish and absurd, and that you had better clear out!"

"Take care," said the youth, holding up a warning forefinger; "better give it up now, for I warn you that otherwise you will spend a lot of money down there, and take a lot of trouble; and when you come back in nine months you will be turned out of the house by Nadejda Fedosievna herself; and if you don't go *then*, it will be the worse for you. Excuse me for saying so, but at present you are like the dog in the manger. Think over it, and be sensible for once in your life."

"Spare me the moral, if you please," began Pavel Pavlovitch furiously; "and as for your low threats I shall take my measures to-morrow—*serious* measures."

"Low threats? pooh! You are low yourself to take them as such. Very well, I'll wait till to-morrow then; but if you—there's the thunder again!—*au revoir*—very glad to have met you, sir." He nodded to Velchaninoff and made off hurriedly, evidently anxious to reach home before the rain.

CHAPTER XV.

"You see, you see!" cried Pavel to Velchaninoff, the instant that the young fellow's back was turned.

"Yes; you are not going to succeed there," said Velchaninoff. He would not have been so abrupt and careless of Pavel's feelings if it had not been for the dreadful pain in his chest.

Pavel Pavlovitch shuddered as though from a sudden scald. "Well, sir, and you—you were loth to give me back the bracelet, eh?"

"I hadn't time."

"Oh! you were sorry—you pitied me, as true friend pities friend!"

"Oh, well, I pitied you, then!" Velchaninoff was growing angrier every moment. However, he informed Pavel Pavlovitch shortly as to how he had received the bracelet, and how Nadia had almost forced it upon him.

"You must understand," he added, "that otherwise I should never have agreed to accept the commission; there are quite enough disagreeables already."

"You liked the job, and accepted it with pleasure," giggled Pavel Pavlovitch.

"That is foolish on your part; but I suppose you must be forgiven. You must have seen from that boy's behaviour that I play no part in this matter. Others are the principal actors, not I!"

"At all events the job had attractions for you." Pavel Pavlovitch sat down and poured out a glass of wine.

"You think I shall knuckle under to that young gentleman? Pooh! I shall drive him out to-morrow, sir, like dust. I'll smoke this little gentleman out of his nursery, sir; you see if I don't." He drank his wine off at a gulp, and poured out some more. He seemed to grow freer as the moments went by; he talked glibly now.

"Ha-ha! Sachinka and Nadienka![2] darling little children. Ha-ha-ha!" He was beside himself with fury.

At this moment, a terrific crash of thunder startled the silence, and was followed by flashes of lightning and sheets of heavy rain. Pavel Pavlovitch rose and shut the window.

"The fellow asked you if you were afraid of the thunder; do you remember? Ha-ha-ha! Velchaninoff afraid of thunder! And all that about 'fifty years old' wasn't bad, eh? Ha-ha-ha!" Pavel Pavlovitch was in a spiteful mood.

"You seem to have settled yourself here," said Velchaninoff, who could hardly speak for agony. "Do as you like, I must lie down."

"Come, you wouldn't turn a *dog* out to-night!" replied Pavel, glad of a grievance.

"Of course, sit down; drink your wine—do anything you like," murmured Velchaninoff, as he laid himself flat on his divan, and groaned with pain.

"Am I to spend the night? Aren't you afraid?"

"What of?" asked Velchaninoff, raising his head slightly.

"Oh, nothing. Only last time you seemed to be a little alarmed, that's all."

"You are a fool!" said the other angrily, as he turned his face to the wall.

"Very well, sir; all right," said Pavel.

Velchaninoff fell asleep within a minute or so of lying down. The unnatural strain of the day, and his sickly state of health together, had suddenly undermined his strength, and he was as weak as a child. But physical pain would have its own, and soon conquered weakness and sleep; in an hour he was wide awake again, and rose from the divan in anguish. Pavel Pavlovitch was asleep on the other sofa. He was dressed, and in his boots; his hat lay on the floor, and his eye-glass hung by its cord almost to the ground. Velchaninoff did not wake his guest. The room was full of tobacco smoke, and the bottle was empty; he looked savagely at the sleeping drunkard.

Having twisted himself painfully off his bed, Velchaninoff began to walk about, groaning and thinking of his agony; he could lie no longer.

He was alarmed for this pain in his chest, and not without reason. He was subject to these attacks, and had been so for many years; but they came seldom, luckily—once a year or two years. On such occasions, his agony was so dreadful for some ten hours or so that he invariably believed that he must be actually dying.

This night, his anguish was terrible; it was too late to send for the doctor, but it was far from morning yet. He staggered up and down the room, and before long his groans became loud and frequent.

The noise awoke Pavel Pavlovitch. He sat up on his divan, and for some time gazed in terror and perplexity upon Velchaninoff, as the latter walked moaning up and down. At last he gathered his senses, and enquired anxiously what was the matter.

Velchaninoff muttered something unintelligible.

"It's your kidneys—I'm sure it is," cried Pavel, very wide awake of a sudden. "I remember Peter Kuzmich used to have the same sort of attacks. The kidneys—why, one can die of it. Let me go and fetch Mavra."

"No, no; I don't want anything," muttered Velchaninoff, waving him off irritably.

But Pavel Pavlovitch—goodness knows why—was beside himself with anxiety; he was as much exercised as though the matter at issue were the saving of his own son's life. He insisted on immediate compresses, and told Velchaninoff he must drink two or three cups of very hot weak tea—boiling hot. He ran for Mavra, lighted the fire in the kitchen, put the kettle on, put the sick man back to bed, covered him up, and within twenty minutes had the first hot application all ready, as well as the tea.

"Hot plates, sir, hot plates," he cried, as he clapped the first, wrapped in a napkin, on to Velchaninoff's chest. "I have nothing else handy; but I give you my word it's as good as anything else. Drink this tea quick, never mind if you scald your tongue—life is dearer. You can die of this sort of thing, you know." He sent sleepy Mavra out of her wits with flurry; the plates were changed every couple of minutes. At the third application, and after having taken two cups of scalding tea, Velchaninoff suddenly felt decidedly better.

"Capital! thank God! if we can once get the better of the pain it's a good sign!" cried Pavel, delightedly, and away he ran for another plate and some more tea.

"If only we can beat the pain down!" he kept muttering to himself every minute.

In half an hour the agony was passed, but the sick man was so completely knocked up that, in spite of Pavel's repeated entreaties to be allowed to apply "just one more plate," he could bear no more. His eyes were drooping from weakness.

"Sleep—sleep," he muttered faintly.

"Very well," consented Pavel, "go to sleep."

"Are you spending the night here? What time is it?"

"Nearly two."

"You must sleep here."

"Yes, yes—all right. I will."

A moment after the sick man called to Pavel again.

"You—you—" muttered the former faintly, as Pavel ran up and bent over him, "you are better than I am. I understand all—all—thank you!"

"Go to sleep!" whispered Pavel Pavlovitch, as he crept back to his divan on tip-toes.

Velchaninoff, dozing off, heard Pavel quietly make his bed, undress and lie down, all very softly, and then put the light out.

Undoubtedly Velchaninoff fell asleep very quietly when the light was once out; he remembered that much afterwards. Yet all the while he was asleep, and until he awoke, he dreamed that he could not go to sleep in spite of his weakness. At length he dreamed that he was delirious, and that he could not for the life of him chase away the visions which crowded in upon him, although he was conscious the whole while they *were* but visions and not reality. The apparition was familiar to him. He thought that his front door was open, and that his room gradually filled with people pouring in. At the table in the middle of the room, sat one man exactly as had been the case a month before, during one of his dreams. As on the previous occasion, this man leant on his elbow at the table and would not speak; he was in a round hat with a crape band.

"How?" thought the dreamer. "Was it really Pavel Pavlovitch last time as well?" However, when he looked at the man's face, he was convinced that it was quite another person.

"Why has he a crape band, then?" thought Velchaninoff in perplexity.

The noise and chattering of all these people was dreadful; they seemed even more exasperated with Velchaninoff than on the former occasion. They were all threatening him with something or other, shaking their fists at him, and shouting something which he could not understand.

"It's all a vision," he dreamed, "I know quite well that I am up and about, because I could not lie still for anguish!"

Yet the cries and noise at times seemed so real that he was now and again half-convinced of their reality.

"Surely this *can't* be delirium!" he thought. "What on earth do all these people want of me—my God!"

Yet if it were not a vision, surely all these cries would have roused Pavel Pavlovitch? There he was, fast asleep in his divan!

Then something suddenly occurred as in the old dream. Another crowd of people surged in, crushing those who were already collected inside. These new arrivals carried something large and heavy; he could judge of the weight by their footsteps labouring upstairs.

Those in the room cried, "They're bringing it! they're bringing it!"

Every eye flashed as it turned and glared at Velchaninoff; every hand threatened him and then pointed to the stairs.

Undoubtedly it was reality, not delirium. Velchaninoff thought that he stood up and raised himself on tip-toes, in order to see over the heads of the crowd. He wanted to know what was being carried in.

His heart beat wildly, wildly, wildly; and suddenly, as in his former dream, there came one—two—three loud rings at the bell.

And again, the sound of the bell was so distinct and clear that he felt it *could* not be a dream. He gave a cry, and awoke; but he did not rush to the door as on the former occasion.

What sudden idea was it that guided his movements? Had he any idea at all, or was it impulse that prompted him what to do? He sprang up in bed, with arms outstretched, as though to ward off an attack, straight towards the divan where Pavel Pavlovitch was sleeping.

His hands encountered other hands outstretched in his direction; consequently some one must have been standing over him.

The curtains were drawn, but it was not absolutely dark, because a faint light came from the next room, which had no curtains.

Suddenly something cut the palm of his left hand, some of his fingers causing him sharp pain. He instantly realized that he had seized a knife or a razor, and he closed his hand upon it with the rapidity of thought.

At that moment something fell to the ground with a hard metallic sound.

Velchaninoff was probably three times as strong as Pavel Pavlovitch, but the struggle lasted for a long while—at least three minutes.

The former, however, forced his adversary to the earth, and bent his arms back behind his head; then he paused, for he was most anxious to tie the hands. Holding the assassin's wrist with his wounded left hand, he felt for the blind cord with his right. For a long while he could not find it; at last he grasped it, and tore it down.

He was amazed afterwards at the unnatural strength which he must have displayed during all this.

During the whole of the struggle neither man spoke a word; only their heavy breathing was audible, and the inarticulate sounds emitted by both as they fought.

At length, having secured his opponent's hands, Velchaninoff left him on the ground, rose, drew the curtains, and pulled up the blind.

The deserted street was light now. He opened the window, and stood breathing in the fresh air for a few moments. It was a little past four o'clock. He shut the window once more, fetched a towel and bound up his cut hand as tightly as he could to stop the flow of blood.

At his feet he caught sight of the opened razor lying on the carpet; he picked it up, wiped it, and put it by in its own case, which he now saw he had left upon the little cupboard beside the divan which Pavel Pavlovitch occupied. He locked the cupboard.

Having completed all these arrangements, he approached Pavel Pavlovitch and looked at him. Meanwhile the latter had managed to raise himself from the floor and reach a chair; he was now sitting in it—undressed to his shirt, which was stained with marks of blood both back and front—Velchaninoff's blood, not his own.

Of course this was Pavel Pavlovitch; but it would have been only natural for any one who had known him before, and saw him at this moment, to doubt his identity. He sat upright in his chair—very stiffly, owing to the uncomfortable position of his tightly bound hands behind his back; his face looked yellow and crooked, and he shuddered every other moment. He gazed intently, but with an expression of dazed perplexity, at Velchaninoff.

Suddenly he smiled gravely, and nodding towards a carafe of water on the table, muttered, "A little drop!" Velchaninoff poured some into a glass, and held it for him to drink.

Pavel gulped a couple of mouthfuls greedily—then suddenly raised his head and gazed intently at Velchaninoff standing over him; he said nothing, however, but finished the water. He then sighed deeply.

Velchaninoff took his pillows and some of his clothing, and went into the next room, locking Pavel Pavlovitch behind him.

His pain had quite disappeared, but he felt very weak after the strain of his late exertion. Goodness knows whence came his strength for the trial; he tried to think, but he could not collect his ideas, the shock had been too great.

His eyes would droop now and again, sometimes for ten minutes at a time; then he would shudder, wake up, remember all that had passed and raise the blood-stained rag bound about his hand to prove the reality of his thoughts; then he would relapse into eager, feverish thought. One thing was quite certain, Pavel Pavlovitch had intended to cut his throat, though, perhaps, a quarter of an hour before the fatal moment he had not known that he would make the attempt. Perhaps he had seen the razor case last evening, and thought nothing of it, only remembering the fact that it was there. The razors were usually locked up, and only yesterday Velchaninoff had taken one out in order to make himself neat for his visit to the country, and had omitted to lock it up again.

"If he had premeditated murdering me, he would certainly have provided himself with a knife or a pistol long ago; he could not have relied on my razors, which he never saw until yesterday," concluded Velchaninoff.

At last the clock struck six. Velchaninoff arose, dressed himself, and went into Pavel Pavlovitch's room. As he opened the door he wondered why he had ever locked it, and why he had not allowed Pavel to go away at once.

To his surprise the prisoner was dressed, he had doubtless found means to get his hands loose. He was sitting in an arm-chair, but rose when Velchaninoff entered. His hat was in his hand.

His anxious look seemed to say as plain as words:—

"Don't talk to me! It's no use talking—don't talk to me!"

"Go!" said Velchaninoff. "Take your jewel-case!" he added.

Pavel Pavlovitch turned back and seized his bracelet-case, stuffing it into his pocket, and went out.

Velchaninoff stood in the hall, waiting to shut the front door after him.

Their looks met for the last time. Pavel Pavlovitch stopped, and the two men gazed into each others eyes for five seconds or so, as though in indecision. At length Velchaninoff faintly waved him away with his hand.

"Go!" he said, only half aloud, as he closed the door and turned the key.

CHAPTER XVI.

A feeling of immense happiness took possession of Velchaninoff; something was finished, and done with, and settled. Some huge anxiety was at an end, so it seemed to him. This anxiety had lasted five weeks.

He raised his hand and looked at the blood-stained rag bound about it.

"Oh, yes!" he thought, "it is, indeed, all over now."

And all this morning—the first time for many a day, he did not even once think of Liza; just as if the blood from those cut fingers had wiped out that grief as well, and made him "quits" with it.

He quite realized how terrible was the danger which he had passed through.

"For those people," he thought, "who do not know a minute or two before-hand that they are going to murder you, when they once get the knife into their hands, and feel the first touch of warm blood—Good Heaven! they not only cut your throat, they hack your head off afterwards—right off!"

Velchaninoff could not sit at home, he *must* go out and let something happen to him, and he walked about in hopes of something turning up; he longed to *talk*, and it struck him that he might fairly go to the doctor and talk to him, and have his hand properly bound up.

The doctor inquired how he hurt his hand, which made Velchaninoff laugh like mad; he was on the point of telling all, but refrained. Several times during the day he was on the point of telling others the whole story. Once it was to a perfect stranger in a restaurant, with whom he had begun to converse on his own initiative. Before this day he had hated the very idea of speaking to strangers in the public restaurants.

He went into a shop and ordered some new clothes, not with the idea of visiting the Pogoryeltseffs however—the thought of any such visit was distasteful to him; besides he could not leave town, he felt that he must stay and see what was going to happen.

Velchaninoff dined and enjoyed his dinner, talking affably to his neighbour and to the waiter as well. When evening fell he went home, his head was whirling a little, and he felt slightly delirious; the first sight of his rooms gave him quite a start. He walked round them and reflected. He visited the kitchen, which he had hardly ever done before in his life, and thought, "This is where they heated the plates last night." He locked the doors carefully, and lit his candles earlier than usual. As he shut the door he remembered that he had asked Mavra, as he passed the dvornik's lodging, whether Pavel Pavlovitch had been. Just as if the latter could possibly have been near the place!

Having then carefully locked himself in, he opened the little cupboard where his razors were kept, and took out "the" razor. There was still some of the blood on the bone handle. He put the razor back again, and locked the cupboard.

He was sleepy; he felt that he must go to sleep as speedily as possible, otherwise he would be useless "for to-morrow," and to-morrow seemed to him for some reason or other to be about to be a fateful day for him.

But all those thoughts which had crowded in upon him all day, and had never left him for a moment, were still in full swing within his brain; he thought, and thought, and thought, and could not fall asleep.

If Pavel Pavlovitch arrived at murdering point accidentally, had he ever seriously thought of murder even for a single evil instant before? Velchaninoff decided the question strangely enough: Pavel Pavlovitch *had* the desire to murder him, but did not himself know of the existence of this desire.

"It seems an absurd conclusion; but so it is!" thought Velchaninoff.

Pavel Pavlovitch did not come to Petersburg to look out for a new appointment, nor did he come for the sake of finding Bagantoff, in spite of his rage when the latter died. No! he despised Bagantoff thoroughly. Pavel Pavlovitch had come to St. Petersburg for *him*, and had brought Liza with him, for him alone, Velchaninoff.

"Did *I* expect to have my throat cut?" Velchaninoff decided that he *had* expected it, from the moment when he saw Pavel Pavlovitch in the carriage following in Bagantoff's funeral procession. "That is I expected something—of course, not exactly to have my throat cut! And surely—surely, it was not all *bonâ fide* yesterday," he reflected, raising his head from the pillow in the excitement of the idea. "*Surely* it cannot have been all in good faith that that fellow assured me of his love for me, beating his breast, and with his under lip trembling, as he spoke!

"Yes, it was absolutely *bonâ fide*!" he decided. "This quasimodo of T—— was quite good enough and generous enough to fall in love with his wife's lover—his wife in whom he never observed 'anything' during the twenty years of their married life.

"He respected and loved me for nine years, and remembered both me and my sayings. My goodness, to think of that! and I knew nothing whatever of all this! Oh, no! he was not lying yesterday! But did he love me *while* he declared his love for me, and said that we must be 'quits!' Yes, he did, he loved me spitefully—and spiteful love is sometimes the strongest of all.

"I daresay I made a colossal impression upon him down at T——, for it is just upon such Schiller-like men that one is liable to make a colossal impression. He exaggerated my value a thousand fold; perhaps it was my 'philosophical retirement' that struck him! It would be curious to discover precisely what it was that made so great an impression upon him. Who knows, it may have been that I wore a good pair of gloves, and knew how to put them on. These quasimodo fellows love æstheticism to distraction! Give them a start in the direction of admiration for yourself, and they will do all the rest, and give you a thousand times more than your due of every virtue that exists; will fight to the death for you with pleasure, if you ask it of them. How high he must have held my aptitude for illusionizing others; perhaps that has struck him as much as anything else! for he remarked: 'If *this* man deceived me, whom am I ever to trust again!'

"After such a cry as that a man may well turn wild beast.

"And he came here to 'embrace and weep over me,' as he expressed it. H'm! that means he came to cut my throat, and *thought* that he came to embrace and weep over me. He brought Liza with him, too.

"What if I *had* wept with him and embraced him? Perhaps he really would have fully and entirely forgiven me—for he was yearning to forgive me, I could see that! And all this turned to drunkenness and bestiality at the first check. Yes, Pavel Pavlovitch, the most deformed of all deformities is the abortion with noble feelings. And this man was foolish enough to take me down to see his 'bride.' My goodness! his bride! Only such a lunatic of a fellow could ever have developed so wild an idea as a 'new existence' to be inaugurated by an alliance between himself and Nadia. But you are not to blame, Pavel Pavlovitch, you are a deformity, and all your ideas and actions and aspirations must of necessity be deformed. But deformity though he be, why in the world was *my* sanction, *my* blessing, as it were, necessary to his union with Miss Zachlebnikoff? Perhaps he sincerely hoped that there, with so much sweet innocence and charm around us, we should fall into each other's arms in some leafy spot, and weep out our differences on each other's shoulders?

"Was *murder* in his thoughts when I caught him standing between our beds that first time, in the darkness? No. I think not. And yet the first idea of it may have entered his soul as he stood there—And if I had not left the razors out, probably nothing would have happened. Surely that is so; for he avoided me for weeks—he was *sorry* for me, and avoided me. He chose Bagantoff to expend his wrath upon, first, not me! He jumped out of bed and fussed over the hot plates, to divert his mind from murder perhaps—from the knife to charity! Perhaps he tried to save both himself and me by his hot plates!"

So mused Velchaninoff, his poor overwrought brain working on and on, and jumping from conclusion to conclusion with the endless activity of fever, until he fell asleep. Next morning he awoke with no less tired brain and body, but with a new terror, an unexpected and novel feeling of dread hanging over him.

92

This dread consisted in the fact that he felt that he, Velchaninoff, must go and see Pavel Pavlovitch that very day; he knew not why he must go, but he felt drawn to go, as though by some unseen force. The idea was too loathsome to look into, so he left it to take care of itself as an unalterable fact. The madness of it, however, was modified, and the whole aspect of the thought became more reasonable, after a while, when it took shape and resolved itself into a conviction in Velchaninoff's mind that Pavel Pavlovitch had returned home, locked himself up, and hung himself to the bedpost, as Maria Sisevna had described of the wretched suicide witnessed by poor Liza.

"Why should the fool hang himself?" he repeated over and over again; yet the thought *would* return that he was bound to hang himself, as Liza had said that he threatened to do. Velchaninoff could not help adding that if he were in Pavel Pavlovitch's place he would probably do the same.

So the end of it was that instead of going out to his dinner, he set off for Pavel Pavlovitch's lodging, "just to ask Maria Sisevna after him." But before he had reached the street he paused and his face flushed up with shame. "Surely I am not going there to embrace and weep over him! Surely I am not going to add this one last pitiful folly to the long list of my late shameful actions!"

However, his good providence saved him from this "pitiful folly," for he had hardly passed through the large gateway into the street, when Alexander Loboff suddenly collided with him. The young fellow was dashing along in a state of great excitement.

"I was just coming to you. Our friend Pavel Pavlovitch—a nice sort of fellow he is——"

"Has he hung himself?" gasped Velchaninoff.

"Hung himself? Who? Why?" asked Loboff, with his eyes starting out of his head.

"Oh! go on, I meant nothing!"

"Tfu! What a funny line your thoughts seem to take. He hasn't hung himself a bit—why in the world should he?—on the contrary, he's gone away. I've just seen him off! My goodness, how that fellow can drink! We had three bottles of wine. Predposiloff was there too—but how the fellow drinks! Good heavens! he was singing in the carriage when the train went off! He thought of you, and kissed his hand to you, and sent his love. He's a scamp, that fellow, eh?"

Young Loboff had apparently had quite his share of the three bottles, his face was flushed and his utterance thick. Velchaninoff roared with laughter.

"So you ended up by weeping over each others shoulders, did you? Ha-ha-ha! Oh, you poetical, Schiller-ish, funny fellows, you!"

"Don't scold us. You must know he went down *there* yesterday and to-day, and he has withdrawn. He 'sneaked' like anything about Nadia and me. They've shut her up. There was such a row, but we wouldn't give way—and, my word, how the fellow drinks! He was always talking about you; but, of course, he is no companion for you. You are, more or less, a respectable sort of man, and must have belonged to society at some time of your life, though you seem to have retired into private life just now. Is it poverty, or what? I couldn't make head or tail of Pavel Pavlovitch's story."

"Oh! Then it was he who gave you those interesting details about me?"

"Yes; don't be cross about it. It's better to be a citizen than 'a swell' any-day! The thing is one does not know whom to respect in Russia nowadays! Don't you think it a diseased feature of the times, in Russia, that one doesn't know whom to respect?"

"Quite so, quite so. Well, go on about Pavel Pavlovitch——"

"Well, he sat down in the railway carriage and began singing, then he cried a bit. It was really disgusting to see the fellow. I hate fools! Then he began to throw money to beggars 'for the repose of Liza's soul,' he said. Is that his wife?"

"Daughter."

"What's the matter with your hand?"

"I cut it."

"H'm! Never mind, cheer up! It'll be all right soon! I am glad that fellow has gone, you know,—confound him! But I bet anything he'll marry as soon as he arrives at his place."

"Well, what of that? You are going to marry, too!"

"I! That's quite a different affair! What a funny man you are! Why, if *you* are fifty, he must be sixty! Well, ta-ta! Glad I met you—can't come in—don't ask me—no time!"

He started off at a run, but turned a minute after and came back.

"What a fool I am!" he cried, "I forgot all about it—he sent you a letter. Here it is. How was it you didn't see him off? Ta-ta!"

Velchaninoff returned home and opened the letter, which was sealed and addressed to himself.

There was not a syllable inside in Pavel Pavlovitch's own hand writing; but he drew out another letter, and knew the writing at once. It was an old, faded, yellow-looking sheet of paper, and the ink was faint and discoloured; the letter was addressed to Velchaninoff, and written ten years before—a couple of months after his departure from T——. He had never received a copy of this one, but another letter, which he well remembered, had evidently been written and sent instead of it; he could tell that by the substance of the faded document in his hand. In this present letter Natalia Vasilievna bade farewell to him for ever (as she had done in the other communication), and informed him that she expected her confinement in a few months. She added, for his consolation, that she would find an opportunity of purveying his child to him in good time, and pointed out that their friendship was now cemented for ever. She begged him to love her no longer, because she could no longer return his love, but authorized him to pay a visit to T—— after a year's absence, in order to see the child. Goodness only knows why she had not sent this letter, but had changed it for another!

Velchaninoff was deadly pale when he read this document; but he imagined Pavel Pavlovitch finding it in the family box of black wood with mother-of-pearl ornamentation and silver mounting, and reading it for the first time!

93

"I should think he, too, grew as pale as a corpse," he reflected, catching sight of his own face in the looking-glass. "Perhaps he read it and then closed his eyes and hoped and prayed that when he opened them again the dreadful letter would be nothing but a sheet of white paper once more! Perhaps the poor fellow tried this desperate expedient two or three times before he accepted the truth!"

CHAPTER XVII.

THE PERMANENT HUSBAND.

Two years have elapsed since the events recorded in the foregoing chapters, and we find our friend Velchaninoff, one lovely summer day, seated in a railway carriage on his way to Odessa; he was making the journey for the purpose of seeing a great friend, and of being introduced to a lady whose acquaintance he had long wished to make.

Without entering into any details, we may remark that Velchaninoff was entirely changed during these last two years. He was no longer the miserable, fanciful hypochondriac of those dark days. He had returned to society and to his friends, who gladly forgave him his temporary relapse into seclusion. Even those whom he had ceased to bow to, when met, were now among the first to extend the hand of friendship once more, and asked no questions—just as though he had been abroad on private business, which was no affair of theirs.

His success in the legal matters of which we have heard, and the fact of having his sixty thousand roubles safe at his bankers—enough to keep him all his life—was the elixir which brought him back to health and spirits. His premature wrinkles departed, his eyes grew brighter, and his complexion better; he became more active and vigorous—in fact, as he sat thinking in a comfortable first-class carriage, he looked a very different man from the Velchaninoff of two years ago.

The next station to be reached was that at which passengers were expected to dine, forty minutes being allowed for this purpose.

It so happened that Velchaninoff, while seated at the dinner table, was able to do a service to a lady who was also dining there. This lady was young and nice looking, though rather too flashily dressed, and was accompanied by a young officer who unfortunately was scarcely in a befitting condition for ladies' society, having refreshed himself at the bar to an unnecessary extent. This young man succeeded in quarrelling with another person equally unfit for ladies' society, and a brawl ensued, which threatened to land both parties upon the table in close proximity to the lady. Velchaninoff interfered, and removed the brawlers to a safe distance, to the great and almost boundless gratitude of the alarmed lady, who hailed him as her "guardian angel." Velchaninoff was interested in the young woman, who looked like a respectable provincial lady—of provincial manners and taste, as her dress and gestures showed.

A conversation was opened, and the lady immediately commenced to lament that her husband was "never by when he was wanted," and that he had now gone and hidden himself somewhere just because he happened to be required.

"Poor fellow, he'll catch it for this," thought Velchaninoff. "If you will tell me your husband's name," he added aloud, "I will find him, with pleasure."

"Pavel Pavlovitch," hiccupped the young officer.

"Your husband's name is Pavel Pavlovitch, is it?" inquired Velchaninoff with curiosity, and at the same moment a familiar bald head was interposed between the lady and himself.

"Here you are *at last*," cried the wife, hysterically.

It was indeed Pavel Pavlovitch.

He gazed in amazement and dread at Velchaninoff, falling back before him just as though he saw a ghost. So great was his consternation, that for some time it was clear that he did not understand a single word of what his wife was telling him—which was that Velchaninoff had acted as her guardian angel, and that he (Pavel) ought to be ashamed of himself for never being at hand when he was wanted.

At last Pavel Pavlovitch shuddered, and woke up to consciousness.

Velchaninoff suddenly burst out laughing. "Why, we are old friends"—he cried, "friends from childhood!" He clapped his hand familiarly and encouragingly on Pavel's shoulder. Pavel smiled wanly. "Hasn't he ever spoken to you of Velchaninoff?"

"No, never," said the wife, a little confused.

"Then introduce me to your wife, you faithless friend!"

"This—this is Mr. Velchaninoff!" muttered Pavel Pavlovitch, looking the picture of confusion.

All went swimmingly after this. Pavel Pavlovitch was despatched to cater for the party, while his lady informed Velchaninoff that they were on their way from O——, where Pavel Pavlovitch served, to their country place—a lovely house, she said, some twenty-five miles away. There they hoped to receive a party of friends, and if Mr. Velchaninoff would be so very kind as to take pity on their rustic home, and honour it with a visit, she should do her best to show her gratitude to the guardian angel who, etc., etc. Velchaninoff replied that he would be delighted; and that he was an idle man, and always free—adding a compliment or two which caused the fair lady to blush with delight, and to tell Pavel Pavlovitch, who now returned from his quest, that Alexey Ivanovitch had been so kind as to promise to pay them a visit next week, and stay a whole month.

Pavel Pavlovitch, to the amazed wrath of his wife, smiled a sickly smile, and said nothing.

After dinner the party bade farewell to Velchaninoff, and returned to their carriage, while the latter walked up and down the platform smoking his cigar; he knew that Pavel Pavlovitch would return to talk to him.

So it turned out. Pavel came up with an expression of the most anxious and harassed misery. Velchaninoff smiled, took his arm, led him to a seat, and sat down beside him. He did not say anything, for he was anxious that Pavel should make the first move.

"So you are coming to us?" murmured the latter at last, plunging *in medias res*.

"I knew you'd begin like that! you haven't changed an atom!" cried Velchaninoff, roaring with laughter, and slapping him confidentially on the back. "Surely, you don't really suppose that I ever had the smallest intention of visiting you—and staying a month too!"

Pavel Pavlovitch gave a start.

"Then you're *not* coming?" he cried, without an attempt to hide his joy.

"No, no! of course not!" replied Velchaninoff, laughing. He did not know why, but all this was exquisitely droll to him; and the further it went the funnier it seemed.

"Really—are you really serious?" cried Pavel, jumping up.

"Yes; I tell you, I won't come—not for the world!"

"But what will my wife say now? She thinks you intend to come!"

"Oh, tell her I've broken my leg—or anything you like!"

"She won't believe!" said Pavel, looking anxious.

"Ha-ha-ha! You catch it at home, I see! Tell me, who is that young officer?"

"Oh, a distant relative of mine—an unfortunate young fellow——"

"Pavel Pavlovitch!" cried a voice from the carriage, "the second bell has rung!"

Pavel was about to move off—Velchaninoff stopped him.

"Shall I go and tell your wife how you tried to cut my throat?" he said.

"What are you thinking of—God forbid!" cried Pavel, in a terrible fright.

"Well, go along, then!" said the other, loosing his hold of Pavel's shoulder.

"Then—then—you won't come, will you?" said Pavel once more, timidly and despairingly, and clasping his hands in entreaty.

"No—I won't—I swear!—run away—you'll be late!" He put out his hand mechanically, then recollected himself, and shuddered. Pavel did not take the proffered hand, he withdrew his own.

The third bell rang.

An instantaneous but total change seemed to have come over both. Something snapped within Velchaninoff's heart—so it seemed to him, and he who had been roaring with laughter a moment before, seized Pavel Pavlovitch angrily by the shoulder.

"If I—*I* offer you my hand, sir" (he showed the scar on the palm of his left hand)—"if *I* can offer you my hand, sir, I should think *you* might accept it!" he hissed with white and trembling lips.

Pavel Pavlovitch grew deadly white also, his lips quivered and a convulsion seemed to run through his features:

"And—Liza?" he whispered quickly. Suddenly his whole face worked, and tears started to his eyes.

Velchaninoff stood like a log before him.

"Pavel Pavlovitch! Pavel Pavlovitch!" shrieked the voice from the carriage, in despairing accents, as though some one were being murdered.

Pavel roused himself and started to run. At that moment the engine whistled, and the train moved off. Pavel Pavlovitch just managed to cling on, and so climb into his carriage, as it moved out of the station.

Velchaninoff waited for another train, and then continued his journey to Odessa.

THE END.

28890343R00052

Made in the USA
Columbia, SC
18 October 2018